"*A Cookbook Conspiracy* is another superb entry—and this one is succulent as well—in Kate Carlisle's witty, wacky, and wonderful bibliophile series . . . highly entertaining."
— Carolyn Hart, national bestselling author of the Death on Demand Bookstore mysteries

"A terrific read for those who are interested in the book arts and enjoy a counterculture foray and ensemble casts. Great fun all around!"
— *Library Journal* (Starred Review)

"Carlisle's story is captivating, and she peoples it with a cast of eccentrics. Books seldom kill, of course, but this one could murder an early bedtime."
— *Richmond Times-Dispatch*

"Well-plotted. . . . Carlisle keeps the suspense high."
— *Publishers Weekly*

"Kate Carlisle weaves an intriguing tale with a fascinating peek into the behind-the-scenes world of rare books. Great fun, and educational too." — *Suspense Magazine*

"Engaging. . . . Delivers the same mix of sharply humorous writing, fascinating details about the world of rare books, and a romance-infused mystery."
— Reader to Reader Reviews

"Who'd have thought book restoration could be so exciting? . . . *Homicide in Hardcover* is good reading in any binding."
— Parnell Hall, author of the Puzzle Lady mystery series

OTHER BOOKS BY KATE CARLISLE

BIBLIOPHILE MYSTERIES

FIXER-UPPER MYSTERIES

PRAISE FOR KA

"Light an
the Biblio
fare. Reco
Rosemary

"With her
This book
who the cu
terests an

PRAISE FOR KATE CARLISLE'S
NEW YORK TIMES **BESTSELLING**
BIBLIOPHILE MYSTERIES

"A delicious, twisty tale, it features food, friends, fiends, and a mysterious antique cookbook that binds them all. Kate Carlisle's most delectable installment yet. Don't miss it!"
—Julie Hyzy, *New York Times* bestselling author of the White House Chef mysteries and the Manor House mysteries

"Saucy, sassy, and smart—a fun read with a great sense of humor and a soupçon of suspense. Enjoy!"
—Nancy Atherton, *New York Times* bestselling author of the Aunt Dimity mysteries

continued . . .

"A cursed book, a dead mentor, and a snarky rival send book restorer Brooklyn Wainwright on a chase for clues—and fine food and wine—in Kate Carlisle's fun and funny delightful debut."
—Lorna Barrett, *New York Times* bestselling author of the Booktown mysteries

"A fun, fast-paced mystery that is laugh-out-loud funny. Even better, it keeps you guessing to the very end. Sure to be one of the very best books of the year! Welcome Kate Carlisle, a fabulous new voice in the mystery market."
—Susan Mallery, *New York Times* bestselling author of *Evening Stars*

"Kate Carlisle never fails to make me laugh, even as she has me turning the pages to see what's going to happen next. . . . Suspenseful, intelligent mysteries with a sense of humor."
—Miranda James, *New York Times* bestselling author of the Cat in the Stacks mysteries

"This is an entertaining cozy mystery that weaves the professional cooking process (and Brooklyn's amateur attempts) into a good old-fashioned whodunit."
—Once Upon a Romance

"Carlisle cooks up a great whodunit. . . . With a wealth of entertaining characters and fascinating facts on bookbinding thrown in, it's a winner!" —*RT Book Reviews*

THIS OLD HOMICIDE

A Fixer-Upper Mystery

Kate Carlisle

AN OBSIDIAN MYSTERY

OBSIDIAN
Published by the Penguin Group
Penguin Group (USA) LLC, 375 Hudson Street,
New York, New York 10014

USA | Canada | UK | Ireland | Australia |New Zealand |India |South Africa | China
penguin. com
A Penguin Random House Company

First published by Obsidian, an imprint of New American Library,
a division of Penguin Group (USA) LLC

First Printing, February 2015

Copyright © Kathleen Beaver, 2015

OBSIDIAN and logo are trademarks of Penguin Group (USA) LLC.

ISBN 978-0-451-46920-5

Printed in the United States of America
10 9 8 7 6 5 4

For Jenel, who saves my life on a daily basis

Chapter One

"It's a monstrosity, isn't it?"

I gazed at the massive structure before us and hid my dismay with a bland smile. "No, not at all. It's ... beautiful. In its own way."

"You're a terrible liar, Shannon," my friend Emily Rose said. "But I appreciate your attempt to make me feel better."

We both stared at the three-story multigabled, over-spindled, gingerbread-laden ... *monstrosity* — there was no better word for it — she'd just purchased. The old Victorian house was shrouded in shadows, making it appear even more forebidding than it might've been if even a smidgen of sunlight had been allowed to peep through the thick copse of soaring eucalyptus and redwood that surrounded the place on three sides. This wasn't the time to mention it, but I planned to suggest a good tree trimming once Emily closed the deal.

"What have I done?" Emily moaned softly. Her soft Scottish accent was thicker than usual, probably because of the stress of deciding to buy a house and then doing so in less than two days.

To be honest, the place was magnificent — if you overlooked the obvious: peeling paint, broken shutters, slumping roof. All of that was cosmetic and could be magically transformed by a good contractor. Luckily for Emily, that was me. I'm Shannon Hammer, a building contractor specializing in Victorian home renovation and repair. I took over Hammer Construction Company five years ago when my dad suffered a mild heart attack and decided to retire. I had grown up working on the grand Victorian homes that proliferated along this part of the Northern California coastline, and I couldn't wait to get started on Emily's.

For many years, Emily had been living in the small but pretty apartment above the Scottish Rose Tea Shoppe she owned on the town square in the heart of Lighthouse Cove. Over the last few years, though, the square, with its multitude of fabulous restaurants and charming shops, had become such a popular destination spot that she'd decided it was time to find a quieter place to live. When an uncle back in Scotland had died and left her some money, Emily decided that with property values being what they were, now was a good time to buy her first home.

She had announced her major purchase earlier today, after gathering together our small circle of friends in the back room of her tea shop. We met there regularly because it was so convenient. Lizzie Logan's stationery shop was just a few doors down, and her husband, Hal, was always willing to man the register when she needed some girl time. Jane Hennessey, my best friend since kindergarten, could walk over from her place two blocks away. Marigold Starling's Crafts and Quilts shop was a quick stroll across the square. My house was close enough that I could walk to the tea shop, too, on the days I did paperwork at home. More often, I drove in from one of the construction sites, careful to slap off as much sawdust as possible before I entered the ultrafeminine domain.

"Champagne?" I'd said when I walked in and saw the yummy spread and the expensive open bottle in Emily's hand. "What's the occasion?"

"You're getting married!" Lizzie said, clapping her hands. She was the only married one in our group, so she continually pushed the rest of us to find a guy and pair up. She persisted in matchmaking despite some rather deadly recent results.

"I'd have told you if I were dating," Emily assured her. "I'm not."

Without missing a beat, Lizzie said, "Did somebody die?"

Jane laughed. "I don't think we'd be drinking champagne if somebody died."

"Are you sure?" Lizzie whispered. "Maybe that's how they do it in Scotland."

Emily, clearly excited, had shushed everyone and held up her glass. "I want to propose a toast to the town's newest homeowner. Me."

"You bought a house?" I said, a little stunned that I hadn't heard. I liked to think I had my fingers on the pulse of the housing market in Lighthouse Cove, but Emily's purchase had slipped past me.

"Cheers!" Marigold cried, clinking her glass against Emily's.

Lizzie gave her a quick hug. "That's fabulous."

"Welcome to the wonderful world of homeownership," Jane said, herself the owner of a B-and-B I'd recently finished renovating.

"Yes, congratulations," I said. "You managed to shock me. I had no idea you were house hunting."

Emily took another sip of champagne before placing her glass down on the table. "I figured it was about time I set down roots in Lighthouse Cove."

"You think so?" Marigold said, laughing. "You've only lived here for fifteen years."

She grinned. "I'm a thrifty Scotswoman. It takes me a while to part with money."

Emily had moved here from Scotland all those years ago her boyfriend, who was going into business with one of our local fishermen. Sadly, a year later, the boyfriend mysteriously disappeared and was presumed lost at sea. Emily was devastated but decided to stay in Lighthouse Cove. She had only recently opened her tea shop and had a few good close friends who saw her through the tragedy.

"Where's the house?" I asked.

"It's over on Emerald Way," she said. "Overlooking North Bay."

I could picture the neighborhood with its glorious pine trees and amazing view of the coast. I'd worked on a number of homes in that area, and as far as I could remember, there was only one available house and it was . . . whoa. "You bought the old Rawley Mansion?"

"Yes," Emily said, and paused to pat her chest. "I get a little breathless when I think about it. I can't wait for you all to see it."

I exchanged a look of concern with Jane and knew she was recalling the Halloween night when we were seven years old and I had dared her to look in one of the windows on the Rawleys' front porch. She took the dare, but after one quick peek, she screamed and ran away. I wasn't smart enough to follow but instead peeked inside myself and saw a beautiful woman with golden hair wearing an old-fashioned dress, sitting at a desk near the window, crying. She looked up and her smile was so sad, I wanted to cry too. I touched the glass, reaching out—until I realized I could see right through her. She was a ghost!

For years, I'd been convincing myself that it was just a silly Halloween trick. What else could it be? I quickly covered my unease with a happy smile. "If you need any help with renovation or with the move itself, I'm available."

"We'll all help," Jane said.

"Thank you. That means so much." Emily blinked, overcome with emotion. "And yes, Shannon, I would love your help with the rehab. It needs a lot of work," she admitted, "but I had to have this house. I can't explain it, but it spoke to me. It's going to look like a fairy castle when it's all spiffed up. I can't wait to move in."

"When do you close escrow?" Lizzie asked.

"Since nobody's living there, I was able to get a fifteen-day escrow."

"Good grief, that's fast," Marigold murmured. She had left her Amish community years ago but still preferred to live at a slower pace than the rest of us.

Lizzie nodded. "The faster she closes the deal, the faster Shannon can get started on the rehab."

"Well, then." Jane raised her glass again. "Here's to Emily's castle."

"May all your dreams come true," Lizzie said fondly, and we drank down the rest of the sparkly champagne.

Now, as I gazed up at the old house, I knew Emily *really* needed help. Still, the place had good bones, and that was what counted. Right?

At the thought of good bones, I shivered. I wondered if Emily had heard the tales of old Grandma Rawley's ghost still haunting the place. It didn't matter. All those scary stories were just silly urban legends and tricks, meant to frighten small children on Halloween. Weren't they?

I brushed those thoughts aside. Everything would be fine. There was no such thing as ghosts. I repeated the mantra as I studied how the roof rolled and dipped in spots.

Emily's delicate features registered doubt as the sun slipped behind a cloud and the house grew even darker. "Perhaps I exaggerated a bit, thinking you might be able to turn it into a fairy castle."

"Don't worry. I'll make it beautiful for you," I assured her, and I meant it. Making Victorian homes look beautiful was my business, after all.

Years ago, our town had been designated a national historical landmark because of all the Victorian-era homes and buildings located here. The Rawley Mansion had once been a gorgeous example of that nineteenth-century Victorian style, before the last Rawley heir died and their gracious home was left to rot. But it didn't have to stay that way. Within a few months, my crew and I would restore it to its original luster and this shadowy eyesore before us would be a vague memory.

"Thank you, Shannon." She slung her arm around my shoulders and gave me a quick squeeze. "If anyone can do it, you can."

"Never doubt it."

She laughed. "I did for a while, but now I must admit I'm starting to get excited."

"I don't blame you. The house is amazing."

She looked up at the imposing structure. "Or it soon will be."

It really was amazing—if you had the vision to see past its dilapidated exterior.

It was a classic Queen Anne Victorian, but with one eclectic detail that must've suited the original owner's idiosyncratic style. The rounded, three-story tower on the left front side of the house was topped by what they used to call a Hindustani roof. Instead of the typical tower roof that came to a point like a witch's hat, this one's undulating profile resembled a large bell. It sat atop a small, round balcony roomy enough for a table and two chairs. Emily said it would be the perfect place to enjoy a cocktail and watch the sunset.

The rest of the home was more traditional, with a deep-shadowed entrance framed by elaborate ornamentation, asymmetrical rooflines, a wraparound porch, fish-scale shingles on the lower half of the house, and four chimneys.

On the downside, a number of the balusters were rotted or simply missing from the porch railing. The stained glass on the door was cracked and faded. Externally, the ravages of time, termites, overgrown plants, and stiff ocean breezes were obvious. Internally, anything was possible. A family of raccoons could've taken up residence. Wooden floors could be rotted clean through. Pipes might be fractured. I just prayed I wouldn't have to rebuild the whole thing from scratch.

I dismissed those thoughts. Why invite trouble? In two weeks when escrow closed and Emily took possession of the house, she and I would conduct a thorough walk-through to determine exactly what the rehab would entail. It all depended on the amount of work, of course, but I estimated that she would be able to move in within three to four months. I had a feeling that that would be cutting it close—like, by a year maybe—but for one of my dearest friends, I was determined to make the timing work. I was already mentally rearranging my crew's schedules. Emily's monstrosity was now at the top of my long priority list.

I wanted her new home to be spiffed up, as she put it, in record time.

"Looking on the bright side," she said with a cheerful grin, "at least there won't be any dead bodies in the basement. I checked."

I swallowed uneasily. "That's good to know." A few months ago, I had come across that very thing. A man had been murdered in the basement of a home I'd been refurbishing. I was the one who had discovered the body, and our new chief of police had not been amused. For a short while, my name was at the top of his suspect list, until the killer decided to focus on me. I never wanted to go through anything like that again.

"I'd better be getting back to the tea shop," Emily said with reluctance, her simple dark ponytail swaying as she turned to walk to her car. "I really appreciate your coming out here to take a look with me."

"I'm glad I did. I can't wait to get started." But as I opened the car door, I took one more look at the old Rawley Mansion and shivered.

I had a sinking feeling that raccoons would be the least of her problems.

Two weeks later, I arose early, threw on old jeans, a sweatshirt and tennies, and left the house to meet my dad for breakfast. I'd made it as far as the sidewalk before I woke up enough to realize that Lighthouse Cove was enveloped in a gray fog so thick I couldn't see the house across the street. It was mid-January on the Northern California coast and I should've expected fog at the very least. I counted myself lucky that it wasn't pouring rain. I jogged back inside to grab my quilted vest for an extra layer of warmth, pulled a warm knit cap over my unruly red hair, and set out again for the Cozy Cove Diner.

Anytime Dad and my uncle Pete were in town, they

met for breakfast at the Cove to chitchat with friends and neighbors and catch up on town business. Meaning *gossip*, of course. My dad and uncle, like everyone else in our small town, thrived on gossip. And wouldn't you know it? I always got the juiciest tidbits from those two men.

I rubbed my arms briskly to chase away the cold as I walked to the town square. Dad and Uncle Pete had just come home from a weeklong fishing trip at the Klamath River. They'd returned last night, dirty, exhausted, and happy to be back. Dad had parked his Winnebago in my driveway and dropped off six large, beautiful Chinook salmon for my freezer. It looked as though we'd be eating fish for the next few months. I wasn't complaining.

While the two men sat at my dining room table enjoying a beer after their long drive, I had filled them in on the most current scuttlebutt around town: Emily's purchase of the old Rawley Mansion; the latest round of infighting among the town's Festival Committee members; MacKintyre Sullivan's new book landing on the bestseller list. I promised to make homemade pizza for them sometime over the weekend since they'd called from the road to say they'd built up a powerful craving for pizza.

Odd cravings could happen when you hung out with a bunch of fishermen all week. Pizza was fairly normal, compared to some hankerings Dad had come up with in the past. The pizza request reminded me of some of his funny old sayings, or truisms, as he called them. One of his favorites went like this: *building a house is like building a pizza*. It took skill and artistry, the right tools, and strong wrists to pound nails into wood—or throw dough up in the air.

It wasn't the smoothest of axioms, especially the part about artistry, but it worked for him.

The thing was, not only had Dad signed this house and his business over to me after he suffered that mild heart attack five years ago, he had also turned over to me his longtime ritual of making homemade pizza. Once the task was safely passed on to the next generation, namely me, he was lavish in his praise of my culinary abilities. Oh, I knew I made a good pizza, but he liked to lay it on thick because he never wanted to have to make one for himself again.

I pushed the diner door open and was greeted with shouts of welcome along with the savory smells of bacon and warm syrup. I suddenly craved something yummy, even though I'd promised myself a healthy bowl of oatmeal.

"Over here, honey," Dad said, and scooted closer to the wall to make room for me in the booth he shared with Uncle Pete. Cindy the waitress arrived seconds later to pour a hot cup of coffee for me.

"Thanks, Cindy," I said, smiling at her. Today her name tag handkerchief corsage was a lacy floral concoction, which covered half her chest. If they were handing out prizes at a waitress convention, Cindy would win the corsage-name-tag competition hands down.

"You know what you want, hon?"

"I'll need a few seconds." I frowned at her. "I had my mind made up until I came inside and smelled bacon."

"Rocky's French toast is excellent today," she said with an evil wink before walking back to the front counter.

"Great," I muttered. So much for my noble attempt to start the day with a healthy breakfast. Cindy knew my weaknesses and exploited them gleefully.

A minute later, she was back to take my order of French toast, a side of bacon, and a fruit bowl. The fruit bowl was my nod to healthiness. It was a pitiful little nod, but it was enough to let me enjoy the rest of my order without feeling too guilty.

While I drank my coffee, Dad and Uncle Pete filled me in on all the latest happenings around town. It was mystifying how two men could go away for a week and come back knowing so much more about my neighbors than I did.

"Have you seen Jesse lately?" Dad asked, referring to Jesse Hennessey, the man who'd been our next-door neighbor for almost as long as I'd been alive. Most mornings, Jesse could be found sitting at the end of the counter reading his paper and nursing the one blessed cup of coffee he was allowed to drink each day.

"Cindy says he hasn't been in here in a few days," Uncle Pete added.

I glanced at the counter where Jesse usually sat and realized I hadn't seen him recently, either. "I hope he's not sick."

Uncle Pete wiggled his eyebrows. "Maybe he's shacked up with his little sweetie."

I almost choked on my coffee. "What're you talking about? There's no little sweetie shacked up at Jesse's house."

Pete shrugged. "So maybe he goes to her place."

"We're talking about Jesse, right? He doesn't have a girlfriend," I assured them. "I would know."

"But he told us all about her," Dad said. "She's supposed to be a hottie."

Good grief, Jesse Hennessey was seventy-seven years old. What was he doing with a hottie? "You know how he likes to embellish the truth. Maybe this is one of those times."

"Could be," Dad admitted. "I know he's told some whoppers in his time."

As I sipped my coffee, I started to feel a little less certain. "I guess he could be dating someone, but I've never seen another car next door. He rarely has visitors. I would notice."

Uncle Pete shrugged again. "He's a private guy. Might not want the neighbors talking."

Private didn't come close to describing my neighbor. *Paranoid* was more accurate. He'd always been a bit of a conspiracy theorist and Jane and I used to be amused when he'd claim that people were watching him. But in the last few years, I had to admit he'd grown to distrust everyone except for his niece Jane, who was one of my best friends. Especially when it came to business and money. I liked to think he trusted me, too, but he'd never introduced me to his hottie girlfriend—if the woman even existed, which I doubted. I would have to ask Jane about her.

"Shannon might be right, Pete," Dad admitted. "I wouldn't be surprised to find out Jesse was pulling our legs. He's always liked the ladies well enough, but he likes his privacy more."

Uncle Pete looked skeptical. "More than the ladies?"

Dad winked at me and I smiled. I knew how much he and Uncle Pete liked the ladies, too.

"So, who are we voting for in the mayor's race?" Dad asked, changing topics radically.

I gave him my two cents, and the subject grew lively as the couple in the booth behind us joined in. Even Rocky the cook tossed out a few salty comments from the kitchen. Local politics had a way of energizing a room.

Uncle Pete abruptly switched topics again. "So, what'd you and your Festival Committee come up with for Valentine's Day this year?"

I almost slid under the booth.

"Yeah, how's that going?" Dad said. "I'm still gonna drive the Hammer Construction float, right?"

"Oh, you bet," I said quickly. "Things are going great. No worries." Seeing Cindy, I added gratefully, "Oh, look, here's my breakfast."

As Cindy unloaded three full plates in front of me, I flashed her a look of appreciation for helping me cut off that avenue of conversation.

Unfortunately she ignored my look. "Is that true, Shannon?" she said, her voice registering skepticism. "Because I heard that Whitney Gallagher and Jennifer Bailey demanded to join the committee."

"Oh no," Dad muttered.

"Yes." Cindy nodded enthusiastically. "And I hear they're causing all sorts of heartburn for y'all."

From across the aisle, Mrs. Schuster gave me a sympathetic nod. "I heard a bunch of vendors dropped out and the festival is going to be a disaster."

All conversation ceased as each person in the place turned to look at me. And herein lay the essential problem with small towns: everyone knew everyone else and we all thrived on gossip. We sucked it up like chocolate marshmallow cream on a hot fudge sundae. It was our lifeblood. And frankly, the more painful or scandalous the news, the more we slurped it up. And nothing was more painful to me than having to deal on a weekly basis with Whitney Reid Gallagher and her BFF, Jennifer Bailey, my worst enemies from high school.

The Festival Committee was headed by my friend Jane and I was her second-in-command. Two years ago, we had stepped up and volunteered to run the committee. It was a little scary putting ourselves out there, but we'd decided it was our turn to give back to our community. Luckily our good deed was rewarded and our eight-member team got along well. We'd been having a great time planning the parades and festivals and events that occurred every month in Lighthouse Cove, and each one had turned out better than the one before.

But a month ago, our luck had run out. Whitney and Jennifer had insisted on joining the committee. They'd heard it was fun. And it *was*. Until they joined. I truly believed that those two women thrived on draining every last ounce of joy the rest of us—especially me—had found working together.

And boy, that burned me up. You'd think that both women would be nicer to me after I saved their sorry butts a few months ago. They would both be goners—I'm talking *dead*—if not for me and my quick action. And while I hadn't been sitting around waiting for the flowers and candy and maybe a thank-you note to arrive, I certainly hadn't expected everything to go back to the same old rotten status quo. I was wrong, sadly. So now the entire committee had to suffer from their obnoxious presence. I blamed myself because it was clear that they were only here to torment me.

Fortunately it wasn't just me who thought the two women were meanies. The others agreed. A good thing, too, because if I was the only one bothered by Whitney and Jennifer, I would've considered seeking professional help for my victim complex.

But no, the other women recognized that Whitney and Jennifer were there to make our lives miserable. The two newcomers questioned every decision and ridiculed every new idea. What made it worse was that the twosome had joined right before Christmas, which really put a damper on our holiday spirits. More recently they drove one of the women to tears after she suggested a Valentine fashion show for dogs and cats with prizes for each category. I thought it was a super idea and the perfect way to entertain the kids in attendance and many of the adults, too. Especially the ones with pets, like me. But Jennifer's groans and Whitney's eye rolls gave a clear indication of their opinion.

Once those two left the meeting, though, Jane assured the rest of us that the pet fashion show was a brilliant idea and would definitely go forward. Right then and there, we began brainstorming some funny categories and prizes for the show.

Jane ran into another problem when she was handing out assignments for the Valentine's Day Festival. She'd asked Whitney and Jennifer to take charge of lining up vendors for the food booths. They had simply refused, claiming they were too busy shopping for Christmas presents. They weren't too busy to complain, of course. Finally Jane was left with no choice but to insist that they resign from the committee, but they refused that, too! They just kept showing up week after week, annoying everyone with their negative vibe.

It didn't make sense to any normal person. But then, their animosity toward me and the town in general had never made sense.

Jane had recently resorted to scheduling secret meetings with everyone on the committee attending except Whitney and Jennifer. We were finally able to get some work done and recapture the camaraderie and fun we'd had before the other two joined the group. Of course, we were forced to keep the meetings hush-hush for fear of reprisals. Nobody wanted to suffer the wrath of Whitney.

Naturally the entire town had heard about the committee's discord, but so far, nobody had found out about the secret meetings. And they never would, if I could help it.

I pasted an innocent smile on my face and looked up at Cindy. "Yes, Whitney and Jennifer have joined the group and we're all getting along great. This year's Valentine's Festival is going to be the best one ever."

"So the bickering I've heard about is just an ugly rumor?" she persisted. "I'm not sure I believe that."

"It's true," I said jovially, waving the idea away. "It was a little shaky at first, but now we're all buddies."

"Huh. Wonder where that rumor came from," she muttered as she walked back to the kitchen.

Oh, I knew exactly where it came from, I thought, my teeth clenched in frustration. The mean girls themselves. But I continued to smile at everyone who was listening and they all smiled back with great relief. Nobody wanted the festival to be a disaster.

I finally gazed down at my breakfast of fluffy French toast drenched in syrup and butter, and bacon. Oh, and fruit. Pineapple chunks, blueberries, and strawberries, all made even better by the presence of syrup.

I should've been blissfully stuffing myself by now, dredging each thick, luscious bite through the melted goodness of syrup and butter. But I'd lost my appetite. I couldn't even down my second cup of coffee. And for that alone, I would never forgive Whitney Gallagher and Jennifer Bailey.

An hour later, after assuring Dad and Uncle Pete that I wasn't sick with some horrible stomach ailment that had caused me to lose interest in food, I headed home to get ready for work. I had a meeting with the Planning Commission at ten o'clock, so I would have to dress a little nicer today than usual. Not that I didn't dress nicely all the time, but let's face it. I worked on construction sites. Most of the time, my wardrobe choices weren't complicated.

I walked down the driveway and through the back gate to my kitchen door. But then I hesitated, recalling Dad's comment about Jesse. It wouldn't hurt to check up on the old guy since I couldn't remember the last time I'd seen him. Maybe three days ago? Four? I recalled glimpsing him out in his yard, kibitzing as usual with Mrs. Higgins from across the street. I remembered because I had just come back from Emily's, where we'd looked through home magazines together so I could get an idea of what she wanted for her new house. Her closing was this coming week. Two weeks had passed in a hurry.

What if Jesse had been sick for the last few days? The least I could do was find out if he needed a ride to the doctor. Or I could offer to deliver an emergency quart of chicken soup from the diner.

I changed direction and headed next door to his place. Jesse's house was one of the smaller ones on the street, a blue-and-white, one-and-a-half-story Victorian with the prototypical pitched roof and wide porch, but it featured a charming white-railed widow's walk that was accessed by climbing out the attic window. Jesse had always talked about turning the attic into his version of a man cave, but he hadn't gotten around to it yet.

His place had grown a little shabby around the edges over the years and I'd repeatedly offered to spruce it up for him, to no avail. Once in a while when I was mowing my lawn, I would go next door and clean up his yard, but it needed a lot more help than that. The front porch was begging for a paint job, and one of the dining room shutters had been missing a few slats for the longest time. Maybe I'd sneak over and fix a few things as a favor to him, especially if he was sick. I could certainly mow his lawn again because it was getting shaggier by the minute.

I knocked on the front door and waited. After a minute, I knocked again. I really hoped he was feeling okay. The old man was crotchety, set in his ways, and had a tendency to tell huge, whopping fibs—or tall tales, as he called them—but I adored him. He'd never married or had children, but he'd always been close to his niece, my friend Jane.

I knocked once more, louder this time, because Jesse seemed to be getting a little deaf. For good measure, I shouted, "Jesse, are you here?"

After another full minute, I took the hint. He obviously wasn't in there. I headed for home, but as I stuck my key into the kitchen door lock, my conscience wouldn't let me relax. What if Jesse was inside the house, sick or in pain? What if he'd fallen down and couldn't reach the telephone or the front door? Darn it, I couldn't walk away without making sure he was all right.

"He won't thank me for this," I muttered, but my decision was made.

Years ago, after a house down the street caught on fire, my father and a few of our neighbors had exchanged house keys to use in case of future emergencies. Dad kept them all on a key ring in the kitchen "junk drawer." Even though he had moved out of the house and into his RV five years ago, I'd never cleaned out that drawer. It was impossible to throw some of those things away because you just never knew.

Pushing aside a stack of yellowed appliance catalogs, an old tape measure, and a dried-up tube of superglue—okay, I definitely needed to clean out this drawer—I found the key ring. Happily most of the keys had small, round descriptive tags attached, so I checked until I found the key that was tagged JESSE'S PLACE.

I jogged back to his house and unlocked the front door, feeling a momentary pang of guilt for invading his privacy. I knew he would hate having anyone walk into his house without his permission, but what could I do?

"It's for your own good," I said under my breath. Later, I planned to lecture him on keeping in better touch with his neighbors.

The house was dark and quiet. It was musty, too, from

being closed up for a while. I was tempted to open some windows, but I figured that would be going a little too far.

"Hello, Jesse? Are you here?"

There was no response, and to be honest, I didn't feel his presence in the house. So maybe he'd gone away for the week. But he'd always told me when he was going anywhere for any length of time so I'd be sure to keep an eye on his house.

Even though I didn't feel his presence—and didn't that make me sound like some psychic nut job?—I was still determined to check all the rooms. If he wasn't home, fine. But what if he'd fallen and couldn't get up? I needed to make sure.

From the foyer, I turned left and tiptoed down the hall to the last room on the right, which I knew was his bedroom. On the way, I took a quick peek inside the other two bedrooms—one of which was his office—to check for him. By the time I reached his bedroom, I was sorry I'd been so eager to find him. Every room was a mess, with dresser drawers opened and clothing tossed everywhere. Even the sheets on the bed had been dragged off and were lying on the floor.

His office was a disaster, too, with the rug pushed back against the wall and the contents of his desk drawers emptied onto the hardwood floor. I had to watch where I stepped to avoid slipping on something. Had he been searching for something? He must've been in one heck of a hurry to leave things scattered everywhere without picking it all up.

I'd visited him countless times over the years and I'd never seen anything like this. Jesse was like an uncle to me and he was one of my father's closest friends. We used to get together all the time for barbecues and neighborhood parties. He didn't go in for grilling much; he generally left that manly chore to my dad. But whenever it got cold and damp, Jesse would whip up a batch of his world-famous chili or, on the rare occasion, a big, rich chicken stew. Both were his specialties, and he'd invite the whole block over for a bowlful, served with his delicious corn bread muffins.

On those occasions, his rooms were as neat and clean as could be. Jesse had spent much of his adult life in the navy until he retired almost twenty years ago, so to say he kept things shipshape around here was an understatement.

But as I looked around now, the only ship this place brought to mind was the *Titanic*. I didn't realize what a slob he'd turned into.

I felt instantly guilty for thinking those thoughts. Maybe I wasn't being fair. Maybe he'd grown depressed lately. That possibility broke my heart, but it could explain the mess. I made a mental note to call Jane as soon as I got home to see if there was some way to help him get through this bad patch.

I returned to the foyer and turned left to go to the kitchen. "Jesse? Are you here?"

He wasn't. But there was more of the same disarray in this room, with drawers pulled open and utensils and kitchen gadgets strewn across the counters and the floor. Cupboard doors were open, the contents shoved to the side or swept haphazardly onto the floor.

I scowled at the mess. Something was really wrong. If this was a sign of depression, Jesse needed help immediately.

But Jesse wasn't depressed; I knew it in my gut. It wasn't in his nature. No, this mess looked more like a desperate hunt to find something and he didn't care if he left a disaster in his wake.

"Jesse?" I called again, more urgently this time. I headed for the small den off the kitchen, where he liked to watch television. And that was where I found him. He was sound asleep on the couch with one arm dangling over the edge.

"Jesse!" I hurried across the room, so filled with relief that I forgot about the mess and everything else. "Thank goodness you're here. Don't be mad that I came into your house, but I was worried."

There was no reaction. The man could sleep like the dead, I thought. The way he'd torn his home apart, I had to wonder if he was simply exhausted. Old people could do some weird things sometimes. I recalled my grandmother going off on all sorts of oddball tangents before she'd died, once tearing up a scrapbook filled with old photographs, and another time bingeing on jars of jalapeño pickles.

I studied Jesse's face and wondered if maybe he was sick after all, because he looked pale, almost gray.

"Jesse?" I knelt down beside the couch and touched his forehead to make sure he wasn't feverish.

On the contrary, his skin was cool. And no wonder, since the poor guy was wearing a pair of tidy white cotton boxer shorts and nothing else.

"Come on, Jesse, wake up." I reached for the afghan draped over the back of the couch and covered him up to give him a little dignity. I lifted his arm onto the couch and tucked the edges of the blanket under him to warm him up.

"Jesse," I said softly, shaking his shoulder lightly. "Can I get you some soup or something?"

His arm slid off the couch again. And I suddenly realized why.

"Oh, jeez!" I scooted backward, away from him, scrambling to my feet as I shouted his name over and over again. "Jesse! Oh my God! Jesse!"

It didn't do any good. He wasn't going to wake up.

Jesse Hennessey was dead.

Chapter Two

I huddled outside on the porch, shaking my head and trembling in disbelief and sadness, not only because Jesse was dead, but also because I'd stupidly approached him as though he were merely sleeping or passed out. I should've known something was horribly wrong when I first saw the disarray throughout his house.

Jesse was gone. My eyes filled with tears and I sank into an old chair by the front door, rocking back and forth with my arms wrapped around my stomach. So many emotions were coursing through me, I couldn't think straight. I was sad, of course. Numb. Shocked. He'd been my next-door neighbor for my entire life, and even if I didn't see him every day, it was comforting to know that I had someone dependable and brave right next door when I needed him. He was raunchy sometimes and terribly corny. He told the world's worst jokes. Jane and I used to laugh and groan at the same time when he would start in on his puns. I could still picture him a few months ago, standing in his front yard with weeds growing all around him.

"What are you doing, Jesse?" I'd asked.

"I'm out standing in my field."

I frowned at him.

"Get it?" he'd said, grinning like an idiot.

Staring at him on the couch a few minutes ago, I'd started to laugh despite the tears rolling down my cheeks. "Oh, Jesse," I whispered. "What happened to you?"

Jane would be here any minute. Would she blame me for his death? Not that I'd caused it or anything, but maybe I could've prevented it if I'd been a better neighbor.

I buried my head in my hands. Oh God, I was a horrible neighbor. I should've checked in on him every day. He wasn't getting any younger and old people had a tendency to, you know, get old.

Okay, I needed to stop beating myself up. Jesse had always been fiercely independent and had never appreciated anyone hovering over him or worrying about him. Even Jane, his only living relative and the one person he loved most in the world, had been lectured more than once. *"Don't worry about me,"* he often told her when she tried to coddle him a little. *"I'm going to live to be a hundred because only the good die young."*

I should've ignored his gruff words and gone ahead and paid more attention to his health and his lifestyle. If I'd been more diligent, made sure he was safe and in good physical shape, he might still be alive.

I heard a siren blast from several blocks away, reminding me that I'd called the police right after talking to Jane. What else could I do? Once I realized that Jesse was dead, I'd immediately wondered about that mess in there. I knew it wasn't normal for Jesse to tear his house apart like that. I wondered if someone else had broken in and done it. The police would be able to determine that, I hoped.

The thought of someone breaking into Jesse's house to rob him after he was dead made me shudder with revulsion. But even worse, what if someone had broken in while he was still alive and scared him to death?

Could something like that have taken place right next door to me without my even knowing about it? I'd like to think I'd hear something or get some kind of strong vibe about it, seeing as how I had gone through such a horrible time a few short months ago.

Maybe that was why my mind was suddenly spinning with thoughts of murder. But there was no way Jesse could've been murdered, because . . . well, just because.

Because things like that didn't happen in Lighthouse Cove. Okay, maybe that one bizarre stretch a few months back, but not on a regular basis. It was crazy to even consider.

Burglaries, yes. We had our share of them, every once in a great while. But why would anyone want to burglarize Jesse's home? He owned nothing of real value. He'd lived nicely on Social Security and his military pension for the last ten years. Everyone in Lighthouse Cove knew it. Not that I would ever accuse one of my own townspeople. No, it must have been a stranger. But really? A stranger just happened to be passing through town and picked Jesse's home to break into? What were the chances?

"Slim to none," I murmured.

So maybe the mess really had been caused by Jesse himself. Maybe he had lost something important and gone on a tear. Or maybe some medication he'd been taking got screwed up and he'd gone a little crazy. Anything could've happened. It would be up to the police to figure it all out. They might find fingerprints that would lead them to conclude that a burglary had taken place.

I swept those thoughts away and concentrated on Jesse himself. It was hard to believe he was dead. I'd known him all my life and all of a sudden he was gone? It didn't seem fair. He might've been getting old, but he'd had plenty of good years left.

I pictured myself talking to him a few minutes ago, tucking that afghan blanket over him, worried that he might have a fever. Then realizing he was dead.

I groaned out loud.

"What a twit you are." Jane would laugh her ass off when I got around to telling her. That wouldn't be anytime soon, of course. I imagined she wouldn't be ready to laugh for a while yet. And I wasn't too anxious to reveal what a major bozo I could be, even to my best pal.

But it wasn't about me, I reminded myself sternly. Jesse was gone and poor Jane would be grieving. Okay, I was, too, but it was time to brush my feelings aside and concentrate on Jane. She would need every ounce of help and support I could give her to get through this.

I sat back in the old wicker chair to wait for everyone to arrive. I thought of Jesse again and how he'd looked so peaceful, lying there on the couch. Was it any wonder why I didn't figure it out right away? He must've died recently, too. Otherwise there would've been some sort of . . . well, deterioration, to put it nicely. But other than that slightly gray pall to his skin, he really did look as if he'd been sleeping. I hated to think what might've happened if I hadn't found him for another week.

I grimaced and rubbed my stomach. I really didn't need to focus on what he might've looked like after a few more days.

The police siren wailed again, interrupting my odd thoughts, thank goodness. Within seconds, the police chief's black-and-white SUV screeched to a stop in front of Jesse's house just as Jane pulled up in her car and parked across the street. I could tell she was crying as she slammed the car door behind her. In seconds, she was up the front stairs, and I was standing up to grab her in a tight hug.

"It can't be true," she said, sobbing. "I can't believe it."

"I'm sorry," I murmured, rubbing her back. Jane and Jesse had been really close. Each had been the other's only family. But Jane had me, too, and I'd remind her of that soon. "I'm so sorry."

"What happened?" she asked, swiping at the river of tears coursing down her cheeks.

"I don't know. I was concerned that I hadn't seen him around, so I decided to check on him. He didn't answer the door, so I used our emergency key and let myself in. I found him in the back den."

She let out a little sob. "That's where he always watches TV."

"I know, sweetie." I realized that the TV hadn't been on when I found him.

Jane buried her face against my shoulder and I held her fiercely. Jesse was Jane's last living relative and now he was gone. I felt my own tears well up again as I contemplated what I would do if I lost my dad or Uncle Pete. It was too awful to think about.

"Jane," a husky voice said from behind us. I opened my eyes and saw Police Chief Eric Jensen standing on the steps leading to the porch. Despite the horrid circumstances, I felt a weight lift from my chest at seeing him. He was a good guy to have around. Solid.

I let go of Jane and she turned. "Oh, Eric."

He stepped onto the porch and held out his arms, and I felt more of my own tears erupt as Jane rushed into his embrace.

"I'm sorry for your loss."

"Thank you," she whispered.

Over Jane's shoulder, Eric's straightforward gaze met mine. I watched his jaw clench and could only imagine what he was thinking. Something along the lines of *Why does Shannon Hammer keep finding dead bodies in my town?*

Funny, I was asking myself that same question. It hadn't been long ago that I discovered that body in the basement of the old Victorian home I'd been working on. At the time, Eric had been new in town and his first inclination was to arrest me for murder, simply because I'd been overheard threatening the dead guy only a few days before his body was found. It was a dumb thing to do — threaten him, I mean — but anyone who knew me would know that I hadn't meant it literally. Unfortunately Eric didn't know me back then.

He knew me now, though, and I considered him a good friend. I wanted him to like me. I prayed he wouldn't jump to that same conclusion this time around. And why would he? Jesse appeared to have succumbed to a heart attack or something equally benign — if a cause of death could ever be considered benign. There was no reason for anyone to assume anything else — except for the minor fact that I'd spent the last twenty minutes *assuming* that very thing. That foul play might have occurred and Jesse's death had been the result.

I was already mentally lining up my alibis and excuses for being inside Jesse's house. Inwardly I winced. I couldn't help it. The thought of being interrogated by Eric again gave me shivers, and not in a good way. I shook my head briskly, hoping to fling those fears away. The only thing the police needed to know about me and Jesse was that he had been my neighbor since I was a little girl and we'd been great friends. I was devastated by his death.

Still, I had been the one who found his body. If Eric could prove that Jesse had died through some kind of foul play, didn't that make me the most likely suspect in his eyes?

"Don't be ridiculous," I whispered. I was letting my imagination run out of control. It was time to wrestle it back into line.

Eric stepped away from Jane but kindly held her arms to steady her until she regained her equilibrium. I almost sighed out loud. He was a nice guy, and pretty darn gorgeous, if you liked that tall, hunky, muscular Nordic god sort of look. And who didn't? I'd been mentally calling him Thor ever since we met. The name suited him, but he probably wouldn't appreciate hearing it.

"Shannon," Eric said, nodding at me.

"Hello, Eric."

"What happened here?"

"I was checking on Jesse. Nobody's seen him around in a few days and I thought he might be sick. He didn't answer his door so I went inside to look for him and found him . . . you know."

"How'd you get inside?"

"We all have keys to each other's houses," I explained in a rush. "My neighbors, I mean. In case there's an emergency. See, a long time ago, we saw smoke coming from the Robertsons' upstairs bedroom and Dad broke down their front door to make sure they were okay. Well, it turned out they were fine, but after that we all decided to swap keys with each other to avoid having to break down doors. I keep the keys in my kitchen drawer, the one by the window. And oh my God, that doesn't really matter, does it?"

I stopped talking abruptly. He didn't need to know where the stupid junk drawer was. I tended to blather on and on when I was nervous. And I had no reason to be nervous, did I?

Eric coughed, probably to keep from laughing out loud at my idiotic chattering.

"Hey, Chief," someone shouted from the sidewalk. It was Tommy Gallagher, my old high school boyfriend and the newly promoted deputy chief of police.

He jogged up the walkway and bounded up the steps to join us.

"Hey, Shannon," he said heartily, and grabbed me in a quick hug.

"Hi, Tommy." I'd known him forever and still thought he was pretty cute, but that wasn't the only reason why I hugged him. No, he was happily married to Whitney Reid, the very same woman who had made my life hell all through high school and continued to do so on the Festival Committee. It was for her sake that I always gave Tommy a nice big hug and a kiss on the cheek when I saw him. I knew it was immature, especially at a moment like this, but it amazed me to know that her spying girlfriends liked to report back to her whenever they caught me anywhere near Tommy. According to Whitney's girlfriends, I showed clear warning signs that I was out to steal him back from her. That couldn't be further from the truth, of course, but Whitney still didn't seem to realize that.

I figured it was Whitney's own guilty conscience that made her so distrustful. Since she herself had stolen Tommy from me back in high school, it figured that I must be lying in wait, biding my time for the chance to take my revenge. It was laughable really. I'd gotten over Tommy's betrayal ages ago and we were good friends now, much to Whitney's disgust.

When he saw Jane, Tommy's ever-present grin dimmed slightly. "Aw, hey, Jane. I'm really sorry to hear about Jesse. What a total bummer. If there's anything I can do, you let me know."

"Thanks, Tommy," Jane said, giving him a light hug.

Eric took my arm and pulled me aside, out of Jane's earshot. He leaned over and spoke quietly. "Where did you find Mr. Hennessey's body?"

"In the room off the kitchen at the back of the house. It's where he watched TV."

"Did you call his doctor?"

"Not yet. I called Jane first and then decided to call the police because of what else I found in the house."

His eyes narrowed. "What else did you find?"

"It's probably easier if I show you."

He stared at me for a long moment before he nodded toward the front door. "Okay, let's see what you're talking about."

He turned and caught Tommy's gaze. "You mind waiting out here with Jane?"

Jane looked affronted. "I appreciate your wanting to protect me, Eric, but it's not necessary. I'm coming inside with you."

Eric glanced at me as if it was my decision.

"He's her uncle," I said, frowning at him. "She'll have to see him sometime."

"Hello?" Jane said. "I'm standing right here."

I smiled ruefully. "Sorry."

She turned to the police chief. "And frankly, Eric, while I'm glad to see you, I'm not sure why Shannon called you anyway. I'm perfectly capable of contacting Uncle Jesse's doctor to have him write out a death certificate."

She started for the door, but I stepped in front of her, holding up my hand when she began to protest.

"Two things," I said.

"What?"

"First, I called the police because it's a mess inside, so prepare yourself."

She frowned. "Okay. What's the second thing?"

"I'm here for you."

Tears sprang to her eyes and she sniffled. "Damn it, Shannon. I know that."

"Good." I grabbed the door handle, pushed it open,

and stepped inside. This time I ignored the chaos of the house and headed straight for the kitchen and the adjoining den, where I'd found Jesse's body.

Behind me, I heard Jane's murmurs of distress as she noted the disarray. Eric was, as always, stoic.

"Oh God," Jane whispered as she approached her uncle. Kneeling on the floor next to him, she touched his cheek. "Oh, Uncle."

Tommy, Eric, and I stood back by the door to give her some privacy. Eric glanced over his shoulder at the chaos in the kitchen and scowled. "Is this how it usually looks in here?"

"No," I murmured. "That's why I called you. The whole house has been torn apart."

"Damn it," he muttered.

"It could've been Jesse searching for something and getting carried away. But I don't believe that. He's always been a tidy guy."

"Okay, let's take a look." Under his breath, he added, "Tom, stay with Jane."

"You got it, boss."

Jane didn't notice we were leaving the room.

In the kitchen, I watched the chief walk around, studying the scene as he tried to avoid stepping on all the stuff that had been pulled out of the drawers and cupboards. After another minute he signaled that it was time to move on, so I accompanied him back to the foyer and told him to check out the bedrooms down the hall. I stayed where I was, not wanting to get depressed all over again.

After a bit of time, Eric returned, his expression sober. "You didn't tell me someone punched a hole in the wall."

"I didn't see any holes."

"There's a big one behind the door in the back bedroom. It goes right through the layer of lath and plaster."

"That doesn't make sense," I said, taken aback. "I can't believe Jesse would do something like that."

"And one of the floorboards in his office was pulled up."

"Wow, I noticed the rug was pulled back, but I missed seeing the floorboard."

"You were looking for Jesse, not trouble."

"True. But I don't get it. I can't believe a burglar would go to all that trouble. It must've been Jesse. He had to have been really desperate to find something he lost. I wish he'd called me. He's not that strong anymore."

"Was he an angry man?" Eric asked.

"No. I mean, he went on a rant once in a while, but it was usually over a barking dog or something the town council did. He would never do anything violent, though, like pound his fist through a wall. Like I said, he wasn't that strong."

"It wasn't done with a fist. Someone used a sledge-hammer."

I shook my head, perplexed. "What should we do?"

"*We* shouldn't do anything," he said tightly. "*You're* going to take Jane back outside and *I'm* declaring this place a crime scene."

"A crime scene?" Jane repeated, once we were relegated to the front porch and the police began searching Jesse's home for possible clues. "But why?"

"Did you see the mess in there?" Had she been so distraught that she hadn't noticed something so obvious? "Someone tore Jesse's house apart. And now he's dead. The police need to figure out what happened."

Her eyes widened. "You think Jesse saw someone break in?" She lowered herself into the porch chair and absently brushed her hair back from her face. "That might've been enough to give him a heart attack. Do you think that's what happened?"

"The thought did occur to me."

"If that's true, it means that he was literally frightened to death." She stared at me. "That can't be possible. It's too awful."

I couldn't think of a thing to say that would make her feel better, so I just nodded in agreement.

"Besides, he looked so peaceful." She cringed. "Oh, what a horrible cliché."

I didn't mention that I'd thought the exact same thing earlier when I first saw him.

"Let's not jump to any conclusions until the police know something for sure."

"I can't sit here doing nothing," she said, gripping her hands together.

"It's just for a little while," I said soothingly.

"Oh, don't act so calm and collected," she snapped. "You have a worse time sitting still than I do."

I chuckled inwardly. At least she hadn't sunk so deeply into despair that she couldn't get riled up about something.

Jane and I had been best friends since kindergarten so we knew each other almost too well. She was right. Sitting out here doing nothing would drive me insane as quickly as it would her.

It probably wasn't a good time to mention it to Jane, but I couldn't wait to get together with Emily, Marigold, and Lizzie, and talk this awful situation out. Even in the worst circumstances, we could always come up with ideas to make things better. Maybe one of them would have a theory to offer. Would they agree that Jesse had been searching for something? Or had his house been burgled? By whom? Maybe the five of us could do a little snooping—I mean, investigating—around town to find out more. We'd gotten pretty good at it, thanks to my own run-in with crime a while back.

"I hate knowing that poor Uncle Jesse died alone," Jane murmured. "Can there be anything sadder?"

I reached over and squeezed her hand. "I'm sorry."

"I should call Mr. Bitterman," she said. "That would give me something to do."

The Bittermans owned the local funeral home and had been serving the dead people of Lighthouse Cove for three generations. Blake Bitterman ran the place now with his son, Bryce, who'd gone to school with us.

"Wait a few minutes before you call Bitterman," I said. "Eric might want to bring in the county coroner."

"But if he does that, it means he thinks Jesse was . . ." She pressed her hands over her mouth, unable to say the word.

Murdered.

We were both silent with our own thoughts for a moment, until I returned to the subject I'd touched on before. "Jane, you did see how badly the house was torn apart, right?"

Her eyes narrowed. "Yeah, I saw it. And I refuse to believe Jesse would do that to his own home. Sure, maybe he left the Sunday paper around for a few days, but that was about it. Most of the time, he was a stickler for neatness."

"I know. And you didn't even see the rest of the place. I walked down the hall, and all of the rooms have been searched. Someone was in a real hurry, because the drawers and closets and cupboards were all open and things were tossed everywhere. Eric told me that someone broke through the wall in Jesse's bedroom and pulled up a floorboard in his office."

"Who could've done that? Because it wasn't Jesse."

"Are you sure? What if he lost something? Maybe he was missing some important papers."

"But why would he be looking under a floorboard or in the kitchen cabinets? I mean, there were spice jars and condiments on the floor. Jesse couldn't have done that."

"I agree."

She blew out a breath. "And seeing all that mess is why you called the police. Duh. Sorry about what I said earlier. My mind has been muddled since you called me."

"Understandable."

She still looked dazed. "So if someone else was in there searching for something, that person could've snuck up on Jesse."

"Right," I said. "Although he wasn't easily scared, he could've been caught by surprise so badly that it gave him a heart attack."

"What if the person knocked him out first and then started searching?"

"It's possible." I thought about finding Jesse on the couch. "But it didn't look like he'd been attacked. I mean, there was no blood or anything. It's like you said. He looked peaceful, not traumatized."

"I hope he didn't suffer."

Depressed by the thought, I shook my head. "We're just grasping at straws. We need to wait and hear what the coroner says."

Jane frowned and shook her head, unwilling to give up theorizing. "If someone was searching for something, what could it be?"

"I don't know. Did he come into some money recently?"

"No, of course not." She wrinkled her nose, puzzled. "You know him as well as I do. If he'd come into money, you'd probably hear about it before I did."

"Maybe so, but only because I'm right next door. My house would've been the first stop on his way to telling every last person in town."

"True," she said, with a light chuckle. "He was private about a lot of things, but he sure liked to share the good news."

I sat up abruptly. "Hey, that reminds me. Did Jesse have a girlfriend?"

Jane looked at me sideways. "Are you kidding? No."

"That's what I figured, but my dad and uncle both claim that Jesse had a girlfriend. A hottie, they said."

She frowned. "That sounds like one of his tall tales."

"I thought the same thing."

"If he had a girlfriend, we all would've met her, right? Especially if she was a hottie."

"Well, of course she would be a hottie," I said, laughing. "Why would he make up a girlfriend and have her be ugly?"

Jane stared at the house across the street. "I wonder if Mrs. Higgins ever saw her."

Mrs. Higgins was Jesse's partner in crime when it came to sharing and passing along the latest gossip.

I winced at the thought of Mrs. Higgins. "I haven't seen her this morning. I'd better go tell her what happened before she sees the police cars."

"It's too late for that," Jane said, gazing at the three cop cars parked on the street. "She's going to be upset. I'll go with you."

"Thanks. It'll help if you're there." I took a long look at the sunny yellow house across the street. "I'm surprised she's not out in her yard, demanding to know what's going on."

Jane frowned. "I hope she's okay."

"Let's go find out."

As we crossed the street, Jane locked arms with me. "I'm sorry you were all by yourself when you found him."

"Yeah, me, too. It was bizarre and sad."

"What made you go inside?"

I told her about meeting my dad and uncle for breakfast at the diner and how they'd missed seeing Jesse. "You know he's usually there in the morning, reading the paper and drinking his one cup of coffee. So I figured I'd stop by to check up on him. I knocked a few times, but he didn't come to the door. I thought he might be sick or something."

"I'm so glad you didn't just walk away. The thought of him lying there alone for a few more days . . ." She shuddered.

"I considered that, too. But it looks like we found him within a few hours of his death—although I'm no expert, obviously. I thought he was sound asleep. I even put a blanket over him."

"Aw," she said, squeezing my arm. "Thank you for doing that."

I glanced at her. "You should thank me. Otherwise you would've caught him in his white boxer shorts and nothing else."

She choked on a laugh. "Oh God. I've been buying him a three-pack of white boxers and white socks for Christmas for as long as I can remember."

"It's what he liked."

She sighed. "Yes."

I knocked on the door of the yellow house and waited. When the door swung open, I could tell that Mrs. Higgins actually did have a cold.

"What is it? What happened? What's wrong?" she asked in rapid order, her voice sounding nasally.

"I'm sorry to bother you, Mrs. Higgins. Are you sick?"

"I've got a touch of something," she said, tugging her housecoat more snugly around her. "I spent the entire morning sleeping. I never do that."

"I wanted to let you know—

"Are those police cars?" she asked, stretching to see beyond me. "What's going on around here? Somebody get arrested? I'll bet it's those drug runners. I've seen 'em sneaking around town in the middle of the night." She folded her arms across her chest and looked directly at me. "Anybody sneaking around at night is up to no good. You can take that to the bank."

Why was she looking at me? I never snuck around at night.

"It's about Jesse," Jane said softly, catching Mrs. Higgins's attention. "He passed away sometime last night."

"What? Jesse? What do you mean?" She glanced from Jane to me, frowning. "No."

"It's true, Mrs. Higgins," I said.

"No, it can't be. Jesse's . . . no." She looked confused and her eyes grew damp. "No." Her knees began to wobble and I grabbed her arm to steady her.

"Let's sit down." I walked into her house and led her over to the sofa in her front room. Jane sat on her other side and we both held her hands for a few minutes while she wept and tried to speak. It was hard. The more questions she asked, the more information we gave her, the more she curled up protectively.

She was clearly devastated. But after a few minutes,

she dried her eyes with a wadded tissue and glared at me. "Why didn't you come and get me sooner?"

That caught me by surprise. "I . . . um, I'm sorry, Mrs. Higgins. I was busy with the police."

She huffed, pointing out the front window. "I missed everything. Look at those police cars. I never heard them arrive."

"Their sirens were blaring," I said a little defensively.

"And I missed it? Dang."

I gave Jane a quick glance and she jumped in. "You should be able to catch the county coroner's arrival in a little while."

"The county coroner?" Mrs. Higgins whispered reverently. "Oh my. Yes, I'll watch for him. The least I can do is watch 'em take the body away." Her eyes darted from Jane to me and back to Jane. "For Jesse's sake, I mean."

"Of course," Jane said, biting back a smile.

Mrs. Higgins patted Jane's hand. "I know he was your family and I'm sorry for your troubles. But all this excitement was happening right in front of my nose and I didn't even get to check it out."

"It's not over yet," I said. "There's still some more excitement to come."

She scowled and shook her finger at me. "You, of all people, should've known to call on me sooner. I need to be a witness. I could've taken pictures. I owe it to that old coot to get all the best gossip before anyone else in town!"

"Sorry, Mrs. Higgins," I said, with an eye roll for Jane. "Don't know what I was thinking."

Mrs. Higgins coughed when she seemed to realize she might've come across as a bit bloodthirsty. "I mean, it would be a fitting memorial to his, er, memory, that's all. I was his closest confidante for the past many years, don't you know?"

"That is true," I said, nodding.

"Of course you were," Jane murmured sincerely.

Mrs. Higgins was a touch addled, even on a good day. I hesitated to ask the next question but realized the woman might actually know something important. "Mrs. Higgins, did you notice anything strange going on at Jesse's house recently?"

"Strange?" When her eyes widened, I knew I'd just spoon-fed her a great big scoop of potential gossip, but what else could I do? I needed information. Her nose was practically twitching as she wrapped her housecoat more tightly around her. "Like what, for instance?"

"Oh, you know. Strangers coming and going. Cars parking on the street that you don't recognize. Loud noises." I figured if a thief had used a sledgehammer to pound a hole in Jesse's wall, somebody must've heard it.

"Noises," she said flatly. "There've been plenty of noises. A car engine was so loud the other night it woke me out of a deep sleep. I heard some pounding late last night, too, but I think it might've been coming from the marina."

The Lighthouse Cove Marina was two blocks away and we could hear late-night party noises occasionally. But I'd never heard pounding coming from over there.

"When was the last time you saw him?"

She pursed her lips, thinking. "Four days ago we talked for a few minutes, but before that, it had been well over a week."

I could remember seeing Jesse and Mrs. Higgins talking every day. What had changed? "Was he out of town?"

"No, just too busy for an old friend." She tried to sound blasé, but I could tell her feelings were hurt.

"Was anything different the last time you talked to him?"

"No, unless you count Jesse being overly jolly. That can get on a person's nerves, I don't mind saying."

"Jolly?"

"What do you mean?" Jane asked.

Mrs. Higgins frowned. "You asked for strange and that's what I'm telling you. He was practically giggling half the time I saw him. I thought maybe he'd been smoking some of that reefer the kids are into."

Jane just shook her head. There was no way Jesse

would ever smoke marijuana. He was as straight-arrow as they came. But giggling? Jesse? That was weird, all right.

"Well, thank you, Mrs. Higgins," I said briskly. "Do you want me to help you outside so you can watch the police activity?"

"No, you girls go along. I've got to make up my face and curl my hair before I go out and see those policemen." She wiggled her eyebrows provocatively.

Jane and I jumped up from the couch and left her sitting alone, smiling to herself.

Chapter Three

"Wow," Jane said as we crossed the street. "She's a piece of work."

"I know," I muttered.

"Assuming she was telling the truth, it does sound strange to hear that Jesse was giggling so much."

"Would dating a hottie cause him to giggle like that?"

Jane actually giggled. "Probably. But I still don't believe it."

"So you never heard him giggling? Never saw him in a jolly mood?"

"Not really. I mean, he laughed and stuff, but jolly? He was mostly a curmudgeon. And crafty. Smart and snarky sometimes. But not jolly. What do you think?"

"I agree. I can think of a lot of ways to describe Jesse, but jolly isn't one of them."

She chuckled. "Definitely not."

"So, when did you last talk to him?" I asked, and wondered if she noticed that I sounded like a cop.

She gave it some thought. "It was Thursday. Four days ago." She smiled softly at the memory. "He was thinking about going on another scuba diving trip with his buddies."

"Since the last one was so lucrative?" I asked, tongue in cheek.

"Oh, wasn't it?" She laughed. "He loved telling that story, didn't he?"

"Yeah," I said, grinning despite the tears that sprang to my eyes. That was happening a lot today.

Two years ago on Jesse's seventy-fifth birthday, he and his old navy buddies, Bob and Ned, had celebrated the occasion by going scuba diving off the coast of Lighthouse Cove. They had gone down to explore the *Glorious Maiden*, an infamous clipper sailing ship that had been lost in rough waters off the coast almost one hundred and seventy-five years ago.

For months after that scuba trip, Jesse had bragged that while he was down there, he'd discovered an old necklace burrowed down behind a wallboard. When Jane finally called his bluff and demanded to see the necklace, he grinned and admitted that he'd been pulling her leg the whole time. He never brought up the subject again.

"I'll miss his tall tales." She sniffled and gulped back tears.

"Me, too." So many memories. But they were good ones. I had a feeling they would help us both get through the next few days.

Jesse was always telling stories to anyone who would listen. He'd go on and on, describing in dramatic detail some exciting adventure he'd experienced or some intriguing person he'd met. Many of his exploits had happened while he was in the navy, assigned to exotic ports on the other side of the world.

He liked to tell us about the time he found a big, fluffy chicken on a dirt road and he picked it up to deliver it to its owner. The local chieftain thought Jesse was stealing his prize chicken and had his warriors chase him all the way back to the ship. He had to run for his life and barely made it. It sounded as though he almost got killed from the spears thrown by the warriors running after him. But then he described the delicious chicken stew he whipped up for the crew that night and Jane and I groaned out loud.

He told that story every time he made his famous chicken stew.

I sometimes thought he made up stories just to entertain Jane, who had lost her parents at an early age. For a
while, the court wasn't sure who would get custody of
her. Her grandmother lived in town, too, but Jesse knew
the high-strung woman wouldn't be able to handle the
sad little girl and make her laugh again. So he made the
decision and stepped forward to take Jane into his home.

That bittersweet thought reminded me that I'd lost my
own mother when I was eight and Jesse had been there
for me, too. The week after Mom died, Jesse planted two
rosebushes along our fence, a red one for me and a white
one for my sister, Chloe.

"Whenever you look at the roses," he told us, "you'll
remember that your mama is always with you."

Those bushes grew and flourished and flowered no
matter how much we neglected the garden. And when
Chloe moved to Hollywood after high school to try her
luck in showbiz, she rented a funky but charming duplex
near Venice Beach. The first thing Dad and Jesse did after they moved her stuff in was plant a white and a red
rosebush in the tiny side yard to remind her of Mom.
Those roses grew like crazy as well, and everyone in her
neighborhood came by for cuttings.

I would have to remember to call Chloe tonight to let
her know about Jesse. There would be more tears.

I tried to lighten the conversation. "Remember when
Jesse started that betting pool at the pub over whether
I'd go home with my blind date or not?"

"Yeah, he bet you'd kick him in the . . . you know."

"That did not end well," I muttered.

"Maybe not for your date, but Jesse won the bet."

True, I thought, but my blind date ended up dead. So
much for lightening up the conversation.

Jane sighed. "Remember how he used to talk like a
pirate?"

"Aye, matey," I said, and we both smiled.

Jesse had always been a little rough around the edges
and his speech could be a bit salty. Maybe because of all
his years in the navy, he had perfected the pirate routine.

He liked to put on a tough-guy act, but he had a heart of gold and was always looking out for me and Jane.

My dad once told me that the day Jesse graduated from high school, he ran away to join the navy. He'd grown up here on the coast, so he'd been surfing, swimming, sailing, and diving his whole life. The navy made good use of his abilities, assigning him first to the Underwater Demolition Teams that were beginning to operate in Southeast Asia, then transferring him to the newly established SEAL Team One in the early 'sixties. He was deployed to Vietnam, first to train their soldiers and later to conduct unconventional warfare in the rivers and deltas of the country. After Vietnam, Jesse moved to Coronado and became a SEAL team trainer until he retired and moved back to Lighthouse Cove to reconnect with his family. Three years later, Jane's parents died and that was when Jesse stepped in to raise her himself.

Jane smiled. "I think that scuba weekend was one of the highlights of his life—not counting all his years in the navy."

"I think so, too. If he wasn't reminiscing about the good old navy days, he was talking about that trip. Those guys had a blast."

Jesse and his two friends had scuba dived for three days straight and camped out on the Sandpiper Islands at night. He still talked blissfully about the fish they fried each night, how it tasted better than any fish he'd had since.

Jane's expression fell. "I hate the thought of calling Bob and Ned."

I grimaced. His two best navy buddies were going to be heartbroken when they heard the news.

"If you'd like, I can be with you when you make the calls."

"Thanks," she said. "I'll think about it." She sat back in her chair. She looked exhausted and it was barely ten o'clock in the morning.

I was glad Jane hadn't yet seen the worst of the destruction inside the house. It would only upset her more.

If all that damage had been caused by Jesse, I hoped he'd found what he was looking for. But if someone else had broken into his house looking for valuables, then I hoped the police would track them down to the ends of the earth. Because somehow something had gone terribly, tragically wrong.

I couldn't think of anything of real value in the house, nothing worth tearing it apart. A crook might've taken the television set and the few electronics Jesse owned. But the television had still been there.

Whoever had broken into Jesse's house wasn't a conventional burglar. So who was it? And what were they looking for? If Jesse had died because of it, I called that murder.

While Jane met with Eric to answer some questions about Jesse, I waited on the porch with too much time to think. I had convinced Jane to spend the night at my house and had contacted Emily and Lizzie and Marigold to come for dinner. Jane wanted to be around people and I knew the girls would want to be with her. And I wanted a chance to talk about Jesse's mysterious death.

After watching the coroner take Jesse away, I was overwhelmed with sadness again. I had more questions than answers and kept trying to recall if I'd seen Jesse at all over the last week or two. Was there really a hottie girlfriend? And if so, why had I never met her before? And when had Jesse stopped visiting Mrs. Higgins? It was his regular habit to walk across the street to kibbitz with her whenever she was in her garden, which was daily. They had been friends forever and enjoyed catching each other up on the latest gossip. They were a neighborhood staple. What had happened to change that?

And now the guilt seeped in because I had no room to judge Jesse for not being around lately. I hadn't been, either. In the past few months, I hadn't bothered to take the time to slow down and chitchat with my neighbors. Ever since I volunteered for the Festival Committee, I'd been pulled in every direction possible.

And in case anyone forgot, I did have a day job. Recently I'd taken on two new construction jobs that were starting to occupy what little time I had left in my day—not that I was complaining. Emily would close the deal on the old Rawley Mansion in a few days and she and I would conduct our first official walk-through. Even without the walk-through, I had already promised she would be able to move in within four months. That meant my crew and I would have to kick things into high gear and quickly but expertly renovate her kitchen, living room, and master bedroom and bath, and also make the exterior presentable enough for her to live there without shuddering every time she looked around. Once she moved in, we would continue renovating, one room at a time.

The only thing that would slow us down was if the ghost of Grandma Rawley decided to play tricks on us. I refused to jinx the project by mentioning that out loud. After all, there was no such thing as ghosts.

Emily was thrilled with my timeline, even though I'd warned her that after she moved in, my guys would continue working on the other rooms and the exterior until she was well and truly sick of us.

The second job promised to be just as challenging, although not quite as time-sensitive. MacKintyre Sullivan, the famous mystery writer, had moved to Lighthouse Cove a few months ago and purchased the old lighthouse mansion two miles north of the pier. The property, though long abandoned, was considered a treasured monument by the townspeople, which meant that I had to submit numerous permits, plans and blueprints and have every single inch of my work preapproved by the town Planning Commission before I could start the job.

Things weren't starting out on a positive note, though. I'd just called the Commission office a few minutes ago to cancel my first meeting with them. Vesta, the secretary who'd been working at City Hall for as long as I could remember, answered the phone. As soon as I explained about Jesse's death, she'd sympathized. But then she had scolded me for disrupting her schedule.

I had no idea how old Vesta was, but she was considered by some to be another treasured town monument. Somewhere in her fifties, I'd guess. She was tiny, barely five feet tall, with blond hair flowing down her back and a face that never seemed to age. She was a walking encyclopedia of town knowledge. People in Lighthouse Cove knew who to talk to whenever they had a question about town history or some obscure law or ordinance. "Go see Vesta," they'd say. I'd known her most of my life and was aware of her obsessive-compulsive disorder, so I'd made my phone call with some trepidation. Any little ripple in her schedule hit her like an 8.5 earthquake, so for her sake, I acted suitably chastised when she reprimanded me for changing my appointment. I figured she'd get over her pique as soon as we ended the call and she could start spreading the news about Jesse, no doubt with the velocity of a Doppler radar signal.

I wrote myself a calendar note to call her back later in the week to reschedule my meeting with the Planning Commission. Happily, there wasn't a lot of urgency to get the plans approved since Mac Sullivan was currently living in one of the comfortable apartments over my garage and seemed in no big rush to move to his new home next to the lighthouse. And truth be told, I was in no hurry to see my ultra-attractive neighbor leave my area.

I had other active jobsites, of course, and over the past month, I'd hired three new workers. My guys and I had recently finished the last of the exterior work on Hennessey House, Jane's elegant new bed-and-breakfast. She had inherited the grand old Victorian from her grandmother. Actually, she and Jesse had both inherited it, but he had immediately signed his share over to her, and Jane and I had worked on renovating it for almost three years. Hennessey House would open its doors to the world in just a few weeks, and the whole town was excited to attend the grand opening celebration.

It was just so sad that Uncle Jesse would miss it. And if I thought about that too much, I would tear up again and I was tired of crying. Instead I replayed the brief, private conversation I'd had with Eric a few minutes before he met with Jane.

It was nice to know he agreed with me that Jesse had probably been the victim of a burglary. Whether Jesse had been dead or alive at the time of the break-in, though, was for the county coroner to determine. One positive note was that Jesse himself hadn't appeared to have been attacked physically. But that meant that the coroner would also have to determine if the shock of seeing an intruder had brought on a heart attack, or if something else had happened.

I figured it was murder either way.

I wasn't about to share my thoughts around town, though, and whether Eric agreed with me or not, it wouldn't change his methodology. He would play by the rule book, as usual, gathering evidence, interviewing neighbors, and waiting for the coroner's autopsy report before drawing any conclusions. It was frustrating, but I was confident in his ability to track down the person responsible for Jesse's death and bring him to justice.

At six o'clock that night, Lizzie showed up at my house with Emily and Marigold and food. Since the three of them owned shops along the town square, it was convenient for them to stop off at Capello's for pizza and salads. I knew the Capello family through their daughter, Luisa, who was a grade behind Jane and me back in high school. Capello's made the best pizza in town.

With the salad in the fridge and the pizza keeping warm in the oven, I opened two bottles of wine and began pouring. Marigold's aunt Daisy stopped by for a few minutes to offer Jane her condolences. She was followed by Mr. and Mrs. Robertson and two more neighbors from down the street who just wanted to give Jane a hug. There were more tears and some sweet stories. Mrs. Robertson recalled the night she was about to give birth to her first child and Mr. Robertson was stuck at a job down in San Francisco. Jesse drove her to the hospital and stayed with her, leading her through her breathing routine and letting her shout obscenities at him until her husband finally showed up.

They'd named their daughter Elizabeth Jesse, E.J. for short.

By the time the Robertsons left, we were all sniffling and dabbing our eyes again.

"Thank goodness there's more wine," Lizzie said, and refilled our glasses.

I brought out plates and utensils as the girls took turns playing with Robbie, my West Highland terrier, who helped lighten the mood. My pretty orange-striped cat, Tiger, was also on hand to give comfort by allowing herself to be petted and held by each of us. She was awfully good at sensing human moods and spent most of her time in Jane's lap, purring softly.

Emily carried the pizza and I brought the salad to the dining room table and we sat to eat and commiserate. Robbie did me proud by staying just outside the dining room, as if held back by the invisible barrier of training, but he couldn't resist a few soft whines as he watched us eat. Tiger ignored us completely, retiring to the living room to curl up on the couch.

"I didn't realize Jesse was sick, Jane," Lizzie began.

"He wasn't," Jane said, still looking a little dazed. "It was a complete shock. We think he might've had a heart attack, but the police—"

"Police?" Lizzie looked at me for the explanation.

"You haven't heard about this?" I said. "I thought it would be all over town by now. I gave Vesta all the details."

"That's the problem," Lizzie said with a knowing nod. "Vesta went home sick this afternoon."

"Well, darn. I went to all that trouble to plant the seeds of gossip, only to have them fall on barren ground."

Jane filled the girls in on the story. "Jesse's house was torn apart, so Shannon called the police. We think someone was looking for something."

Lizzie frowned. "Someone broke into Jesse's house?"

"A burglar?" Emily moaned. "Not in Lighthouse Cove."

"Oh, Jane, I'm so sorry," Marigold said.

I was momentarily distracted by Marigold's ability to weave her long strawberry blond hair into a neat braid, which stayed out of the way while she ate. If only my hair would be that cooperative.

"Thanks, Marigold," Jane said. "I . . . I don't know for certain. . . ."

I could hear her voice growing misty so I jumped in to explain. "We can't be absolutely sure someone broke in until the police go through the evidence. For all we know, it could've been Jesse himself, looking for something he lost. But the place was a mess. It didn't look like something Jesse would do to his own house."

Marigold patted Jane's hand. "It's horrible not knowing what happened." Marigold was a true nurturer. She'd been raised in a loving Amish community, although she'd left her family years ago to join our English world, as she called it.

"It is," Jane said with a nod. "I hate to think poor Jesse might've seen an intruder and died of fright."

"That's a ghastly thought," Emily whispered.

"I'm convinced that didn't happen," I insisted, attempting to persuade Jane while trying to believe it myself. "He really did look like he died peacefully in his sleep. Maybe while watching TV."

But the television was turned off, a little voice in my head reminded me. I ignored the voice because it didn't mean anything. Jesse had probably turned off the set himself.

"So the police were there," Lizzie prompted, reaching for her wineglass. "Does that mean Eric was on the scene?"

I met Jane's gaze. We both knew Lizzie was fishing for some juicy gossip on the handsome police chief, but I didn't have any to give. "Yes, he was here. He was very thorough. He won't make any judgment calls until he's seen all the evidence and talks to the coroner."

"He's such a good person," she said fondly.

"And he's very attractive," Marigold said, egging Lizzie on in her own subtle way.

"And how nice that he showed up himself," Lizzie added, "instead of sending an underling."

"There were plenty of underlings around, too," I said dryly. Ever since Eric first suspected me of murder a few months ago, Lizzie had been lighting votive candles and praying that he would ask me out on a date. She was a natural-born matchmaker and thought a crime scene was as good a place as any to meet an eligible man.

I loved Lizzie like a sister and her husband, Hal, was a sweetie pie. But there was not enough love in this world to ever make me go out on another blind date again. Not after the last guy she set me up with was found dead.

I didn't blame her for that, of course. And I didn't blame her for thinking Eric would make a nice boyfriend for one of us. He was a great guy. But that didn't mean I would allow myself to be set up on blind date with him. On the other hand, it wouldn't be a blind date since I already knew him, right? And why were my thoughts headed in this crazy direction? It must've been the shock of finding Jesse today. There was no other explanation for it.

Marigold pushed her plate away and sat back in her chair. "Jane, I'd like to help you with the funeral arrangements. I'll do whatever you need me to do."

"Yes, let's figure out what needs to be done," said Lizzie, always the organizer, pulling a pad of paper from her purse. "Have you scheduled a time and place for the service?"

Jane sighed. "I thought I'd ask Mr. Bitterman to handle everything. Jesse wasn't particularly religious, but I would like a memorial of some kind. And he was a veteran, so I'd like some recognition of his service. And afterward, I thought about inviting everyone back to Hennessey House, but . . ."

"But it won't be open for business yet." I finished the sentence for her because I knew what she was thinking. "Having a funeral service so close to your grand opening will put a pall on your party and might even affect your reservations."

She sighed. "When you say it out loud like that, I feel so shallow."

"Don't," Lizzie insisted. "You can have a lovely party at the Inn on Main Street and nobody will think anything of it. Well, I guess it's not a *party* exactly, but—"

"No, let's call it a party," Marigold said. "We're celebrating a life well lived."

Jane nodded more firmly. "That's right. I want to have a party and I want everyone to have a good time celebrating Jesse's life."

"Sounds perfect," I said. "He would love that."

"I'd be happy to cater it," said Emily, who ran a successful catering company with her tea shop employees. "Unless you have something else in mind."

"No, that would be wonderful," Jane said. "Can you include a full bar? Something tells me we'll all be in the mood for some liquid refreshment."

"Absolutely. A full bar, hearty appetizers, and bite-sized desserts. How does that sound?"

"Wonderful. Thank you all so much." She gazed around the table. "I couldn't ask for better friends."

"Oh, now you've done it," Emily said, grabbing one of the tissues I was already handing out.

I'd placed tissue boxes strategically around the room, figuring there would be plenty of tears tonight along with a few laughs. All of us had known Jesse and loved him, so we told plenty of funny stories and jokes and made some somber guesses as to what had happened to him.

Yes, we'd loved Jesse, but more important, we all loved Jane and wanted to lighten her mood for a while.

Finally Emily returned to a subject I'd been wanting to revisit all evening but hadn't brought up for fear of upsetting Jane. "I'm concerned about the possible break-in at Jesse's. I think we should ask around town, see if anyone else has had their home broken into."

I was happy to see Jane perk up. The last time the five of us had joined forces like this, we helped find a killer.

But then Jane frowned. "Shouldn't we hold off until

we know what actually happened at Jesse's place? I would hate to frighten people with the idea that someone is breaking into houses around here."

Lizzie lifted one shoulder, unconcerned. "I'm surprised the whole town doesn't already know about the possible break-in. By morning, it'll be front-page news."

"True enough," Jane said, and glanced around the table. "We wouldn't have to make a big deal of it, right?"

"Of course not," Marigold said quickly. "We'll just ask people if they've heard about any other break-ins around town."

"That's straightforward," I said.

Lizzie nodded in agreement. "Always best to keep it simple."

"But that brings up another question," Emily said as she refilled our wineglasses. "Don't you think if someone else was burglarized, we'd have heard about it already?"

"Well, yes," Marigold allowed. "Ever since the police department Web site started listing the local crimes, everybody knows everything."

To be honest, we didn't need a Web site to spread the news. Our local grapevine was amazingly effective. But the Internet did speed things up a little.

"In that case, we can just look online," Jane said.

I sipped my wine. "But there might be someone who didn't bother calling the police. It couldn't hurt to ask around."

"No, it couldn't hurt," Jane said.

Marigold grinned. "It'll be fun and it might lead to some interesting conversations."

Jane chuckled, and I savored the sound. She turned to the other three. "I'm still surprised you guys didn't hear the gory details before you got here."

"I heard that he died," Lizzie said, "but nothing about the possible break-in."

"I'm still disappointed in Vesta," I said, then added, "Oh, but I hope she feels better soon."

"She thought it might be a twenty-four-hour bug," Lizzie said.

"But think about it," I said, my eyes narrowing. "Vesta knew, Mrs. Higgins knew, half the police force knew, and word still didn't get around town?"

Marigold's eyes widened in mock horror. "That sounds like one of the seven signs of the apocalypse."

I snickered. "All the best gossips knew and said nothing. It's definitely a sign from above."

"I should've come down and told you all myself," Jane said, glancing around the table. "But I've been such a space case all day. I can't focus on anything."

"Nobody expects you to, love," Emily said, her soft brogue a soothing balm. "You're grieving, after all. I brought you some special tea that'll calm your nerves and help you sleep. I'll brew some right now."

The next day I ran around to three jobsites where I had crews working. I had planned to get in at least a few hours of work, but my foreman chased me away the second time I messed up a template for replacing the decorative wood shingle siding on the old Victorian we were rehabbing. Clearly, I wasn't thinking straight. Since I couldn't focus on work, I drove home and decided to get the ball rolling and survey some of my neighbors about Jesse. It turned out that Mrs. Higgins wasn't the only one who'd heard a driver gunning a car engine. Several neighbors reported hearing the sound of tires screeching down the street around two in the morning the night before. But when I asked my neighbor Hester, who lived four doors down on the corner, if she'd heard the same noise, she smiled ruefully. "Yeah, sorry about that. Lisa has a new boyfriend and his car makes an awful racket. It woke me and Joe up, too, so we've both warned him to either get a new muffler or stop seeing Lisa."

I laughed. "Does Lisa know you told him that?"

Hester confessed that she'd rather have the guy dump her daughter than keep coming around. "He's from San

Francisco and I'm scared to death she'll move away with him."

"I thought she wanted to go to Cove College."

"She does," Hester said, shaking her head. "But he's got those sexy eyes that reel a girl in and make her forget her goals and dreams."

So that answered the puzzle about the loud car in the night. Nobody else had heard the pounding that Mrs. Higgins had mentioned, but perhaps the sound had carried directly from Jesse's house to hers. Or maybe she had imagined it.

But Eric hadn't imagined the hole in the wall in Jesse's bedroom.

By the time I got back home, the only thing I knew for sure was that my innocent questions would send the gossip levels soaring over the next few days. That wasn't such a bad outcome.

"My work here is done," I murmured, smiling inwardly. But before I could make it down my driveway and escape into my backyard, Mrs. Higgins flagged me down. "Yoohoo! Shannon, dear! Can you come here, please?"

"Hi, Mrs. Higgins." I crossed the street to the picket fence, where she was watering her roses. Today she wore a bright green housedress covered in purple plumeria. "How are you doing?"

"Oh, there's just so much to think about and do in any given day."

"There sure is," I said amiably.

"But weighing most heavily on my mind is the fact that my birdbath is leaking."

For two longs seconds, I was befuddled. Then I remembered who I was talking to.

"That's too bad, Mrs. Higgins," I said, gritting my teeth. I'd installed a birdbath last year to replace the leaking one I'd installed the year before that. The woman just wanted a new birdbath every year, and if she could blame the leak on my handiwork, she could wangle a new one and not get charged for my labor.

Not that I would've charged her. It wasn't a lot of

work and it made her happy. My father had been replacing Mrs. Higgins's birdbaths for years before I inherited the duty.

"And boy howdy! I've got a beauty picked out this time. Wait right here." She toddled up the walkway and disappeared inside her house. A minute later, she was back, waving a mail-order catalog. "I ordered it just this morning. Isn't it glorious?"

"Oh my." My eyes boggled at the fountain she wanted installed in her backyard. It was a hideous statue consisting of children and dolphins and fish and birds and a puppy. Water cascaded over everything and ended up in a small pool at the base. There were even angels. Big ones, with wings.

The children were actually two naked boys dancing on the backs of two dolphins. The dolphins cavorted in the waves with a school of fish swimming beneath them. A bird perched on a puppy's lifted paw, and other birds flitted over its head. A throng of overgrown cherubim frolicked above them all.

Water spewed from every conceivable orifice.

I tried to catch my breath. That thing would scare away any bird that came near it.

"My goodness," I managed, "that's quite a birdbath."

"I know." She smiled at the catalog. "There's space at the base of the fountain and I plan to add a plaque, dedicating it to Jesse."

Now I felt like an idiot. "That's very thoughtful, Mrs. Higgins. I'll be happy to install it as soon as it arrives."

"Thank you, dear. It's being delivered to Sloane's sometime next week. I was hoping you'd run out and pick it up for me."

"Of course." Sloane's Stones was a brick and masonry yard out by the highway. They had an enormous inventory and I did a lot of work with them. "Just let me know when it arrives."

"I will, dear. You're a good girl." She turned and continued watering her roses, indicating that I'd been dismissed.

Chuckling, I crossed the street to my house.

"You look like you just heard a good joke."

I glanced in the direction of the voice and saw my neighbor and tenant, Mac Sullivan, smiling as he held open the gate leading to my backyard. "Hi, Mac."

The man had a beautiful smile and I took a moment to enjoy it. There was no getting around it: Mac Sullivan was drop-dead gorgeous. With dark hair and blue eyes, he had a dangerous look about him that was utterly masculine and sexy. He was also a bestselling mystery author whose hero, ex-SEAL Jake Slater, had become a worldwide household name in the tradition of James Bond. I still wasn't sure why Mac had chosen Lighthouse Cove to call home, but the women in town were eternally grateful he had.

Heck, the men liked him, too. He was a great guy and a wonderful writer.

"I was just talking to Mrs. Higgins," I explained.

"Ah, no wonder you're smiling. She's a pip, isn't she?"

"The word suits her, whatever it means."

He laughed, and there went that tingling sensation again. Was there anything more appealing than a man with a great laugh? Not in my book.

"Did you get any writing done today?" I winced. "Sorry. I imagine writers hate that question. And it's none of my business. But I hope you had a good day."

"I had a great day. And I don't mind you asking about my writing. It went well." He grinned. "I killed two people."

I headed for the steps leading up to my kitchen door. "Sounds delightful."

"It was," he said, and leaned against the stair railing. "And to celebrate, I was hoping you'd join me for dinner."

For a few brief seconds I reflected on the fact that after years of avoiding the dating scene, I found myself interested in two attractive men at the same time. I didn't know what would happen in the future, but for the moment I was determined to enjoy myself. "I'd love to. Give me ten minutes?"

"I'll meet you right here."

We ate dinner at Rosie's Crab Pot, which, despite its name, was a lovely restaurant with an old-world clubroom atmosphere and an excellent wine list. From our quiet corner booth, we gazed out at the ocean and shared a dozen oysters and a bottle of Chardonnay. I ordered salmon and Mac had sea bass. We talked about Jesse and I told Mac how I found him among the chaos inside his house.

"I'd like to get into his house and see it for myself," Mac said before taking his first bite of fish. He nodded his approval. "You have a key to the place, right?"

"Well, yes." I bit into my salmon. It was perfectly prepared, not overcooked, with a light butter and lemon sauce. "But you know, it's probably still a crime scene."

"I'll talk to Eric."

"Good idea," I said, relieved that he wasn't going to put me in a precarious position with Eric. Now that I had finally won the police chief's trust and we were friends, I didn't want to go back to the days when he had looked at me with suspicion.

Mac gazed at me as he sipped his wine. "Would you let me into the house without my talking to the police?"

I thought for a minute. "I guess I might, but I wouldn't feel comfortable doing it."

He nodded and took a bite of baby potato. "One of the many things I like about you is that you believe in following the rules."

Nonplussed, I said, "I'm a simple small-town girl. I don't generally break the rules."

He chuckled and shook his head. "You're anything but simple. And not everyone in a small town follows the rules. What I meant was that you instinctively and regularly choose to do the right thing."

"Oh." Why did it feel as if I'd just been insulted? Maybe I was projecting. I knew myself well enough to accept that I'd always been a little afraid to walk on the wild side. Still. "You should know that I've skirted the law on occasion."

"I'm shocked." His smile widened. "What'd you do? Wear white shoes after Labor Day?"

I scowled at him. "Maybe."

"You're a bold and dangerous woman."

"And don't you forget it," I muttered, and stabbed at my green beans.

He laughed. "I remember a high school rule that nice girls never wear black and red on Fridays. I'll bet you break that rule constantly."

Ignoring him, I sipped my wine. "I've been mocked by better men than you."

"Really?"

I glanced over, caught his infectious grin, and gave up any pretense of annoyance. "No, you're about the best."

His eyes widened—with pleasure?—and he leaned over and kissed me. My mind went blank for a moment. The man was an amazing kisser.

"You are a dangerous woman, Shannon Hammer."

I blinked at the seriousness of his words. "Thank you, I think."

"You're welcome." He sat back and picked up his fork. "And because you care, I do intend to follow the rules in this case. I'll talk to Eric tomorrow and get his okay for you and me to go inside Jesse's house."

I ate my last bite of salmon and green beans before nodding at him. "Good."

"Eric won't be happy," he said, dredging his final piece of sea bass through the sauce.

"Why not? He likes you."

His smile was vague. "I talked to the mayor today and got his approval to hang out and follow the cops wherever they go around town."

"Why do you need the mayor's approval?"

"Because I'm starting a new mystery series set in a small town and I want complete access to everything the police do."

"Oh." I grabbed my wineglass and took a long drink. A mystery series in a small town? Written by MacKintyre Sullivan? This was big news. I had so many questions I didn't know where to start. "The police don't generally like having civilians tagging along with them, do they?"

"Not one little bit." He popped that last piece of fish into his mouth. "Should be fun. I'll keep you posted."

Chapter Four

On the walk home from dinner, I asked Mac if he'd heard any of the various noises the neighbors had described hearing over the last few weeks.

"Loud engine noises?" he said. "Pounding? No. I haven't heard much of anything, but then, my schedule is all screwed up lately. For some reason, I've been falling asleep early and waking up at the crack of dawn to write all day."

"I thought you wrote at night."

"I usually do," he said, scratching his head. "I can't explain why it all switched. I've got this new series in my head and it seems to want to be written in the light of day."

"Interesting," I said.

"Weird."

"That, too."

He grabbed my hand and held on to it as we walked the rest of the way home in companionable silence. At my kitchen steps, he said, "Thanks for coming out with me."

"Thank you," I said. "It was fun."

He touched his forehead to mine. "Maybe one of these nights you'll invite me in."

"Maybe I will."

"There's no rule against it."

I laughed. "Shows what you know."

He pressed his lips lightly against my cheek. "My small-town girl has rules I've yet to discover."

"Maybe one or two."

"Sounds fair." With a half smile, he added, "Good night, Irish."

"Good night, Mac."

The following day, Emily became an official homeowner and I drove over to meet her at the Rawley Mansion to do our first inspection of the interior. I'd taken lots of notes based on our many conversations and now I wanted to get a good, close look to figure out what it would take to bring the house into the new millennium. My foreman Wade Chambers joined us.

"The walls look solid," he said, knocking his knuckles against them as he walked into the foyer. "Good proportions in this entryway. Well-lighted landing. Nice."

"You can see why Emily fell in love with it," I said to Wade, marveling at the stunning lacework of the wrought-iron staircase. The ironwork was topped by a wooden handrail that I could imagine shining after being burnished to a high gloss. The newel post at the foot of the stairs with its lovingly carved appliqués required only a coat of varnish to shine again.

An intricate vine-and-leaf motif added interest to the otherwise simple cornice. In the middle of the ceiling was an elaborate fleur-de-lis medallion, or ceiling rose, as the Victorians called the round plaster moldings that often served as a base for a chandelier.

The archway leading to the living room was embellished on either side by stylish plaster corbels, adding formality to the space.

"It's a beautiful home," Wade said.

"I think so," Emily said dreamily, "or it will be, with a few improvements."

He took a closer look at the corbels, reached up, and scratched the surface of each one. "This one here is disintegrating. We'll use the other one to make a mold."

"Will that be difficult?" Emily asked, a frown line marring her forehead.

Wade grinned. "No."

As I took a step inside the living room, Wade grabbed my arm. "What the hell was that?"

"What was what?" I asked.

"Didn't you hear it?" He whipped around in every direction, looking for something. "It sounded like a sick cat."

"What're you talking about?" I started to laugh but noticed Emily staring up at the living room chandelier, which was swaying slightly.

"Did we just have an earthquake?" I wondered.

"I felt something," she said.

I studied her face. "You do realize there's supposed to be a ghost living here, right?"

"You're not the first one to mention it." She wore a worried expression as she glanced around.

I gulped. I never would've believed it if I hadn't seen the crying woman all those years ago. But my memory had faded enough that I was willing to believe that she had been an elaborate trick. Now, seeing Wade's reaction to some strange noise no one else heard, I didn't know what to think. "It couldn't hurt to say nice things about her house. Maybe she'll leave us alone."

"I love her house—I mean, *my* house." She raised her chin defiantly. "I'm sure we'll get along just fine."

"So you believe in ghosts?" Wade asked.

"I'm Scottish. We practically invented the concept."

Wade still looked a little flipped out, but since I hadn't heard a thing, I moved on to the formal dining room.

Wade followed but stopped inside the doorway. "Wow, look at that fireplace. It's stunning." He crossed the room to study the arched marble mantelpiece, the ironwork of the screen, and the hearth with its intricate jade and marble tile pattern. The firebox space was almost big enough for Wade to stand inside. "This feels like the heart of the house."

Emily beamed. "That's exactly what I thought." She

wandered over to the far wall and pressed her hand against it. "It's warm. It practically vibrates with life."

"And look at this built-in breakfront," I said, gazing at the wall opposite where Emily stood.

Wade turned and approached the cabinet that filled the wall to our left. "That's a beauty. All that scrollwork." He opened a few of the glass-paned cabinets to examine their inner workings. "This hardware looks like new. And the mirrored backings are in good shape."

Emily joined us. "Don't you love it?" She glided her hand along the smooth center surface, which was big enough to serve as a buffet space for a good-sized party. Glass-fronted cupboards on each side of the open space would hold an entire service for twenty or more, as well as stemware and various display pieces. The wood-paneled cabinets below would store other items. "I can picture my mother's bone china displayed here."

Given Emily's skill in the kitchen, no wonder she considered the dining room one of the most important rooms in the house. I could see why she'd been so attracted to this property. She would be entertaining guests in grand style in this room.

Wade wandered to the far wall and checked the surface for weaknesses in the plaster. He looked over his shoulder at me. "This wall really is warm."

"I told you," Emily said, pressing her cheek against the surface.

I walked over and touched it. It was warm and I could feel a mild vibration. I wasn't prepared to explain that, so I just grabbed Emily's arm. "Let's go check out the kitchen."

"All righty."

I glanced at Wade. "And since I've got you here, we should inspect the basement." I led the way to the kitchen. I presumed the door to the basement would be located somewhere in here, too.

Inside the swinging door, I stopped to admire the room. It was a sprawling space, big enough to fit two modern kitchens inside it. But it would have to be completely rebuilt. I glanced under the old sink to check the subfloor and backboard beneath and behind the pipes. On my hands and knees, I reached in to knock on the wooden wall. It felt solid, but I would take another look while the plumbing was being redone. This was a prime area for water damage and termite infestation.

Off the kitchen was another good-sized room with polished wooden counters on three sides, under which a cabinetmaker had built large cubbyholes that pulled open.

"It's a winter pantry," Emily said, her voice giddy with excitement.

"For storing root vegetables and such?"

"Yes. That's what I'm going to use it for."

"Clever," Wade murmured as he studied the cabinetry for damage and jotted down notes.

We finally found the door to the basement in the butler's pantry on the other side of the kitchen. Wade confirmed that the stairs leading down were solid. The two of us checked the beams and posts while Emily wandered the cavernous space. There were a few joists where termites had done their worst. Replacing the center horizontal beam was already at the top of my list of priorities, and Wade concurred. Shoring up a couple of load-bearing posts would be critical as well.

Otherwise the house appeared to be structurally sound. Wade did a quickie survey of the bedrooms and bathrooms upstairs and we reevaluated my three-to-four-month target to get Emily moved in. We might be able to get more done in that time frame than I had first estimated.

Emily was delighted and that was important to me. Whether the ghost of Mrs. Rawley would be equally delighted was a different question altogether.

Jane heard from Chief Jensen the next day. The coroner had given a preliminary time of death, and according to his estimate, Jesse died sometime during the night before I found his body. Jane and I were both relieved to hear it, glad to know that his body hadn't been lying there on the couch in the den for longer than a few hours. Unfortunately there was still no word on cause of death.

Even though Jesse's house was still considered a crime scene, and even though the coroner's final autopsy results had not yet been announced, Jesse's body would be released to Bittermans' mortuary tomorrow, Friday, and his funeral was scheduled for the following Monday.

I had a hard time getting to sleep that night, knowing that Jesse's body would be laid out in some casket at the Bittermans' funeral home all weekend. But I read for a while and finally dozed off, hoping I wouldn't toss and turn all night long.

I couldn't say what woke me up, but all of a sudden I was sitting up in bed and wondering what was happening. Had I heard a loud noise? Had I dreamed of something? I checked the clock and it read one a.m.

I glanced over at the doggie bed against the wall, where Robbie slept peacefully. Tiger was sound asleep at the foot of the bed, so all was right with their world.

I punched my pillow to get comfortable again, hoping I could fall back to sleep immediately. But all of a sudden a light flashed outside. It was startling and I wondered if that was what had woken me before. It must've been a car's headlights turning down the side street half a block away, so I decided to let it go. I gave the pillow one last scrunch and was prepared to lay my head down when the light flashed again.

"That's closer than the side street," I muttered. Flipping the covers back, I climbed out of bed and walked to the front window. My movements woke up Robbie, who grabbed his favorite toy, a floppy skunk, and trotted over to join me. As long as he had something in his mouth, I could trust him not to bark.

Was Mac just getting home from somewhere? I rarely saw his lights go on or off, because my bedroom was at the front of the house facing the street and he lived in the back apartment over the garage. But the light could've come from his car driving up.

I slipped into my bathrobe and continued looking up

and down the street. Except for a streetlamp at the end of the block, the area was dark. I almost went back to bed, but another ray of light suddenly swept the front of Mrs. Higgins's house. So it had to be coming from my side of the street. Was Mac using a flashlight to find his way around?

The light flashed again and I leaned closer to the glass to get a look at where it was coming from. That was when I realized someone was inside Jesse's place with a flashlight.

With Robbie watching my every move, I threw on jeans, a sweatshirt, and sneakers. I was on my way out of the room when Robbie began to whimper. "It's okay, sweetie," I said, lifting him up and giving him a hug. "Go back to bed."

I set him down in his bed and petted his back a few times until I felt him settling. "Good boy," I whispered, and closed the door to keep him and Tiger safe in the room. I tiptoed down the hall to avoid waking Jane, who had spent the night. Then I ran down the stairs to the kitchen to get Jesse's key. Seconds later I was out the kitchen door, skulking over to the gate so as not to make any noise. I had to press down on the gate to keep it from squeaking when I pulled it open.

"Maybe Jane's in there," I muttered, although I couldn't imagine why she would go over to Jesse's house alone at this hour of the night. I could understand if she'd stopped to wake me and drag me along, but she hadn't.

I snuck up Jesse's walkway and saw another beam of light flash across the draped window. And that was when I stopped walking. My sensible inner voice was starting to shriek at me. *Who are you? One of those dumb heroines in a trashy horror movie? The one who goes running into the swamp and ends up being eaten by monster crocodiles?*

No, that wasn't me.

I should've called the police rather than confront whoever was inside. And there was definitely someone inside Jesse's house. I could see the flashlight beam moving around. Was it Jane, after all? Or was it the same person who had trashed Jesse's house before? What was he, or she, looking for? Was it the same person who killed Jesse?

It had to be the same person.

Time to go home and call the police, I thought. But before I could do anything, I heard a noise behind me. I whirled around and saw a dark figure approaching.

I screamed.

"Shush!"

I recognized the voice and clapped my hands over my mouth, officially embarrassed. I sounded like such a girl. I mean, I am a girl, but I was only now realizing how vulnerable I was.

"What are you doing out here?"

"Mac," I whispered. I wanted to faint with relief, but that would be stupid. "What are *you* doing here?"

"I asked you first," he whispered. "Never mind. I was following you."

"I saw a light," I said.

"Yeah, me, too. And then I saw you sneaking around and knew I'd better find out what the hell you were up to."

Mac pulled me off the walkway into the shadows under a sycamore tree. "So, what's the story?"

"We don't have time to talk," I whispered impatiently. "Whoever's in there could be the same person who killed Jesse."

"*Killed* Jesse?" he repeated. "Has the coroner determined cause of death, then?"

"No, but I'm pretty sure he didn't die of natural causes. If you'd seen his house, you'd think so, too. The place is a mess." I turned toward the house. "We have to find out who's in there."

"Okay," he said, easily pulling me back. "I'll go check things out and you wait here."

"No way," I said, affronted. "You're a writer. You know what'll happen if we split up."

"Right. You'll get lost in the woods and trip over a rock and sprain your ankle."

"Exactly." Wasn't that what always happened? And then the girl would either die of exposure or be killed by a diabolical ax murderer. Luckily that was all in my head and not something I said out loud.

"Okay," he said, acknowledging my point. "But you stay behind me. Got it?"

"All right." I had no problem agreeing to that. "Here's the key."

He led the way up to the porch and over to the front door. "Hold on to my belt so I know you're back there," he said, and quietly inserted the key in the lock.

Mac opened the door silently and pulled me inside. He closed the door behind me and we stopped and waited in the foyer, listening to every sound. The creaks and groans of the old house seemed to be magnified at this hour of the night.

He leaned close to whisper in my ear, "We'll start with Jesse's room."

"It's this way," I said, nudging him toward the hall. And that was when I noticed that Mac was carrying a gun. My knees began to shake. Not that I hadn't ever seen a gun before. Of course I had. I'd even gone to the firing range a few times, but that was for fun. This was deadly serious. Someone could get killed.

After a few steadying breaths, I figured Mac knew what he was doing. After all, he'd been a Navy SEAL just like his protagonist, and he wrote about crime all the time.

He walked down the hall to the master bedroom at the end. I walked close behind him, praying we didn't run into anyone he thought he should shoot.

We searched the entire house, including the basement, but didn't find anyone.

"They must've heard me scream and escaped out the back door," I whispered, disgusted with myself.

"Yeah, maybe."

We checked the back door and found it unlocked.

"I can't believe the police forgot to lock up the place."

"They didn't," he said. "Whoever it was, they left through this door in a hurry."

He walked outside onto the back porch and then jogged down the steps and carefully searched the perimeter of the lawn. His attitude was casual, but I could tell he was checking every inch of grass, looking for a clue that might lead to the identity of the culprit. It was helpful to have the full moon shining down on things.

"I'll talk to Eric tomorrow," he said. "He's going to want to check out this whole area. The soil at the edge of the lawn may be damp enough to provide some footprints."

He took one last glance around, and then we locked up Jesse's house and returned to my place. Robbie yipped from behind the closed bedroom door, so I let him out and shushed him so he wouldn't wake up Jane. Back downstairs, with his tail end wiggling madly, he greeted Mac. Tiger followed lazily, yawning when she finally settled at Mac's feet.

"Your animals are so unfriendly," he said, making me laugh. We discussed the fact that we were both too wired to sleep right away, so I invited him to stay for a cup of hot chocolate.

We chatted about nothing in particular while I heated the cocoa and he sprawled in a chair at the kitchen table. Tiger was now curled up on his lap while Robbie was in thrall at his feet. Lucky pets, I thought to myself, feeling a little ridiculous for being jealous of my animals.

Once I'd divided the cocoa into two cups, I placed a small bowl of miniature marshmallows on the table and joined him. "I'm sorry I screamed out there."

"I'm sorry I scared you," he said.

"You did, but it's not your fault. I just know the intruder heard me and got away."

"He'll be back," he said easily.

"I didn't realize you had a gun."

"Is that a problem?"

I thought about it. "It was a surprise—that's for sure.

I guess it made sense to have one with us, but I'm not a big fan."

"I'm not, either, but it seems foolish to walk into a dark house in search of an unwanted visitor without carrying some protection."

"You're right. I didn't think about protecting myself. I just went running over there. By the time I realized I might be confronting a killer, I was already in front of Jesse's house."

"You were very brave."

I heard what he wasn't saying. "But stupid, I know. Thank you for not adding that."

His lips twisted into a wry smile. "You're welcome."

I laughed. "Okay, it was idiotic, but the thought of catching the guy who might be responsible for Jesse's death was too compelling. Like I said, I didn't think. Next time I'll bring a baseball bat." On that satisfying thought, I savored a sip of cocoa.

"If there is a next time," Mac said, "promise me you won't go by yourself. Call me or call the police. Or both."

"I promise. And I'm pretty sure there will be a next time. There's something inside that house that somebody wants really badly. At first I thought it was Jesse doing the searching, but now I know there's someone else."

"And that's why you think he was killed."

"Yes, don't you? I mean, it's obvious to me. Now I just have to convince the police."

Mac didn't respond. He sat back in his chair and stirred the chocolate with his spoon. He added a few more marshmallows and stirred some more.

"Did you spend much time with Jesse?" I asked.

He glanced up at me. "Yeah, I got to know him pretty well in the last few months. We were both in the navy, both had SEAL training. We bonded pretty quickly."

"He must've loved having you around to talk to."

"Yeah, it was great for me, too. The military's a strange world and not everyone can relate."

"I get that."

Mac frowned. "Something was bothering him lately. I

don't know what it was, but I had a feeling he would've told me eventually. Now I'll never know."

Little shivers of alarm streaked down my spine. Had Jesse known he was in danger?

Mac said, "One thing he really wanted to do was go diving out in the bay again. You've got a shipwreck out there that he wanted to see one more time."

"The *Glorious Maiden*," I said.

"We made plans, and I would have loved to take him, but it didn't work out."

"He went out there a few years ago with a couple of his navy friends."

"Yeah, he told me. Bob and Ned. I've met them."

"They're sweet old guys." I sipped my cocoa. "Did Jesse say why he wanted to go scuba diving again?"

He gazed at me. "Have you ever done it?"

"No?"

He chuckled softly. "I didn't think so. Otherwise you wouldn't ask. There's nothing like being down there. It's a whole different world."

"I guess that's another thing you two bonded over."

"You could say that. He liked going on adventures. He told me about the last time he got together with his buddies. They went exploring around that old naval shipyard. Just sneaking around, really."

"Is that the place they call the graveyard about twenty miles down the coast?"

"Yeah, that's it. Most of the boats are mothballed and in dry dock. The guys were just goofing around, checking out some of the old tubs and daring each other to climb on board."

I frowned. "Did they find anything interesting?"

"They came across some old weapons and explosives." He shook his head.

"You realize these guys are close to eighty years old, right?"

"Yeah, but they're still kids at heart. I think it's great."

"But . . . explosives? Ordnance?"

"They didn't do anything stupid. They went directly to

the commander in charge of the yard and reported what they found. The guy gave them a reward."

"He gave them money?"

"No, he bought them all beers at a local dive bar."

I smiled. "That's way better than money."

"Absolutely."

But just thinking about Jesse and his pals rooting around an old, rusty ship that had unspent bombs stashed on board gave me the chills. "They could've been hurt."

"Yeah, I know," Mac allowed, "but they got out of there without incident and they did a good deed by reporting it."

"I just hope Jesse didn't bring anything home," I grumbled, then winced, knowing I sounded like somebody's mother. But good grief, those old codgers could've gotten themselves into a lot of trouble.

Mac's eyes twinkled, so I figured he was trying not to laugh at me. "You mean, like some kind of trophy?"

"Exactly. I can just see him bringing home a trophy bomb." And wouldn't that be special? I thought. Living next door to a live bomb. *Oh, Jesse.*

"Don't worry," Mac said. "He would never have brought back anything dangerous."

"You promise?"

He thought for a minute. "I'm almost certain."

I shook my head. "Men are weird."

"You got that right," he said with a grin. "And on that note, I'd better get going and let you go back to sleep. I'll call Eric first thing in the morning to have him check out Jesse's backyard."

"He should probably check inside the house again, too," I said.

"Right." After a surprisingly chaste kiss on the cheek, Mac murmured, "Sweet dreams, Irish."

Eric paced the room, wearing a scowl on his face so intense I thought it might become permanent. I was seated in a side chair in my living room, feeling at a distinct disadvantage since he towered over me even when I was standing.

He had been at Jesse's house earlier that morning with a team of investigators, searching for possible clues and evidence of the break-in the night before.

"I want to know," he said, "if you experienced even the smallest inkling of doubt before you ran over to Jesse's house in the middle of the night without first calling me."

I started to speak, but he held up his hand to stop me.

"You ran over to Jesse's house," he reiterated, "where, I might remind you, the man died recently. A man you seem to think was murdered. And you still gave no thought to making a quick call to the police because that might be the smart thing to do."

"I—"

He stopped me again.

"Okay, go ahead," he said two seconds later. He wore a determined grin and I thought he might be kind of proud of himself for keeping me from talking again. I had to give him that.

I took a deep breath and said, "I realize it was a dumb thing to do. I was halfway up Jesse's driveway when I turned around to go home and call the police."

"That's so weird," he said, thinking back. "I didn't get a call."

"I know, because right at that moment was when Mac showed up."

"Oh, Mac showed up." Eric pressed his hands together in a sign of conciliation. "In that case, everything's okay. Sorry I yelled at you."

"Really?"

"No," he bellowed. "Don't go into that house again without first calling the police. That's an order."

Two hours later, I was still smarting from Eric's lecture. I felt stupid and small and a little bit misunderstood, so I decided to work in the garden for a while. That always calmed me down and soothed my spirit. I called Wade to tell him I'd be available by phone and justified my staying home by pledging to work on payroll over the weekend. Besides, I'd stayed up way past my bedtime last night, so I wouldn't be of much use at any of the jobsites anyway. I wasn't too proud to admit to him that I'd screwed up. Wade told me to lighten up and go pull some weeds. Sound advice, I thought.

After two hours, I had cleaned and weeded all the beds, throwing out wilted leaves and spindly vines and fallen fruit. My last task was to tidy up my pumpkin patch, which, for some unnatural reason, was still producing fruit. My father claimed I grew happy pumpkins and I had to agree.

As I raked out the bed and checked for any blossoms, I found a small spot of powdery mildew on one of the leaves. I knew it would spread fast if I didn't nip it, so once I'd removed all the old plant debris, I dusted what was left with an organic sulfur product I liked. I hoped it would do the trick because I had big plans to spawn another winner for the Harvest Festival later that year.

I heard footsteps and looked up to find Mac coming down the garage stairs.

"You look wrapped up in your work," he said.

"I got yelled at, so I thought I'd take refuge here for a while."

"Eric?"

"Yeah. He was right. I was wrong. I'll get over it."

"Sure you will. He gave me an earful, too."

I smiled. "That's something, I guess."

Eric probably hadn't yelled as loudly at Mac, I thought. Still, I knew I was wrong, so I wasn't going to hold it against the chief of police. Or Mac.

"What're you up to?" I asked.

"I was going to drive up to the lighthouse. Want to come?"

"I'd love to," I said, then glanced down at my grubby gardening duds. "But I'll have to change. You might want to go without me."

"I'd rather go with you," he said. "I can wait."

"Give me twenty minutes."

*　　*　　*

Mac had moved to Lighthouse Cove and bought the mansion last fall. I'd heard about his purchase but I hadn't met him yet when I rode my bike up to take a look at the exterior in hopes of bidding on the rehab job. We'd met that day under strange circumstances having nothing to do with his home purchase. Since then, Mac had officially hired me to renovate the mansion, but because of some conflicts in his schedule—deadlines, book tours, film premieres, meetings with his publishers in New York City—we hadn't done an official walkthrough of the place yet, never mind starting the job. And now Jesse's death had pushed the start date even further out.

Mac parked his car a dozen yards away. I grabbed the blueprints and we walked over to the house. Approached from this angle, the stalwart lighthouse seemed to jut right out of the middle of the roof. In reality, it was separated from the house by thirty feet or so.

"It's so beautiful out here," Mac said, gazing around. "I can't believe the town was willing to sell this place."

"We were only willing to sell it to the right buyer," I said. "You were the one."

He bent his head to gaze at me. "Why?"

"Because you love it. Because you won't change it. Because you'll take good care of it."

"How do you know? I might want to paint it purple and turn it into a den of iniquity."

I laughed. "Purple is so very much your color."

"I think so."

"The iniquity suits you, too."

Chuckling, he slung his arm around my shoulders and we strolled to the stairs leading up to the front porch. As he unlocked the door, I heard a squealing sound.

"Those hinges need to be oiled."

"Yeah." After a long moment of struggling with the front door key, he got the door opened.

"I'll check that lock on my next trip out here," I murmured as I walked inside. "It's probably rusty from years of neglect."

"Same goes for a bunch of stuff around here."

"That's what I'm here for," I said, glancing around.

He followed my gaze. "The most important thing before I move in is to get the roof fixed and update the kitchen as much as the Planning Commission will allow."

"I don't think they'll care too much what we do to the kitchen," I said. "As I mentioned before, they're mostly concerned that we stay true to the original exterior look and also be mindful of the interior walls. In a lot of Victorians, the rooms are compartmentalized, and the first thing new owners want to do is open them up. But the interior walls are often load-bearing, so it can present a problem."

His lips twisted into a frown. "I was hoping we could open up the wall between the master bedroom and that second bedroom to make room for a sitting area. Doesn't have to be big, but I'd like to have a couch and a chair, at least, for sitting around upstairs. And I'd like a walk-in closet. Not that I'm a clotheshorse, but the closets are way too small. I like having the extra space."

"Let's see what it looks like." I walked into the kitchen and spread the stack of blueprints out on the counter. I rifled through them until I found the second-floor plan and spread it out. After a minute of studying the line drawing, I said, "Here's the master bedroom, and, yeah, this is a load-bearing wall. But look. Instead of tearing out this entire wall, we could build a wide doorway here and another regular doorway here." I used my pencil to point out the spots. "This area would be your sitting room, and this here would be the closet. You could add French doors or just leave it all open. We'll add a four-inch molding around the doors and crown molding at the top to make it look really elegant."

He stared at the drawing, then nodded. "So it'll be more like a suite of rooms. I could live with that."

"We can run upstairs and take a closer look if you want to."

"Okay, but first I want to look at the electrical plan. My biggest concern is that the wiring is updated. I need super-high-speed Internet along with every cable channel known to man." He grinned wryly. "Gotta keep my finger on the pulse of popular culture."

"Right." I found the electrical plan and spread it out, bending the ends back and forth to flatten it enough to keep it from rolling. "We're required by law to rewire the whole house because it's still got the original knob-and-tube wiring throughout."

"I wouldn't even know what that was if I hadn't seen it with my own eyes," he said, referring to the old-fashioned ceramic tubes and knobs that held electrical wires in place. "It's a miracle the house hasn't burned to the ground by now."

I tapped my pencil on the drawing. "It looks like most of the upstairs rooms only have one outlet each, so we'll add one or two more to each wall. And same goes for the light sockets. We can revamp the lighting to make it whatever you want it to be."

"Good." He shoved his hands into his pockets. "You want to go upstairs and look around?"

"Sure." I made a few quick notes on the electrical blueprint, then rolled it back up with the rest of the stack. Glancing around the kitchen, I spied a cabinet on the far wall. "And before we leave, I want to check out the dumbwaiter."

"Is that what that is? Cool."

I turned and took one step—and screamed.

A tiny white rat skittered across the floor, ran right between my feet, and escaped into the living room. It might have been sort of cute—if I weren't so horribly freaked out by rats. Even a tiny one that looked like a family pet.

It was lowering to admit it, but I scrambled out of the room and ran straight out the front door. Mac followed right behind me. I didn't stop moving until I reached his SUV, where I wrapped my arms around myself and shivered uncontrollably.

"Sorry," I muttered, when I could speak again. "Rats creep me out, no matter what size they are."

"They creep me out, too." He pulled me close and we huddled together for a long time in silence.

"Call me a wimp," I said finally, rubbing my arms to get rid of the goose bumps. "But I don't think I can go back inside. If there's one rat, there's probably more."

Mac nodded in understanding. "I'll call the Pied Piper."

I gulped. "I know a guy."

He smiled. "Of course you do."

Chapter Five

The Bittermans had arranged a lovely service in the somber granite-walled auditorium on their sprawling property. The American flag was draped over Jesse's casket at the front of the room, and chairs fanned out from there. Everyone who attended received a beautiful program designed by Marigold.

I had plenty of time to make some casual observations during the hour-long service.

The mayor and several members of the town council spoke, as did some of Jesse's closest friends, including his two oldest buddies, Bob Madderly and Ned Darby. I'd met them a few times in the past when they got together over at Jesse's house, so I recognized them. These were the two men who'd gone scuba diving with Jesse on his seventy-fifth birthday.

Both men were around Jesse's age, but Ned appeared to be younger, taller and healthier than Bob. Ned also struck me as the more formal of the two, with his patrician profile, thick gray hair and charming smile. Bob had a bit of a gut, but despite the paunch, he seemed to be a spry old coot with a devilish gleam in his eye, very much like Jesse. I liked them both straightaway. Ned had briefly introduced his son, Stephen, to us before the service began. Stephen was probably about thirty-five years old, tall and nice-looking like his father, with sandy-colored hair and warm brown eyes.

Glancing around the filled room, I noticed three young uniformed servicemen standing in the back. At the end of Ned's eulogy, Mr. Bitterman said a few more words followed by a short prayer. Then he left the podium and two of the military men approached the casket from either end. They took hold of the flag and began to fold it, first lengthwise, then back and forth in a triangle pattern, thirteen times, until there were only stars showing. As they folded, the third serviceman began to play a haunting rendition of Taps on his trumpet. It was a poignant performance with the notes echoing through the granite-walled room, giving me goose bumps.

The last man holding the flag tucked the edges securely into the fold, walked over to Jane, and presented it to her.

"On behalf of the President of the United States and the Chief of Naval Operations," he said, "please accept this flag as a symbol of our appreciation for your loved one's service to this country and to a grateful navy."

"Thank you," Jane whispered, her eyes wet with tears. She wasn't the only one. I was sniffling like crazy and I was willing to bet everyone else had shed a tear during that touching moment.

A minute later, Blake Bitterman announced that the indoor service was ended and quickly segued to the procedure to be followed for anyone accompanying Jesse's casket to the burial plot.

Before the service, the girls and I had agreed that at least one of us would stay close by Jane's side at all times. She was usually so capable and strong, but all of these rituals had to be agonizing for her.

Lizzie and I accompanied her to the burial ceremony while Emily and Marigold rushed over to the Inn on Main Street, a lovely old hotel where the reception would be held in the main banquet room.

A few of Emily's employees at the tea shop were helping out the Inn's permanent staff and would surely have everything under control so that once the two girls arrived, they would only have to check that each guest had plenty to drink and nibble on.

Jane and I showed up an hour later, after a brief, sad ceremony at the grave site. We were both surprised and pleased at the number of people who'd come to the Inn to pay their respects. A few of them, mostly old navy friends, had traveled up from San Diego in Southern California.

Jane did a quick survey of the kitchen, said hello to the staff, and then joined the gathering in the main room. The first thing she did was find Bob and Ned.

"Your words were so wonderful," she said, hugging them both. "Thank you so much. Jesse would've loved hearing what you said."

"I think he would've," Ned said, "if only because that would mean the son of a gun was still here with us."

Bob chuckled. "I think he is anyway. After all, they're serving his favorite Irish whiskey at the bar."

"You may be right about that." Ned turned and grabbed his son's arm. "Stephen, let me introduce you to Jesse's niece. Jane Hennessey, this is my son, Stephen Darby."

"We met briefly before the service," Jane said, shaking his hand. "Hello, Stephen."

I was standing next to Jane, so I had a good view of Stephen's expression as he was introduced to her. He appeared instantly smitten, which was not surprising since Jane was a tall, beautiful blonde with a kind heart and a ready smile.

"Stephen's a financial planner," Ned said proudly, "so if you have any money problems, talk to him."

Stephen rolled his eyes at his father and turned to Jane. "I'm no longer working in finance. My father tends to forget that I recently graduated from the Culinary Institute and have become a chef."

"A chef?" I said, before Jane could react. "How fun."

"I feel I was born to do it."

"That's exciting, but quite a departure from the world of finance," Jane said. "Are you planning to work somewhere in Northern California?"

"He plans to work in Lighthouse Cove," Ned explained before Stephen could answer for himself. "He got a job up here so he could be closer to me."

"That's so nice," I said to Ned.

"He's a good kid," Ned said, elbowing his son good-naturedly. "He's about to start working at some French place. What's the name, son?"

"Tre Mondrian," Stephen said, smiling indulgently at his dad for calling him a "kid."

It was pretty obvious that his father wished he'd remained a financial planner, but Stephen apparently loved cooking more. And who didn't like a guy who could cook?

"Tre Mondrian is a wonderful restaurant," I said, thinking of the one meal I'd had there a few years ago. It was very expensive but worth it. Nowadays, reservations were required three months in advance and plenty of people drove all the way up from San Francisco just to have dinner there.

"I'm really stoked about it," Stephen said. "I'll start out as a sous-chef, but I'm hoping to move up the ladder eventually."

"Have you found a place to live in the area yet?" Jane asked politely.

"I'm still looking. I'll probably stay in a hotel or rent a room for a few months, then buy something."

"I'd offer you a room at Hennessey House, my new bed-and-breakfast in town," she said lightly, "but we haven't even opened yet and we're already booked for the first two months."

"I wish I'd known," Stephen said, staring intently at Jane. He couldn't seem to look anywhere else.

"Jane," Ned said, "you should talk to Stephen about Jesse's estate. He can advise you on the best investment strategies in this fluctuating market."

"Dad, I'm not doing that work anymore." Stephen looked at Jane. "But I'd be happy to help you with anything you need."

She smiled. "Thank you, but I have a financial consultant. And honestly, Jesse didn't leave me much worth worrying about."

"His house has got to be worth something," Ned said.

"Please excuse my father," Stephen said, smiling. "He has a one-track mind sometimes."

Ned held up both hands in good-natured surrender. "Okay, I can take a hint. But it's not just the house. There might be items inside the house that could be worth something. You might have to hunt for them, though. Jesse liked to hide his treasures away from prying eyes."

"Do you know something I don't know?" Jane asked, her tone playful.

"No, no," Ned said, laughing. "But you know Jesse. He was always telling stories about his exploits. Who's to say he didn't bring home some booty from those adventures?"

"I always called Jesse's tales a stretch of the truth," Bob added, flashing us a grin. "It would serve us all right if he really did have some treasure tucked away somewhere."

I exchanged a quick glance with Jane. Did these two men know something about the break-in? I found it hard to believe they had anything to do with it, but they'd both made it sound as if Jesse had something worth stealing.

They were probably capable of breaking into the house, but there was no way they could've done all that damage. Ned's son, Stephen, on the other hand, looked strong enough to pound holes through walls.

But why? I shoved my suspicious thoughts away and walked over to the bar with Ned and Bob, where I left them to chat with one of the people visiting from San Diego.

As I took a sip of juice, Emily sidled up next to me. "Who's the tall, good-looking stranger?"

I turned and saw Ned's son still talking to Jane, his eyes riveted on her.

"His name's Stephen," I said quietly. "He's the son of Ned, one of Jesse's old navy buddies. He used to be a financial planner but quit to become a chef at Tre Mondrian."

"Ooh la la," she whispered. "He seems smitten with our Jane."

"I believe he might be."

We watched them interact for another minute. Stephen seemed charming and Jane could certainly use a distraction. I just hoped she didn't get hurt. She had a romantic soul and believed in her heart that someday she would find her one true love. We teased her that she got that delusional idea from reading too many romance novels at an impressionable age, but she always insisted there was no such thing as too many romances.

I really hoped she'd meet her one true love someday. It was just bizarre to think she might meet him at a funeral.

Ned summoned his son to the bar to talk to someone else, and Jane was left alone. Emily and I hurried over to join her.

"He's awfully cute," Emily whispered loudly.

Jane smiled. "Yes, isn't he?" She still looked a little dazed, but I didn't think it was from talking to Stephen— even though he was indeed cute. No, I was pretty sure the events of the last week were catching up to her. She'd been going nonstop, ever since I called to tell her about Jesse. She had to be emotionally drained.

I glanced over to where Stephen and his father were talking together. Both men were frowning and I wondered what their topic of discussion might be.

Before I could speculate further, my father and Uncle Pete walked into the room. I waved and marched over to greet them.

"Hey, kiddo," Dad said, enveloping me in a big hug.

Uncle Pete did the same, whispering, "This is a lousy way to spend an afternoon."

"Don't I know it?" I said. "How're you guys holding up?"

Dad shrugged. "I had some of the fellas over for a wake of sorts last night. We told stories about Jesse and tried to keep each other laughing."

"Jesse would've enjoyed himself," Uncle Pete said, chuckling.

"I assume the whiskey was flowing."

"Whiskey?" Dad looked affronted. "Hell, no. You know we only drink iced tea and lemonade."

I laughed. "Of course. How could I forget?"

He grinned. "You're forgiven. Listen, sweetie, we're going to mingle for a little while and pay our respects to Janey. Then we'll be heading out to the winery. I'll be there for the next week or so, remember?"

"Oh, that's right." I'd forgotten Dad was helping to design the new reserve tasting room off the main hall of Uncle Pete's popular winery. I'd seen the architect's renderings and knew it was going to be a spectacular room. "I'll miss you."

"I'll miss you, too. But you can call or drive out there anytime you want." He added, "I've always got an extra set of tools."

I laughed. "Thanks for the offer. I might take you up on it, but things are pretty busy around here these days."

"I know the company's doing great," he said. "I'm proud of you."

"Thanks, Dad." I gave him a kiss on the cheek and watched him drift through the crowd until he found Jane and gave her a warm hug. I crisscrossed the room, smiling and greeting friends and acquaintances as I moved. At the bar, I traded in my juice for a glass of water and sipped it slowly, happy to be alone with my thoughts for a moment.

I set my glass on the tray next to the bar and turned to look for Jane. Dad and Uncle Pete had moved on and Jane was standing by herself. None of our friends was nearby, so I walked briskly across the room to keep her company. But just as I reached her side, an older woman approached.

"Jane?" she asked, her voice tentative.

"Yes?"

Glancing at me, she said, "I hope I'm not interrupting. I'm Althea Tannis. I was a friend of Jesse's. I wanted to express my condolences for your loss."

"You're not interrupting," I said, and stepped back a few inches to give her clear access to Jane. Althea Tannis was a pretty woman somewhere in her fifties or sixties, wearing an attractive black pantsuit with a dark gray silk shirt. The suit was perfectly tailored and showed off her slim figure. Her shoulder-length blond hair was held back by a black velvet headband.

"Hello, Althea." Jane shook her hand and the woman held on to it.

"Jesse was a wonderful man and I'm so grateful I had the chance to spend time with him before . . ." She sniffled and delicately blew her nose into her lacy white linen handkerchief. "I'm sorry."

"That's all right." Jane smiled attentively. "Did you know Uncle Jesse from the navy?"

"No, no." Althea's eyes were filling with tears and she quickly blinked them away. "Oh gosh, I promised myself I wouldn't cry, but . . ."

"You won't cry alone today," I said.

That brought a brief smile to her face. "No, I probably won't."

"Oh, Althea, this is Shannon Hammer."

We said our hellos.

"Shannon is one of my dearest friends and she was also Jesse's next-door neighbor," Jane explained as part of a more formal introduction. "She knew him her whole life."

Althea shook my hand. "It's a pleasure to meet you, Shannon, despite the circumstances."

"He was a sweet guy and a wonderful neighbor," I said. "I miss him every day."

"I do, too."

"Tell me how you knew Uncle Jesse," Jane prompted her.

"Oh, well, we met a few months ago in a senior aerobics class, believe it or not. We were all hot and sweaty—and I don't mean that in a particularly glamorous way." She laughed lightly and we joined her. "But we hit it off. And for the past six months, we've been . . . well, I guess you could say we were dating. If anyone our age actually dates anymore."

"You were dating my uncle?" Jane's eyes widened and she glanced at me.

Althea smiled at Jane's reaction. "Yes. I can see he never told you about me. It figures. He really guarded his privacy. But he told me so much about you, Jane. He was so proud of you." She pressed the white linen to her cheeks where tears were starting to stream down. "I'm sorry to make a scene. I'd better go."

Jane looked completely stunned, but she recovered quickly. "No. Don't go. Please. Let's sit and talk."

I was pretty darn shocked myself. My father and Uncle Pete had claimed that Jesse had a "hottie" girlfriend he was keeping all to himself, but I'd brushed it off, thinking the girlfriend was yet another one of Jesse's tall tales.

So this was the hottie?

I followed, studying the woman more closely as Jane led her over to a small circle of lyre-back chairs near a corner table where we could talk more privately. Althea didn't look that *hot*—at least, not in the way most men would define the word. But she was lovely and refined and seemed sweet and intelligent and was apparently in mourning for her deceased boyfriend.

Boyfriend. That was about the most bizarre term I'd ever used to describe Jesse. Even more bizarre was that they'd met in an aerobics class. I couldn't believe it. Jesse? Aerobics? The two words didn't belong in the same universe. Sure, he stayed in shape, but he was more of a push-ups and calisthenics kind of guy. But that just showed what I knew about my neighbor.

I felt a little invisible and that was probably a good thing as I listened to the woman open up to Jane, explaining that she had rarely had a chance to visit Jesse here in Lighthouse Cove because he usually drove over to see her in her hometown of Blue Point, a quaint village about fifteen miles down the coast.

"He preferred to visit me rather than the other way around, and that was fine with me," she said. "He was always saying that he liked to keep his private life private. You know, because of all the gossip it would've created if I had come to see him. He really hated gossip, but I guess you probably knew that."

He hated gossip? I almost laughed out loud. Jesse Hennessey was the king of the gossip mill! But it would probably be rude to mention it out loud at that moment. Besides, now that I thought about it, even though Jesse did like to dish the gossip, he probably would've hated to be the center of it.

It was a little surreal to realize that just last week, Jane and I had had a good laugh about Jesse claiming to have a hottie for a girlfriend. Jane had called it yet another figment of Jesse's overactive imagination. But now that figment was here, in person. The girlfriend we hadn't believed existed.

Althea was talking about the last time she saw Jesse. "He came over and I cooked dinner. I'm not the world's best cook, but I can stuff pork chops like a real pro." She chuckled at the memory and Jane smiled. Seconds later, Althea dissolved into tears.

"I'm so sorry," she said, soaking her handkerchief with all the additional tears. "The memories are catching up to me. I can't seem to stop sobbing."

"Please don't worry," Jane whispered. "You have every right to be upset."

"Oh, but you must be so tired of all this crying by now. Let's please talk about something happier." She blew her nose. "Jesse told me about your new bed-and-breakfast and I hope I'll have a chance to see it one of these days. He claimed it was simply beautiful and I'll bet he was right."

"Thank you. We're having the grand opening soon. I hope you'll come and stay there sometime once we're up and running."

More waterworks threatened and Althea pressed her hand to her lips. "That's so sweet. I would love to. And will these damn tears ever stop?"

Jane laughed softly. "I know how you feel. It's just

rotten that we had to meet on such a miserable occasion."

"It really is." Althea took a deep breath. "I know you need to mingle and talk to your other guests, but I would love to keep in touch with you. Maybe we can have lunch sometime."

"I would like that, too." Jane reached over and squeezed her hand.

"You're as sweet and generous as Jesse said you were."

It was true. Jane had such a generous soul, and that was what concerned me. She was so open and giving anyone could come along and take advantage of her.

Was I wrong to be suspicious of Althea Tannis? What did she want from Jane? She seemed so genuine and it was obvious that Jane really liked her, but I wanted to find out more about her before I would be willing to accept her at her word.

"Oh, Shannon," Jane said, turning my way. "Can you believe we're just meeting Althea for the first time?"

"I'm in complete shock." I hesitated, then plunged ahead. "Do you mind if I ask you a question, Althea?"

"Not at all." She looked slightly mystified.

"Did you two really meet in an aerobics class? Because I can't picture Jesse walking into one, ever."

She laughed. "We really did. He confessed a few weeks after we started dating that he'd set the whole thing up. He happened to be visiting an auto shop in Blue Point and he saw me walking into the gym. He pulled his car over and followed me inside. When he saw which class I was in, he enrolled."

"That devil," Jane said.

I grinned. "You've got to give him points for determination."

"Oh, I do," Althea said with a laugh. "Later he confessed he'd never been to an aerobics class before."

"Then he must've been very impressed by you," I said.

"You're being kind," she said, touching my arm. "Thank you."

We chatted for another minute; then Althea handed

Jane a card. "This is the number for my shop in Blue Point. It's also got my personal cell phone number on the back. I hope you'll call me soon. Or come down and go shopping. It's a fun shop. If I don't hear from you in a few days, I'll call you and we'll set up a lunch."

"Wonderful," Jane said, and gave her a warm hug. "I'm so glad you came today."

As Althea walked through the crowd to the door, I realized I was going to have to shift my opinions around. I hadn't believed that Jesse had a girlfriend, and yet here she was. I'd just met her, talked to her. And much to my surprise, I liked her. I could tell Jane really liked her, too.

A few minutes later, on a trip to the bar for a glass of water, I glanced out the front window of the inn and saw Bob, Jesse's navy buddy, standing out on the sidewalk, talking to Althea. Did they know each other? Of course they did. It made sense that if she was Jesse's girlfriend, he would've introduced her to his oldest friends. Even if none of us had met her.

Bob looked dazzled by her and I couldn't blame him. She was very pretty and she wore a kind smile as she listened to him. A few moments later, she laughed, patted his cheek fondly, and walked away.

Bob stood transfixed, staring as she walked down the block and turned the corner, disappearing from his view.

"Having fun?"

I whipped around, instantly guilt-ridden for spying on the private interaction. My stomach did a little dip when I saw who was standing inches away from me. "Oh. Hi, Mac. Yes, I'm having a good time, considering the circumstances. How about you?"

"This is a great send-off. The old man would've loved it. He'd have been right over there, spinning tales."

I smiled. "He told some good ones."

"I'll say." He gazed at me. "Why'd you look so guilty just now?"

Darn it, the man read me too easily. "Me? Nothing. No reason."

He laughed. "Irish, you're a terrible liar. I saw that couple talking outside. And I saw you observing them closely. I'm just wondering why you seem so mortified about it."

"Because," I whispered, annoyed to be pinned down, "I didn't believe my dad when he told me Jesse had a girlfriend, but he was right. And now I'm wondering why we never met her before today. She said that Jesse didn't want to bring her around, that he was guarded about his privacy. And I know that's true, but I'm not sure it makes sense when it comes to a woman like Althea. If she was interested in him, I think he would've risked stirring up gossip just to show her off to the people in town. But he never did, even after six months of dating. I mean, she's very pleasant and I don't have any reason to disbelieve her, but . . ."

"But you're suspicious. Is she lying? What's her story? And more important, what does she want from Jane?"

I pouted. Nothing got past him. "Maybe."

"Relax," he said with an easy grin. "Suspicion is a good thing. It can keep you alive."

I thought about that for a moment and decided he was right. Morbid, but right. "I guess that's true. But I still feel bad about spying on her just now."

"It's human nature. Let it go."

"You probably spy on people all the time."

"Of course I do. It's fun. And people-watching helps me develop the characters in my books." Gazing around, he lowered his voice. "Just look at the plethora of peculiar people in this room alone."

I smiled at him. "Are you plotting a murder?"

"Always," he murmured, and continued to scan the room as he sipped his beer.

I followed his gaze. "I see plenty of suspects."

"It's an embarrassment of riches." He grinned. "I love this town."

I had to admit we did have a few eccentric types, and to my dismay, I saw one of them heading straight for

Jane, who stood alone by the French doors that opened onto the Inn's small terrace and pool area. I looked back at Mac. "Excuse me for just a minute."

I rushed across the room in time to hear the man wheeze Jane's name and see her turn.

"Oh. Hello, Mr. Clemens," Jane said. Her smile was forced, for good reason.

"Cuckoo" Clemens, the owner of the Treasure Chest antique shop on Main Street, was about to corral Jane. Clemens was a local fixture but not particularly well loved. He advertised nationally on late-night cable TV and had admittedly brought a lot of business to Lighthouse Cove. He always dressed in bird feathers on TV and made a big deal about his prices being "so low they're cuckoo."

Not to put too fine a spin on it, but the man was an abrasive blowhard. On television he appeared to be tall, but in reality, he was about my height, maybe five foot eight, and sort of skinny, although he came across as bulkier on-screen. Maybe the feathers added ten pounds. These days he considered himself the main reason Lighthouse Cove was a successful resort town. Some of us wondered how many potential visitors he was scaring away each year.

"Hi, Cuckoo," I said, gently shoving my way into the space between him and Jane. "How's it going?"

"Good day, Miss Shannon," he said. "Just paying my regards to the lady of the hour."

"That's so nice, but she's had a long day and was just about to go take a nap. Weren't you, Jane?"

Jane gave me a fulminating look that I interpreted loosely as *A nap? Are you insane? Buzz off. I'm perfectly capable of handling this clown.*

So I gave her a look back that said, *You sound a little cranky. Maybe you really do need a nap.*

Before she could silently flip me off, I turned to Cuckoo. "How's the junk business, Cuckoo?"

"I sell *antiques* and business is booming," he said with

his teeth clenched. "Look, I've got something to discuss with Jane here, so you ought to mosey along and—"

Jane cut him off. "Shannon's my best friend, Mr. Clemens. Anything you have to say to me can be said in front of her."

I grinned at Jane, knowing she'd give me hell later.

"Fine." He ignored me and said to Jane, "I want to know what your plans are for liquidating the necklace."

I almost laughed. I couldn't believe Cuckoo had bought in to Jesse's old fib about finding a necklace. I had to hand it to Jane, though. She didn't bat an eyelash. "Necklace?"

"Don't play dumb, now," he said, before Jane could play dumb. "I deserve the right to bid on it first. After all, your uncle came to see me two days after he found it on the sunken ship. I saw it before he showed it to anyone else."

Jane swallowed and I could tell she was speechless.

"Jesse claimed that the story about the necklace was untrue," I said. "So you must realize we're having a hard time believing you. Can you prove that you've seen it?"

He leaned over and looked me in the eye. "You're playing a dangerous game here, missy."

"No, I'm not." I backed away a few inches. He really was a little cuckoo.

Jane recovered quickly. "Mr. Clemens, Shannon's just trying to make sure you're not trying to trick me. Can you describe the necklace?"

He expelled an angry breath. "Gold, three-tiered, with a couple dozen of the biggest rubies, emeralds, and diamonds I've ever seen. Man, that thing sparkled enough to blind your eyes."

Jane didn't dare glance at me. "So Uncle Jesse came to see you in hopes of selling the necklace to you?"

"That's right."

"And when was this, exactly?"

His forehead furled tightly as he calculated. "Almost two years to the day."

"But you didn't buy it."

He coughed and blustered. "Well, no. I was having a little cash flow problem at the time, but things are different now."

"I'm happy for you."

"Look, the piece is too garish to be worth much in this market. I'd be doing you a big favor by taking it off your hands for five thousand dollars."

"Five thousand dollars." Jane seemed to be considering the offer, but then gave him a smile of regret. "That's an interesting offer, but since I can't verify that the necklace exists, I can't possibly sell it to you."

"Don't pull that crap on me," he said with a hiss. "I've seen it with my own eyes."

"I don't believe you," Jane said quietly.

His teeth clenched and he fumed silently for a moment. "All right, all right, damn it. Ten thousand, but that's my final offer."

"I doubt it," I muttered. If the gems were as big as he claimed, the necklace had to be worth many thousands more than he was offering. If there really was a necklace at all, which was a big "if." But since Cuckoo was making such a fuss, I figured it had to exist. And there went another one of Jesse's so-called myths blown wide-open.

"You know, Mr. Clemens, Shannon was right." Jane touched her forehead dramatically. "I'm really very tired."

"Then just say yes and we can close the deal right now."

"Why don't I stop by your shop next week and we can discuss it again?"

He scowled so intensely that his dark, bushy eyebrows had to be blocking his vision. "Don't wait too long, missy," he warned. "I'm in the mood to do business now and I won't be played for a fool."

"And I won't be bullied. Thank you for your advice," Jane said graciously. "Good-bye, Mr. Clemens."

Chapter Six

"He must've sold it," Jane said. She had her eyes closed as she tried to rest on the comfortable couch in my living room.

After the party, we had escaped back to my house for a restorative glass of wine and a snack. All of the girls had gone home except for Emily, who had remained at the Inn on Main Street to help her team with the cleanup.

Upon hearing Cuckoo's claim, Jane and I were obsessed with the possibility that Jesse might've actually found treasure in the sunken clipper ship, just as he'd once claimed.

I spread a dollop of Brie onto a cracker and took a bite. "That would explain why Jesse was searching the place like a madman."

Jane opened her eyes. "I can't believe he'd forget where he put it."

"I can't, either. He was forgetful sometimes, but that doesn't mean he was getting senile."

"He did get a little confused once in a while," Jane admitted.

"I know. A few times lately he called me Jane."

"Oh." Her lower lip trembled. "That's sad."

"No, no," I said quickly. "I think it was more to do with being preoccupied than actually losing his memory. And he would laugh about it with me. I mean, you and I are both tall, but that's where the similarity ends. You're blond and beautiful, while I'm—"

"Redheaded and gorgeous," she finished. "Plus, you have the best arms of anyone on the planet. I wish I could get my arms to look like yours."

I grinned. "You could come work on my crew."

"I guess swinging a hammer all day is one way to get there." With a sigh, she returned to the subject of Jesse. "But no, Jesse wasn't getting any younger."

She picked up her wineglass from the coffee table. "I still don't think he would tear up his own house like that."

I thought about the mess I'd walked through. "I don't, either."

Jane scowled. "If it's true that the necklace exists, I hate that we had to find out about it from Cuckoo Clemens."

"He's so rude, isn't he? And a little scary, too." I shivered, remembering how he got right in my face.

"I don't want to think about him right now," Jane said, waving his image away as she closed her eyes again.

Something occurred to me. "Do you think Cuckoo could've been the one who was tearing Jesse's house apart?"

Jane's eyes popped open. "Oh my God, Shannon. Yes. Why else would he approach me like that if he wasn't anxious to get his hands on that necklace?"

"If it was him, he obviously didn't find it. Otherwise he wouldn't have tried to buy it from you."

"Wait." Jane pressed her hand to her lips. "What if he threatened Jesse?"

"Let's take our time and think this through." I sipped my wine and mentally went over everything that had happened recently. "Suppose Jesse really did find the necklace while scuba diving. The first thing he would do is try to sell it, right?"

"Wouldn't that get him into trouble? Aren't there salvage laws involved?"

"I don't know." I squeezed my eyes shut. "I'm trying to remember our sixth grade history class."

In our local schools, every child learned the history of Lighthouse Cove and the *Glorious Maiden*, the clipper ship that sank off the coast in 1839.

The fast sailing ship had made regular round-trip runs from British Columbia down to San Francisco, and while it was purported to carry tea and textiles, its main cargo was often opium. They also transported wealthy travelers along with their money, jewelry, and other valuables. Legend had it that a Spanish princess and her royal entourage were passengers on board that fateful night, and when the ship sank, the princess and all her jewels were lost at sea.

Allegedly.

In the aftermath, a number of gold coins washed up onshore, bringing an onslaught of treasure hunters to town. After a time, the gold fever died down, but every once in a while, another gold coin would show up and another wave of treasure seekers would inundate the area.

Pawnshops and curio shops cropped up around town to provide seekers with a place to trade their worldly goods for cash to last them another few months while they tried to hunt for more treasure. But except for the occasional gold coin, no fancy jewels were ever found.

A few of the shops were still in business, though, and one of them was owned by Cuckoo Clemens.

Two local scuba diving shops and a company that specialized in geocaching, or treasure hunting, continued to thrive as well. The lure of finding treasure was no longer the draw, of course. Now our bay was simply a popular diving spot for the fun of exploring a nineteenth-century sailing ship.

But none of that information answered Jane's question about salvage rights.

"I'm no expert in maritime law," I admitted. "But if the legend is true and a Spanish princess really did die on that ship and Jesse found her necklace, I imagine it would rightly belong to Spain."

She opened her eyes and sat up. "Maybe Jesse did the right thing and contacted the Spanish embassy."

I thought it through. "I doubt it."

"Me, too." She smiled ruefully. "Jesse wasn't exactly the type to follow through on the kind of complicated paperwork that would entail. He might've planned to do it, but whether he ever got around to it . . ."

"Right," I said. "So maybe in the beginning he just wanted it appraised and figured Cuckoo's shop was as good as any to get it done. Once Cuckoo turned him down, maybe he sold it somewhere else. Or not."

"It's too complicated," Jane said, reaching for her wineglass.

"My mind is spinning with several theories."

"Do share."

"What if Cuckoo kept offering to buy the necklace, but Jesse always said no? But then, just recently, Cuckoo offered him money again, and Jesse told him that he was planning to give the necklace to Althea?"

Jane stared at me for a long moment. "Oh, that's good. Althea's presence could've changed everything. Cuckoo realized he was running out of time to get his hands on that necklace."

"He grew desperate," I speculated.

"Cuckoo went cuckoo."

I laughed. "It's all ridiculously hypothetical, of course. First of all, Jesse wouldn't give a priceless treasure to a woman he just met a few months ago."

"I hope not," Jane muttered.

"It's more likely that he went ahead and sold the necklace to another antique dealer a few years ago and that was the end of it."

"So why was his house torn apart?"

I frowned. She had a point. "Good question."

"And if he sold it, what did he do with the money?"

"He didn't spend it on himself—that's for sure." I looked at her. "Did he leave a will?"

Jane thought for a moment. "Not that I know of. He mentioned a while ago that he wanted to hire a lawyer, but I don't know if he ever did."

"Did he tell you why he needed a lawyer?"

"No, darn it. But I'll bet it's about this necklace."

We drank our wine in silence for another minute, and then I asked, "Are you going to talk to Cuckoo?"

"No way."

"Good. I think we should talk to Eric and let him know that Cuckoo threatened you. And I also think we should start searching for the necklace."

Jane yawned. "Okay. Maybe tomorrow. I need to figure a few things out."

I put down my glass. Now wasn't the time to bother Jane with a list of things to do. "I should let you take that nap."

She laughed. "You know I don't take naps. I almost smacked you when you said that."

"I could tell. But I didn't like seeing Cuckoo barreling toward you the way he did. He's such a jerk."

"He really is." She was quiet for a moment, then seemed to come to a decision. "I know you've got more than enough work to do, but I would so love to get Jesse's house rehabbed and ready to sell. I don't want any more crazy people breaking in and ripping down the walls, looking for a necklace that was probably sold years ago."

"Good idea."

"So you'll do the rehab?"

"Of course." I was happy to have some concrete way to help Jane. "I'll rearrange a few things on the calendar and try to get started in the next week or so."

"Thank you, Shannon. I'll have a cleaning crew go through and get rid of the mess in there as soon as Eric tells me it's not a crime scene anymore."

The next day, I held an early-morning meeting at my house with my two foremen, Wade Chambers and Carla Harrison. We had worked together for years, so I knew that Wade would be happier attending an impromptu meeting with the boss if I made blueberry muffins to go with our coffee.

As we munched on muffins, I went over everyone's

schedules and then I mentioned that I'd added Jesse's house rehab to our workload.

"Wow, we're going to be busy," Carla said, counting items on her calendar program.

"I would never turn her down," I said.

"Of course not."

"We can handle it, boss," Wade said, making notes.

"I know, but now I've promised both Jane and Emily that we'll get their projects done quickly."

"Working with friends," Wade muttered, shaking his head.

"Your friends are wonderful," Carla said, smacking Wade's knee. "We'll make it happen. He's just grumpy because Sandy's away with the kids, visiting her sister."

I gave him a sympathetic look. "Cooking your own meals, huh?"

"I'm starving," he moaned.

Carla and I snickered at the sound of whining from such a big, tough bear of a man.

"Don't laugh. I tried to make spaghetti but had to throw it away. I think I poisoned myself."

I smiled. "Well, you can take the rest of the muffins home if you'd like."

"Yeah?" He looked pitifully grateful. "Thanks, I will. These are great."

Carla grinned at me. "He wangled an invitation to have dinner with me and Chase tonight. I promise I won't let him wither away on my watch."

"I appreciate that."

After we finished rescheduling the jobs and reassigning the crew, I gave Carla and Wade the payroll checks to hand out to the guys. They took off for their jobsites and I spent the day doing more paperwork, my least favorite thing. I went over Mac's blueprints and began a preliminary list of tools and supplies we would need for the electrical redo on his place.

At the end of the day, the telephone rang and I grabbed it. I was desperate for human contact, even by phone.

Jane said, "Eric called to let me know he's finished with Jesse's house. It's not a crime scene anymore."

"Great."

"I'm going to call a cleaning crew, and as soon as they're done, you're free to start. No pressure. I know you have other jobs."

"I've already talked to Wade and Carla. We plan to get started as soon as you give us the word."

She thanked me and we talked for another minute, then ended the call.

I spent Wednesday and Thursday working at my various jobsites, filling in for Sean, who was sick in bed with some kind of icky flu. It felt good to be back on-site after a full week of mourning with Jane and helping arrange things for Jesse's sendoff. Wade and Carla kept me busy at the sites, too busy to worry about anything except the job at hand.

For me, one of the best aspects of construction work was that sense of accomplishment you got from starting a project and seeing it through to the end. When you put down your hammer or nail gun, you could look around and see a finished room, or a new deck, or a sparkling-clean new bathroom. Sure, it was just a bathroom and not the Nobel Peace Prize, but what the heck? It made me feel good, especially when I saw the homeowners smiling with delight at what my guys and I had just done for them.

Friday morning, I decided to squeeze in a preliminary survey of Jesse's house. I didn't want to sacrifice any of my crew to join me, and Jane had a meeting at her bank that morning, so I poured myself another cup of coffee and walked next door to Jesse's house by myself.

It was weird to return to the house while the sun was shining, weird to think that I'd found Jesse's body all those days ago. It was no longer a crime scene. Jane's cleaning crew had come through and done a great job. I couldn't see a trace of that fine black soot the police liked to leave on every surface after they'd dusted for fingerprints. I knew how hard it was to get rid of that powder residue because the police had dusted for fingerprints in my garage a few months ago and had left it for me to clean.

I was actually looking forward to doing the work on Jesse's dilapidated home, even though he was no longer here to enjoy it. I'd offered to help him fix the place a bunch of times over the years, but he'd never taken me up on it. His house was charming, or it would be once I was finished with it.

It was one story, but it had a steeply pitched roof and a large attic with a dominant front-facing gable. The porch was roomy enough to create an outdoor sitting room if someone wanted to, and the widow's walk that circled the attic was instantly appealing from the street. I knew the house would sell quickly.

I had my computer tablet with me, and as I walked through the main living areas, I took pictures and typed out notes. Later, I would prioritize the work. On most jobs, that meant starting with the basement, reinforcing the support posts and beams before doing anything else. Otherwise an old house like this might collapse on top of itself.

The only time I'd ever been in Jesse's basement was the night Mac and I came looking for the intruder, but it had been so dark that night that I couldn't see whether there was any damage or not. Now I walked into the pantry, found the brass ring set into the floor, and pulled up the trap door leading to the basement.

I ignored the instant chill that shot up my spine. After finding that body in the basement a few months earlier, I got a little flash of terror whenever I had to go down into the bowels of a house. Not that I would ever mention that aloud to another human being, especially my guys.

"Part of the job," I grumbled. "Don't be a wimp." Besides, next time I ventured into Jesse's basement, I would be with a few of the crew and wouldn't have to worry. It was just when I was alone that the thought of these dark, dank spaces creeped me out.

I switched on the light at the top of the stairs, took a bracing breath, and strolled down the steps as if I didn't have a care in the world. Shining the flashlight around the large space, I confirmed that there was no dead body and sighed with relief. I could handle cobwebs, grime, even spiders if I had to. But I'd rather not.

Walking around the room, I checked the strength and condition of each post. I studied the horizontal beams overhead for signs of sagging or rotting. Damage to something down here could mean we'd have to jack up the entire house, and that was always a tricky move, even though we were experts at it.

I was surprised but happy when I didn't find any water or termite damage and the posts looked and felt solid. But the brick walls around the foundation told another story. There was crumbling in spots, and in several places where I pushed my thumb against the mortar, it turned to powder.

I checked the next wall, cautiously pushing a few more random bricks to test the wall's strength. I reached as high up on the wall as I could stretch, and also got down on my hands and knees to check near the base. Then I moved on to the third wall and did the same. It wasn't the most scientific way to survey for possible damage, but it would give me a preliminary idea of the work necessary to bring the house up to a level that would fetch Jane the best price.

As I thumped my knuckles against a random brick, a big mama spider swung out at me. I screamed so loud I was afraid the neighbors might call the police.

"You just surprised me, that's all," I grumbled to the spider, who had already crawled back between the bricks.

I admit I wasn't a big spider fan, especially when I came across a whole cluster of them scattering in angry confusion. At least, they looked angry to me. This was another little secret I preferred to keep to myself. If my crew ever found out about my spider phobia, they would tease me mercilessly. I would probably find plastic spi-

ders in my sandwiches or my toolbox. I shivered invol-
untarily.

The fourth wall was under the stairs and not easy to
access. But since the steps butted up against the main
load-bearing wall of the house, I knew I had to check this
one even more carefully than the others. I ducked my
head to get under the stairwell, close enough to the wall
to study each brick as the flashlight beam hit it. I pushed
and scraped as I went, making sure the bricks were still
holding up after about a hundred and fifty years. I
worked my way down the wall, following the descent of
the stairs and finally ending up on my knees in the corner beneath the lowest step I could fit under. Here the
mortar wasn't as solid and a few of the bricks moved
easily when I prodded them.

It just figured that the most inaccessible area would
need the most work.

Dismayed, I fiddled with one of the bricks until I'd
worked it almost completely out of its space. I pulled the
brick out and laid it on the floor next to me, then worked
on the one above it. A third brick loosened from my
pressure on the one next to it. They all came out after
only a little prying.

There were a few reasons besides regular aging that
might've caused the bricks to separate. I just hoped they
weren't suffering from water damage or an infestation of
subterranean termites. I got down on my hands and
knees and wiggled closer, directing the beam of the
flashlight into the cubbyhole I'd made. But the space was
too far out of my range of vision, so I knew I'd have to
stick my hand inside the space to assess the thickness
and integrity of the wall. The hole was too small for me
to wear my work gloves, so I pulled one off, blanked out
all thoughts of giant mother spiders, and thrust my hand
in there. All I felt was something cold and metallic.

My first thought was that the original builder had
used steel posts to bolster the brick foundation. But that
didn't make sense. Jesse's house was only one story and

didn't need that much reinforcement. Besides, the metal I was touching wasn't as strong as a steel post. I moved my hand and realized the metal was thin but solid. It was a box of some kind.

I pulled at the next brick over and managed to ease it away from the wall. Now I was able to grab what was in the cubbyhole and pull it out. I pushed myself off the concrete floor and sat against the wall with my flashlight trained on what I'd found.

It was a small metal box similar to a cookie tin, the kind sold at Christmas, with a decorative latch on the front and hinged on the back. The top was dented and didn't open easily, but I finally managed to pry it loose. Inside was some crumpled old tissue paper.

I didn't realize I was holding my breath until it whooshed out in disappointment.

"That's it?" I muttered aloud. "A bunch of paper?"

Halfheartedly, I rooted through the paper until I heard a clink and felt something hard. My heart raced as I pulled a very old, very beautiful necklace from the paper it was wrapped in.

Upstairs at Jesse's kitchen table, recently cleared of all the dishes and newspapers that had been there since Jesse died, I sat to examine more closely what I'd found downstairs.

I opened the box again, unsure if I'd dreamed it or not, but sure enough, the gold necklace was there. Holding it up, I watched it glow radiantly in the sunlight pouring through the window.

I stared at it in awe—and a touch of fear.

This was what Jesse had bragged about finding on his scuba diving trip two years ago. It was spectacular, at least a hundred and eighty years old if I just dated it from when the clipper ship sank in Lighthouse Bay in 1839. But it was probably much older. It looked as though it could've belonged to a Renaissance queen.

Cuckoo was wrong. It wasn't garish at all. It was luminescent, as though lit from within. I allowed that it would be considered ornate by today's standards, but it was beautiful, made of thick, hammered gold and encrusted with diamonds, rubies, and emeralds. Big ones. Each of the larger jewels was surrounded by dozens of tiny diamonds. I couldn't count them all. On more careful study, I noticed that three large gems were missing from their settings. Had they fallen out or had someone removed them?

Despite the missing jewels, it was a gorgeous piece. There were three tiers, each hammered to a fine sheen and each inlaid with the three kinds of stones. The lowest tier curved to a point, and hanging from the point was a single, magnificent diamond in the shape of a teardrop.

The diamond would rest at the apex of a woman's cleavage and a man wouldn't be able to avert his gaze.

If it was real, that diamond alone had to be worth millions of dollars. And I had no reason to doubt that it was real.

I hefted the necklace in my hand and thought it might weigh close to a pound. I couldn't believe that some woman had once actually worn it. A very wealthy woman, no doubt, with a strong neck. It made sense that it had belonged to a Spanish princess, because who else but royalty could afford a piece of jewelry so lavish back then?

And if something this extravagant had been found inside that sunken ship, wasn't it possible that there was more treasure to be found out there?

I'd never learned to scuba dive and now I wondered if maybe I should've. For anyone who grew up in Lighthouse Cove, the sinking of the *Glorious Maiden* on a stormy night in 1839 was a familiar story. Maybe I should've shown more of an interest in exploring our famous underwater attraction.

I shook myself out of all that history to realize I'd been staring at the necklace for too long. What if someone broke into Jesse's house at this very minute and found it in my hands? I could wind up as dead as Jesse.

"Yikes," I muttered, and started to wrap it up, but then stopped. I pulled my phone out of my purse and took a few pictures of the necklace from different angles, just to have a record of it in case of . . . what? In case it was stolen? Ripped from my hands? I shivered again.

I quickly wrapped the priceless jewelry in the old tissue paper and put it back in its tin box. For a few seconds, I wondered where I could hide it without taking it back to the basement. Then I decided I wasn't about to let it out of my sight for one millisecond. Shoving it into my bag, I grabbed my phone and called Jane.

"What's the big hurry?" Jane asked when I answered the door at my house.

I grabbed her arm and pulled her inside, shoving the door closed behind her.

"What's wrong with you?" she said. "You've gone crazy."

"I have something to show you," I said, leading the way to my dining room table. I nudged Jane into a chair and sat down next to her.

"Stop pushing me around," she groused.

I laughed. "I hardly ever push you around, but you'll be glad I did this time." I placed the tin box on the table in front of her.

"What's this?"

"Open it, for God's sake."

"All right, all right." She had to fiddle with the latch to get it open and then waded through the mass of crumpled paper. "Oh, Shannon. It's paper. How exciting! Thank you for calling me over."

"Keep digging while I ignore your mockery."

She found the heavy piece at the bottom and unwrapped it. The necklace fell into her hands. "Oh my God."

I grinned. "I know."

She stared at me with her mouth open. "You found it. Where? How?"

"In Jesse's basement, under the stairs. It wasn't easy. He hid it behind a couple of bricks in the wall."

"Not exactly in plain sight," she murmured as she studied the gorgeous piece.

"I wasn't looking for it. I went over to do a quick inspection and found it completely by accident."

She held the necklace up to the light and gazed at it in amazement. "That is a gigantic diamond. It sure looks real."

"I think all the stones are real."

"It's fantastic." We were silent for a moment while she continued to gaze at the treasure. She hesitated, then asked, "Do you think this explains why Jesse seemed to be getting more paranoid over the last year or so?"

"Could be," I said. "I know I would be plenty paranoid if that thing were hidden in my house."

"I just thought he was getting old," Jane said. "I was worried that he might be . . ."

"Did you really think he was going senile?"

"I didn't know," she said, looking bummed. "He acted so weird sometimes."

"I'm sorry."

"Yeah, me, too." She held up the necklace. "This is amazing. I'm so grateful you found it."

"I'm just happy I found it before someone else did."

She exhaled softly. "Someone else had to be looking for this. It wasn't Jesse. He couldn't have simply misplaced it."

"I agree. It's not like he slipped it inside some drawer and forgot about it. I had to crawl under the basement stairs, break loose some bricks, and pull it out of the wall." Shaking my head in admiration, I thought of just how clever Jesse had been. "That took some planning and hard work."

"I'll say."

"I had to get down on my hands and knees to feel around behind those bricks."

"Ew, spiders," Jane said, rubbing her arms.

I made a face. "Tell me about it."

"It was worth it, though." She cast another glance at the necklace. "This thing is magnificent. I guess I don't blame him for being paranoid."

"He may have been paranoid, but he wasn't going senile. More likely, he was just scared to death that someone might find it and steal it."

She stared at the necklace for another full minute, turning it this way and that, touching the jewels, rubbing her fingers over the hammered gold. "I can't believe Cuckoo Clemens saw this two years ago and didn't buy it."

"Not enough cash, he said."

"Oh, right." Jane rolled her eyes. "He looks guiltier by the minute."

"He seemed pretty desperate to buy it from you."

"I don't trust him at all," Jane said, scowling. "I wonder if Jesse felt the same way."

"I can't imagine anyone trusting him."

"I know, but his story was true. At least the part where Jesse showed him the necklace. I'm not sure I believe the part where Jesse wanted to sell it to him. He might've just wanted it appraised."

"But why go to Cuckoo?" I wondered. "He could've gone to a reputable jeweler."

"They've known each other forever. He probably figured it was easier to deal with Cuckoo than some stranger."

"The devil you know," I said.

"Exactly."

Jane's cell phone rang. She pulled it from her purse and checked the screen. "It's Eric."

"Put it on speakerphone," I said.

She touched the speaker icon so I could hear the conversation. "Hello, Chief, how are you?"

"I'm well, Jane. Listen, I've got the autopsy results on your uncle and I have a few questions for you, if you have time to talk right now."

"Oh. Sure." She glanced at me, her eyes wide. "Go ahead."

"Was your uncle having trouble sleeping lately?"

Jane frowned. "Not that I know of. He liked to fall asleep in front of the TV, but I think he slept soundly most nights. Why do you ask?"

"Because the coroner ruled his death accidental."

Jane and I frowned at each other.

"Accidental?" she said. "What does that mean?"

"It means that according to the coroner, your uncle died of an accidental overdose of sleeping pills."

Accidental overdose?

That was impossible! I grabbed a piece of paper and wrote "No way!"

Jane nodded her emphatic agreement and said to Eric, "I'm sorry, Eric, but I don't believe it."

"I'm afraid that's his finding," Eric said, his tone gentle.

"I mean, I really don't believe it. You saw the condition of his house. Something happened there."

"I appreciate your concern," Eric said, "and I have some of my own as well. We haven't closed the books on this yet. My crime scene team is still investigating a few angles and I promise we won't stop until we've got conclusive evidence either way."

"Thank you, Eric." Jane swallowed hard. "Jesse wasn't absentminded. He hated taking pills and he never would've taken too many."

The chief thanked her for the information. Jane ended the call and looked at me. "I couldn't tell him about the necklace. I'm just not ready to talk about it. Not until we figure out our next move."

"I agree." I might regret it later, but for now I was willing to go along with Jane's wishes. "We've got to tell him soon, though. Otherwise he'll close the case without knowing that someone had a really excellent motive for murder. And we won't even mention what'll happen if he finds out about the necklace on his own. We'll be dead as doornails."

"We won't let that happen." Jane opened the tin box and removed the tissue paper to wrap the necklace. "What's this?" She pulled out a folded piece of lined paper.

I frowned. "I didn't see that in there."

"It was under all the tissue paper." She opened the

sheet, flattened it on the table, and gazed at me. "It's a letter to me."

I felt my mouth drop open. "From?"

"Uncle Jesse."

In the letter, Jesse retold how he'd found the piece of jewelry while diving with his friends a few years before. He found it in one of the passenger staterooms where a wall had begun to disintegrate. The necklace must have slipped behind the wall, probably while the boat sank in the storm. Jesse grabbed it and hid it in his fanny pack so his friends never saw it.

He wrote "I hope it'll ease your mind to know that I hired a lawyer to research the salvage laws. He believes the necklace belongs to me, fair and square. Finders keepers, you might say, but you never know when the laws will change. If you're reading this letter, Janey girl, it means I'm gone and the necklace belongs to you now. Rule Number One, don't show it to anyone. There are too many conniving people out there in the world. Rule Number Two, call Demetrius for more instructions. He's a good guy—for a lawyer."

In the letter, Jesse explained away the three missing gems. He needed cash a few months ago, so he pried them loose and took them to a jeweler in San Francisco.

"Does he say why he needed the cash?"

Jane frowned. "No."

Jesse also explained that he had originally shown the necklace to several antique shops in the area, but grew suspicious and obsessive when they showed too much interest.

"How did he know we would ever find the box?" I wondered.

"He says he left instructions with this lawyer." Jane checked it again. "Demetrius."

"I don't know a Demetrius, do you?"

"No, but I guess I can Google lawyers with that name."

"What if I'd never found the box in his basement?"

"Demetrius, whoever he is, would've contacted me eventually."

I slumped back in my chair. "I feel guilty. I'm beginning to think we should've believed everything he ever said."

She took a deep breath and let it out. "Don't feel guilty. He told plenty of wild tales that you know aren't true."

"We just couldn't tell the difference between the true stories and the whoppers."

I reread the letter as she carefully wrapped the necklace in the tissue paper and put it back in the box. I handed her the folded letter and she placed it on top and shut the box.

"We have to hide this."

"I don't want to return it to the wall," I said. "It was in a good hiding place, but if I could find it, someone else could, too."

She thought for a moment. "I'll open a safe-deposit box at my bank."

I smiled brightly. "I already have one."

"You do? Why did I never know that?"

"Because I have hidden depths?"

Shaking her head, she said, "I have nothing to say to that."

I grinned. It was always good to surprise people who thought they knew you so well. "Did I blow your mind just now?"

She snorted a laugh. "No, but you scared me."

"I scare myself sometimes."

Jane stood and grabbed her purse. "Do you have time to go to the bank right now?"

"I do." I placed the tin box at the bottom of my bag and found my keys, then stopped as something occurred to me. "I wonder if the cops found sleeping pills in Jesse's medicine cabinet."

"Sleeping pills," she said in disgust. "I don't believe it. But we can go next door and look."

I hoisted my purse. "I'd rather go to the bank first. It's

Friday and I hate the idea of either of us walking around with this priceless hunk of jewelry all weekend."

"Okay, bank first, then Jesse's house."

"It's a lot of hassle just to visit your safe-deposit box," Jane said forty minutes later as she parked her car back in front of my house. "I thought you only needed to show them the key to get access to the vault."

"It used to be that way," I said as I pushed the door open and climbed out. "But now they've got signature verification and a PIN and the thumbprint analyzer. It's all very high tech."

"It's a little disconcerting."

"You get used to it," I said. "I'm surprised you don't have one. You must have plenty of important documents for your business."

"I have a lockbox in my closet."

"Oh, that's high tech," I said.

"I know it's dumb," she said. "Don't worry. Before I open my doors to the public, I'll get a safe-deposit box."

"They're only a few dollars a year. Totally worth it."

We walked up to Jesse's front porch and Jane unlocked the door. I took a step inside, but she hesitated on the threshold.

"Are you okay?" I asked.

"It's the first time I've been back since he's been ... gone. It's a little sad."

I took her hand. "Come on. I'm right here with you."

"Okay."

We walked arm in arm to the end of the hall and into Jesse's bathroom. I recalled what it looked like before the cleaning crew arrived. The medicine cabinet had been plundered. Pills, bandages, and all sorts of medical stuff were scattered all over the floor. Some had been flung across the room and into the shower. The drawers had been emptied as well. Now it was tidy, and we found nothing stronger than ibuprofen.

We did the same thing in the smaller guest bathroom, rummaging around in the cabinets under the sink and above the commode, but found nothing more exciting than a can of instant tanning spray. Who knew Jesse had ever used that stuff?

"I'll check his bedroom," I said.

"Better check the floors and carpets in case the cleaning crew missed something."

Talk about creepy. But I didn't want Jane to have to do it. The bathrooms were bad enough, but Jesse's bedroom would be a lot more difficult for her.

"I don't see anything in here," I called out after a few minutes of searching his nightstand and around and under his bed.

Jane came back down the hall. "I checked the kitchen. I didn't see anything there, either."

I gritted my teeth. "Now we've got to figure out a nice way to ask Eric if his crime scene guys already found the sleeping pills and took them back to the lab."

"Why does it matter?" she asked as she locked the front door behind us.

"If Jesse had his own prescription, they would've found the pill bottle and we'll know for sure that he had sleeping pills. But if they didn't find sleeping pills anywhere in the house, then it's likely that someone brought them in from the outside and drugged him."

Jane looked at me with something resembling awe. "That's so smart. How did you think of that?"

I assumed an unfocused gaze into the middle distance. "I've had some experience on the dark side."

I was happy to hear her laugh. "Spare me. Let's get out of here and go see Eric about those pills."

Chapter Seven

I was pleasantly surprised when Eric smiled and welcomed us warmly to his office. I could only conclude that it was Jane he was happy to see, because even though he and I were friends—or we had been before he was forced to lecture me—he still had his doubts about me. It hurt a little, but I'd have to get over it.

Standing, he gestured toward the two visitors' chairs in front of his desk. "Have a seat, please."

"Thanks," I murmured as we both sat.

He moved around the desk and sat down in his chair. "How are you doing, Jane? I know this is a rough time for you. Is there anything you want from me?"

And with that, he won my complete approval.

"Oh, I'm fine," she said quickly. "Thank you. That's not why we're here."

"Then to what do I owe the pleasure? Are you having problems with the Valentine's Parade?"

I laughed. "None that you can fix, but thank you for asking." Oh, if only he could arrest Whitney and Jennifer on general principle, but Tommy would probably protest his wife being locked up in jail. He was such a killjoy.

"We had a question about the coroner's results," Jane said, then hurried on before he could comment. "Can you tell me if your investigators found any sleeping pills in Jesse's house with his name on them?"

Eric's smile faded and he glared right at me. It was

unfair, but not unexpected. And probably well deserved since the sleeping-pill theory was mine.

I held up both hands in a show of peace. "We're not trying to interfere. Jane's simply concerned that you have the wrong idea about her uncle. Jesse was a real straight shooter when it came to things like sleeping pills and painkillers. He never took them. We're hoping you'll keep looking for evidence of foul play, because there's no way he popped a bunch of sleeping pills."

He took a deep breath that expanded his muscular chest even farther. "Don't even think about investigating this on your own, Shannon."

I blinked. "I'm not." Okay, maybe I was, a little. My girlfriends and I had asked a few questions around town, but he didn't need to know that. Especially since we hadn't turned up much.

Jane rushed to my defense. "It was my idea to come see you."

Eric's disbelief showed plainly on his face.

I jumped in. "The thing is, we figured that if your guys didn't find a bottle of sleeping pills with Jesse's name on it, then somebody must've brought them into his house and tricked him into taking them. And that means he was murdered."

Jane clutched her hands together in her lap. "If Uncle Jesse had resorted to taking sleeping pills, I want to know why. Because he was never into anything like that. He used to pride himself on being able to tough it out, probably because of his Navy SEAL training."

Eric sat back and crossed his arms over his formidable chest. "So you would feel better if you knew someone else was responsible for overdosing him?"

I frowned, not liking the way he put it.

Jane pressed her lips together to keep her composure. "Nothing is going to make me feel good about any of this, but at least I would know that Uncle Jesse hadn't been suffering from insomnia or something even worse."

If Jesse had been suffering insomnia, I knew the reason, for it was sitting in my safe-deposit box right now. Having that priceless necklace in the house would keep anyone awake at night.

Eric glanced from me to Jane and slowly back to me again, then shook his head in resignation. "Don't make me regret this."

"You won't," Jane said instantly.

"I'll tell you what you want to know, but it doesn't leave this office—do you understand?"

Both Jane and I nodded rapidly.

"If I find out either one of you talked to anyone else in this town, I'll toss you both in a cell and throw away the key."

He meant it, I could tell.

"We won't say a word," I said.

"Never," Jane insisted. "I promise."

"I'm only telling you two because you knew Jesse so well and because . . . I can't believe I'm saying this, but oddly enough, I trust you both." He shook his head, probably because he was breaking one of his own cardinal rules. "The crime scene techs didn't find a prescription bottle, but—"

"I knew it!" I said.

"But," Eric repeated loudly, "that doesn't mean he didn't have one. We're following up with his doctors and pharmacy."

"Won't it be a problem getting that information?" I asked. "Sometimes doctors aren't willing to—"

Jane cut me off. "If you have any problems at all, let me know and I'll talk to Jesse's doctor and pharmacist. I used to take him to the doctor and I picked up his prescriptions, so I know everyone involved. I'll get the information for you."

Go, Jane, I thought, silently cheering her on.

"I might take you up on that," Eric said, sitting back in his chair. "But so far, we haven't run into any resistance."

I took a breath and plunged ahead. "So it was murder."

He went back to scowling again. "Let's end this conversation right now while we're all still friends."

Jane jumped up. "Great idea. Thanks, Eric. Come on, Shannon." She gave me a look and tipped her head toward the door.

I took the hint and stood. "Thank you, Eric. Not knowing would have driven Jane nuts."

"Yeah, yeah," he said, his tone caustic. "Just remember to keep your mouths shut. Because, trust me, you won't like sleeping in a jail cell."

"I need to cook."

I wasn't about to argue, because Jane was a fabulous cook, so we stopped at the market to buy the ingredients for beef stroganoff and took everything to my house. She confessed that she didn't want to go home alone after talking to the police chief. And since we couldn't tell anyone else about Jesse being murdered or about the priceless necklace I'd found, we decided we'd better stick together.

I opened a bottle of wine and poured us each a glass. "We need to tell Eric about the necklace. It's got to be the main reason why Jesse was murdered."

"I know, I know." Jane began heating up beef stock, adding a carrot, some thyme sprigs, and a bay leaf. While that bubbled, she chopped up a chuck roast into bite-sized chunks. She didn't believe in dredging the meat in flour, instead dropping the chunks into olive oil and frying them until they were lightly browned. She added onions to the meat and cooked them down, then poured cognac over everything and cooked it until the alcohol burned off. Finally she added the flavored beef stock, stirred it up, and covered it to keep it simmering.

She sat down at the kitchen table and took a sip of wine. "That has to cook for about an hour and a half."

"Okay, I'll make a salad while we wait." I walked outside to my garden to pick some fresh veggies. The fog had rolled in and the air was cold and damp. I found three different types of tomatoes, a small head of romaine, some purple leaf lettuce, green onions, and a cucumber. After washing everything, I went to work at the chopping block on the counter.

"I just wish we could tell Lizzie and Emily and Marigold about the necklace," Jane said. "It feels odd to be keeping secrets from them."

"It won't be a secret for long." I tossed some cut-up cucumber into the salad bowl and reached for my wineglass. "But yeah, the true meaning of misery is trying to keep a secret this big all to ourselves."

"Two big secrets," she said.

"Right." We had to keep quiet not only about the necklace, but also about the possibility that Jesse was murdered. I lifted my glass. "Wine helps."

She laughed softly. "Always."

"This is the problem with living in a small town," I griped. "There are no secrets. I guess we've gotten used to that, because now I'm about to burst with all this news."

"Well, try to control yourself," she said, pointing at me as she clutched the stem of her wineglass. "I don't plan to spend even one night in jail. And you know that wasn't an idle threat."

"Believe me, I know." I popped a cherry tomato into my mouth and handed one to Jane. "Eric wasn't happy telling us about the pills, but I'm glad he did."

The cooking time passed quickly, and before long, Jane was heating up butter and sautéing mushrooms and garlic and more thyme. She added the cooked meat along with some sour cream and more seasonings.

I was in charge of the noodles, which meant I had to open a package and pour them into boiling water. I fancied myself a pretty good cook, but I couldn't begin to compete with Jane.

Once we sat down with our plates, there was silence as we tasted the first few bites of the amazing food. After a minute, Jane shook her head. "I don't know how Jesse ever managed to keep that necklace a secret."

"He didn't in the beginning."

"True," she said, frowning. "But at some point, he hid it away and never mentioned it again."

"I have a whole new level of admiration for him. How he managed to keep quiet all that time is as big a mystery as what happened to him the other night." I dragged a small chunk of beef through the buttery, creamy mushroom sauce, took a bite, and almost moaned.

"He kept the necklace a secret for a couple of years. We only have to keep our secrets for a few days."

"I know, and yet I worry that I won't be able to do it."

"Just picture yourself inside a prison cell."

"That's good advice," I said.

Jane sighed and swirled her wine. "I won't have a problem keeping what Eric told us a secret, but the necklace is another story."

I gave her a look. "It might help to remember that the reason we can't talk about the necklace is because we don't want Jesse's killer to know we have it."

She grimaced. "Oh yeah."

"If we told one person, you know word would get out somehow."

"Including Eric?"

"No, we have to tell him, but this time we'll be the ones swearing him to secrecy."

"Still, you know somebody in the department will find out at some point. And that's all it'll take for everyone in town to know about it."

"Within about five minutes," I added dryly.

I didn't add that if the wrong person heard that the necklace had been found, Jane's life would be in danger. I was convinced of it, and the realization put me in a somber mood during the rest of our dinner. Maybe Jane had figured that out, too, because she was awfully quiet in the end.

It was barely nine o'clock when we finished washing the dishes.

"Do you want to watch television?" I asked, although I could hardly keep my eyes open.

"I'm exhausted," Jane said, tossing the dish towel into

the laundry basket. "I'm going to bed. Thanks for letting me spend the night. I just didn't want to be alone after going through Jesse's house and worrying about the necklace and talking to Eric."

"I'm glad you're here." We climbed the stairs and said good night. I fell asleep the minute my head hit the pillow.

Sometime in the middle of the night, a flashing light woke me up.

"Jesse's house." I jumped out of bed and grabbed my clothes, then stopped. What was wrong with me? Did I want to rot away in a prison cell?

Robbie and Tiger awoke in an instant and watched in rapt silence as I reached for my cell phone and called Eric. Robbie's tale twitched excitedly, and rather than wait for him to beg, I picked him up and held him in my lap. Tiger kneaded the covers a few times before cozying up next to my leg.

Eric answered on the first ring. "Jensen."

"It's Shannon."

"What a pleasant surprise."

"Someone's inside Jesse's house."

"I'll be right there. If I see you outside your house, I'll—"

"I know, I know. You'll toss me into a cell and throw away the key."

"Very good."

I could tell he was grinning from ear to ear.

It wasn't like me to kowtow to anyone, but the chief of police had spoken and I didn't dare push back.

I sat on the edge of the bed, wondering what to do. I wanted to see what was going on next door, but I didn't want to incur Eric's wrath again. I knew I wouldn't be able to fall back to sleep anytime soon, but I lay down on the bed to ponder the universe and my place within it. Robbie and Tiger kept me company and I dozed off within minutes.

Saturday morning I should have known Jane was already up when I stumbled out of bed and Robbie and Tiger were nowhere to be seen. I took a quick shower to wake myself up, and when I got downstairs, the two beasts were sitting at Jane's feet, begging for scraps. When Robbie saw me, he raced over, circled me once with his back end wiggling like mad, and then returned to his proper begging position. Tiger was too cool to bother acknowledging me.

"Good morning," Jane said. "I made coffee."

"I love you," I muttered, and poured myself a cup. After several healthy sips, I sat at the table. "We missed all the excitement last night."

"What happened?"

I told her how I woke up from the flashes of light next door and how Eric had strongly suggested that I stay inside. "And then I fell asleep."

"Someone broke into Jesse's house again? I hate this." She slapped the paper onto the table. "I'm going to hire a security company."

"That's a good idea."

"I'll look up some companies and call them this morning. There'll be someone patrolling the place tonight."

"Okay." I gazed out the window and saw Mac jogging down the stairs. "I'll be right back."

I went running outside before Jane could say another word. "Hey, Mac."

He smiled. "Good morning, Irish. You sat it out last night."

I hoped he couldn't tell I was pouting on the inside. "I didn't want another lecture."

"Can't blame you for that."

"So, what happened?"

"Nothing," he said, disgusted. "Once again, they ran out the back and got away."

I shook my head in dismay. "It's like Jesse has a secret tunnel leading from his house to somewhere down the street or something."

"I had that same thought."

I realized he was wearing a jacket and a tie with his jeans. "You're all dressed up."

He checked himself out. "Hardly, but I do have a lunch meeting in San Francisco."

"Oh, then I won't keep you. Good luck and safe travels."

"Thanks, Irish. See you later."

I watched him exit through the gate before I returned to the house.

"Where's he off to?" Jane asked.

I told her and we talked about the joys of having handsome men around to look at. As I poured myself another cup of coffee, something occurred to me.

"You know," I said slowly, "maybe you could hold off on calling those security companies for a day or two."

"But why?"

"Because I'm thinking that if there's a guard on duty, our intruder won't come back. And I really want to catch him in the act."

"That's a really bad idea."

"I mean, I want the police to catch him. Not me. The police."

"Sure," she said, clearly not believing me.

"I mean it. I've learned my lesson."

"Look," Jane said. "If this guy is desperate to find the necklace, nothing will deter him. He'll be back."

"But if he sees a guard walking around wearing a uniform, he'll leave and maybe he'll give up. And I want him to come back. Does that make sense?"

"I'm afraid it does in a sick and twisted way."

"Right. Because it's almost a guarantee that whoever broke into Jesse's house is the same person who killed him."

Her lips puckered into a stubborn pout, but finally she said, "Yeah, okay. I'll wait a few days. But I still don't want you going in there again without the police around."

"Believe me, I got that message."

"I don't think you did."

"I did." I confessed to her about Eric's lecture and how miserable it made me feel.

"You never told me."

"I felt humiliated. But he was right. It was stupid to go over there without calling the police first."

"I agree," Jane said, smiling brightly.

"Thanks." I picked up the newspaper and studied the headlines. War. Disease. Destruction. Degradation. A day like any other day. I set the paper down and sighed. "I'd better get to work."

"I'll be leaving shortly," Jane said. "I'll probably spend the night at home."

"I'll miss having you here."

I gave her a hug, then fed Robbie and Tiger, who were delirious with gratitude. At least Robbie was. Tiger was much too dignified, but she still seemed happy with her food. I filled up a thermos with iced tea and finally left for work. Since it was Saturday, I only had one construction site to visit today and I planned to spend most of the day there.

Twenty minutes later, I parked my truck in front of the Stansbury home, a frothy pink gingerbread confection that stood on a rise overlooking Lighthouse Cove and North Beach. From there, you could see our famous lighthouse and most of the coastline for miles in either direction.

The old pink Victorian had weathered well and the walls and exterior siding were still in good condition. The Stansburys insisted on having the house painted every few years to maintain its perky pink hue. They had four young daughters, and those little girls loved living in a pink house. And who could blame them? I happened to be a big fan of the color pink myself. I owned every type of pink tool known to womankind, plus a pretty pink hard hat, goggles, tool belt, the whole deal. It was fun to be a girl contractor.

It wasn't the house itself but the roof that was causing problems for the Stansburys, and we were in the process of giving them a brand-new one. In many cases, this simply entailed adding another layer of shingles onto the existing roof. But the Stansburys' roof had been replaced numerous times in the past, so a lot of the existing layers were beginning to rot from dampness and termite damage. We had recommended removing all of the old shingles and all the decaying layers beneath the surface and putting down an entirely new roof. Happily they had agreed.

They had also agreed to go with a lighter-colored shingle this time around. The existing black roof looked dramatic against the pink, but black roofs retain more heat in the summer without having the same insulating effect in the winter when the sun's rays are diffused and indirect. The Stansburys would also get a generous government rebate if they used the lighter shingles and thus conserved more energy, so they were all for that.

The pale gray shingles I recommended looked beautiful against the pink wood and the white trim. I knew the family would be thrilled when the job was done.

I grabbed a few tools out of the truck bed and strolled up the long front walk, gazing up at the roof the whole time. Victorian roofs were notoriously steep, so we had constructed a massive pipe scaffolding across the front of the house and had also brought in our hydraulic lift to reach some of the trickier spots. I didn't like my guys climbing on roofs, although most of them thought it was the most fun part of the job.

And, of course, to do the job right, they had to stand directly on the roof, so I insisted that they all wear tethered safety harnesses. There was a lot of good-natured complaining, but that didn't matter to me. These days, my site could be shut down if a building-and-safety inspector happened to cruise by and see one of my guys working on a pitched roof without a harness.

Years ago, I'd watched one of my dad's crew slip and fall off a steep roof, an image I never got out of my head. He was unbelievably lucky, though, breaking only his arm and a couple of ribs. But I still got chills whenever I thought about it.

From where I stood, I could see that the entire front part of the roof had been stripped of all the old wooden shingles. While wooden shingles were more authentically Victorian, we preferred to use an asphalt composite that came in layered sheets that had the look of real shingles. The material was fire-resistant and guaranteed to last forty years. And it looked pretty, which counted for a lot in my book.

I had a tendency to gush about the products I believed in, like those shingles. With all the PR work I did on their behalf, my guys thought the company should send me residuals. My friends, on the other hand, just thought I needed to get out more.

I spotted two of my guys, Sean and Billy, ascending the scaffolding pipe like two monkeys climbing up a tree. I'd gone to high school with both of them and had known them most of my life. I loved having them on my crew because they worked like maniacs and showed little regard for my status as their boss.

"Sean," I shouted.

He turned around, saw me, and waved. "I'm not contagious and I'm feeling a lot better, so don't lecture me."

"I won't lecture you, but if you have a relapse, I'll kill you."

"It's a deal," he said, laughing.

I shook my head. The guy had been home in bed with the flu for most of the week. "Just stay away from me. And . . . be careful."

"You got it, boss" he said, and kept climbing.

Johnny, another hard worker, was already on the roof, hammering down the last sheathing layer of oriented-strand board, or OSB. These boards looked similar to a piece of plywood but actually consisted of a combination of thin wafers of wood, resins, and wax. The product was amazingly strong and was meant to resist heavy weight, strong winds, and the contractions and expansions that occurred in humid areas like ours along the coast.

Today we'd be covering the sheathing layer with roofing felt, a water-resistant underlayment that kept the deck boards dry. It was similar to tar paper, but heavier and better at deterring moisture. It came in a roll and was attached to the sheathing by means of a staple gun, and that was why I was there. I needed to get rid of some excess irritation, and there was nothing better than a staple gun for that. Painting walls or measuring drywall wouldn't do it for me and pounding wood with a nail gun was too intense. My staple gun provided me with a great way to work out my frustrations without having to punch someone's lights out. That was a big joke, of course. I wouldn't dream of actually hitting anyone. But sometimes things drove me a little crazy, and believe it or not, pounding out a few thousand staples in rapid succession often helped calm my nerves and put things in perspective. Besides, it was fun and good exercise if you did it right.

The mystery surrounding Jesse's house had been raising more questions than I had answers for. I was frustrated and unsure what to do next. We had a priceless necklace to deal with, an intruder who was possibly a murderer, and a handsome police chief who said he trusted me but still didn't always expect me to do the right thing.

I couldn't wait to wrap my hands around that staple gun and go to my happy place for a few hours.

"Hey, Shannon," Billy called. "You've got company."

It took me a few seconds to realize Billy was talking to me. I really had zoned out, and it felt good. I scanned the roof and noticed for the first time that I'd finished almost half of the front side of the house. Not bad.

I stretched my back and turned to take in the view from the roof. In the distance, maybe a quarter mile up the coast, the pure white tower of the lighthouse stood tall and solitary. I loved that image of the stalwart spear shooting up from the rocky breakwater to light the way on a stormy night.

"Yo, Shannon," It was Sean shouting this time. I turned to see him pointing down toward the front yard. "Wake up, boss. Look who's here."

I blinked and shook my head a few times. I really had been in a zone. Staring down, I saw Eric Jensen standing on the front walk, looking up at me. No wonder Sean and Billy were trying to get me to move my butt.

I waved at the police chief. "I'll be right down."

Looked as though my good times were over.

When I was back on solid ground, I unbuckled my harness, grabbed my thermos, and chugged down a big gulp of iced tea. I had worked up quite a thirst on the roof because while the air was still cool, the late January sun was bright enough to make me sweat a little. And Eric's presence didn't help.

He found me at the side of the house where our work-table was set up and covered with open tool chests and roofing materials. He scrutinized the harness and then gazed up at the roof. "That's a long way up. Ever get dizzy up there?"

"No, not dizzy. I'm not afraid of heights, but I am afraid of falling. I would wear the harness even if it wasn't required."

"Smart."

"I could've come to see you," I said, leaning my hip against the sturdy table. "You didn't have to track me down."

"You weren't hard to find, and it's a nice drive." He turned and looked to the west. "And this is a great view."

"The best in the world," I said. "It's even better from up on the roof."

After a moment of appreciation for the amazing blue of the ocean and the gorgeous dark green of the redwood trees that lined the crest of the hill to the south of town, I turned back to Eric and tried for a lighthearted approach. "So. I'll understand if you want to lecture me again. I should've called you. It was stupid, but it was also the middle of the night. I wasn't thinking too clearly."

"I figured you got my message, so I won't be giving another lecture."

"I appreciate it."

"I thought you would," he said wryly. "I also felt you should know that since we've found evidence of an intruder breaking into Jesse's house these last few nights, it gives more credence to your notion that someone killed Jesse rather than the coroner's theory that he died of an accidental overdose."

"Really?" I said. "You agree with me?"

"I'm starting to," he hedged.

"That's close enough." I patted my heart. "I'm all choked up."

"I doubt it," he said, biting back a laugh. "You shouldn't make too much of it."

"I'll try not to, but this is a big moment for me."

Eric rolled his eyes, but at least he was smiling at me.

We were flirting all of a sudden and it felt good, despite my guilty conscience. When he wasn't suspecting me of murder or accusing me of contaminating his crime scene, Eric Jensen was awfully cute. No, cute didn't describe him at all. Rugged. Blond. Tall. Fantastic smile. He was *Thor*. Superhero. In my mind, of course. Not out loud. I didn't want to spoil the moment.

And speaking of my guilty conscience, I really had to talk to Jane. We couldn't keep the necklace a secret. At least, not from Eric. I took another long sip of iced tea.

He brought up the topic of Jesse and his friends exploring the old shipyard down the coast.

"You heard about Jesse finding the live bombs on board?" I asked.

"Yeah. I called the naval station about it."

"I'm glad."

"The last thing I need is someone bringing bombs into my jurisdiction. So the navy plans to use bomb-sniffing dogs and some high-tech electronics to sweep the entire shipyard for any possible explosives still there."

"Good," I said. "I can only imagine some kids thinking it would be a fun place to start a fire or something."

"Yeah." He blew out a breath. "I had that thought, too. If three old codgers could break in there and stumble across actual active ordnance, I'd say they need to tighten their security."

"You should talk to Jesse's friends Bob and Ned. They were with him. They could tell you how they got inside."

"I've got their names on my interview list." He pulled out a small notepad and pen and made a note to call them.

I set my thermos down on the table. "Looks like you've got things under control."

"If only that were true."

"Of course it's true. Now you just have to find Jesse's killer."

"Let's not jump the gun," he warned. "We still haven't concluded that there was a killing."

"But you said—"

"I said your notion had some credibility. We still have to study the evidence and determine conclusively what happened."

"Oh." I made a grumpy face. "Okay."

"And despite what you think," Eric added lightly, "in a case like this, and in a place like Lighthouse Cove, it's not always an easy task to find a killer."

"Why do you say that?"

"Because there are so many people who knew the victim well." He shifted to take another look at the spectacular view and spoke as if thinking out loud. "Old jealousies and treacheries abound. You never know who in town has been waiting patiently to mete out revenge even after twenty or thirty years."

I smiled. "That's almost poetic."

He glanced at me. "I'm a complex guy."

We both laughed but sobered quickly.

"Guess I'd better get going," he said, pulling car keys out of his pocket.

"Wait."

He turned. "What is it, Shannon?"

I swallowed nervously, then gave up. I couldn't tell

him about the necklace. Not until I talked to Jane. But now I had to say something. I took a quick sip of iced tea to quench my dry throat. "I—I know you have to study the evidence, but I hope you'll hurry up and find whoever did it fast."

He glanced at me sideways. "I hate to be the one to point this out, but the person who has the most to gain from Jesse's death is your friend Jane."

I choked on my iced tea. "You must be joking. Jane is the gentlest creature alive."

"No doubt," he said smoothly. "But if I wanted this investigation to conclude quickly, I would arrest her and that would be that."

"No, that would be insane." He had to be kidding. Thor would never pick on Jane. All of my nice, companionable feelings for Eric were being swept aside in a tidal wave of outrage. "Don't you dare arrest Jane! There are a lot more suspicious people around here than her."

He gave me a look. "Do share."

I scowled, knowing I'd walked right into that one. "Well, it's not that I'm accusing anyone, but have you talked to the other neighbors? And his old navy buddies, Ned and Bob? Or Ned's son, Stephen? Have you talked to him?" As I said all this out loud, I really warmed to my ideas. Jane was a ridiculous suspect, especially when there was a veritable banquet of iffy people to consider instead. "Stephen just suddenly moved here. What's up with that? And there's Jesse's mysterious girlfriend, Althea. Not that she's all that mysterious. I mean, she's lovely, but still. They might've had a fight or something."

"Or something," he said sardonically.

"And you must've heard about Jesse's treasure necklace, right? I mean, not that it exists," I added quickly, making another mental note to talk to Jane about coming clean. Seriously, I am not a good liar. "He used to talk about this thing he found on the old shipwreck, a jeweled necklace. I don't think it exists, but someone else might've believed him and . . ."

Oh, dear God, I needed to shut up while I still had half a brain left. "Never mind. That's pretty far-fetched."

Eric placed his big, strong hands on my shoulders and gave me a little squeeze. "Shannon, if it'll ease your mind, I'm in the process of talking to all those people you mentioned. I hadn't heard the story about that necklace, but whether it's true or not, I won't stop investigating until I get some answers. But the fact remains that Jane probably had the most to gain from Jesse's death."

"But—"

"That doesn't mean I'm going to arrest her," he said, holding up his hand to cut me off. "It just means that the investigation is ongoing. I know I'm relatively new in town, but I'm not an idiot. I know Jane isn't a killer."

"You do? Okay. Good. And I don't think you're an idiot."

"I appreciate that."

I frowned. "Were you trying to teach me a lesson there?"

"Maybe." He leaned closer and whispered provocatively, "How'd I do?"

"You're good," I said reluctantly. "Scary, but good."

He walked away grinning.

On the way home from work later that afternoon, I called Jane to talk about the necklace situation. We simply had to tell Eric that I'd found it. But before I could say anything, she told me that she had just arranged for all the locks on Jesse's doors to be changed.

"Good. It'll slow the intruder down, but it won't scare him away. Not like a security guard roaming around."

"I talked to Eric a little while ago," she said. "And since there was no sign of forced entry, he assumes that the intruder somehow got ahold of a set of Jesse's keys. So if that's true and the guy tries to sneak inside again, his keys won't work."

"Okay." But I hoped the intruder would break in anyway. Did that make me a crazy person?

"And by the way, I slipped a new key under your front doormat."

"Thanks. That was smart."

"I thought so. Oh, there's my landscaper," she said suddenly. "I've gotta go. Talk to you later."

She hung up before I could say a word about the necklace. I was going to have to call her back tonight because my guilty conscience couldn't take this much longer.

I stopped at the market for a few things and ran into Lizzie in the produce department.

"Hello, stranger," she said as she grabbed a head of romaine and plopped it into her basket. "I know it's barely been a week, but I feel like I haven't seen you in forever."

I gave her a quick hug. "We have to get together for a girls' night."

"Yes, please," she pleaded. "I need a break from sports. It's all football all the time at my house."

"Okay, how about Wednesday night? You talk to Marigold and Emily and I'll talk to Jane and we'll make a plan."

"It's a deal."

I walked away, happy I'd seen Lizzie, but in the next aisle I was attacked with even more guilt than I'd felt with Eric earlier. Jane and I had sworn each other to secrecy, and that meant keeping information from our dearest friends. I hoped they wouldn't be furious with us when they found out about the necklace.

I had known Lizzie for as long as I'd known Jane. In other words, for most of my life. Lizzie's family had lived down the street from me, and because she was five years older than me, she had been my babysitter while I was growing up. In those days, I had looked up to her as an older, smarter woman and had shared all my deepest, darkest thoughts and secrets with her. And now I couldn't tell her my current deepest, darkest secret!

Emily and Marigold had moved here more recently,

but I felt almost as close to them as I did to Lizzie and Jane.

I hurried out to the parking lot, but the guilt followed me.

When I got home, I called Jane's cell while I put away my groceries. When there was no answer, I didn't leave a message for fear of someone overhearing me. As soon as I ended the call, I realized how ridiculous that was. I was in my own kitchen, leaving a message on a cell phone.

"Oh great," I muttered, as I stashed the pint of half-and-half in the fridge. I was getting to be just as paranoid as Jesse had been.

Somewhere in the middle of the night, I was woken by another flash of light coming from next door. I jumped out of bed, wondering how someone got in there. Jane had just changed the locks today. I reached for my cell phone and called Eric to report it. When I got his voice mail, I had to leave a message.

"Damn it. Now what?" But I knew what I had to do. I threw on my clothes, grabbed my baseball bat, and ran downstairs with Robbie at my heels, the floppy stuffed skunk dangling from his mouth. "Stay," I whispered, and once he was curled up on the rug under the table, I slipped outside my kitchen door and found Mac waiting.

"You saw it, too," I whispered.

"I was going to give you another five minutes."

"I called Eric, but I had to leave a message."

"I got ahold of him," he said. "Hey, you've got a baseball bat."

I held up the bat. "It's not quite as effective as a gun, but it can't hurt."

"It can, actually, if you swing it too close to my head." He grabbed my free hand as we walked down the driveway.

It felt oddly as if we were going on a date. To a dead man's house. To find a killer. I suppose I'd been on weirder dates.

Since the police arrival was imminent, we didn't venture onto Jesse's property but stayed on my driveway and out of the way. Eric's SUV approached quietly and parked a few doors away. He searched Jesse's house high and low but found no one inside. He scoured the backyard, too, but there was nothing. No clues, no sign of an intruder, nothing.

I thought Mac and I had been as quiet as little mice, but whoever was searching Jesse's place must have heard us coming. Or maybe they never got inside. Maybe the change of locks had discouraged them. But I'd seen the flashes of light. So maybe they'd only used their flashlight to check the lock and a few windows and then left when they realized they couldn't get in.

Both Mac and Eric walked me back to my kitchen door and we all whispered good night. They waited until I was inside and the door was locked before Mac returned to his place up the stairs and Eric left through the gate and down the driveway. Holding Robbie, I watched from the kitchen window until everyone was out of sight before I went back to bed.

These late-night missions were oddly thrilling, especially with two good-looking men escorting me around. I wondered what I would do for excitement when we finally caught the culprit.

I mentally smacked myself at such a foolish thought. I mean, we were on the hunt for someone who might have killed my sweet old neighbor. How could I possibly consider it exhilarating—except in the murkiest way possible?

Then call me murky, I thought as I punched my pillow into shape, because I was having way too much fun. And why not enjoy it for now? The thrills would end soon enough and I would go back to my usual routine of sleeping peacefully through the night without all the flashing lights and guilt-spawned nightmares.

And Mac would move out of my garage apartment as soon as the lighthouse mansion—his new home—was fully refurbished. After that, we would see each other around town every so often, but it wouldn't be the same. And since that thought depressed me more than anything else, I picked up Tiger and held her close. As her steady purring lulled me to sleep, I prayed I'd make it through one night without dreaming of dead bodies and dark basements.

I spent most of Sunday cleaning my house and playing quietly in the garden with Robbie and Tiger. It wasn't until Monday morning while I was waiting for the coffeepot to fill that I recalled what Eric had said about Jane being the most likely suspect. I knew he'd been teasing me and was only trying to scare me, but he'd succeeded. I was frightened and disturbed to think that the police might actually conclude that Jane was guilty. I couldn't believe Eric would ever be that short-sighted—unless he found out about the necklace and the fact that we'd been hiding it from him.

That thought sent a chill skittering down my spine. He would probably arrest both of us. That settled it, I thought. It was time to sit down and figure out who really had killed Jesse.

"I'm going to need your help," I said to Robbie as I pulled out a notepad and pen.

He shivered with energy and barked twice, telling me he was up to the task.

"You, too, Tiger," I said to the cat as she prowled the kitchen. I sat down at the table with a cup of coffee and a piece of cinnamon toast, and made my own list of suspects and their motives.

"Definitely Cuckoo, right?" I said.

Robbie whined and I laughed. "I don't like him either." I glanced at my list. "What do you think of Bob and Ned?"

The little dog tilted his head as if to question why those two old guys were on my list.

"Yeah, they probably can't swing a sledgehammer or an ax and pound a hole in the wall too easily at their age. But Stephen, Ned's son?" I glanced down and Robbie barked enthusiastically.

"I think so, too," I said, chuckling as I added his name to the list.

I checked the clock. It was too early to call Jane and discuss the necklace, but it wasn't too early for Lizzie. I made the call and firmed up Wednesday night for our girls' get-together.

I couldn't wait to tell my friends what I'd found in Jesse's basement and give them the names of the possible killers and motives I'd come up with. With luck, the girls would have other names to add to my list.

That was what we'd done a few months earlier, when I was the one on top of the suspect list. My girlfriends and I had tracked down information it would've taken the police months to find out, simply because we knew this town and the people who lived here so well.

In lieu of girlfriends this time around, Robbie and Tiger sniffed and snuggled at my feet and made me feel as if I ruled the world. Or at least, my little corner of it.

I poured a second cup of coffee and returned to my suspect list. In spite of Eric's taunting, I refused to put Jane's name on the list. I knew she didn't kill Jesse. But there were plenty of others who might have.

I studied the names again. At the top of my list was Cuckoo Clemens, an old grouch and a conniver. He was mean to boot. Even Robbie agreed with me. I could picture Cuckoo fighting with Jesse over the necklace. The way he had demanded that Jane sell him the necklace for an outrageously low amount showed his desperation.

Next came Jesse's old navy pals, Bob and Ned. I didn't really suspect them of killing Jesse, mainly because they were too old. They might've been able to slip him some sleeping pills, but they couldn't have caused all that damage in his house. But Ned's son, Stephen, a strapping young man, as his father might describe him, could have done it. So his was the next name on my list.

Robbie perched attentively on the rug, waiting for me to name my next suspect. "I'm adding Althea," I said, and smiled as the dog seemed to ponder that suggestion.

"I know what you're thinking, but she's an obvious choice. The girlfriend nobody knew."

He tossed his head, shook himself, and then lay down to gnaw on his floppy skunk.

"Yeah," I said. "I can't see that she had much to gain by Jesse's death, but she'd been seeing him regularly, which means she had plenty of opportunity. That has to count for something, right?"

I glanced down and saw that Robbie had lost interest. I couldn't blame him because I was out of ideas after that. I squiggled little circles and spirals, then wrote Mrs. Higgins's name on the list. Then I laughed out loud and removed her name. Honestly Mrs. Higgins was barely able to walk outside her front gate, never mind sneak into Jesse's house and smash a hole in the wall.

Tiger jumped up onto my lap and I put my pen down to pet her. As she settled, I remembered Eric's words about small-town revenge. Could it be someone in town? A neighbor I'd known forever? I thought more about Jesse. Who were his enemies? It was possible that he had plenty of them because he had been a bit of a curmudgeon. I'd always gotten along with him, but did the rest of our neighbors? Had he ever caused trouble for one of them? I knew that the family living on the other side of Jesse used to have a noisy dog that drove him nuts. The family didn't have that dog anymore. Had Jesse set it loose and caused it to run away? Would the neighbors have killed him for it?

I was grasping at straws.

What I needed here was a long talk with my dad. He had to know plenty of details about Jesse that I didn't. I dialed his cell phone, but there was no answer. Dad didn't always carry his phone with him when he was busy. I would have to try him later.

I stared at my list again and wondered who among Jesse's friends and acquaintances had seen the necklace. My instinct told me that the necklace was the key to Jesse's death. Why would anyone kill him otherwise?

We already knew that Cuckoo had seen the necklace.

Who else had Jesse shown it to? Other antique dealers? Pawnshop owners?

He couldn't have shown it much around town. If he had, everyone would have been talking about it. And that realization left me exactly nowhere.

I did an online search of such businesses within a ten-to-fifteen-mile radius of Lighthouse Cove. I found a number of possibilities and printed out their names and addresses, determined to visit them and find out if any of them had seen the necklace.

Feeling good about taking some concrete action, I headed out to my truck. Across the street, Mrs. Higgins shuffled out her door and down the walkway. At her front gate, she stopped and waved. "Yoo-hoo, Shannon, dear, can you come over here?"

I felt instant guilt and remorse for adding her name to my suspect list. It didn't matter that I'd removed her name almost as quickly—my guilt was a living, breathing thing.

I shook it off and I walked across the street. "Hi, Mrs. Higgins. How are you?"

"I'm superfine like Chablis wine," she said, snapping her fingers in a Z formation.

Oh, dear. Had she been drinking already? She wore a satin pink housecoat with kitten-heel slippers with little tufts of pink fur on the toes. Her hair was in curlers, and her rhinestone-studded bifocals completed the look.

"You look very glamorous today," I said.

"Thank you." She touched her curlers gingerly. "*Celebrity Wheel of Fortune* is on today and I want to look my best."

"Ah." I nodded. "What can I help you with?"

"I got a call from Sloane's telling me my bird fountain is ready for pickup. Can you drive out there and get it for me today? I don't want them to send it back."

"They wouldn't send it back, but I'll be happy to pick it up for you." Anything to assuage the guilt, I added silently.

"And you'll install it for me?"

"Of course."

"By tomorrow?"

I mentally checked my schedule and my level of guilt. "Sure, I can pick it up today and install it tomorrow."

She reached out and pinched my cheek. "You're a good girl."

"Thanks, Mrs. Higgins." I returned to my truck, rubbing my tender cheek where she'd squeezed it like a Vise-Grip. Maybe the old gal *was* strong enough to punch a few holes in Jesse's walls, I thought, and was tempted to add her name back onto the suspect list, just for spite.

Chapter Eight

"You've got to be kidding," I said, staring at the bird fountain Mrs. Higgins had ordered. It was even bigger and uglier than I'd thought it would be.

"Nope." John Sloane laughed again. He'd pretty much been laughing his ass off since I drove onto the lot.

"Have I mentioned that your customer relation skills suck?" I felt comfortable telling him that since I'd known him forever. My father and I had been shopping at Sloane's Stones for almost that long, too.

My critique just made him laugh harder.

"I don't think it'll fit in my truck," I said.

"Oh, we'll get it in there," he assured me with a chuckle. "Because there's no way we're keeping it here."

"Thanks, John. You're a peach."

His shoulders were still shaking as he walked off to find a couple of guys who could help him squeeze that gargantuan atrocity of a birdbath into the back of my truck.

It took four of them, plus me. It wasn't that the fountain was too heavy. In fact, it was light enough for me to lift on my own. The thing had been carved out of polystyrene foam, coated in plastic, and then spray-painted a bronze color to make it look much heavier than it was.

No, it was just a big awkward thing, at least eight feet long, four feet wide, and seven feet tall, with odd angles everywhere and all those naked boys and dolphins and angels sticking out all over it. Fitting it back there took some clever maneuvering, but we managed it.

"There you go," John said, slapping my tailgate. "All set."

"You've got to lend me a tarp," I said. "I can't be driving around town with this thing exposed to the world."

He frowned. "What do you mean? Are you implying that it's ugly?"

"I'm saying it's hideous," I said, laughing. "I've got stops to make between here and home. I don't want to scare any small children."

"All right," he said. "But I think you're going to need more than one tarp."

On the way back to town I stopped at another construction site to talk to Wade about getting some of the guys started on rehabbing Jesse's place. I would've stayed to chat longer, but I had a strong urge to get home with Mrs. Higgins's fountain before anyone I knew saw it and gave me a hard time.

I had to make one more stop at the supermarket to pick up a few essentials I needed. I ran inside and was out in seven minutes, but it was too late.

Whitney had just stepped out of her Jaguar and was headed straight toward me. She wore stiletto heels and skinny jeans with a strategically torn T-shirt that was tie-dyed and glitterized. It was what all the housewives in Lighthouse Cove wore when they had to dash off to the market to pick up dinner.

"Hello, Whitney," I said breezily as I unlocked the truck and tossed my small grocery bag onto the front seat.

"Always a pleasure," she lied, flipping in dismissal her keratin-treated straight black hair. As she passed the back of my truck, a bungee cord snapped and one side of the tarp began to flap in the wind, smacking her in the face.

She screamed and ducked, waving her hands over her head as if she were being attacked by bats.

"Jeez, freak out much?" I grabbed the bungee cord

and the edge of the tarp and was about to reattach it when she gasped.

"Holy Versace," she cried, as one shaky finger pointed at the item under the tarp. "What is that horrible thing?"

Even though I agreed with her description, I felt indignant on Mrs. Higgins's behalf. "It's a one-of-a-kind fountain. A very wealthy client just ordered it. What do you think? Beautiful, isn't it?" I raised the tarp a little higher to give her a better look.

She recoiled in horror. "That is the most hideous, gauche piece of garbage I've ever seen. It figures a client of yours would think it was fabulous."

"Sticks and stones . . ." Although I couldn't disagree about the hideous-gauche part of her statement. I tried not to snicker as she made a face and stomped off.

"Always great to see you," I called after her, then chuckled as I jumped into the truck and drove off.

The next morning, I got one of my guys to help me haul the fountain into Mrs. Higgins's backyard and install it. I had already removed last year's rejected fountain and easily attached the hoses and pump to this new one.

Mrs. Higgins watched from the edge of her small patio, twenty feet away.

"We're going to turn the water on now, Mrs. Higgins," I said. "I'm not sure if all the water will wind up in the fountain itself or spray the yard, so I think you should stay back where you are."

"I'm ready, I'm ready," she said, clapping her hands. "Hurry. Turn the water on."

"Coming up." I twisted the handle and the fountain spurted and coughed to life. Water began to trickle from the mouths of the dolphins and the birds, and after a minute they were spitting water everywhere. The naked boys began to pee.

The water tumbled down and collected in a small pool at the base of the fountain and then recycled through the pipes. It was actually a clever design if you ignored its outer shell.

"Oh, it's stunning," Mrs. Higgins whispered, clasping her hands to her bosom. "I've never seen anything like it before in my entire life." She walked closer, grabbed my hand, and clutched it tightly. "Thank you, sweetie. I'm just thrilled."

"I'm glad, Mrs. Higgins. I hope you'll enjoy it for many years."

"Oh. Oh." She looked around the yard, mystified. "Is that music?"

"I think it's coming from your fountain." It had started as soon as the water reached the three angels that stood at the highest point of the fountain. When they began spitting, the sound started. There had to be some sort of mechanism inside their mouths that created the high-pitched heavenly choirlike humming noise whenever the fountain was running. Unbelievable.

It was all too much for Mrs. Higgins, who collapsed in ecstasy into a patio chair.

"Are you all right?" I asked.

She gulped. "I am sublime and on time."

Where did she get those lines?

"That's a good thing, right?" I asked, just to make sure.

"Right and tight," she muttered, and closed her eyes. She looked happy, but the fountain experience had exhausted her. I just hoped we wouldn't have to call the paramedics.

I gathered my tools and took off, hoping this particular fountain would keep her interest for more than a year, unlike the previous two. But then I figured, what did it matter? If having a gaudy new fountain brought her a little bit of happiness, who was I to pee on her parade?

That night, I finally reached Jane, who was excited about the idea of getting together with the girls at Emily's apartment the following evening. I emphasized the fact that we were guaranteed a delicious meal prepared by Emily herself or her fabulous catering crew.

"Wonderful. I had tentative plans," Jane said, "but I'll cancel them. I'll have much more fun with the girls."

"Tentative plans? With someone I know?"

"It's not important," she said, and quickly changed the subject. "Hey, don't forget my big gala is this weekend."

"How could I forget? It promises to be the party of the year."

"Of the decade," she said, and laughed. "I'm so thrilled to be opening my doors at long last. Everything is ready. I'm just waiting for it all to begin."

"You've worked really hard to make this happen and I'm so proud of you."

"Now you're going to make me cry."

"Save your tears for Wednesday night with the girls."

"Good idea. Maybe I can make everybody cry."

"There's a goal," I said with a laugh, and ended the call a minute later. As soon as I did, I realized I hadn't even mentioned the necklace to her. I'd completely forgotten. And I had hardly heckled her at all about her *tentative* plans. I was really falling down on the job of BFF.

Before I could call her back, though, I received a call from my second foreman, Carla. She had a lot to talk about, and by the time we finished the conversation, it was too late to call Jane back. I'd have to catch her before we got to Emily's, and talk it through. One way or another, we had to spill the beans.

Of course, Jane and I played telephone tag all day, so Wednesday night, I got to Emily's early to try to grab Jane. We had to discuss strategy. Would we tell our friends about the necklace? Would we tell them that Jesse had been murdered? And we absolutely had to tell Eric about the necklace. My hair was turning gray just worrying about what he would say.

But Jane didn't show up until after everyone else had arrived. So we were going to have to wing it, but I was determined to tell them about the necklace.

"I know it's only been a week or so," Marigold said after giving me a warm hug, "but I feel like I haven't seen you in months."

"I said the exact same thing to Shannon," Lizzie said. "I've been so busy with work."

"And a few of her men have been busy at *my* place," Emily said dramatically as she poured wine into five glasses.

"How's that coming along?" Marigold asked.

"It's fantastic," Emily said. "I can't wait for you all to see it."

Even though I hadn't been back to her place since we did the walk-through with Wade, he'd been keeping me apprised of the progress. It seemed that the ghost of Mrs. Rawley was still very interested in what was going on there.

Emily passed me a glass. "You'll be happy to know that Wade and Douglas and the others have been doing amazing work."

I smiled. "That's why I pay them the big bucks."

"And they deserve every penny," Emily said, and turned to the others. "They have not only me to deal with, but an interfering ghost, as it turns out."

Lizzie's eyes widened. "The Rawley ghost. I've heard about it for years. Do you think it's real? Have you seen it?"

"Let's say I've felt her presence," Emily said, swirling her wine.

It was more than just a presence, I thought, if my experience at age seven was any indication. And Wade had been filling me in on a few incidents that had happened since they started the job. Nothing too scary, he'd said, but still a little nerve-racking to work with a *ghost* in the house.

"That's so fascinating," Marigold whispered. "Is it scary? Do you feel cold air in spots?"

"Not at all," Emily said. "I just feel she's there, taking an interest in everything happening around her house. There hasn't been much to occupy her for the last five years that it was on the market, so now she's fairly active."

"How can you tell?" Lizzie wondered.

"It's an energy. Plus, you know, the lights going on and off by themselves."

"Seriously?" Marigold's mouth hung open.

"Yes," I said. "And the guys assure me it's not the wiring. The first time we walked through with Wade, he heard a yowling sound, like a cat."

"Was it a cat?"

"Maybe," I said, "but nobody else heard it."

"It's a presence," Emily said. "I can't describe it. You'll all have to come over once I move in."

"I wouldn't miss it for the world," Jane said.

"Me, neither," Marigold said. "I can't wait to meet your ghost."

"She seems to show up in whatever part of the house the men are working in," Emily put in.

"Smart ghost," Lizzie murmured.

Emily grinned. "Yes. Sometimes their tools get moved. The other day a paint can tipped over, but it was on the tarp, so no damage was done. I don't know if she wants to observe the work itself or if she just likes watching the men, period."

"Don't we all?" Jane said.

Emily winked. "They're awfully cute."

"Yes, they are," Jane said. "When Johnny and Douglas were working on my place, it was hard to ignore them with those tool belts hanging low around their hips and those muscles bulging as they hammered and sawed."

"Tell me more," Marigold said, fanning herself.

I laughed. "You're talking about guys who are like brothers to me."

"I'm sorry for you, then," Emily said, "because they're quite adorable."

Lizzie carried a bowl of guacamole into the compact dining space. "This is so much nicer than meeting at a restaurant."

"I agree." Emily brought a platter of pâté, cheese, and

crackers to the table. "It might be the last gathering I have in this cozy little place, so I want to enjoy it while I can."

I raised my glass to her. "I hope you'll be even happier in your beautiful new home."

"Oh, yes, absolutely," she said, clinking her glass against mine. "I can't wait to get started."

"The guys are making pretty good time," I reported, both to Emily and the others. "I think we're right on schedule."

"I know you are." She watched as Lizzie placed a large bowl of pasta with a thick red sauce on the table. "But I don't want to force you to talk shop tonight."

Not that I would've minded talking shop, but the table was now crammed with food. We all took our seats and I glanced around. "How about if we talk about Jane's 'tentative plans' for tonight?"

They all turned to look at Jane, who shot me an evil glare. "I'll get you for that."

"Let me rephrase the question," I said, laughing. "Jane, are you seeing anyone lately?"

"I figured I couldn't keep it a secret for long." She sighed and reached for a marinated olive. "If you must know, I've gone out with Stephen Darby twice now. We were supposed to do something tonight, but I canceled."

"Stephen who?" Emily said.

"Who's Stephen?" Marigold asked, glancing around the table.

"Darby?" I said. "Ned's son?"

"Yes," Jane said, her tone defensive, knowing we were poised to pounce on her every word. "He called and asked me out and I said yes. We've gone out twice and I've enjoyed myself. He's very tall. And, um, nice. He likes good food."

"Ooh, tall," Lizzie said.

"And *nice*." Marigold emphasized the word since Jane hadn't made it sound very appealing.

"That's something, isn't it?" Lizzie glanced around the

table, clearly hoping we would support Jane in her quest to find true love. As the self-proclaimed matchmaker of the group, she wanted everyone to be as happy as she was in her marriage. Of course, each of us wanted that for ourselves, too. Eventually. Lizzie wanted it to happen right now.

Marigold gave Jane a smile of encouragement. "Are you having fun, at least?"

Jane groaned. "Oh, God, he tries so hard. He's become a chef and he loves to eat, so we've gone to two fabulous places."

"Food is good," Lizzie said firmly. "A man who likes food is a . . . a good man."

"I thought he was handsome," Emily said.

Jane buried her face in her hands and laughed at our obvious attempts to make Stephen sound interesting.

I patted her back. "So he doesn't float your boat. Just enjoy yourself for now and someday you'll meet someone who knocks your socks off." And, I added silently, someone I didn't maybe, sort of, almost suspect of murder. Possibly.

"Someday," she echoed quietly.

"Nothing wrong with someday," Emily said.

"True." Jane waved her hands to put an end to the topic. "Anyway, yes, Stephen is *nice*, but oh, so boring, poor guy. So, Marigold, how are you these days?"

"Things are pretty quiet in my life," Marigold said, "unless you count Goofus, Aunt Daisy's new puppy."

She passed her phone around and we oohed and aahed at her adorable pictures of little Goofus, a tiny golden retriever whose paws were bigger than his head. The dog was going to be gigantic one of these days.

I glanced up and saw Jane looking right at me, her forehead furrowed. Something was up with her. "What is it?"

"I want to tell them."

"So do I." We hadn't discussed it, but it was the right thing to do. These women were our best friends. In this little group, we shared everything.

"Tell us what?" Emily asked.

Jane sat up a little straighter and cleared her throat. "Shannon found a priceless antique necklace in Uncle Jesse's basement. It's made of gold and encrusted with diamonds and rubies and all sorts of other jewels."

"Good heavens," Marigold said.

"We believe he found it a few years ago," Jane continued, "while scuba diving around the *Glorious Maiden* shipwreck."

"We believe he showed it to a few people at first," I said. "He was probably trying to get an estimate of the cost or maybe trying to sell it, but he kept it hidden after that."

Jane glanced around. "We think it might've been the reason he was killed."

I gasped. "Jane, no!"

"Oops." Jane pressed her fingers to her lips.

Lizzie pounced. "Why 'oops'? What's the story? Come on, spill it."

Jane winced, and shot a glance at me. "He didn't say we couldn't mention it was murder. Just, you know, the means by which it was done."

I gave her a withering look, although, technically, she was right. We had only promised Eric we wouldn't mention the fact that the investigators hadn't found a prescription for sleeping pills inside Jesse's house. Still, if he found out about this conversation, I had no doubt that Jane would escape unharmed while I would be thrown into that jail cell he'd threatened us with.

"Fine," I said. "We think Jesse was murdered, but we're not allowed to say how it might've been done. So I don't want to hear this conversation repeated outside this room."

Jane nodded, on board with me here. "Or he'll kill us."

"He'll kill *me*," I muttered, then glared at everyone seated around the table. "So all of you must promise not to say a word."

I must've scared them with my intensity, because they all swore not to breathe a word of it to anyone. I gave them all a tight smile, took a sip of wine, and confessed,

"And the necklace presents another problem. We weren't going to tell you about it, because we were afraid that if word got out, Jane's life would be in danger."

"In danger?" Lizzie cried. "But why?"

"Because if someone was willing to kill Jesse to get it, they might think nothing of hurting Jane, too."

A couple of tense seconds of silence passed before we seemed to take a collective deep breath.

"Jane," Emily said, "you must give it to the police."

"I will," she said. "For now, it's in a safe place."

"Not on your premises, I hope."

"No." She stared at each one of us in turn. "Now, look, you're all sworn to secrecy until after my grand opening."

"Jane," I said. "That's—"

She held up her hand to silence me. "I know it's selfish and silly of me, but I want my grand opening to be the focus of everyone's attention for the next few days. Not the necklace."

"I'm going to tell Eric," I warned, knowing the penalty for holding out on the chief of police. "He'll keep it quiet."

Lizzie nodded. "And he can help protect Jane."

And not imprison me, I thought. Besides, now that the girls knew, it was only a matter of time before the secret leaked out. It wouldn't look good if Eric found out through another source.

"Why did you want to wait to tell everyone until after your opening?" Marigold asked.

Jane frowned. "Because if people start talking about the necklace, it'll consume every conversation. And then they'll inevitably talk about Jesse, too, and rumors will fly and I just don't want my guests to show up and be confronted with gossip about a possible murder and burglary and . . . well, you know."

Emily reached over and squeezed Jane's arm. "You don't want word to get out that murder has once again tainted our little town."

I sighed, knowing that that was exactly the way the gossip would go.

"So, if it's possible," Jane pleaded, "can we please keep the news among the five of us for now?"

We all looked at Lizzie. She was the only one who was married, so of course she would tell Hal.

"I can keep a secret," she insisted.

"If you want to tell Hal, go ahead," Jane said, then gave me a worried look. "There's no way we can contain it."

"Your party is in two days," I said. "We can all keep a secret for two days, can't we?" I glanced around the table. "It's important."

"I promise we can," Marigold asserted. "It's not just Jane's grand opening we're concerned about, but her safety. For that, we can all keep our lips zipped. Yes?"

Emily extended her arm. "Promise."

I did the same and grabbed her hand. "Promise."

The others joined in. Once we were all holding hands, we raised our arms in the air and shouted, "Promise!"

"That was stirring," Emily said, chuckling, as she reached for the wine bottle.

Jane smiled. "Just like cheerleader camp."

"Minus the pompoms," Lizzie said.

We laughed and the serious vibe was broken for the moment. Emily poured another round of wine, which helped enormously. Lizzie wanted to hear more about the necklace, so we described it to her. I got a few laughs and shudders when I told them how I'd found the darn thing in the darkest, least accessible place in Jesse's house.

Marigold sighed. "The necklace sounds fantastic, but I hate to think your uncle was killed because of it."

"I hate it, too," Jane said.

"You really think someone killed him?" Lizzie asked. "It wasn't a heart attack?"

Since they knew the basics, Jane shared the news about the autopsy report. "There's no way he took a bunch of pills on his own," Jane said. "We think someone drugged him."

I sighed but didn't point out that she had just revealed the one piece of information we'd agreed to hold back.

Wine had a way of making Jane—and everyone else in the world—indiscreet, so I could only hope that our friends would be satisfied talking about this with each other and not with anyone outside of our little group.

Oh, who was I kidding? I needed to make it clear all over again just exactly what the stakes were.

"Excuse me," I said, lightly tapping my spoon against my wineglass. "But that little piece of information about the pills is exactly what you cannot repeat outside of this room."

"Oh no," Jane said, slapping her forehead. "Shannon's right. Cone of silence, okay? Or Eric will really be mad."

"Yeah, really mad," I repeated. "So mum's the word."

"Poor Shannon," Marigold said, rubbing my shoulder. "I know you're worried, but you can trust us to be discreet."

I smiled at her. "Thanks, Marigold." She could read people's emotions better than any psychic in the world.

"But who would do such a thing to Jesse?" Emily wondered, bringing us back to the subject at hand.

"That's the fifty-thousand-dollar question," Jane said. "Who did it?"

"And *why*?" Lizzie added.

I cleared my throat. "I made a list."

They all gaped at me and Emily laughed. "That's our girl."

Early Friday morning, I was surprised when Mac knocked on my door and invited me to walk with him down to the Cozy Cove for breakfast. The sky was clear but the air was cold and crisp as we made our way toward the town square. We chatted about his new house and our upcoming meeting with the Planning Commission. I'd made a list of all the additional changes we'd talked about and had gone over the list with my dad. He was even more familiar with the personalities involved and would know what changes they would—and would not—allow us to make to the lighthouse mansion, our town's beloved landmark.

Mac insisted that it wouldn't bother him if they turned down one thing or another. As he'd told me the other day when we drove out to see the place, he didn't plan to change much of the outside of the building. He just wanted a comfortable home on the inside. Free of rats, of course.

"I'm with you there," I said, shivering a little at the memory of that tiny, squealing rodent skittering across the wood-plank floor. Once we were seated and our coffee was poured, I added, "We'll get everything approved, I guarantee it."

"I'm not worried," he said. "Between you, with your awe-inspiring ability to secure all those permits and read those blueprints, and me along to dazzle them with my fancy footwork, they'll be putty in our hands."

I smiled broadly, held up my coffee mug, and we toasted our two-pronged plan of attack. The Commission members wouldn't know what hit them.

Saturday was Jane's gala grand opening and everyone in Lighthouse Cove was invited to the party. Tonight would be the first time Jane welcomed guests to the Hennessey House Bed-and-Breakfast. Besides the guests who would be checking in for the first time, the entire town would be stopping by to wish Jane well. Those who hadn't yet gotten a look inside the town's newest, most elegant establishment were eager to see it.

It had taken me and Jane and my crew almost three years to renovate her grandmother's disheveled old mansion and turn it into a world-class small hotel. The place had been standing there for over one hundred and fifty years, and in that time, it had been a family home, a brothel, a boardinghouse, a private residence, and finally an elegant bed-and-breakfast.

I stood on the sidewalk and gazed with pride at the beautifully restored Queen Anne with its wide wrap-around porch, wonderful three-story tower, and six chimneys. Hennessey House featured fourteen uniquely decorated guest suites, many with balconies and fireplaces. The entire house was furnished with beautiful Victorian-era pieces that were not only authentic but also comfortable and elegant.

The gardens had been completely renovated months ago and now they were gorgeous and green, a lush paradise with flowering plants everywhere. Charming rustic pathways invited strolling guests to discover a small bench or sitting area behind a tree or next to the koi pond, where they might read a book or drink their morning coffee or enjoy a glass of wine at dusk.

Jane had planned the party as an open house from three in the afternoon until eight o'clock that night, so people would be coming and going and the kitchen staff had been told to keep the appetizers hot and plentiful.

Jane's small, permanent kitchen staff had been practicing for weeks, learning Jane's recipes and creating new ones of their own. Jane's friends had been used as guinea pigs, happily, so we knew they would do a great job. Tonight they had help from some of Emily's tea shop staff, who were used to catering larger affairs.

An open bar was set up in the living room area off the lobby foyer, and another one was outside on the deck overlooking the gardens. It was a beautiful afternoon, cold but clear, and space heaters were stationed at each seating area.

Most important, my friends and I had our marching orders. Jane had invited everyone on my suspect list to the party, so we planned to do whatever it took to corner each of them and pump them for information—in the friendliest, most polite and discreet way possible, of course.

I arrived early and helped Jane with a few of the last-minute details, such as arranging stacks of cocktail napkins on the end tables and testing the baby quiches for flavor. "Yep, they're perfect," I said with my mouth full.

"Thanks so much," Jane said wryly. "I have to go to the kitchen for a minute, and guests are starting to arrive. Please behave yourself."

"I'll be delightful, as always."

She walked away shaking her head, and I proceeded

to go to the bar, where Ian, one of Emily's staff waiters, was serving drinks.

"Hey, Shannon, what can I get you?"

"I'll have a glass of the cabernet."

"Hello there, Shannon," a woman said.

I turned and found Althea Tannis standing behind me.

"Althea, hello." We shook hands. "How are you?"

"I'm fine, dear," she said wistfully. "You know, taking it one day at a time."

"Yes, I know what you mean."

"It's still such a shock," she said, obviously referring to Jesse's death. "I'm sure it hasn't been easy for anyone."

"No, it hasn't."

Ian took her order for a vodka gimlet and I tried to check my guilt once again. The woman had known Jesse, so of course she had to be on my suspect list. It was nothing personal. No reason to feel guilty, but there it was.

Ian handed her the cocktail and she set the glass on the bar before turning to me.

"Don't you look pretty in green?" she said. "Your eyes just sparkle next to that color."

"Oh, thank you." The forest green sleeveless cocktail dress with the low-draped back was one of my favorites. "I like your dress, too."

She glanced down at the strawberry polka-dotted silk dress she wore with short red heels. "Isn't it fun? It's from my shop. I sell lots of new things, too, besides vintage clothing and accessories. You should come by sometime."

"I will. It's in Blue Point, right?"

"Yes, you have a good memory. It's such a pretty little town. Smaller than Lighthouse Cove, but just charming."

"I've been to a few restaurants down there, and you have a great little bookstore, too."

"That's right," she said, looking pleased that I remembered. "My shop is just a few doors down from the bookstore."

She really did seem nice. So why was I still grappling with suspicion? "I might stop by one of these days. I'll probably drag Jane along, too."

"That would be wonderful." She glanced around. "Speaking of Jane, I haven't seen her yet."

"She should be in the kitchen."

"I hope she won't mind giving me a little tour later. This is one of the loveliest B-and-Bs I've ever seen."

Okay, well, I had to admit the way to my heart was to flatter my friends and my own work. "It is, isn't it? I'm sure Jane would love to give you a tour. The gardens are beautiful, too."

She glanced in the direction I'd pointed. "Oh, it all looks lovely." She picked up her drink. "I might just peek around on my own until I find her, if you'll excuse me."

"Of course. Enjoy yourself."

I watched her walk outside onto the deck and wondered just how close Jesse and she had been. I mean, if it had been serious, he would have said something to Jane, right? I would think so, anyway. And if they weren't serious, why was Althea suddenly becoming so at home in Lighthouse Cove?

And why couldn't I stop asking dumb questions? Althea was here because Jane had invited her, duh! There was nothing nefarious about her presence here this afternoon.

Deliberately I turned back to Ian. We talked for another minute until someone behind me ordered a drink. I turned and bumped into Stephen Darby. "Oh, I'm sorry."

"No damage done," he said, smiling as he extended his hand. "Hello. We met the other day. Stephen Darby. You're . . . Sharon?"

"Shannon."

He winced. "Sorry, Shannon. You were Jesse's neighbor."

"And you're Ned's son."

"Right." We smiled at each other. He turned to Ian and asked for two scotch and waters for Bob and Ned, and a glass of white wine for himself. I waited for him, sipping my wine as Ian worked.

"Here, let me help you," I said, and took one of the cocktails Stephen had ordered. We delivered them to the two older men, who were involved in a stirring discussion with Mac about navy policies.

Mac winked at me by way of greeting before continuing his conversation with the two men. I turned back to Stephen. "I remember you said you were working at Tre Mondrian. How's it going?"

He raised an eyebrow. "You have a good memory."

"I love that restaurant," I said brightly, "so naturally I remembered you talking about it. Is it working out okay?"

"It's, uh, yeah, it's going great. It's part-time for a few months and then I'll go full-time this summer." His gaze flitted restlessly over the crowd and I wondered if I was boring him as well as the other way around. He clearly wasn't interested in my charms, shocking as that was.

"That's good to hear." We strolled around the room and outside onto the deck while I tried to find something to talk about. Not usually an issue for me, but Jane was right. Stephen wasn't exactly electrifying company. "And you've found a place to live?"

"Not yet," he said, sounding sheepish. "I'm starting to look at houses in town, but meanwhile, I'm bunking with my dad."

"You'll find the right home."

"I hope so." He took a big gulp of wine, glancing around, looking desperate to find someone else. Jane, no doubt. "I'd like to get something near the beach."

I wished I hadn't vowed to stay close to him, because I was so ready to walk away. Would he even notice? I tried to think of a way to steer the conversation toward what I needed to know without being obvious about it. Such as, where was he the night of the murder? Did he know about the necklace?

Did he murder my friend Jesse?

"I don't blame you," I said. "The coastline is beautiful."

"Especially around Lighthouse Cove," he said. "I love

this area. I think it's the prettiest part of Northern California."

"I think so." I tried to smile, but it wasn't easy. I didn't believe a word he was saying. It was my own fault for striking up a conversation with someone whose name was number four on my suspect list. My judgment was already clouded by that, and now every little thing he said, the tone of his voice, his facial gestures, felt false.

"Are you looking to buy something or rent? I usually know which houses are on the market so I'd be happy to help."

"Oh." I must've caught him off guard with my offer, because he looked stymied. "I've actually been looking for a place similar to the one Jesse owned. Smaller, one story, but still in the Victorian style."

I smiled tepidly. "Sad to say, Jesse's home will be on the market eventually."

"Of course. I didn't mean to sound crass. I just remember visiting him once and really liking the feel of the place."

Wasn't that fascinating?

And also, it was the first time in all these minutes that I wasn't bored by his presence. Maybe because it was the first time he seemed genuinely connected to what he was talking about instead of just muttering small talk. Before he had seemed so distracted. Not exactly flattering to the person he was with.

"How long ago did you visit him?" I asked.

"It's been a few years." He set his drink down. "Maybe I should ask my Realtor to contact Jane to ask what her plans are. I don't want to pressure her by asking her directly."

Oh, really? I thought. *Ask Jane?* Jesse's place would be available when I said so. *Meow!*

I knew it wasn't fair to be influenced by the fact that Stephen's name was on my suspect list, but there it was. He bugged me. I managed to keep talking though, because I was on a mission of sorts.

"So, do you scuba dive like your father does?" I asked.

"I got certified a few years ago, but I'm not as gung ho about it as Dad is." He chuckled. "If he could throw on a wet suit and jump in the water every weekend, he'd be a happy man."

He looked almost animated again. Score another point for me.

"We have some great diving areas around here," I said. "Did he tell you about our amazing shipwreck right in the middle of Lighthouse Bay?"

"He said something about a clipper ship sinking out there."

"Yes, the *Glorious Maiden*. That's where your father went on a diving trip with Jesse and Bob a few years ago."

"Oh yes."

"Rumor has it that it sank with a huge stash of gold, payment for the opium it had delivered to San Francisco. These days we get our share of diving enthusiasts who show up every year, hoping to find some kind of treasure down there."

I watched his face for any reaction to the mention of gold and treasure.

"Does anyone ever find anything exciting?" His eyes flickered with interest. A good sign.

"A gold coin might wash up on the beach every few years, and that seems to be enough to keep some of the more adventurous people interested and coming back." While that was true, most normal people returned to Lighthouse Cove for completely different reasons such as the great weather, the beauty of the coast, the Victorian charm, and the welcoming warmth of the townspeople.

"A lot of folks want to get something for nothing," Stephen said, frowning.

"True enough." I took a sip of wine and savored the flavor. "Jesse used to boast that he'd found some fabulous piece of jewelry while diving around the *Glorious Maiden*."

"Jewelry?" he said, perking up again. "Now, that's exciting. Did you ever see it?"

"No." I chuckled. "Jesse had a tendency to tell tall tales once in a while."

"But if he found it, what would he do with it?"

"Sell it? Or give it to a museum? I don't really know."

"Would he hide it?"

"Maybe. What would you do with something like that?"

He blinked and seemed to catch himself. "Uh, yeah, I'd probably give it to a museum. But you don't think it exists? Too bad." He glanced around at the walls and ceiling and I could feel his attention slipping away again.

"Jane's place is fantastic," he said.

"Isn't it? It took us a few years to get it into shape, but it was worth it. It's beautiful."

"It sounds like you had a hand in it."

"My construction company helped Jane renovate the entire building." I gazed around the room. "But the furnishings and color schemes and the warmth are all due to Jane."

"She is a warm person," he said, his gaze focusing on someone behind me. Was Jane back there?

"Yes, she's got a loving and generous heart and she's smart and beautiful. She's been my best friend since kindergarten." *So don't play games with her,* I added silently.

I thought maybe he got the message, because his jaw tightened ever so slightly. "That's great to hear."

"Hello, you two," Jane said from behind me. "Having fun?"

"Sure are," I said.

"Jane, I've been looking all over for you."

"Hello, Stephen."

"I was hoping we could take a walk in the garden."

"Maybe a little later," she said vaguely, and gave him her most gracious smile. "Help yourself to some appetizers. They're delicious."

"Don't mind if I do. Thanks." He rushed away and Jane gave me an accusing look.

"What did you say to him? He ran off like a scared rabbit."

"I didn't do anything. I thought we were having a pleasant conversation. I guess he was hungry."

"I know he's on your so-called suspect list, but that doesn't make him guilty of anything."

"Then why does he act so suspicious?" I whispered.

"Shannon," she warned.

"Okay, but you were right about one thing." I leaned in and said, "He's boring."

The truth was, I hadn't tried very hard to frighten Stephen, but he'd looked awfully uncomfortable talking to me. And he'd seemed a little too interested in Jesse's house and in what Jesse might've done with the necklace if he found it. Made me wonder what kind of secrets he was hiding and how I might find out what they were.

Jane was right. Stephen's discomfort didn't mean he was guilty of anything—except maybe boring me to death. One thing was certain, though: I would be keeping an eagle eye on Stephen Darby from now on.

Chapter Nine

"How do you think the party's going?" Jane asked an hour later as she cast an anxious look around. "I'm too involved to see it objectively."

"It's going great," I said. "It's a fabulous party. Try to relax. Everyone is raving about the great food and excellent wine, and your place looks fantastic. Did you redo the lighting in here?"

"Just tweaks here and there." Jane's smile was tinged with pride. "I think we cleaned up well."

"I'd say so," I said, laughing. "Everything looks elegant and welcoming. Have any guests arrived yet?"

"Yes, two darling couples drove up from San Francisco earlier this afternoon and were the first people to check in."

"How exciting."

"It was. I gave them each a champagne basket to celebrate."

"Cool."

"Three more couples arrived shortly after that, and five singles and a couple streamed in over the past few hours. I suspect at least one of them is a reviewer. Sandra is showing them to their rooms."

"Who's Sandra?"

"Sandra Larsen. Didn't you meet her? She's my new assistant manager."

"I guess I haven't been around lately."

"I'll introduce you. She's a cousin of Sean's."

"Then she must be okay," I said, grinning. "So any more guests expected?"

"Yes, I'm expecting a family to arrive later tonight. And I had one dropout, which bummed me out a little. But then someone just called a few days ago and reserved the room for a week starting Monday afternoon. So that's all fourteen rooms."

I grabbed her hand and squeezed. "A full house. It's all happening, Jane."

"I know." She giggled and let out a little squeal. "I'm an innkeeper for real!"

"You're a hotelier," I said, raising my glass to her.

"Yes, much classier."

I gave her a quick hug. "I'm thrilled for you. Congratulations."

"I couldn't have done it without you."

"That's so true." I laughed and shook my head. "No, I helped rebuild the walls and the floors and the facades, but you added your own special touch of beauty and grace and friendliness. That's what your guests will take away and talk about for years to come."

"Oh." She pressed her fingers to her lips. "Don't you dare make me cry again."

"Ooh, I see a tear," I said, peering at her. "I believe my work here is done."

She smacked my arm. "Beast."

"That's me." I grinned. "Hey, did Althea find you?"

"Althea's here?" She glanced around. "Where is she?"

"She took herself off on a little tour of the place, but that was a while ago."

"Oh, good. I'll go track her down."

At that moment, Jane's assistant tapped her on the shoulder. "I hate to interrupt, but we've had a cancellation."

"Oh no." Jane gave me a quick glance before turning to follow Sandra through the door to the check-in desk tucked under the main stairway off the foyer. I tagged behind.

Jane looked at the phone message Sandra handed her. "Andrew Braxton. He was involved in a car accident."

"His doctor called from the hospital," Sandra added. "He's had to cancel his entire trip."

"Must've been a bad accident," I said.

"I hope he's okay." Jane wrung her hands. "He's the one who reserved the last room, and he even paid for the entire week in advance. I'll have to issue a refund to his credit card. We should find out what hospital he's in and maybe send flowers."

"I can call around and take care of it," Sandra said.

"Thank you, Sandra. You're the best."

"Come on," I said. "Let's get you a glass of wine." I wound my arm through Jane's and we walked back to the living room bar.

"And he was booked into my favorite room," she said dejectedly.

"They're all your favorite rooms," I said.

"I know, but he was booked in Desdemona, the one with the pretty pale green walls and the little balcony that overlooks the Buddha Garden."

"That's a nice one," I admitted, remembering vividly the work we'd done to refurbish that room with its peeling paint and rotted wooden walls, not to mention the crumbling balcony. Steel-reinforced beams had been extended out from beneath the floor to buttress the small terrace, and the softly curving iron rail and elaborate fretwork in the balusters had cost a small fortune to replicate. But it had been worth it, if Jane's overwhelming delight was any gauge.

Jane had named each of her fourteen suites after Shakespeare's heroines. She'd also named different areas of her garden after the various statuary she'd placed there. So there was the Buddha Garden with its statue of the laughing Buddha set at the base of a young redwood tree, surrounded by verdant ferns and pink cyclamen. A standing statue of Walt Whitman had his own miniforest of pines at the end of the garden walk. And a family of deer stood guard near the copse of bay laurels, earning it the whimsical name of Bambi Bay.

"I hate that the room's going to be empty all week," Jane said.

"I know. I'm sorry."

She took a sip from the wineglass I handed her. "I just wanted to be able to say that I had a full house our first week in business." She waved her problems aside. "Never mind. The important thing is to find out if he was badly injured. I hope not."

"Did I hear you say you have an empty room this week?"

We both turned and saw Stephen Darby hovering nearby.

"Yes, I've had a cancellation," Jane said. "My guest was involved in a car accident."

"I'm sorry," he said, touching her arm in a show of sympathy. "And I hate to gain from your guest's loss, but I would love to take that room for as long as it's available."

"Oh, Stephen, you don't have to do that."

"But I want to," he insisted, then leaned closer. "I really want to get out of my father's house."

Jane laughed softly. "In that case, the room is available and it looks like it's yours."

That was convenient, I thought, as Stephen ushered Jane back to the registration area. First he wined and dined Jane and now he was renting a room in her B-and-B? Was he so enthralled with Jane or was there something more sinister going on? I had already decided to keep an eye on Stephen, so what else could I do but traipse along behind them?

"Here we go," Jane said, settling herself behind the check-in desk. "If you'll fill out this information card and let me know which credit card you'll be using, I'll get things started." She looked a bit flustered. "Oh, but I guess you don't have any luggage."

"No, I'll go back to Dad's later and pack a few things. Here's my credit card."

"Perfect," Jane murmured, taking the card and sliding it through the mini credit card processor.

"Oh, there you are, Jane," Althea said.

"Althea," Jane cried, glancing up from the card reader. "I'm so happy you made it."

"I'm happy, too. But you look busy, so I'll find you later."

"No, wait." Jane skipped around the desk and gave the older woman a warm hug. "It's so good to see you. Are you finding your way around?"

She giggled. "I hope you don't mind, but I just gave myself a little tour through your beautiful garden and lost track of time. This place is magnificent. I'm so proud of you and I know Jesse would've been bursting with pride tonight."

"That means a lot. Thank you." She hugged her again. "Just give me a few minutes to take care of some business, and we can sit down and have a little talk."

"I would love that," Althea said. She waved her hand in the general direction of the living room. "I'll be around, mingling."

"Good." Jane returned to her seat and stared at the readout. "Oh. Oh dear." Her shoulders tensed slightly as she gazed up at Stephen. "I'm sorry. Your card was rejected. Let me run it one more time."

"No, no," he said, his face turning pink. "I'll just give you another card."

"Of course." Jane stood waiting patiently, her face a mask of professional discretion.

"This is awkward," he muttered.

"It happens all the time," Jane said. "Don't give it another thought."

He fumbled through his wallet, yanked another card out of its slot, and stared at it for a few seconds before handing it to her. "I see the problem. I gave you my old business credit card, but I'm no longer working there, so it's not active. I wasn't thinking. Sorry."

"No apologies necessary." Jane handed him the rejected card and took the new one. "Let me run this through for you."

She sat down and swept the card through the machine. We all held our collective breaths for the fifteen seconds it took for the card to be accepted.

"There we go," Jane said, peppy and perky again. "All checked in. Whenever you bring your luggage back, please ring the bell and I'll have someone carry it upstairs for you."

"Don't worry about that. I'll just have a small bag with me."

"Well, then, welcome to Hennessey House." Jane stood and handed him a room key. "Sandra will show you to your room. You'll find a notebook on the dresser filled with every bit of information you could possibly want to know about our bed-and-breakfast and about Lighthouse Cove and the surrounding area. We have free Wi-Fi in every room and bicycles available anytime you'd like to take a spin around town or ride down to the beach. We begin serving breakfast at seven, but coffee is available starting at five in the morning."

I beamed at her and she smiled back. I knew she'd worked extra hard to memorize that speech.

"Good to know," Stephen said. "Thank you. I won't go up to my room just yet. I'd rather enjoy the party for a while longer."

"Please do." Jane handed off the desk to Sandra, who nodded and slipped back into professional greeter mode.

Stephen's embarrassment seemed to dissipate as he chatted with Jane while Sandra stacked his information card and initial hotel bill printout and slipped both into a drawer. Having a credit card refused was a fairly common problem, but I had to wonder how a financial adviser could make that mistake.

I knew I wasn't being fair to him. Maybe he'd been so blown away by Jane's beauty that he handed her the wrong card. No offense against Jane's beauty, but that sounded like a load of baloney.

Stephen finally wandered off to find his father, and Jane went to find Althea. I saw the two of them slip outside to have an intimate chat, and I walked back to the parlor and found Lizzie and Hal. I hugged them both and we toasted to Jane's success.

"It's about time we found you," Lizzie said in a quiet voice. "We've been talking to Bob and Ned for the past twenty minutes." She winked meaningfully at me and I almost laughed.

"So maybe we'll talk tomorrow," I said.

"You bet we will," she said, nodding with purpose.

Hal just rolled his eyes. "I don't want to know what you two are cooking up this time."

Lizzie patted his cheek, gave me another wink, and they took off for home.

Seeing Lizzie and Hal made me realize I'd lost track of Mac. I'd spied him momentarily a while ago when I was talking to Stephen, but now I didn't see him anywhere. It wasn't as if we were here on a date, so it was none of my business if he'd already left the party. Still, I couldn't help feeling a bit disappointed. It would have been fun to hang out with him for a while.

"Hello, Shannon."

I whipped around. "Eric! Hello."

He smiled. "Can I get you a drink?"

I glanced at my glass and saw that it was empty. "I'll go with you."

"Good." He grinned and held out his arm, and I weaved mine through his. It was odd to be walking arm in arm with the man who had reprimanded me so thoroughly the other day. The man who'd promised to lock me in a prison cell and throw away the key. Maybe he'd been partly kidding about that, but still, I was nervous, especially as I mentally ran through all the information I was presently keeping from him.

"This place is fantastic," he said, admiring the features of the room. "I heard you had a lot to do with renovating it."

"My company helped out."

"Something tells me you're being too modest." He ordered a glass of cabernet for me and a beer for himself. When we had our drinks, we walked out the French doors and into the garden.

"This is spectacular," he said, looking around.

I took a sip of wine and almost spilled it down my dress. I was too nervous to think straight and knew I had to tell all. "Eric, we have to talk."

He gazed down at me. "Right now?"

"Yes, please."

"Let's go for a walk."

"What's this all about?" Eric asked when we'd walked half a block from Jane's.

I stopped and turned to him. "It's about a priceless jeweled necklace I found in Jesse's basement. Jesse used to tell us about it, how he'd found it while scuba diving on the *Glorious Maiden*."

"But he later denied that he found it."

"Right." We continued walking toward the town square. "He finally admitted to Jane that he'd been joking, and that was the end of it."

"But it wasn't."

"No." I took a deep breath and forged ahead. "I found it. See, Jane decided she wants to rehab Jesse's house and sell it, so last Tuesday I did a preliminary inspection. I don't think it'll take too much to clean it up, paint it. It'll sell well, I think, but I need to ... um, anyway, I found the necklace hidden behind the brick wall in his basement."

I had a tendency to veer dangerously off topic when I was nervous.

"Where is it now?"

"In a safe-deposit box at the bank." I gave him the name of the bank without him asking. And then I started describing the necklace while he alternately nodded and scowled.

Eric had this clever, insidious way of not saying anything, thereby forcing me to fill the gap and blather out all sorts of information. I told him everything—except the part where I'd been the one who wanted to tell him about the necklace right away, but Jane had insisted on waiting. I wasn't about to throw Jane under the bus.

I made a mental note to remind her what a good friend I was.

"I'm telling you about the necklace," I said, "because I'm afraid it might be the reason someone's been breaking into Jesse's house and searching for something."

"Yes, I got that connection," he assured me. "Any reason why you waited so long to tell me?"

"I was . . . afraid."

"Afraid of me?"

"No, afraid that if the intruder knew I found it, then Jane or I might be in danger."

He stopped walking and gazed down at me. "So you didn't tell the one person who could keep you safe?"

"You mean, you?"

"Yeah, me."

I frowned. "I think I've already proven that I have odd ways of dealing with things."

He wasn't in the mood to be cajoled. "Why didn't you say something, Shannon?"

"I–I wanted to, but there was so much going on. I've got all these jobs, plus Jesse's funeral and Jane's opening gala and the Festival Committee meetings. Plus I was scared to death that if I told anyone, word would get out and Jane would be in danger." I was blathering again.

"I understand your worry about your secret being exposed," he said. "That's a problem in small towns."

"Thank you."

"But look at me." It almost hurt to stare up at him, he was so good-looking. He was *Thor*. With dimples. "You can trust me," he said quietly. "Always. Do you get that?"

"I do," I said, letting go of the breath I'd been holding. "I really do."

He stared at me for another long moment, then nodded, apparently satisfied with what he saw in my eyes. We walked for six more blocks while we talked about nothing in particular, all the way around the town square and back to Hennessey House, where he left me, explaining that he had a few more hours of work before he could call it a day.

I stared at his back, wondering how he could smile so beautifully and sound so casual while leaving me feeling so nerve-racked.

I went straight to the bar for another glass of wine.

"Hello there, miss," a man behind me said.

I turned and smiled at Bob, Jesse's old buddy. "Hi, Bob. I'm Shannon. Do you remember me?"

"Sure do. I believe you're the only lovely lady I haven't chatted with this afternoon."

"Are you having a good time?"

"I am now," he said, and winked. The man was a flirt!

I slipped my arm through his and we strolled outside with our drinks. "I didn't have much of a chance to talk to you at Jesse's memorial service, but I've heard about you for years."

"It's all lies," he said, holding up both hands in surrender.

I laughed. "I don't think so. Jesse never stopped talking about all the fun you had on that diving trip you took for his birthday."

"That was a great time," he said with a sentimental nod. "There won't be another one of those anytime soon."

"Did you get all the way down to the shipwreck?"

"We sure did. That's a big chunk of history right there. But you've got to be careful. Got to know what you're doing. Of course, we were all in the navy, so diving was our life for many years."

"What was it like to swim around inside the old clipper ship?"

"Didn't go inside. I'm a little too tall and hefty." He chuckled and patted his belly. "If I swam into the bowels, I might get stuck. One small shift of the current and an old ship like that could rise or sink a little and kill you."

"I never thought of that. Sounds dangerous."

"It can be. So I was perfectly happy swimming around the wreckage. It's spread across a big area of the sea bottom."

"I didn't know that."

"Yep. I could've spent a few days down there and not seen it all. And of course, I might not have made it back."

"We wouldn't want that to happen."

"No, ma'am. Jesse made it, though. He explored some of the staterooms and the hull. Those are some tight squeezes for a man my size."

"Did Ned go inside?"

"He managed to work his way down to the main dining room belowdecks, but that was it."

"Did any of you find anything worth bringing back?"

"Oh, there was some talk at the time that we should tell everyone we found some precious gems or coins, but it was all a big joke. The real treasure was the experience itself. The memories. That's what I brought back."

"It sounds like you had a wonderful time."

"We sure did. Jesse was able to explore most of the ship, but then he was a few years younger than me." Bob nudged me and winked again. "But I've got stamina on my side."

"You're a devil," I said.

He laughed until he wheezed. I had to grab his drink to keep it from dropping. When he finally caught his breath, he chuckled hoarsely. "Haven't laughed like that in years. I like you, Shannon. You're a firecracker."

"Thank you." I was pretty sure it was a compliment.

"I'd better get you inside," he said, rubbing his arms. "It's turning chilly out here."

I left Bob at the French doors and watched him shuffle back toward the bar. It was interesting to know that he and Ned had not gone into any of the staterooms of the *Glorious Maiden*. And he considered the talk about finding treasure a joke. So chances were good that he and Ned had never seen what Jesse found.

I hadn't expected Bob to confess to murder, but I was a little bummed that he'd turned out to be such a sweetie. My list of suspects was shrinking.

"There's my girl."

I whipped around instantly and felt my disappointment slide away. "Dad, you made it."

"Wouldn't have missed it for the world." He gave me a bear hug and kept his arm wrapped around my shoulder. "Our Jane's in the big time now."

"I know. Isn't this place grand?"

"Sure is." Dad glanced around the room, taking in the finishings. I followed the direction of his gaze, grateful that he would notice the raised-panel wainscoting I'd designed, the double-ringed ceiling medallion that so perfectly accented the chandelier, the way the aging moldings were fitted together at each corner, the rebuilt decorative cornices and brackets at the edges of the alcove, the completely redesigned fireplace panel.

"You did a fantastic job, sweetheart." He nodded to himself as his experienced eye examined everything. "I couldn't be prouder."

What could I say? That meant everything. "Thanks, Dad. I learned from the best."

"Hey, guess you did." His chest expanded in mock self-importance and we both laughed.

"I'm so glad you're here," I whispered as I hugged him again. He'd dressed up in his best navy suit and wore a white shirt and the beautiful silk tie I'd given him last Christmas. He rarely dressed this elegantly these days, so I was especially pleased that he'd done so for Jane.

He took a good long look at me. "Something going on. What is it? What's bugging you?"

"Nothing," I said blithely, but I should've known better. He knew me too well.

"Nothing," he mocked. "How many times have I heard that before? You realize I haven't bought that line since you were fifteen and brokenhearted because Deputy Tommy didn't call when he said he would?"

I sighed and mentally kicked myself. No way should I have expected to fool my dad.

"But I'll let it go for tonight," he said, tweaking my chin. "Tomorrow, though, I'm coming over for breakfast."

I blinked. "Okay. Thanks for the warning."

"Be prepared to spill your guts."

Chapter Ten

Dad was already flipping pancakes when I stumbled down the stairs Sunday morning. Robbie, well aware of Dad's lack of kitchen coordination, stood at the ready to catch any misflipped flapjacks. I couldn't complain that Dad had broken into the house, since the house was still his, officially. Five years ago, after a heart attack scare, he had handed the house over to me and bought himself a Winnebago, a big one. He wanted to hit the road, explore the great outdoors, just as he and my mom had always planned to do. Dad got as far as the Oregon border before he turned around and came back home.

Traveling alone wasn't all it was cracked up to be, he realized. He found the best of both worlds when he decided to live in the motor home while it was parked in my driveway. That way, Dad could live in his bachelor pad and still have a place to do laundry. And I still had my dad around most of the time.

Dad especially loved the "man cave" aspect of the RV, with its wide-screen television and comfortable swiveling lounge chairs. His buddies joined him regularly to watch sports and play poker, and at least once a month, he would take off to go fishing with Uncle Pete.

So to find him in my kitchen every so often, whipping up a batch of pancakes and bacon, wasn't much of a shock. In truth, almost anyone willing to make me breakfast was welcome to break into my house anytime.

"Pour yourself a cup of coffee and sit. Breakfast will be ready in two minutes."

I did as I was told and sat down at the kitchen table, where a glass of orange juice and a multivitamin were waiting for me.

"Thanks, Dad. You didn't have to cook."

"I figured if I was invading your space, I owed you a meal."

"Okay, but I don't ever mind you invading my space."

He placed a big plate of pancakes, bacon, and a fried egg in front of me. "Syrup's hot, so help yourself."

"Are you eating?"

"I sure am." He pulled another plate from the oven and sat down across from me.

Robbie was trained not to enter the dining room, but he had no compunction against begging at the kitchen table. Fortunately he was a polite beggar, keeping a bit of a distance and letting the power of his big brown eyes do the work for him.

I glanced at Dad's plate. "Only one pancake?"

He patted his stomach. "I've got to watch my girlish figure now that I'm retired." He poured a bit of syrup on his pancake and began to eat. After the first bite, he put his fork down. "Tell me what's making you unhappy. Is it a man? Can I kick somebody's butt for you?"

"Nobody's making me unhappy, but thanks for the offer. It means a lot." I loved him so much it hurt. The worst day of my life was the day I received the call from Uncle Pete, telling me Dad had had a heart attack.

"I'm always willing," he said.

"I know, and I appreciate it. No, it's not about a man. It's mostly dealing with Jesse's death. We're sort of in a holding pattern with the police."

"Police? What do you mean? I thought he died of a heart attack. Why are the police involved?"

"Sorry, Dad. I forgot you haven't been around much." Even though we had talked a few times during the week while he was working at Uncle Pete's, I hadn't let him in on all the news about Jesse and the necklace.

I reached across the table and touched his hand. "It's being kept under wraps, but there's a strong possibility Jesse might've been murdered. According to the coroner, he died of an accidental overdose of sleeping pills."

"Sleeping pills? Jesse?" He shook his head vigorously. "I don't believe it."

"Jane and I don't believe it, either. And there wasn't a prescription bottle of pills anywhere in his house." I didn't even feel guilty about revealing the secret this time. This was my dad. Eric had to allow an exception for my dad, didn't he? "So how did he OD? Somebody must've helped him along."

"Aw, jeez." He dropped his fork and slumped back in his chair. "You're tangled up in another murder?"

"I found his body, Dad."

He grimaced, leaned forward, and squeezed my hand. "I know that part, sweetie. I'm sorry. Sounds like it's still tough for you."

Dad had made it to Jesse's funeral service but had been out at Uncle Pete's ever since then. I had told him about finding the body, but not much else. There hadn't been enough time for a sit-down talk at the service.

"It's been pretty awful," I admitted. "Here's the thing, Dad. Somebody had been inside Jesse's house, searching the rooms and making a real mess. There's a hole punched in the wall and one of his floorboards was pulled up. Stuff was thrown on the floor. I don't think Jesse would do that to his own home, do you?"

"Absolutely not." He shook his head. "He was darn proud of that place. And neat as a pin most of the time."

"Exactly. So it had to be someone else."

Dad's face twisted as he thought. "And whoever it was probably killed Jesse. What were they looking for? It can't be money. Jesse didn't have much worth stealing."

"Remember that antique necklace he used to brag about finding?"

"Oh, yeah, that time he went scuba diving. I thought he finally admitted that was a fib."

"He did, but it turns out there really was a necklace. I've seen it. And it really is priceless."

Dad's eyes went wide.

"And I know he showed it to at least one person in town."

"Do you know who?" he asked.

"Cuckoo Clemens."

"Ah." He nodded. "That figures. He and Jesse were buddies at one point, but they had a falling-out a few years back. Might've been over this necklace." He picked up his fork, swirled a bit of pancake in the syrup, and took a bite. He palmed a small piece of bacon and slipped it to Robbie, who almost melted in gratitude. Dad was always doing that and I always pretended not to notice. Robbie was his granddog, after all. "Sounds like Jesse got in over his head. Damn it, the man might have made a foolish mistake, but he didn't deserve to die for it. You think Cuckoo was in there searching for the necklace?"

"He's our best guess. It's worth asking him about it anyway."

Dad shook his head and got his I'm-worried-about-Shannon expression again. "Not a good plan, sweetheart. He's a hard man to talk to. I don't think he's got all the brain cells clicking in unison, if you know what I mean."

"Tell me about it," I muttered.

"Hey," he said, pointing his fork at me. "You're not actually trying to track down this guy, are you? I know you've got your theories, honey, but leave it to the police to find the answers. I don't like the idea of you getting tangled up in another murder mystery."

Eric Jensen had said something similar. It was too late to worry about it, I told myself. I was already thoroughly tangled up.

"I just think that the longer the police take to investigate, the more Jane is in danger. If someone believes she has the necklace, they could attack her like they did Jesse."

"*Does* she have the necklace?"

"No, we put it in a safe-deposit box."

"But the thief doesn't know that."

"No," I said. There was no way for the thief or anyone else to know that the necklace was no longer in Jesse's house.

"That does it," Dad said, setting down his fork. "If you don't call the police, I will."

"You don't have to," I said quickly. "The police are on top of this."

"They'd better be."

Oh boy. I mentally rolled my eyes, knowing that Eric would not appreciate an irate phone call from my father, telling him to stop allowing me to do the job the police should be doing. Eric would probably throw me in jail just to teach me another lesson.

It was time to change the subject. "So, how's your love life, Dad?"

He chuckled. "Doing just fine. Maybe better than yours. Which reminds me, how's Mac? When's his next book coming out?"

"He's great and the book will be out in the fall. We haven't started rehab on the lighthouse mansion yet because he's been too busy. But we have an appointment with the Planning Commission next week."

"Good. If you have any problems there, you know who to call."

"Ghostbusters?"

"Ha. Very funny. Let me know if they give you a hassle."

"I will, but they won't."

"I don't know. People get itchy when you start talking about refurbishing a beloved landmark."

"I won't be touching the outside except to paint it."

"They won't believe that. Even if you show them the blueprints, they'll want more information and assurances."

Dad would know. He'd been pitting himself against the town's Planning Commission for years.

"I've got all the permits lined up and the blueprints speak for themselves. Mac intends to make a speech, too.

I think we'll get through it, but I'll call you if anything goes wrong."

"Good." He sipped his coffee. "Something else is still bugging you. Talk to me."

I sighed. "It just bothers me that you knew Jesse had a girlfriend and I didn't. How could I be so blind?"

"Don't take it so hard," he said. "Guys talk about things around other guys that they wouldn't think of bringing up in front of a woman—especially one young enough to be their daughter. Jesse was old school. A man's man. Went into the service when he was a kid and stayed there until he was old enough to retire. He would no more talk to you about a woman he was dating than he would wear flowers in his hair."

"I guess so." But even if Jesse never said anything, I still felt silly for never having noticed that something in his life had changed so dramatically.

"Did you ever meet her?" I asked.

"The girlfriend? No, but I heard she was hot."

"Oh, please." I laughed at the typical male response. "She was at the memorial service and she was at Jane's party last night. I'm surprised you didn't chat her up."

"She was there?"

"Yeah. She was talking to Jane for a while out in the garden."

"Oh." He nodded slowly. "I think I saw her but didn't get a chance to meet her. Nice-looking woman. Does she live in the area?"

"Why do you ask?"

"Just wondering."

Great. All I needed was to have my father start dating the woman who still held the number-five spot on my suspect list. I supposed that if she was as pleasant and innocent as she seemed to be, maybe I wouldn't mind if Dad wanted to get to know her better.

"She lives down in Blue Point," I said.

"You should see your face," he said, laughing. "Don't worry. I'm not looking for a steady girlfriend."

I smiled. "No, you prefer the one-week Wilma types."

He grinned wolfishly. "Nothing wrong with that."

"You're right," I admitted. "I just want you to have a good time, be safe, and don't get tied up with some gold digger."

He laughed again. "You sound like me lecturing *you*."

I joined in the laughter, but inside I was serious. There were plenty of women who would love to get their hands on Dad's bank account. He had been a successful contractor for most of his life and had built many of the luxury homes around town and a number of mansions out on the Alisal Cliffs. He had a hefty bank balance, even if he came across as a working-class guy.

Uncle Pete was similar. He owned vineyards and a popular winery and the best Italian restaurant in town, but he wore old jeans and flannel shirts rolled up to his elbows and still liked to toil in the fields with the rest of the guys.

Together, they were quite the twosome when it came to the ladies. Any older woman visiting Lighthouse Cove for a week or two was fair game. Dad and Uncle Pete didn't date the locals. One-week flings were their specialty. So I didn't have much hope of Dad settling down with a nice, attractive woman like Althea Tannis anytime soon. It was just as well, since Althea was still getting over Jesse's death. More than anything else, she would temporarily need a man for his shoulder to cry on.

Dad made me promise again to be careful and to call him if I needed help with anything. Once he left, I cleaned up the kitchen and then telephoned Lizzie to see if she could meet me to talk about her chat last night with Bob and Ned. Funny how I thought of the two men as a duo, since they weren't. Either one of them could've been out to get Jesse.

Lizzie said she was about to take a thirty-minute break from Paper Moon, the books and paper arts store that she and Hal owned, so I grabbed my purse and dashed down to the town square. We met at the coffeehouse three doors down from her shop.

"What did you find out?" I asked as soon as we each

had a café latte and were able to snag a table far enough away from prying eyes and ears.

"I doubt Bob or Ned had anything to do with Jesse's death," she said. "First of all, they're both sweet guys and I can't see them doing something so awful."

"Yeah, I know." I had come to the same conclusion, but I was still disappointed to hear Lizzie validate it.

"Second," she continued, "they're really old. I mean, Ned could probably swing a tennis racket, but a sledge-hammer? No way. And I doubt that Bob could even manage the tennis racket. How could either of them punch that hole in the wall?"

"I agree." I sipped my latte. "I didn't have much hope of either of them being viable suspects, but we had to start somewhere."

"Well, hold on, now," Lizzie said, wearing a smug smile. "Ned did manage to throw his son under the bus, to some extent."

"What?" I set my latte down. "Tell me everything."

"Okay." She scooted her chair around to get closer so she could whisper. "Ned said that a few months ago, he was showing Stephen around town because he wanted him to move here."

"Yeah, that's what he said."

"So they stopped at Jesse's house to say hi. Stephen had been there before and fell in love with the place. He asked for the full tour and Jesse told him it wasn't for sale. He said it nicely, but it was a definite no on giving him a tour. Stephen asked two more times and finally Jesse freaked out, according to Ned. Told him he didn't show off his house to anyone and to stop asking. Stephen hinted that maybe he'd sneak in sometime and take a look around. Jesse was really pissed off about that, and it didn't help when Stephen suggested that he must have something to hide."

I scowled. "I think I'd want to kick him out of my house at that point."

"Me, too. Now, all along, Ned is insisting that Stephen was only teasing Jesse with that comment, but Jesse wasn't taking it. Ned had to calm Jesse down and convince him that it was all a big joke on Stephen's part. But it wasn't, of course."

"Jesse didn't think it was a joke."

"Nope."

Lizzie shook her head, looking baffled. "Why would Stephen keep insisting after being told no? He sounds like my kids when I won't let them stay up late to watch TV."

"It does sound immature." I finished my latte and tossed the cup into the nearby trash receptacle. "I spent some time talking to Stephen, who really is kind of boring, by the way."

"Oh no," Lizzie groaned. "Poor Jane. She doesn't need a guy like that. Immature and boring, what a combination." She stared into her latte. "At least my kids aren't boring."

I chuckled. "No, they aren't. Anyway, Stephen told me that Jesse used to come over for barbecues and parties and things. He made it seem like they were practically family."

Lizzie frowned. "Doesn't sound like Jesse considered Stephen part of his family."

"No."

I considered what she'd told me. "So I guess you got all the info from Ned and I got what I could from Bob."

Lizzie thought about it. "It's probably better that we split it up that way, so neither man would be suspicious if both of us asked the same questions."

"Probably so."

We sat in silence for a minute and then I grinned. "Good detective work, miss."

"I know, right? That was fun."

After Lizzie went back to the store, I digested what she had told me. It was anecdotal and probably didn't mean anything in terms of proving that Stephen was a cold-blooded killer or a thief or anything else. But it was something to add to the list of interesting coincidences.

I spent the next four hours at home doing paperwork and following up on supplies and orders for my jobsites.

For dinner, I baked a whole chicken and ate a portion of it with tortillas and salsa. Afterward I watched a little television with Robbie and Tiger and went to bed early. Surprisingly I slept well, even knowing I had to deal with a ghost in the morning.

I hadn't been back to Emily's since the walk-through, so Monday morning I drove across town to see how the renovation was going.

As I opened the front door, I heard a loud thud. And walked into chaos.

A gallon of rich forest green paint had been thrown against the wall at the far end of the dining room. Thick rivulets streamed down, puddling on the floor. I was relieved to see there was a tarp to catch a lot of it. And none of the paint had hit the breakfront or the beautiful tile work surrounding the fireplace. I considered that a stroke of luck.

Emily had bought several cans of paint in different shades to start experimenting with room colors. Anything that didn't work could be primed again and repainted.

"What's going on?" I asked Wade, who was crouched on the floor by the big tool chest in the far corner. He was clutching a hammer. Sean must've run from the room, because he was now peeking around the kitchen door.

"Where's Douglas?" I asked.

"He ran outside," Sean said. "Total chicken."

"As opposed to a partial chicken?" I wondered.

Sean scraped his fingers through his hair as he walked back into the room. "Yeah, well, you would've run, too, boss, if you'd seen what we just saw."

I was getting a bad feeling. "Are you going to tell me a ghost did that?"

"Well, it wasn't one of us," Wade groused.

"I didn't think it was," I said mildly. "But do you know why it happened? What were you guys doing just before it happened?"

"We weren't doing anything," Sean insisted.

Wade snorted.

Sean shook his head in self-disgust. "I mean, we were busy, boss, but not doing anything unusual or dangerous. That's what I meant."

I smiled. "I know what you meant."

"Okay." Sean exhaled gruffly. "So I was about to peel off the last panel of wallpaper and then we were going to pull that wall down to check for problems."

I glanced at Wade. "What problems?"

He approached me, still clutching the hammer. "There's a weird scent emanating and I can't figure out what it is. So we're going to check it."

"What kind of scent?"

"Musky. Not unpleasant, but very weird."

That did sound weird. "Some kind of chemical leak, maybe?"

"Could be."

Sean continued the story. "But as soon as I took out my pry bar and hammer, the paint can went flying."

"Scared the hell out of us," Wade admitted, lowering his voice. I wasn't sure why, since I figured a ghost could probably hear everything he said.

"The old girl's been pretty calm lately. You know, we still get the occasional vibe and know she's around, and the lights have gone off a few times, but otherwise nothing violent. And then all of a sudden, she's throwing things."

I looked around at the guys, including Douglas, who had just snuck back into the room, looking sheepish. "Did any of you read up on the family history?"

Lizzie's store stocked a number of books on the history of the town and its prominent families and homes. Many of the great houses in the area came with their own folklore, and I liked to read up on them when I had the chance. I hadn't read much about the Rawley family, but that was because I'd heard a lot of the legends while growing up. I made a mental note to call Emily about it. She might know if something had happened in the dining room so that we could be more careful in there from now on.

My mind instantly went to murder. Was somebody killed in the Rawley dining room? But as soon as I thought of it, I brushed it away. If a murder had occurred here, it would be a town legend by now and everyone would know about it.

Wade tapped the hammer absently against his leg as he studied the paint streaks. "You think something happened in here that she's particularly sensitive about?"

"It's a thought."

Sean fumed. "It would be helpful if she just told us what her issues were instead of trying to kill us with paint cans."

"That would be helpful," I said.

"B-boss."

I whipped around and saw Douglas pointing at the wall of paint. His eyes were as big and round as moons.

I turned and saw what had mesmerized him. Halfway up the wall, an arrow had appeared in the paint, pointing down toward the floor, as though a child might've been finger-painting.

"Holy crap," Wade muttered.

"Anybody home?" a man called from the front door.

Who was that? I wondered. I glanced at my guys for a clue, but they both shook their heads.

"We're in here," I said loudly.

Footsteps sounded against the wide wooden planks of the foyer and stopped at the entry to the dining room.

"Hey, Shannon, how's my favorite contractor?"

"Gus." I walked over to greet him and couldn't help melting a little when he gave me a big, warm hug. "How are you?"

"I'm even better than I look."

I laughed. Gus was joking around, but the fact was, he looked really, really good. The man was a walking chick magnet and had been since first grade. He'd also been my auto mechanic for as long as I'd been driving.

Augustus Peratti, *Gus* to his friends, owned the best auto shop in Northern California together with his father, uncle, and brother. The shop had been in business for three generations and catered to every type of automobile made. A good thing, because I was pretty sure that every woman within a five-hundred-mile radius brought her car to them.

The Peratti men were handsome devils with beautiful smiles, gorgeous dark eyes, and thick black hair. I couldn't swear to it, but based on the sort of attention he'd always received, I had a feeling that Gus had slept with every girl in my senior class except me. Maybe that was why we had remained friends all this time.

The best thing about Gus was his sense of humor and his intelligence. He had a ready laugh and he always got the joke. What woman could resist that in a man?

He greeted the guys with waves and nods. "How's everybody doing?"

"Pretty well, Gus," Wade said. "Except for a little mishap over here."

"That's quite a mess," he said, gazing at the wall of green paint. He turned back to me. "I thought I'd find Emily here."

"She hasn't been around today," Wade said.

"Is she catering a party for you?" I asked.

"Uh, yeah," Gus said. "She told me to meet her here."

The chandelier in the middle of the room began to sway directly above Gus's head.

I grabbed his arm and pulled him over to the side.

"Holy crap," Wade muttered, staring at the ceiling, where the chandelier grew steady.

"What was that?" Gus asked.

All of a sudden he started to tremble.

"Are you okay?" I asked.

His eyes rolled back in his head and his body began to undulate from his shoulders down to his hips and back up again.

"Gus!" I shouted. I grabbed his arm again and shook it. "Are you sick? Somebody call 911!"

"I'm calling now," Douglas said.

"Do it," Wade demanded. "Now." He grabbed Gus's other arm and we tried to hold on to him. But he shook us both off.

"Tell them to hurry!" I shouted.

Gus stopped moving as suddenly as he'd started. After shaking his head back and forth a few times, he bent over and leaned his elbows on his knees, trying to catch his breath. He gave up, slid down the wall, and sat on the floor. "What the hell is going on here?"

We all stared at him for a minute.

"Wow," Douglas whispered.

"What just happened to you?" I asked, kneeling next to him.

"Here, drink this." Wade handed him a bottle of water.

He took a long gulp. "I . . . jeez." He was still breathing heavily. "It felt like my whole body was taken over by . . . something. I know that sounds weird, but it's the best I can do."

"Are you in pain?"

He patted his stomach and chest as he mentally checked himself out. "No. I feel pretty damn good, actually. Really damn good." He pushed himself up off the floor and stood, but he had to lean against the wall as he brushed his hair off his forehead.

Wade stared at me, but I was clueless.

"I don't believe it," Wade muttered.

"What?" Gus demanded, glaring at Wade. "What was that? You know something. Tell me."

I gulped. "Do you believe in ghosts, Gus?"

"Sure, babe," he said, his tone casual. "Why not?"

"Okay," I said, nodding slowly.

We all stared at him some more and now he stared back.

"Is that what that was? Huh." He rubbed his chest some more as it slowly dawned on him. "Oh, yeah, the Rawley ghost. Damn. I never thought I'd see the day." He turned and gazed around the room, beaming that sexy smile that had won countless ladies' hearts all through high school. "Hello there, Ms. Rawley."

The lights abruptly began to flash off and on and the chandelier started to sway again. A strong wind came up from nowhere and swept through the room.

Gus grinned. "Yeah, nice to meet you, too."

Suddenly one of the breakfront windows cracked. I let out a little shriek and I was pretty sure Douglas jumped at least two feet off the floor.

Gus's grin just grew wider. "Damn, lady. You are one powerful ghost."

Everything calmed down at once.

I shook my head, not quite believing what I had seen. But one thing was for sure. "I think she likes you, Gus."

It was almost four o'clock when I left Emily's. Gus took off at the same time, first calling Emily to let her know that he would meet her at the tea shop instead.

The guys and I moved all the tools and paint and supplies out of the house for safekeeping. We still couldn't figure out what was going on in there, but we needed to find a way to keep working without distractions—and having Gus there was a definite distraction. Of course, he'd been a distraction ever since first grade.

Wade and I agreed to meet back here first thing tomorrow morning to discuss everything that had happened since we'd first started the job. I wanted Emily to be here, too, to hear about Gus's encounter and to help figure out if there was any possibility of danger to her or my crew.

I headed for home, intending to finish paying the bills this afternoon. But I decided to stop off at Jane's to see how her second day as a high-class innkeeper had gone. I found her sitting at the check-in desk, working on her computer.

"Hey, you," I said. "How's it going?"

"Wonderful," she whispered, not wanting to be overheard by any of her guests. "We had the best breakfast. The girls made my recipe for stuffed French toast croissants."

"The one with mascarpone cheese and blueberries?"

"Yes, only they added raspberries and strawberries and bananas and sweetened the mascarpone cheese with orange liqueur and sprinkled chopped caramelized pecans over the top. And served it with bacon, of course."

"Oh my God." I sat down in the guest chair. "Are there any leftovers?"

"Everyone was raving about it, Shannon. We had all the juice and coffee and muffins and the usual spread, of course, and we even had a gluten-free version for one of our guests, and she was delighted. I'm so happy."

"And I'm so happy for you." I felt silly whispering, but I understood her need to be discreet. She actually had paying guests walking around the place!

"Excuse me. I'd like to check in."

I turned and saw a nice-looking man standing in the foyer behind me with two suitcases and a briefcase. With a bright smile, I stood and stepped out of the way. "Of course. You can do that right here."

Jane stood up, wearing a look of concern. "I'm Jane Hennessey, but I'm afraid we're booked solid for the next four days. I'll be happy to recommend—"

"But I have a reservation," he said.

"Are you sure?" She sat back down at her computer. "Under what name?"

"Andrew Braxton. I reserved a room for the week."

She looked up at him. "Oh dear. I was so sorry to hear about your accident, Mr. Braxton, but I understood that you were canceling your entire trip."

"What accident?"

Jane was perplexed and uneasy. "I—I got a telephone message Saturday afternoon saying that you'd been in a bad car accident and that you wouldn't be able to make your trip. I'm sorry. There's clearly been a misunderstanding."

"Clearly." He gave her a thin-lipped smile, which was no smile at all. "Because as you can see, I'm here now and I'm perfectly fine. If you'll show me to my room, there won't be any problem, right?"

"But . . . we understood that you wouldn't be coming.

Your room has been taken." Jane stood again. Her eyes were wide with distress as she bit her bottom lip. "I can't tell you how sorry I am."

His mouth opened and closed in shocked anger. "But . . . but this is unacceptable. It's outrageous. I've paid for the entire week in advance."

"Yes, I know," Jane said calmly. "But when I got the news about your accident, I refunded your credit card. You probably haven't seen the statement yet."

He shook his head, unable to speak.

"I appreciate that you're upset," Jane said. I really admired how she handled herself so professionally. Still, I ached for her. This was a bad mix-up. "I would never have given away your room if I hadn't received the message from your doctor saying you weren't coming at all."

"But that's the problem. There was no accident. No doctor of mine ever sent that message."

Jane's gaze met mine. What in the world had happened? Sandra had taken the message and she wouldn't lie about it, would she?

"I can only apologize profusely for all the confusion," Jane said, "and I'll be happy to pay for your room at a comparable hotel in town. The Inn on Main Street has several rooms available and it's a lovely hotel, closer to the beach, with its own highly rated restaurant in-house."

"But I wanted to stay here," he said, and his tone was almost whining. I couldn't fault him, though. "I've heard so much about it."

I almost said something like *Why don't you kick Stephen out of his room?* But that probably wouldn't have been the most professional decision for Jane to make in this situation.

She took a deep breath and let it out slowly. "Let me see what I can do." She sat and began to click the computer keys rapidly. I could tell she was upset, for good reason. Something weird had happened and she was the one who would take the blame, whether it was her fault or not.

"Here's what I can do," Jane said finally, looking up from her computer screen. "As I said, I'll be happy to comp you a room at the Inn on Main Street for the next four nights. On Friday, I can have your things brought back here and move you into the Rosalind Suite for the rest of your stay . . . also comped."

I could tell that Andrew Braxton was taken aback. Jane was amazing. She was obviously rattled by the situation but was willing to make things right for Mr. Braxton.

"I . . . I guess that's as good a deal as I can ask for. I appreciate your willingness to accommodate me."

"There's been an unfortunate mix-up and I will certainly find out what happened. But you shouldn't have to pay the price for someone else's error. I'll have my assistant manager walk with you to the Inn on Main Street and make sure that everything is to your liking. And then on Friday, we'll be happy to move you out, pack your clothing if you want us to, and bring you back here for the rest of your stay."

"Well, thank you," he said, and shook Jane's hand. "I appreciate it." He held on to her hand and smiled. "Maybe I can buy you a drink some night and we can laugh about it."

Jane smiled at that. So now he was flirting? Maybe the guy wasn't such a stuffed shirt after all. But his emotions sure ran the gamut. I wasn't certain Jane should be flirting with this guy, but that was none of my business.

Once he had left with Sandra, Jane looked at me. "What just happened here?"

"That was quite a mix-up. You should ask Sandra about it as soon as she gets back."

"I will. Maybe she can shed some light."

"I hope so." I remembered hearing Sandra say that she'd follow up on the accident. Had she talked to someone about it?

Jane twisted her lips in puzzlement as she stared at her computer. "Maybe I'm hallucinating."

"You're not. I was right here the other night when you got the message that he was canceling his trip because of a bad car accident."

"Right. I guess that'll teach me to follow up on things like this myself. Particularly when a message to cancel a room comes in." She sighed. "At least he went away somewhat mollified."

But as I drove home, I wondered why Andrew Braxton had been so adamant about staying at Hennessey House in the first place. How could he have heard so many great things about it when it had only opened two days ago and hadn't even been rated by any of the travel associations yet?

Had he heard about the necklace? Was that why he was so anxious to stay here? Did he think Jane had it? Who else did he know in town? Maybe I was being paranoid, but I wanted to know who in the world Andrew Braxton was. I intended to find out before Friday when he'd be moving back into Hennessey House.

I mentally added his name to my suspect list because why not? His odd, mistaken cancellation and untimely arrival were weird. I couldn't wait to get home to my Google machine.

And I couldn't forget about Stephen Darby, who was already staying at Hennessey House, thanks to a fraudulent telephone message about Andrew Braxton being in a car accident. Did Stephen have sinister plans to find the necklace as well? According to Lizzie, Stephen's own father had admitted that Stephen had been desperate to get a good look at Jesse's house that time he and Ned stopped by. Were Stephen and Ned in cahoots? Were they responsible for Jesse's death?

I thought about Stephen's credit card being rejected when he had checked in Saturday night. I knew things like that happened all the time, but it made me wonder about his competence as a financial adviser. Working as a part-time chef wasn't exactly a big moneymaking occupation. Did Stephen need money? Did he think he could find the necklace and sell it for ready cash?

And who could forget that he'd already asked Jane out on two dates? Of course, what guy wouldn't want to ask her out? But did he have an ulterior motive for getting close to her?

And if Stephen wasn't responsible for Jesse's death, who was?

And who was Andrew Braxton?

Stephen and Andrew were only two of the names on my newly revised suspect list. Which reminded me that I still needed to visit some of the pawnshops around the area to see if Jesse had shown the necklace to anyone else. Beginning tomorrow, I would start looking. Because people and things were closing in on Jane and I had a feeling we were running out of time.

Chapter Eleven

Early Tuesday morning after gulping down two cups of coffee to steel my nerves, I drove over to the Rawley Mansion to meet Wade and Emily. I was concerned about my crew working there while an errant ghost haunted the premises. I wouldn't have believed it if I hadn't seen it with my own eyes. And I still couldn't explain what had happened to Gus. Luckily he hadn't been hurt, but his possession—what else could we call it?—was about the weirdest thing I'd ever witnessed.

I parked my truck on the street and walked up to the front door. It was open, so I walked inside. And felt the grief hit me like the heat of a blasting furnace.

"Wade?" I called.

"In here, Shannon."

I heard pounding and ran into the dining room, where three of my guys stood with Emily near the wall of green paint. Sean was using an ax to tear into one of the wall panels—directly at the spot where the arrow was pointed.

"What're you doing?" I shouted over the sound of the ax slamming and tearing the wood.

"There's something in here," Sean said. "I'm sure of it."

"How do you know?"

Wade glanced at me. "He saw it in a dream."

I smiled, then instantly sobered when Wade gave me a warning look. "No, really. He saw it in a dream."

"I felt something here, too," Emily said. "Remember the other day when the wall felt warm?"

"I remember." It had been vibrating, too. So maybe that meant something.

"Couldn't hurt," Wade reasoned. "If nothing's there, we can always patch up the wall and call it a day. Weirder things have happened, right?"

No, not really, I thought. All in all, the ghost of Mrs. Rawley was about the weirdest thing I'd ever experienced.

Sean pulled the last of the wood shards away and we all stared into the wall. Wedged inside was a small book. Sean grabbed it and held it up for us to see. He handed it to me.

"It's a journal of some kind," I said, staring at the faded red leather cover. I opened it to the first page and read the delicate handwriting. "The Diary of Winifred Rawley."

I glanced at Sean. "Was this part of your dream?"

"No." He leaned the ax against the wall. "I dreamed I was being shoved into this room and the ax floated up and into my hands. And I started tearing into this wall. Then I woke up."

I held the book out to Emily. "Do you want to read it?"

"I do." I started to hand her the book, but she waved me off. "You should read it first. It might indicate if your men will be safe here or not."

"Okay, I'll read it." I looked around at my guys. "Are you okay working here today? If not, I'll pull you off this job and send you to another site."

Sean was defiant. "No way am I leaving."

"I think we'll be okay, boss," Wade said. "I don't feel the same vibes anymore."

"Nor do I," Emily murmured, meeting my gaze. "There's a sadness still, but it's mixed with a sort of positive resolve. And you're looking at me as though I've lost my mind."

"Then we've all lost our minds," I said. "So I guess we'll carry on."

*   *   *

After sensing a grieving ghost that morning, I figured
nothing else could scare me. At least, I hoped not as I
strolled into Cuckoo Clemens's shop on Main Street.

Cuckoo turned at the sound of the doorbells chiming
and I saw that he was rearranging a clothing rack stuffed
with old tuxedos along the back wall of the store.

"Well, well," he said in a sarcastic tone. "If it isn't Miss
Pinky Tool Time herself."

I'd been called "Pink" and "Pinky" plenty of times in
my life and it rarely bothered me, but I didn't like hearing it from him.

The nickname had started after my mother died,
when my dad used to bring my little sister, Chloe, and me
to his construction sites in lieu of hiring babysitters. The
guys on Dad's crew began teaching us how to build bird-
houses and other small projects like that. That led to
them buying us little pink tool chests and hard hats.
Chloe was too much of a tomboy to go crazy over the
pink thing, but I loved it. Because of that, the guys would
sometimes call me Pink or Pinky, and the nickname
stuck for a while. I still liked using pink tools because
they were just as functional and strong as regular tools;
plus, my guys didn't walk off with them.

These days, none of my crew dared to call me Pinky.
To my face, anyway.

"Hello, Cuckoo," I said, attempting to sound cheerful.
I tried to calm my nerves by taking in the ambience of
the shop. It was clean, at least, and well stocked. Six shiny
vintage guitars were hanging on the left wall with several
old amplifiers, a drum set, and an electronic keyboard
placed below them.

One shelf featured all sorts of items purported to have
come from the *Glorious Maiden*, including a brass port-
hole, several old jars, an old apple peeler, and various
other types of shipboard kitchen appliances, circa 1839. A
stuffed moose head stared down at me from the wall
above the cash register, its glassy eyes following me
through the store until I had to look away. If that wasn't

creepy enough, there was a display of marionettes hanging from a rack in the center of the store. At any minute I expected them to start talking to me.

"To what do I owe the pleasure?" Cuckoo asked, sneering at me.

"I've been thinking about that necklace you claim Jesse had."

He leaned against the front counter and folded his long, bony arms across his sunken chest. "I don't *claim* it, little girl. I *know* it."

As a female contractor, I'd been dealing with sexist attitudes all my life, but his arrogance really irritated me. I stood up straighter and found myself actually looking down at him. I mentally gave myself a high five for wearing two-inch heels. The guy was barely five foot eight with his shoes on. Where did he get off calling me *little girl*?

"I saw the thing with my own eyes," he asserted, "and Jesse offered to sell it to me more than once. I didn't have the money then, but I do now. And since I was the first one he showed it to, I should have first dibs on it."

I hadn't known how I would approach Cuckoo when I first walked in, but now I had the urge to shove him. Hard.

"But these deals usually favor the *highest* bidder," I said, flexing my fists reactively. "Not the first one."

He chuckled without humor. "I haven't seen anyone else bargaining for it, so I just might be the highest bidder, too."

"Yes, you might. If we were certain that the necklace existed."

"What did I just tell you?" he shouted. Spittle gathered at the corners of his mouth, and his eyes took on a wild edge that left me with no doubt about why people had started calling him Cuckoo. "I said I've seen it with my own eyes."

"That's what you've said, more than once." I prayed my tone was reasonable despite my desire to run screaming out of the store. But if I wanted answers from him, I needed to keep things calm. "It's just that Jane has never seen the necklace and neither have I. Did Jesse tell you where he kept it? Maybe he sold it somewhere else. Or maybe it's in a bank vault. If we could find it, you might be able to make the deal with Jane."

His face was turning red. "How the hell should I know where he squirreled it away?"

"You really don't know?"

I was baiting him, so I shouldn't have been surprised when he came even closer and began shouting, "It's in his house! Look around! That place is full of secrets!"

So much for my smooth facade. I inched back a few millimeters because his rage was alarming. "I don't know where it is, and I've lived next door to Jesse my entire life. He used to tell me everything, and I've got to be honest. He admitted flat out that he was making up the whole story about finding a necklace. Said he'd told a big lie. So now why should I believe you?"

"He changed his tune," Cuckoo admitted, calming down a little. "Told everybody he'd been lying about it because people were starting to get a little too curious. Too aggressive. They wanted to see it, wanted to display it. They offered him money for it. He realized it was worth a lot more than he thought it was at first, so he had to regroup. But he was going to sell it to me eventually."

"I wonder where he put it."

"In his house," Cuckoo said softly, as if he were talking to himself. "He would want to see it all the time, and touch it. He was obsessed with it. It was a priceless treasure."

"Does that mean your offer of five thousand dollars is less than it's worth?"

His eyes narrowed warily. "That was an opening bid. Now I'm willing to pay eight thousand dollars for it."

"*Eight* thousand?" I said. "Last week you offered ten thousand."

"Maybe I'm willing to pay twenty," he said, his upper lip twisted in a snarl. "Why the hell am I negotiating with you, anyway? You've never even seen the damn thing. This is between me and Jesse."

"You mean, between you and Jane."

He blinked, suddenly looking a little disoriented. "That's what I said."

"You said Jesse, but Jesse's dead."

"Dead. Right." He shook his head. "I know that. I know he's dead. I'm not stupid."

"I didn't think you were." I tried another tack. "Do you know where Jesse originally found the necklace?"

"Of course I do. He was scuba diving out there by the *Glorious Maiden*."

"Do you know any of the other people he showed it to?"

"Yeah." He shoved his hands in his pockets and paced the floor in front of the counter. "That pawnshop down the coast a few miles. And there was some dinky little knickknack shop around Point Arena. Probably a few other places he didn't tell me about."

"One more question and I'll leave you alone. Do you think the necklace was worth killing for?"

"What's that supposed to mean?"

I held my palms out. "Jesse's dead, right?"

His eyes widened. "Hold on. Nobody's killing anybody."

"I didn't say that."

His cheeks puffed out like a fish's. "So . . . what? What're you saying? Somebody killed Jesse? Is that what you're saying? Nobody killed him. He died, and that necklace belongs to me."

"Legally it belongs to Jane."

"Exactly. And I'm willing to pay her six thousand dollars for it."

"*Six?*" I choked out a laugh. "You're crazy."

He waved his hands in the air. "Hell, yes, I'm crazy!" He swooped in close to my face and stared at me through empty eyes. "Why do you think they call me Cuckoo?"

I flinched, afraid he might attack me physically. I began creeping backward toward the door.

"I'm Cuckoo because I'm crazy!" He shrieked with

laughter. And not happy laughter. It was high-pitched and hysterical and disturbing. "Certifiable! And I want that necklace before he gives it to—"

I whipped around. "Gives it to whom?"

But his eyes were unfocused and I was pretty sure he had just blasted off to another planet. But then he whispered, "Get out."

And I did. I continued backing out of the store, my jaws aching from the stiff smile I continued to flash him.

I ran all the way to my truck parked three doors down. As I unlocked the door, I had to inhale deeply a few times. That was when I realized I'd been holding my breath for the past few moments.

I climbed into the driver's seat and slammed and locked the door. To whom did he think Jesse was going to give the necklace? Was it Althea? Jane and I had theorized that Althea's presence in Jesse's life might've been the catalyst for Cuckoo to start searching for the jewels in Jesse's house. Could it be true?

One thing I couldn't figure out was why Jesse had been friends with Cuckoo. The man was seriously nuts. Jesse had never been known for his patience and he didn't put up with a lot of crap. Cuckoo, on the other hand, was completely full of it.

Over the next few hours, I visited three more pawnshops and spoke to several antique shop owners outside Lighthouse Cove proper but still within the fifteen-mile circumference I'd set up for myself. It was just a hunch, but if Cuckoo had overreacted to the necklace the way I thought he probably had, Jesse might've regretted showing him the piece or even talking about it around town. So maybe he had quietly visited some reputable shops a longer distance away from Lighthouse Cove.

Pretty early on, Jesse had claimed the story of the necklace was a fabrication, so he might've decided to go farther afield to sell it in a different town where he wasn't known. That way, he would avoid the inevitable gossip that would snowball around Lighthouse Cove once people found out that the priceless necklace was a reality. I was frankly surprised that Cuckoo hadn't spread the news, but he'd probably wanted to keep it under his hat in hopes of buying the piece before anyone else heard about it or saw it.

I stopped at the first shop I found on the other side of the interstate and struck out. Maybe it was too close to town, or maybe I was on a wild-goose chase.

I decided to keep going, to a pawnshop I'd read about six miles down the coast. I was pretty sure this was the place Cuckoo had referred to earlier. The shopkeeper, an older man who looked as reputable as any pawnbroker I'd ever seen—meaning he looked completely disreputable—looked at the photo of the necklace I'd snapped with my phone and told me he had indeed seen it and had been willing to take it, but only on consignment.

Jesse had refused the stingy offer and claimed the guy was trying to get something for nothing. Which, privately, I agreed with. I smiled and thanked him and couldn't get out of there fast enough. While he didn't shriek and hoot like Cuckoo, the pawnbroker came across as quietly menacing, as though he would willingly hock his first-born son if he could get a decent trade out of the deal.

At another shop called the Chic Antique near Point Arena, a woman remembered seeing the necklace in the photo I showed her and told me she would love to have bought it. But she turned it down, telling Jesse she couldn't afford the insurance it would cost her to keep it in her shop.

I was on a roll, so I drove a few miles inland to Greitsburg, another tiny, picturesque town along Highway 128. I stopped at Christa's Cache and talked to Christa herself, who remembered the necklace and also recalled that Jesse had accused her of trying to cheat him.

"The guy was a little paranoid," Christa said apologetically. "Not that I could blame him. The necklace was a really beautiful antique and worth so much more than he was willing to sell it for. I recommended that he take it into San Francisco, where he could get a heck of a lot more money for it than he could up here."

"Do you remember how long ago that was?" I asked.

"Oh gosh." She stared at the ceiling, trying to think. "Had to have been at least two years ago."

Why had Jesse been so willing to sell the necklace so cheaply? Why wouldn't he have made the trip into the city to see what price he could get from a bigger buyer?

Christa was so helpful that I took a few minutes to browse around her shop and found an unusual quilted tea cozy for only seven dollars that I knew Emily would love.

Since I was down the coast anyway—and since I was basically nosy—I drove a few more miles west until I reached the town of Blue Point where Althea lived. I was curious to see the clothing shop she'd told us about. Oh, hell, I wanted to find out if there even was a shop. Was she telling the truth or had she made up the whole story?

I found the bookstore I'd visited before, the one I'd mentioned to Althea, and sure enough, three doors down was Althea's Attic, a vintage clothing shop. I felt a little embarrassed to think I'd questioned the woman's honesty. I mean, any of us could've driven down to see the shop for ourselves. But if Jesse's death had taught me anything, it was to verify everything before assuming or jumping to conclusions.

So now what? I parked the truck directly across the street, just as Althea walked out of the shop. Without thinking I ducked to hide my face—good grief!—so she wouldn't see me as she strolled down the sidewalk. It was lunchtime, so I assumed she would be gone a good ten or fifteen minutes at least.

I felt a little silly for avoiding her, but I hadn't prepared myself to face her today. I jumped out of the truck and jogged across the street to the shop. A younger woman was standing at the counter as I walked inside. It was the kind of place that made guys shudder. In other words, completely feminine and wonderful. Soft music played in the background, and the air smelled like flowers. The antique dress forms that displayed some of the clothes were topped with fascinator-type hats that I wished I could get away with wearing. So much prettier than a hard hat, even a pink one.

"Hello. Can I help you find anything?" she said.

"I'm just looking right now. Is this Althea Tannis's shop?"

"Yes. Do you know her? She just stepped out for half an hour or so, but she'll be back soon enough if you'd like to wait for her."

"That's okay. I just met her recently and we talked about the shop and it sounded so intriguing. I was in the area and thought I would stop by."

"Well, do take a look around, and if you have any questions, please ask me."

I started riffling through one of the racks of vintage silk blouses. "It must be fun to work in a store like this, with so many beautiful things."

"Oh, I love working here," she gushed. "Althea saved my life by hiring me."

"That's lovely to hear."

"It's true. I couldn't ask for a more wonderful, supportive boss." She walked over to another rack and pulled out a rich copper-colored raw silk jacket. "This would look gorgeous on you with your hair and skin tone," she said, holding it up for me to view.

"Oh," I said, almost gasping for breath. The jacket was amazing and I experienced an immediate visceral need to have it. "It's . . . stunning. Oh my God, I think I have to buy it right now."

She laughed. "Try it on first. And we have some earrings up at the counter that will look fabulous with it."

"You're killing me." I was a sucker for fun earrings, and they had a nice collection.

"I'll bring them to you in the dressing room. And since you're a friend of Althea's, I'll give you a fifteen percent discount off your first purchase."

Wow, I was feeling guiltier by the second for ever doubting Althea's veracity.

Ten minutes later, I walked out of the store with my new favorite jacket and a great pair of earrings tucked inside an adorable bag with lots of pretty pink tissue paper.

On the drive home, I managed to rein in my adoration for Althea. Just because she had a beautiful shop—where I would be spending my money from now on—didn't mean she wasn't a cold-blooded killer and potential necklace thief.

But she hadn't lied about her shop or where she lived. Her employee loved her, and that counted for a lot. It seemed that Althea's only crime, so far, was that she'd allowed Jesse to keep their relationship under wraps so we'd never had a chance to meet her until after he was gone. He had evidently found her to be a delightful companion, and I was beginning to share his opinion.

I stopped at Emily's Tea Shop and surprised her with the tea cozy. After she thanked me profusely and I refused her offer to pay for it, I asked if she'd like to go with me to Jane's later on. I explained a little bit about her mix-up with Andrew Braxton the day before.

"I'm worried about her," I said. "I hope it didn't dampen her spirit too much."

"Let's make sure," Emily said. "Sarah can close up for me, so I'll be ready to go at four."

"I'll pick you up."

When we arrived at Hennessey House, Jane was in the living room, serving wine and cheese to her guests, who were scattered throughout the first floor and grounds, chatting and sipping wine and getting to know one another. People were in the living room, the library, outside on the deck, and in various nooks and crannies around the garden. One woman had snuck into the kitchen and was chatting up Jane's cook, attempting to steal one of the recipes Jane had perfected. I wished her good luck.

"Here she is," Emily said.

Jane stopped in the doorway. "Hey, you two. To what do I owe this happy visit?"

"We're here to check up on you," I whispered.

She squeezed my arm affectionately. "I'm fine. Just some first-week cracks in the system that I'm quickly patching up so they never happen again."

"Did you talk to Sandra about the botched reservation?"

"Yes." Jane fiddled with a doily on the sofa before walking us to a more private spot across the room. "She spoke to the emergency room doctor who told her Andrew had told them about his vacation and then slipped into a coma. The doctor was the one who called us."

"How weird. Was the doctor a man or a woman?"

"The connection wasn't good, but she says it sounded like a man."

That answer wasn't as helpful as I'd hoped it would be. Anyone could disguise their voice if they had to.

"I think you need a glass of bubbly," Emily murmured, slipping her arm through Jane's. "Can we entice you to join us?"

"Jane, there you are." Stephen Darby was about to take hold of her arm when he realized she wasn't alone.

"Oh. Hello, Shannon," he said, then noticed Emily and extended his hand. "Hello. You look familiar but I'm afraid I don't remember your name. I'm Stephen Darby."

"Emily Rose," she said, shaking his hand. "A friend of Jane's."

"Any friend of Jane's is a friend of mine."

I glanced at Jane, who was doing her best not to make eye contact with me.

"Can I pour you a glass of wine?" Stephen asked Emily.

"No, thanks. I'll wait."

"Stephen," Jane said, attempting to take charge. "Why don't you go help yourself to some wine?"

"I was waiting for you."

"I'll be along in a minute," she said, gesturing toward the great room. "You go on ahead."

"All right. Don't be long."

Making himself right at home, I thought, and wondered why he struck me as being so wrong. Maybe it was the fact that he came across as both pretentious and presumptuous at the same time. He walked away and I finally caught Jane's gaze. "He's awfully friendly, isn't he?"

"Yes," she hissed, "and I don't know what to do about him. I went out with him twice and now he's living here and treating me like I'm his girlfriend."

"That's got to stop," Emily whispered.

Just then another tall, good-looking man walked through the front door. He smiled brightly and it took me a moment to realize it was Andrew Braxton. He glanced around, found Jane, and approached. "Hello. Remember me?"

"Of course I do," she said, smiling as she shook his hand. "How are you, Mr. Braxton?"

"Doing much better, and please call me Andrew."

"Andrew. And you must call me Jane. These are my friends Shannon Hammer and Emily Rose. Andrew Braxton."

After we'd all greeted one another, Andrew turned to Jane and spoke in a low voice. "I thought I'd take a chance and see if you were free later. I'd love to take you to dinner to thank you for being so accommodating."

"I'm still so sorry for the mix-up."

"I thought you showed true grace under fire," he said. He had a really attractive smile and I liked his approach, but I still wondered why he was so intent on staying at Hennessey House and why he was showing Jane so much attention. Not that she didn't deserve it, but under the circumstances, I felt rightfully nervous on her behalf.

Jane didn't look nervous at all. She seemed happy and flirtatious and interested in Andrew Braxton.

Emily and I stepped away to give them a moment alone. I wasn't sure why, because now I couldn't eavesdrop on their conversation. What was I thinking? My only excuse was that I knew Jane would tell me everything he said later.

Men had been taking notice of Jane since middle school. But why all of a sudden, right after Jesse's death and the discovery of the necklace, were these particular men trying to get cozy with her? My every instinct was on high alert.

Stephen walked into the room just then, carrying two glasses of wine. "Here you go, my dear. Oh, hello."

Jane turned. "Stephen. Have you met Andrew Braxton? Andrew, this is Stephen Darby."

The two men shook hands, clearly recognizing that they were rivals.

"We should go," Emily murmured.

"And miss this show?" I protested. "You can't be serious."

She elbowed me. "Jane's doing just fine. Besides, we'll get all the good dish later."

I'd just had the same thought, but now I wasn't so sure we should leave her. But there was a difference between being worried and being paranoid. It wasn't as if Jane was alone in the house with those guys. There were plenty of other guests around.

"I don't know," I whispered. "The way those two men are bristling around her, it could get ugly."

We giggled all the way out to the sidewalk.

That night I climbed into bed with Winifred Rawley's diary to learn her story and find out if we could do anything further to calm the restless spirit residing in Emily's new house.

As a single debutante, Winifred had lived a life of whirlwind parties and carriage rides and visits to the beach, where everyone showed off their latest swim fashions, which surely covered them from head to toe. It was an entertaining account, but I felt like a voyeur as I read her most intimate thoughts.

She had fallen in love with a man her father didn't approve of, and he was forcing her to marry another man, Ronald Rawley, whose father was one of the pillars of Northern California society. It was a good business decision, and Winifred was expected to sacrifice herself for the family fortunes.

Winifred defied her father's wishes and snuck out of the house one night to meet her handsome young lover, an Italian immigrant who'd moved to Lighthouse Cove the year before to join his brother. The two had opened a small shop that provided parts and services for the horseless carriages and motor buggies that were sweeping the haut monde in the year 1906.

After poring over several pages filled with the couple's amorous and highly secretive exploits, I turned the page and read her young man's name. Giuseppe Peratti.

Peratti? Gus's great-grandfather?

"No wonder she freaked out over Gus," I murmured. His family had lived in Lighthouse Cove for over a century.

Winifred snuck back home late that night and was greeted by her irate father, who whipped her and sent her to her bedroom with a guard stationed at the door. The following week, she was married to Ronald Rawley. It wasn't the happiest marriage, especially after she gave birth exactly nine months later to a baby boy with an olive complexion and dark hair. Her blond husband wasn't amused, nor was her father. She and the baby were shunned by her entire family, although the child was given the name Rawley in order to quell rumors that he was a bastard.

Winifred begged for a divorce, but her husband refused and, in fact, she later gave birth to three more babies, who were her husband's. They were sickly, though, and none of them survived childhood.

Her son with Giuseppe, on the other hand, survived and thrived. She had named him Joseph, the English version of Giuseppe. And as Joseph Rawley, the young boy stood to inherit everything.

I fell asleep reading and dreamed of poor Winifred and her darling dark-haired baby boy.

Late Wednesday morning Jane revealed to Lizzie that Stephen Darby had asked her out twice more and Andrew had already called her three times that morning.

Lizzie was thrilled that Jane had two suitors to choose from and knew she was sure to find true romance any minute now, but the rest of us were still wondering about the motives of both men. Why were they being so pushy? Yes, Jane was smart and beautiful, as I'd mentioned countless times, but she was also kindhearted and in love with romance. These two men weren't worth Jane's love. They seemed to be growing more and more interested in competing with each other than simply being with Jane.

After dealing with Cuckoo Clemens and spending the night reading Winifred's diary, I had no patience for arrogant men.

Having observed Jane with the two men, I thought of a more sinister possibility. Why had Stephen been so adamant about getting a tour of Jesse's house? Had Ned mentioned to his son that Jesse had found the necklace? Were Ned and Bob in cahoots with Stephen doing the heavy lifting?

Of course, after talking to Bob and hearing what Lizzie had found out from Ned, I was pretty sure neither man even knew about the necklace. How could Jesse have kept it secret from them? I suppose he could've simply tucked it into his fanny pack and never shown it to them. But they had camped out for three days together. A sparkling jeweled necklace seemed like something that would be discovered in such close quarters for three days.

It was possible that despite what Lizzie and I had gathered from our conversations, Bob and Ned really did know about the necklace. Had they been biding their time, waiting for Jesse to grow more vulnerable? Had Ned told his son, Stephen, about the rare piece and urged him to find a way to get it?

I sighed, frustrated that I kept going over and over the same territory without making any progress. One positive thing I could do, though, was warn Jane that Stephen might have an ulterior motive for spending time with her. That went double for Andrew. Even though I couldn't figure out a connection, the way he had appeared at Jane's B-and-B was suspicious all on its own.

I had a roof to finish today, but later that afternoon I planned to drive over to Hennessey House to talk turkey with her.

It didn't go well.

I drove home from Jane's, wondering where I'd gone wrong.

I had shown up at happy hour again, just as Jane was pouring wine for the guests. Andrew was already there and Stephen was vying for her attention, as well. I was glad to see her having a good time, but I couldn't afford to ignore any possible threats.

When I finally got a chance to speak to her in private, all I said was please be careful. Okay, that wasn't all I said, but the rest came out once Jane started to attack my basic premise.

"What do you mean, be careful?" she demanded when I happened to mention that I was worried about her dating Stephen and Andrew.

I pulled her into the powder room and locked the door. "You know Stephen is a suspect in Jesse's death. I'm worried that his interest in you is related to the necklace. Don't forget that one of his credit cards was rejected when he tried to check in. He might be hard up for money."

"Now, listen to me," she said in an angry tone I'd rarely heard before. "Stephen is only a suspect on *your* list, Shannon. I don't happen to like him in that way, but that doesn't make him a murderer. He is my guest here and I will not tolerate you being rude to him."

I started to comment on that, but she shut me up fast.

"And another thing," she said. "Everyone in the world has had a credit card rejected, so you can't possibly hold that against him. And finally are you saying that the only reason a man might show some interest in me is that stupid necklace?"

"No, of course not. You're fabulous. But as far as we know, he could be cozying up here because of the necklace. Maybe he thinks you have it stashed upstairs in your bedroom."

"How would he know about the necklace?"

I frowned. "From his father?" I was losing the argument, so I added, "Besides, a week ago you were claiming to be bored by him."

That was a mistake.

Jane scowled. "Yes, I was and I feel terrible about that. He has been nothing but polite and helpful since he checked in. He seems to be a very nice man and his attention is . . . flattering. You can't argue with that.

I could, but that wasn't the point. "Fine. But what about Andrew Braxton? Who is this character, anyway? Why is he so insistent on staying here? And then he comes over and flirts with you? I don't get it. I'm just . . . I'm worried. Don't you think it's kind of weird that Jesse dies and suddenly these two guys show up and . . ."

I realized halfway through my rant that she was glaring at me. I stopped talking instantly. How much bigger and deeper could I dig the hole in which I was about to bury myself?

I held up my hands. "Never mind. I love you, you're my best friend, and you deserve every bit of joy any man can bring you."

"Oh, thanks so much for your blessing." Jane huffed out a breath. "Jeez, Shannon, can you really not spare one little teaspoon of happiness for me? You know me. I never go out. I rarely date. And now all of a sudden, my life is different. I have the bed-and-breakfast and I have two fascinating men who want to spend time with me. Can you not enjoy the moment with me?"

"Stephen's fascinating?"

She frowned at me. "Focus, Shannon."

I felt so awful for hurting her feelings I was going to start crying any second. But before I could say another word, Jane stomped out of the powder room and returned to her guests.

I slunk out through the kitchen and drove home.

I don't know how word got around that Jane and I had had a little tiff, but the very next afternoon, as I was preparing to hang drywall in the bedroom of one of the Victorians I was rehabbing, I heard through the grapevine—my foreman Carla called me because she'd heard from her sister, whose best friend worked for Jane's chef—that Whitney Reid Gallagher had shown up at Hennessey House to invite Jane to lunch.

How had Whitney discovered that Jane and I were fighting? It was a mystery. The woman had radar when it came to finding opportunities to interfere with my life.

And because I was paranoid about Whitney in general, the feeling was spreading to other areas of my life, such as, why had Whitney joined the Festival Committee? Had she done it as a way to get close to Jane and try to drive a wedge between us? It wouldn't surprise me.

Jane had never been as much of a target of Whitney's ire as I'd been, even though we were both considered "townies" by the mean girls in Whitney's crowd. The real conflict between Whitney and me had grown out of the fact that I was Tommy's girlfriend. He was adorable, the quarterback on the football team, and the most popular boy in school. I was popular, too, and very friendly. In those days, I was head of the high school welcoming committee, so whenever new kids came to town, I would befriend them or find out their favorite pastimes and introduce them to others who had the same interests. I wanted everyone to be happy and get along. Just call me Little Mary Sunshine.

Whitney and her group of snooty pals disdained my friendliness from the start. Since I'd never met anyone like her before, I thought maybe she was just shy, so I doubled my efforts to get to know her. Big mistake.

It didn't help that I liked to dress in jeans and T-shirts and work boots so that I could join my dad at his construction sites after school. The rich girls teased me mercilessly over my outfits, not to mention my mop of red hair and lack of interest in makeup. They assumed I was poor and bashed me for that, too. The irony was that my father made as much money as theirs, but that didn't matter to the kids whose parents had moved into the gorgeous modern Victorian homes along the Alisal Cliffs—most of which were built by my father.

To Whitney's group, my friends and I were the working-class people who existed to make life easier for them. It was an age-old struggle, and Whitney and her friends played right into the stereotype, ridiculing us and making our lives as miserable as they could. Usually they failed because we just didn't care about them as much as they cared about us.

"Enough melodrama," I muttered as I mixed up a batch of mud to slather across the drywall joints. I'd gotten over my high school angst a long time ago, but unfortunately Whitney was still around, trying to ruin my life. And she couldn't have found a better way to do it than to come between me and Jane.

I admit I'd screwed up where Jane was concerned, but my heart had been in the right place. If Jane couldn't see that . . .

But I was still worried about her. Whitney was evil incarnate. Sweet Jane would be putty in her hands. I wasn't about to mention that point to Jane, though, because her reaction wouldn't be pretty.

Naturally the town grapevine conspired to make sure I found out that Jane had accepted Whitney's invitation to lunch.

Furious with that skinny interloper Whitney, I drowned my sorrows in piles of drywall and mud. I worked ten straight hours that day and tried to avoid any more news about the damn Lunch that Rocked the World.

And as if this day couldn't get any worse, I had to drag myself to a Festival Committee meeting that night. Even though this was an officially announced meeting, Jennifer and Whitney were no-shows. But I still had to contend with Jane's frosty behavior toward me. I was relieved that none of the others seemed to notice her curt responses to my comments.

We turned to the topic of the Pet Fashion Show and began coming up with all the possible categories we would offer. I listed what we'd settled on so far. "We have Most Glamorous, Most Dignified, Cutest, Scariest, Most Creative Costume. What else?"

"Most Sporty?" Ellie suggested, and I wrote that down.

Sylvia raised her hand. "How about the one who Most Resembles Food?"

"Oh, like a Dachshund dressed like a hot dog," Jane said.

"Right. Or a cat dressed as a pizza."

I checked my list. "We should also decide whether the same animals will parade around together or whether it should be cats with cats and dogs with dogs. Or should we just have a free-for-all?"

We had a hearty debate and finally decided that they should all compete with each other. It was a "pet" show, after all. Not a dog show or a cat show.

"Let's give it a cute name," Ellie said. " 'Pet Fashion Show' is boring."

"What do you have in mind?" Jane asked.

Ellie looked hopeful. "How about the Pet Parade? That's a little jazzier."

Sylvia raised her hand. "I'm entering my cat. I was thinking we could call it the Cat Crawl?"

"The Mutt Strut," Judy said.

"The Bunny Hop," Ellie cried.

By now we were giggling as some of them came up with truly silly names, depending on the pet. Procession of the Parrots. The Cavalcade of Cows. Pigs on Parade.

I'd been trying to avoid eye contact with Jane because I hated seeing that scowl on her face. But now I looked at her and she was smiling and so was I. A moment of connection happened and then she looked away.

So there was hope.

Chapter Twelve

In her insatiable need to ruin my life, not only did Whitney try to go after Jane, but she also convinced her husband, Tommy, to nag me until I confessed the reason behind my fallout with Jane. That way, Whitney would be able to casually drop all the right little barbs and stoke Jane's anger at me and separate us further.

I was probably being a little paranoid about the whole situation, but honestly Whitney was a thing to be feared. Still, Jane knew all about my past with Whitney, so maybe, despite her anger, she might see the truth. It was my only hope.

I ran into Tommy at City Hall that morning when I stopped by to drop off another building permit. He pulled me aside and asked what was going on between me and Jane.

"Why do you ask?" I said.

"Don't tell Whitney I said anything, but she's really concerned about you two."

"Oh, that's so nice of her," I said, inwardly rolling my eyes. Tommy was so naive.

"She's just that way," Tommy said with a shrug. "She hates it when the people she cares about are having problems. The thing is, she knows you'll be fine. You're strong. But she thinks Jane could use a friend right now and is trying to set up a lunch with her."

I fumed silently. "Your wife is really generous."

He nodded vigorously. "I know, right? She's the greatest. I think she'll be able to give Jane some good advice about her bed-and-breakfast. Whitney is fantastic when it comes to running a business."

Seeing as how she'd run exactly zero businesses in her life, I could see how he would believe that.

"Oh, Tommy, you're so lucky you married her." My voice was as sweet as sugar while in my head I was dreaming of ways to torture the conniving little witch. Like, maybe chop off the stiletto heels from all her shoes when she wasn't looking.

The thing was, Tommy really was a kindhearted, good-natured guy who believed his wife was as sweet and kind as he was. Tommy was as honest as the day was long, and he wouldn't think of hurting anyone's feelings on purpose. He hadn't changed much since high school when we were dating. Back then he liked surfing, playing football, and me. Probably in that order. These days, I knew that he loved his job and was devoted to his kids and his wife. Probably in that order as well.

And because he was so agreeable, his wife found it pitifully easy to manipulate him. Whatever I said to him would get back to Whitney, so I was always careful when he and I talked. I tried not to abuse his good nature, but right now I was the one who needed information.

"What time is their lunch?" I asked. "Do you know where they're going? Um, because I would love to send a split of champagne to their table."

"Hey, that's a cool idea," Tommy said, and provided me with the intel I needed.

I gave him a big kiss—because that was how I rolled— and left for my jobsite, where I gleefully pounded nails for two hours straight.

It was twelve noon and I was about to take a lunch break and call the restaurant where Jane was meeting Whitney, when Douglas, who was helping me with the nail pounding, got a phone call.

"I've gotta take this," he shouted.

I relaxed my hammering arm so he could talk on the phone. A minute later he disconnected the call, looking puzzled.

"What happened?" I asked.

"You know my brother, Phil, works at the Inn on Main Street."

"Yeah, sure."

"He just told me that some guy committed suicide in his hotel room."

"Oh my God. That's terrible."

Douglas looked stunned. "Phil found the body."

My stomach dipped. "How awful."

"He said the guy ordered breakfast from room service, and when Phil brought the tray up, he found him slumped over his computer keyboard. There was a suicide note on the screen and a syringe hanging out of his arm."

"Oh no. That poor man. That's so upsetting. Is your brother all right? Is he traumatized?"

My mind was already spinning with questions. Namely, why would anyone order room service and then kill himself before the food arrived? I didn't say that out loud. I figured I was focused on food because I hadn't gone to lunch yet.

"Phil's a little shaky, but he'll be fine." Douglas lowered his voice to add, "He thinks the guy was having an affair."

"Really?"

"Yeah. Every time he went to the guy's room, he smelled perfume."

"Interesting. Did Phil see the woman?"

Douglas shrugged. "I don't think so."

"It was probably his wife."

"Maybe. Phil said the guy was in town for a conference out at the Zen Center."

"Your brother found out all that?"

"Yeah. He's pretty chatty sometimes. And he'd been delivering room service stuff to the guy since he arrived a few days ago."

I smiled. "Phil's got a future as a detective."

"I know. He can be sharp when he wants to be."

I went back to hammering, but a minute later, my phone rang. I checked the screen and saw that it was Jane. My shoulders fell a little. Was she going to yell at me some more for being an idiot or maybe tell me all about her fabulous lunch with Whitney? I sighed. "Hello."

"Oh my God, Shannon," she cried. "Did you hear?"

"Hear what?" Was her lunch with Whitney that bad? I checked the time. I'd missed my window of opportunity to send a bottle of champagne to their table.

"Andrew Braxton is dead! He committed suicide in his hotel room!"

I met Jane across the street from the Inn on Main Street.

"This never would've happened if only I'd kept his room open."

I wound my arm through hers for support. "Jane, this isn't your fault. He might've killed himself in your Desdemona Suite if you hadn't sent him off to the Inn."

She gasped and pressed her hand against her mouth. "Oh my God. I hadn't considered that. It would have been horrible."

"Yes." And the publicity would've been awful, too. Nobody wanted to stay in a room where a death had just occurred. I didn't mention that part out loud.

"Oh no," she cried. "Shannon, today is Friday. He was supposed to move back to Hennessey House today. What happened?"

"I don't know," I muttered. Peering through the crowd, I spotted a familiar face. I grabbed her arm. "There's Tommy. Come on. Let's try to find out what happened."

As soon as we reached Tommy, he held up his hand. "I can't tell you anything, Shannon, so don't ask."

I gave Jane a quick look, then said, "I wasn't going to ask, I swear. But Jane thinks she knows the guy. He was supposed to check into Hennessey House today so she's pretty upset and wonders if maybe the thought of changing hotels pushed him over the edge." I was stretching credulity, but I was willing to do whatever it took to get info from Tommy. I leaned in closer and whispered, "We already know the guy committed suicide. And somebody said he was having an affair. Can you tell Jane anything that will help ease her mind?"

"Jeez," he said, smacking his forehead. "Can't anyone keep a secret in this town?"

I almost laughed, since I got a lot of my best information from Tommy himself. Then again, this wasn't a good time to mention that.

"We heard that he typed out the suicide note on his computer," I added.

"Yeah. Right after he swept the room of any fingerprints," Tommy muttered in disgust. "Not to mention every strand of hair and any other evidence a normal person would leave in a hotel room."

It was my turn to gasp. "It was murder."

Tommy looked skyward, as if some great Being would come down and save him from women who could manipulate him so easily.

I patted his arm. "I didn't hear you say a single word. But wait. Were the computer keys wiped clean, too?"

He glared at me. "You know I can't tell you, so stop asking questions."

"Because if the computer keys were wiped clean of prints," I continued, "then that pretty much confirms it was murder."

He pressed his lips together and refused to speak.

I frowned. "But if the keys had his fingerprints on them, indicating suicide, why would he bother to wipe off his prints in the rest of the room?"

I glanced at Jane, who nodded vigorously. "He wouldn't. Which means it's obviously murder."

I smiled in triumph. "Either way, it was murder."

Tommy grabbed both of our arms and walked us down the sidewalk away from the crowd. "You two troublemakers, get out of here before Chief Jensen sees you."

We both pulled away from him and I said, "Okay, we're going. Thanks a lot, Tommy." I planted a kiss on his cheek.

Jane kissed his other cheek. "Thanks, Tommy."

We walked together for another block until I finally stopped and turned to look at her. "I'm so sorry about Andrew, Jane. I know you liked him. And I'm sorry I hurt your feelings. I didn't mean to. It's been a weird week and I was just concerned that those guys might be taking advantage of you. I know you can get any man you want and I don't begrudge you that ability. You're gorgeous and fun and you're my best friend and . . . I was . . . just . . . so stupid. I'm sorry."

She grabbed me and gave me a big hug. "You're forgiven. I was being ultrasensitive. Let's not even talk about it anymore."

"Well, there is one more thing," I said, staring at the ground. "Did you enjoy your lunch with . . . she who must not be named?"

"Whitney?" She laughed. "I ended up not going. It was just so creepy to have her fawning all over me." She shuddered and rubbed her arms. "I knew her sudden interest in me and my business and all that was totally fake. She's so transparent. I told her I was too busy and asked for a rain check."

"A rain check. So you'll go out to lunch with her some other time?"

"Only if you come with me."

"That's a big no way, no how, never."

"Exactly what I thought."

We walked together back to Hennessey House and went straight up to Jane's suite. Jane looked ready to pass out so I poured her some tea and we nibbled on the shortbread biscuits her chef was quickly becoming famous for.

Once the adrenaline rush wore off, Jane admitted she was really shaken by Andrew's death. She still blamed herself and I continued to insist that it wasn't her fault.

"Tommy practically admitted it was murder," I said. "So how can it be your fault?"

"Murder," she whispered. "That's so awful. I know the

two can't be connected, but isn't it weird that so soon after Jesse, someone else turns up murdered?"

I stared at my teacup, knowing she was right. The two murders had to be connected. But how?

While we sat in her room commiserating and drinking tea, Whitney called twice. Jane recognized the number and didn't answer the phone. Apparently, thanks to the gruesome turn of events, Whitney's devious plans to destroy our friendship were dashed for now. So at least one good thing had happened that day.

There was a knock on Jane's door.

"Come in," she called.

The door opened and Althea poked her head in. "Hi there. Mind if I come in for just a moment?"

"Althea, what a surprise." Jane jumped up and walked across the room to hug the woman. "It's so good to see you."

"I was delivering a package to a customer in town and I thought I'd take a chance and stop by."

"Perfect timing. Come in, won't you?"

She hesitated by the door. "I really should get back to the shop, but I wanted to see if you'll have lunch with me tomorrow. Just for fun, you know, girl talk, get to know each other better." She glanced at me. "You're more than welcome to join us, Shannon."

"I'd love to have lunch with you," Jane said, and flashed me a look. "Please come with us. You knew Jesse so well for so many years, we can all reminisce and have some laughs."

"In that case, I'd love to." To tell the truth, I wouldn't miss it for the world. Althea might just be the nice, warm woman she seemed to be. On the other hand, weird things were happening and I couldn't be sure that she wasn't a part of them. No way was I letting Jane go off with the woman alone.

Not that I would say that to Jane. I'd learned my lesson with Andrew and Stephen.

"Wonderful," Althea said. We settled on the time and

place, and after hugs all around, she took off back to her shop. Jane and I continued talking and sipping our tea.

"I have a confession to make," I said.

"Am I going to get mad again?" she asked, but I could tell she was kidding.

"I hope not. I drove around on Tuesday and stopped at a couple of pawnshops and antique stores, hoping to find more shop owners who might've seen Jesse's necklace. I figured if he showed it to Cuckoo with the intention of selling it, he probably showed it to others, too."

"That was smart." Her eyes widened. "Wait. One of those owners could be the person who's been searching Jesse's house. He might've killed him for it."

"That's exactly what I was thinking."

"Oh my God, Shannon, you *weren't* thinking. You could've put yourself in danger."

"Nobody's going to kill me for asking the question," I insisted. "They were all perfectly normal shopkeepers. Well, except for Cuckoo. He really is crazy. And there was this one pawnbroker who was pretty ominous, but I got out of there okay."

"Oh, jeez, you're scaring me."

"Don't worry." The odd thing was that I hadn't been scared at all. Well, except for that one guy at the pawnshop. And Cuckoo, of course. Okay, I was scared. But I managed to leave both shops without a mishap.

"Anyway, the reason I'm telling you this is that I was halfway down the coast and decided to drive the rest of the way to Althea's shop in Blue Point."

She tilted her head. "You saw Althea on Tuesday?"

"Not exactly. She was leaving for lunch just as I arrived. I waited—and she never saw me—and then I went inside. And ended up buying a pretty new jacket."

Jane shook her head at me. "You were snooping."

"Maybe." I smiled. "Yes, I was snooping. Anyway, the point is, I talked to Althea's salesclerk, who raved about her being the best boss who ever lived. So that's reassuring, right?"

Jane thought about it. "Yes, very. I'm glad to hear it."

With a sigh, she took a sip of her tea. "It makes me think that Jesse was happy spending time with her."

"I hope so." I laid my head back against the soft-cushioned chair and stared at the view of trees out the window. "I still feel bad that I doubted him so often. The necklace was real, the girlfriend was real, and there's probably other stuff that I thought was made up but was really real. I should've had more faith in him."

"Well, he did spin some stories," Jane admitted with a soft chuckle.

"Yes, he did."

We sat silently for another few minutes. I was lost in thoughts of Jesse and of all the things I should've told him. Like how my life was made richer and more fun because of him, and how he made me laugh with his salty language and silly puns, and how I learned from him not to take things so seriously all the time. But I wouldn't have the chance to tell him anything ever again.

Later that afternoon on the way home from Jane's, I stopped at the post office and ran into my buddy Palmer Tripley, who owned and edited our local newspaper, the *Lighthouse Standard*. Years ago, my father had rehabbed his parents' house and we had all become friends. Our fathers still got together to watch sports every so often.

"Did you hear about the suicide?" I asked right away.

"A little. What have you heard?"

I smiled at the way he hedged his answer. I had a feeling he knew plenty, being a good reporter. "I'll tell you what I know if you'll do the same."

"Okay. You go first."

"Oh, all right." We walked outside to a private spot where we wouldn't be overheard and I proceeded to give him the information I'd received from Douglas and Tommy. "But you didn't hear it from me."

He grinned. "Of course not."

"So, what do you know about it?"

He thought for a moment. "Let's see. Andrew Braxton drove up from Long Beach in Southern California for a pharmacology conference out at the Zen Center."

The Zen Center was located outside town in what we called the Redwood Crest area. The actual name of the center was the Sanctuary of the Four Winds. It was run by our local Zen master, Kikisho. People came from all over the world to study with him, and some of them had even moved to Lighthouse Cove permanently to be close to their master.

The center was also well-known as a good place to hold small conferences with an emphasis on team-building and New Age wellness. I figured that was the focus of Andrew Braxton's business conference.

So much for wellness, I thought grimly. Andrew was dead in an apparent suicide, although I knew it was really murder.

"Anything else?" I asked.

"Yeah," Palmer said. "According to his business associates, Andrew had been in good health and was happily married to a nice gal and they had three loving kids."

Hmm. Andrew had a wife and three kids. So why had he been flirting so outrageously with Jane? He'd asked her out on at least one date while I was standing right there, listening in on their private conversation. And Jane had admitted later that he had called her three times to ask her out.

Just how happily married had he been? Not very, it seemed. Maybe the turmoil of being *un*-happily married had driven him to commit suicide.

But he didn't commit suicide, I reminded myself. Not if what Tommy said was true, that the hotel room had been scrubbed of fingerprints and other evidence. That sounded like murder.

Maybe his wife knew about his philandering and snuck up to Lighthouse Cove and killed him. It was a longshot, but if that were the case, it was just as well that he hadn't been staying at Jane's B-and-B. I shivered at the thought that Jane could've been involved. But that was ridiculous. It was more likely that Andrew Braxton was involved in some kind of industrial espionage and was killed by a business partner. Or, even more likely, I didn't know what in the world I was talking about.

I tried to remember what Palmer had just said. Oh yeah, the happily married man.

"If he was so happy, why did he commit suicide in a hotel room in Lighthouse Cove?"

"Good question," Palmer said. "Was he drunk? Was he coerced?"

"Was it murder?" I was more or less putting the idea into Palmer's head.

"Could be," Palmer mused. "One more thing. Braxton was scheduled to give a presentation this afternoon on the latest psychotropic drugs on the market. He had been traveling with a briefcase filled with samples of the drugs he intended to discuss during his speech."

"Really?"

"Yeah. But no such briefcase was found in his hotel room."

That evening, Jane and I were able to gather the Festival Committee for a short, secret meeting at my house. We planned to spend one quick hour together to settle all of our remaining issues. Three of the food vendors hadn't handed in a menu. We had come up with all the fun categories for the Pet Parade, and we were all thrilled with our choice of grand marshal, Chief Eric Jensen, who would lead the float parade. But we still had to determine the order of the rest of the floats and participants.

As I was placing a platter of cookies on the dining room sideboard, the doorbell rang. And rang. And rang.

"Good heavens," Lily said. "Who's that?"

Pat glanced at me. "Somebody's desperate to see you."

"I'll be right back." But as I approached my front door, a chill zipped across my shoulders. And as I reached for the doorknob, I knew why.

Whipping the door open, I said, "Hello, Whitney, Jennifer."

"My, my, what have we here?" Whitney said as she brushed past me to enter my house.

"Do come in," I muttered.

Whitney stood at the dining room entry. "Look at this."

"It looks like a Festival Committee meeting," Jennifer said, scowling. "I think you forgot to invite a few of us."

"Didn't you get the e-mail?" I asked. "We've been waiting for you."

"That's a lie," Jennifer declared.

Whitney blocked my way into the dining room. "Did you really think you'd get away with it?"

I stared at her with what I hoped was an insipid smile. "Whatever are you talking about?"

Jane didn't miss a beat. "Hello, ladies. We've been waiting for you. There's coffee and cookies, so grab what you want and have a seat so we can get started."

Jennifer frowned at Whitney as I nudged them toward the table.

"We've made a list of the parade floats and we're working out the order." Jane passed them the list. "Some of us think the Baby Batoneers should come after the fire engine brigade, but before the Surf City Band." She gazed blandly at Whitney. "What do you think?"

"Huh?" Jennifer said.

Whitney made a face. "Why would I give a fig?"

"Okay, then, all in favor of the order as posted?"

Six of us raised our hands.

"Opposed?"

We all turned and stared at Jennifer and Whitney, who looked at each other in confusion for the briefest moment but quickly recovered.

"I oppose it," Jennifer said loudly, for no reason other than the fact that she was a knucklehead.

Whitney made a sound of disgust. "Let's get out of here." She shoved her chair back and stood. Jennifer did the same and they both stormed out of the room. I was quick to follow to make sure they left my house.

"The ayes have it," Jane said brightly.

*   *   *

At noon on Saturday, Jane and I met Althea for lunch at Francois, the French bistro on the town square. The older woman turned out to be just as charming and easy to talk to as she'd seemed before.

I wore my rust-colored jacket and Althea spotted it immediately. "You. You're the customer who came in the other day while I was at lunch, aren't you?"

I modeled the jacket. "I am. I was down there on business and took a chance on stopping by. I'm sorry I missed you, but I did manage to snag a few fabulous items." I pulled my hair back and flicked my new earrings.

"And you bought the earrings, too. Aren't those great? Margot told me she sold the jacket to someone who knew me and I couldn't for the life of me figure out who it was." Althea studied me for another moment before nodding in approval. "That color was created for you."

"I think so, too." I spun around. "I really love it. And your shop is so adorable. I could've spent another hour in there."

"You should both come down sometime to shop. We'll do lunch on the pier."

"I'd love that," Jane said. "I'm terribly jealous of Shannon's new jacket."

We ordered lunch: a salad for Jane, an omelet for Althea, and a burger and french fries for me. "I'll split the fries with you both," I said.

"You'd better," Althea said, laughing as we handed our menus to the waitress.

"Your salesclerk was so charming," I said. "And she had lots of great things to say about you. And need I mention, she is one heck of a saleswoman."

Althea laughed. "Don't I know it? I have no idea what I would do without Margot. I feel so lucky to have her working there."

"That's how I feel about my chef," Jane said. "It's so important to work with good people."

Our lunches arrived and the conversation never stopped. It was as if we'd known Althea forever. She grew up in Southern California but moved north to open a vintage clothing shop after visiting Blue Point just once. She had a feeling in her bones that it would be the right move. She gushed about her shop, explaining that she'd always had a love of fine fabrics and clothing from when she was a little girl and played dress-up with her mother's high heels and slinky dresses. She admitted she loved life in general.

"I think that's why Jesse and I hit it off so well. We both enjoyed doing so many different things. Boating and yoga and traveling and golf. We had plans to travel and . . . well . . ." She tried to swallow but had a difficult time as tears gathered in her eyes.

Jane reached for her hand and gave it a light squeeze. "I know. It's hard."

Althea blotted her tears with a small white handkerchief. "Jesse always said he wanted us to be friends, Jane. I would love that, and I know it would make him happy, too."

I discreetly lifted my napkin to dab my own tears. If this wasn't real, then Althea deserved the Best Actress of the Year award.

Althea turned and patted my hand. "And you, too, Shannon. I know you were close to Jesse and I'd love to get to know you better, too."

"I'd like that," I said, sniffling delicately. "And not just because I intend to keep shopping in your store."

We all laughed and Althea called for the check, insisting on buying us lunch. I left the restaurant feeling much more inclined to be friends with Althea than when we'd come in.

That night, I was getting into bed when I caught another dim flash of light over at Jesse's place. I was surprised that the intruder was back because Jane had changed the locks and the guy knew it. Plus, the police had been driving by on a regular basis lately. That was obviously Eric's doing, and I was happy he'd thought of it. But none of those precautions had scared off the crook, apparently.

This time I wasn't going to let whoever it was get away. I put on my sweats and sneakers and grabbed my heaviest flashlight. Robbie must've been getting used to my late-night sojourns because he barely stirred in his bed. He just lifted his head, gave me a "You're crazy, lady" look, and went back to sleep. Tiger ignored me as well. Downstairs, I called the police to report the break-in and then left the house as quietly as I could. When I reached the gate, I saw Mac jogging down the garage stairs.

"You saw the light?" he whispered.

"Yes, and this time I intend to nab him."

"Did you call the cops?"

"Yes. But I'm sick of someone breaking into Jesse's house. Jane even changed the locks. How did they get inside?"

"Pure determination," Mac said. "Or else they stole the new keys somehow. Come on."

We tiptoed silently down my driveway and snuck up Jesse's front walk before Mac spoke again. "How about if you wait by the front door and I go around to the back?"

I hated the idea of splitting up, for all the reasons I'd come up with before, but we'd lost the guy several times when he ran out the back way, so I agreed.

After a ten-minute wait on the front porch, I didn't see another flash of light or hear any sounds, so I jogged around to the back door to find Mac. "Did anyone come out?"

"No."

"I can't believe we came up empty again."

"Does Jesse have a secret side entrance somewhere?"

"Not that I know of."

"Maybe he's still inside," Mac suggested, "hiding in some crevice somewhere."

"Maybe. We could wait out here all night, but I think whoever was in the house is long gone."

I'd been so sure we would catch him this time, I was feeling extra bummed. Eric's SUV arrived and he parked in front of my house.

"Uh-oh," I whispered.

"Let's go meet him."

We jogged back to my place just as Eric made it to the sidewalk.

"We didn't go inside," I said immediately.

"Nobody came in or out," Mac added.

"Then he's probably still inside. You two wait out here."

"Yes, sir," I murmured.

He flashed me a sardonic look, as if he didn't believe my cooperative, good-citizen act.

Mac and I waited until he came back outside.

"Nothing," Eric said. "I'll bring a team by tomorrow to see if we can find any evidence. But he's long gone tonight."

Early Sunday morning, the police were already at Jesse's, trying to find anything that would lead to the capture of this wily intruder. But there was nothing, Eric reported. Not a fingerprint or a footprint anywhere.

The three of us regrouped in my kitchen around the coffee machine. Robbie was beyond thrilled to have two great big men paying attention to him, so he showed them all his tricks: sat politely for a treat, rolled over, played dead. Tiger was more subtle, winding herself in and around their legs until Mac stooped down and picked her up. Now she was in heaven.

"So how did he get inside again?" Mac asked.

"The locks haven't been jimmied," Eric said, "so he must've used the new key."

"This guy just won't give up," I said.

"I'll beef up the drive-by surveillance for the next few days," Eric said.

"Okay, thanks." I didn't know what else to do. "Do you want another cup of coffee?"

"Thanks for the offer," Eric said, "but I've got to get back to the station."

"I'll take one," Mac said, and helped himself.

We sat at the kitchen table in silence for a moment. Robbie rested at his feet and Tiger was curled up in his lap. "I like your animals."

"They're pretty great, aren't they?" I said, reaching over and scratching Tiger's soft neck. "If you were writing a book and plotting out Jesse's death and its aftermath, would you have things happening so haphazardly like this?"

"Actually I would," Mac said.

"What do you mean?"

"I mean, human nature is pretty straightforward," he said. "In real life, events and situations are often self-explanatory and relatively simple, even murder. But for a mystery novel to be intriguing, an author needs to write as complex and elaborate a plot as possible to keep readers guessing. Because believe me, mystery readers are so damn smart, they always figure it out."

I sighed. "This situation is ridiculously convoluted."

"Yeah." He scratched his head. "I should be taking notes."

I got up and found the little bag of shortbread cookies I'd coaxed out of Jane's chef and put a few on a plate. "I so want to catch this person. Chances are he killed my neighbor and now he's trying to steal something. And to do it, he's destroying Jesse's house. Or he was, until Jane changed the locks and Eric started having someone drive by a few times a night. But it's still so frustrating because he keeps coming back and we never catch him."

"Why doesn't Jane just hire a security guard or two?"

I winced. "I talked her out of it."

"You what?"

"It made sense at the time," I insisted. "We weren't going to catch Jesse's killer if the intruder was scared off by a guard."

He sighed heavily. "Okay, that makes sense in a perverse way."

I fiddled with my coffee spoon. "I thought so."

"What can they be looking for?" Mac wondered out loud.

I pressed my lips together, trying to decide how much to tell him.

His eyes narrowed. "You know something."

What did I say? How did this guy read my mind like that?

"Look, Shannon. Whatever it is, we need to find the damn thing before anyone else gets hurt. Something tells me you know more about it than you're saying. So spill."

He was right. Besides, all of our girlfriends knew and so did Eric. And my father. Mac had a right to know after spending all these nights chasing down the intruder with me.

"Jesse found a necklace when he went scuba diving with Bob and Ned."

"I heard that was an old wives' tale."

"Yeah, well, it's not. I found it."

"You . . . you found it." He stared at me in disbelief and I could swear the temperature dropped ten degrees. "The necklace. And you didn't tell anyone about it?"

"Jane knows, of course." Along with half of Lighthouse Cove. But I felt too guilty to mention that fact to Mac.

"Jane knows," he echoed as he absently turned his coffee cup around in slow circles, his gaze never leaving mine. "Of course she would, because at this point, it probably belongs to her. But you know, you and I have gone to Jesse's house at least four times in the middle of the night to investigate what's going on. So, when were you planning to tell me the truth?"

The guilt swept over me in waves. "I'm sorry, Mac. Jane and I swore each other to secrecy. I was so worried that if anyone knew the truth, her life would be in danger. But I should've trusted you."

"Yeah, you should've," he said, reaching for my hand.

"I feel awful." His warm palm felt good against mine.

"Good. As long as you're feeling really guilt-ridden, I'm okay with that. Do the cops know?"

"I told Eric."

"That was smart."

"I know. You might not speak to me again, but he could throw me in jail."

He allowed himself a half grin. "Makes sense."

Was it my imagination or was some of the ice in his eyes melting?

"Sorry."

"Apology accepted," he said. He let go of my hand and got up to pour more coffee. "You don't know me really well, but I'm a good guy."

I smiled. "I know that much."

He sat down again. "But now you owe me."

"Oh." I frowned as he grabbed my hand again and pressed it lightly between his two palms. It felt secure and warm.

"You owe me the truth," he said softly. "All of it. Right now. I want to hear the whole story."

I told him how I found Jesse's body. How a week later, I was checking the foundation for Jane and came across the cracked bricks in Jesse's basement where he'd hidden the necklace. I told him about my conversation with Jane about keeping the discovery a secret so that Jesse's killer wouldn't come after her. And how we'd immediately put the necklace in the safe-deposit box.

"That was smart," he said. "Good move. But here's the deal. It doesn't do any good to put it in the bank if the bad guy still thinks it's somewhere inside Jesse's house." He gave my hand a squeeze and I liked it a lot. Not just the warm, solid contact, which was really nice, but also the feeling that I wasn't in this alone. That Mac was willing and ready to charge into battle by my side.

"I agree," I said.

"Because someone is still breaking in and searching for it. He won't stop until he either finds it himself or hears that someone else found it."

"You're right," I said, still feeling the guilt seep back in. "And that's why we didn't tell anyone else. We didn't want the bad guy coming after Jane."

"I understand. But this time when he comes after Jane, we'll be waiting for him."

A few hours later, I dressed in my prettiest springtime frock, even though it was February. I'd been invited to a

Sunday afternoon garden party at one of the "Grande Dame" Victorian mansions on the Alisal Cliffs. It was a beautiful sunny day, but I grabbed a sweater to wear in case the wind got too brisk out on the cliffs.

I'd invited Mac to go with me to the home of Mr. and Mrs. Perry, the art collectors who owned the house. My crew and I had recently done a bit of remodeling for them, turning their downstairs office into a glass-walled solarium. I was pleased with the work and had uploaded some pictures of the pretty, plant-filled room onto my Web site.

The reason for the garden party was to unveil a new sculptural masterpiece that the Perrys had shipped back from Florence. I couldn't wait to see it after hearing Mrs. Perry rhapsodize over it.

Mac was an immediate hit, of course, and I was considered brilliant for bringing him. There was plenty of great conversation, luscious champagne, and waiters carrying trays of yummy hors d'oeuvres. The only fly in the ointment, so to speak, was that Whitney and a few of her unpleasant friends were among the guests. I should've known, since she was one of the Perrys' neighbors as well as a charter member of the rich folks' society. Those people really stuck together.

The good news was that Tommy was on hand, too, so I flirted with him every chance I got.

Whitney didn't like that and she nailed me with a combination cold shoulder and haughty look down the nose. But she couldn't have been sweeter to Mac, who caught on to her right away. He'd been in town long enough to figure out who was to be avoided. Whitney was one of those.

Which was only part of why he so appealed to me.

Mac was enjoying himself, perfectly at ease among the snooty and friendly alike, and the champagne was lovely. After an hour of socializing, Mr. and Mrs. Perry approached the large canvas-covered statue at the corner of the terraced patio.

"We're about to reveal our masterpiece," Mrs. Perry

cried. A few people clinked their glasses together to get everyone's attention.

We all gathered around and Mac grinned. "They're really drawing out the suspense, aren't they?"

"I'm breathless with anticipation," I joked, but I really could feel the excitement building.

He chuckled, and Whitney, standing on the other side of Mac, turned and glared at me. I was happy to ignore her.

Mrs. Perry began to count. "Five! Four! Three! Two! One! Reveal!"

Mr. Perry and another man grabbed either side of the canvas covering and pulled, exposing the masterpiece to the world.

Whitney gasped.

I snorted with laughter.

The Perrys' masterpiece was an elaborate fountain in the classic Italian tradition made of rich marble and beautiful copper—and an exact replica of my neighbor Mrs. Higgins's huge backyard eyesore. Water spewed from the hands and mouths of the angels and tumbled down over the creatures cavorting below.

The only difference I could discern between the two fountains was that the Perrys' was worth many thousands of dollars more and would age to a fine patina in those spots where the surface was burnished copper, while Mrs. Higgins's was constructed of faux plastic and foam and would probably crumble and collapse in a year or two. Otherwise the two fountains were identical.

Whitney began to choke, probably from the shock of seeing a duplicate of what she'd once called "the most hideous, gauche piece of garbage" she'd ever laid eyes on. That was exactly how she'd described Mrs. Higgins's version, the one she'd seen in the back of my truck in the supermarket parking lot.

Tommy and Mac grabbed her from both sides and gave her a few firm slaps on the back. She finally waved them both away, having recovered from her choking bout. But her face still looked a little green.

The crowd oohed and aahed at the splendid display, and as the angels began to hum shrilly, Mrs. Perry made the rounds, asking all the guests what they thought of her new treasure.

Whitney gulped, then exclaimed, "It's beautiful! I'm so envious! The silhouette of the angels is so glorious against the afternoon sky. It's all so . . . so stylishly whimsical, yet sensual. I've never seen anything so utterly splendiferous in all my life."

"I'm so happy you love it, Whitney," Mrs. Perry said, giving her an enthusiastic hug. "You absolutely must see the original fountain once before you die. The Boboli Gardens of Florence are beyond description." She moved on to the next guest and proceeded to gush all over again.

"You are so full of it," I muttered in Whitney's ear.

"Shut up," she hissed.

A minute later, Mrs. Perry approached me. "What do you think, Shannon?"

"It's truly unique, and yet . . ." I paused. "It reminds me of another work I've seen recently."

I gave Whitney a quick glance and saw her eyes shooting poison-tipped daggers at me.

I turned back to Mrs. Perry. "Now I remember. I believe it's similar in style and grace to something I saw in the Boboli Gardens in Florence, Italy, a few years ago."

"Yes!" Mrs. Perry cried. "Exactly! We took our inspiration from the Boboli."

"I knew it!" I said. "It's truly . . . splendiferous."

"Thank you, my dear." She walked over to another guest and I took a big gulp of blessed champagne.

Whitney tried to walk away, but I grabbed her arm and yanked her back, saying, "You owe me one."

"Don't hold your breath," she snarled. "Splendiferous, my ass."

I laughed and downed the rest of my champagne.

Chapter Thirteen

Jane called early Monday morning as I was pouring my first cup of coffee. "It's bad news. Bob has slipped into a coma."

I must've been half-asleep, because I shook my head and stared at the phone for a long moment. "Who? What?"

"Bob Madderly. Jesse's navy pal. He's slipped into a coma. They're not sure he'll survive."

"Survive?" I gulped at my coffee, hoping for clarity. "What the heck happened to Bob? How did he get into a coma? And how did you find out so early in the morning?"

"Bob's a diabetic and they think he forgot to take his insulin. Or maybe he took too much. I'm not sure."

"That's so sad." I'd grown to care for the sweet old guy. I remembered him winking and flirting with me at Jane's party.

"I know."

"Does he have any family nearby?"

"A younger cousin, but Ned and Jesse were his real family. And Stephen. He's taking it hard."

"That's horrible for everyone." I gulped down my coffee because if I didn't, I would never figure out what happened to Bob.

"How could he forget to take his insulin?"

"I don't know. He's old. Maybe he forgot."

I frowned. Like Jesse, Bob was somewhere in his seventies, which could be considered old, I guessed. But he was still spry and had all his faculties. If he'd been dealing with diabetes for any length of time, he was not going to "forget" his meds. What was going on around here?

Coming so soon after Jesse's "accidental overdose," Bob's mishap with a prescription drug was indeed suspicious, but I didn't say anything to Jane, because she was so upset. I was upset, too. I wondered if Jane might be flashing back to the moment when she first heard about Jesse's death. If that was the case, I didn't want her suffering alone.

"I'm coming over," I said.

"Okay," she said, sounding relieved. "I'll be here."

Ten minutes later, I walked into Hennessey House and found Stephen and Jane sitting in the living room, commiserating. Jane jumped up and hurried over to greet me. "Oh, Shannon, thanks for coming."

"I wanted to make sure you were okay."

"I was planning to call you later. I set up a lunch with Althea for tomorrow and I was hoping you'd come with me. But now with Bob in the hospital, I think we'd better cancel."

"Yes, we should," I said. "Do you want me to call her?"

"No, I can do it." She pressed her hands together and glanced around. I could tell she was on her last nerve.

"Jane, sit down, please?" I said quietly. "You're entitled to relax once in a while."

"I'm fine. It helps to keep busy. Let me get you a cup of coffee."

"No, I'll grab a cup in the dining room and join you in a second."

"Okay."

I really wanted to know what Stephen was up to. Why was he always just there, by Jane's side, like a new puppy looking for treats? I knew that now wasn't a good time to dwell on it, but the guy was really starting to bug me.

I sat down with my coffee and tried to smile at Stephen. "I'm really sorry. I know you and your dad are close to Bob."

"I'm going to miss him," Stephen whispered. "He was a great guy."

I frowned at Stephen. "Did he die?"

"Well, no, but it's only a matter of time."

"But he could still come out of it," I insisted. "Don't write him off just yet."

Jane clutched her hands together. "Shannon's right. As long as he's alive, there's hope."

I was familiar with diabetes because my mother had had it. I was too young to know much about it at the time she died, but as I grew up, I did a lot of reading on the disease. I was willing to bet that I knew as much about it as anyone else who didn't actually suffer from it.

One way Bob could've fallen into a coma was if he overdosed on insulin. I was tempted to call the hospital.

"My dad said that he found Bob passed out in his silk boxer shorts," Stephen said, with a feeble grin. "That's all he was wearing when he was rushed to the hospital."

I didn't find that tidbit of news worth smiling about. Especially when it reminded me that Jesse was dressed the same way when I found him.

"That poor man," Jane said.

Stephen stared into his coffee mug. "Who knew old Bob was sporting silk boxers all this time? I must admit, silk does feel nice against the skin, although I prefer going commando."

I exchanged a look with Jane. Did he say stuff like this on a regular basis? Was he nuts? He was socially inept for sure.

But Jane, always the perfect hostess, took a steadying breath and tried to smile. "Silk is wonderful, isn't it? And if it made Bob happy, where's the harm?"

Perfect hostess or not, Jane couldn't possibly be buying in to Stephen's weirdness, could she? I supposed some people behaved oddly in crisis situations, but discussing fabrics and boxer shorts and—God help us—going commando was a whole new level of bizarre.

*   *   *

Later that day, I posed the question to Mac over a couple of bottles of ice-cold beer. "Are boxer shorts a navy thing?"

He looked at me as though I were crazy, and I had to wonder if I was nuts, too. Had I drunk the same Kool-Aid as Stephen and Jane?

"A navy thing?" Mac laughed. "Uh, no. You can wear tighty whities or anything else in the navy if you want to. Uncle Sam's not all that interested in your underwear."

"Right, right," I said, feeling a rush of embarrassment at the conversation I'd started. "Of course not."

"Is something going on, Shannon? I mean, you'd tell me if you were onto something else, wouldn't you?"

"I'm not." I frowned at the beer bottle, then gazed at him. "It's just that Jesse died wearing only his boxer shorts. They were white and cotton, but I guess that's not relevant. And now Bob was rushed to the hospital wearing only a pair of silk boxers. Just seems weird, that's all."

I glanced over and saw him looking at me in precisely the same way I'd been looking at Stephen a few minutes ago.

"Never mind," I said quickly, waving away the question. "Oh, hey, there's a game on TV. Want to watch?"

"A woman who loves to watch sports?" Mac grinned. "Count me in."

A few hours later, Jane telephoned. "I spoke to Althea. We'll schedule a lunch sometime next week."

"Good," I said.

"I told her about Bob. I think she met him a few times with Jesse, so I wanted her to know he's not doing too well. She was so sweet, said she was going to send a card to Ned because they're buddies."

I remembered seeing Bob and Althea together the day of Jesse's memorial. I told Jane about how they'd been talking so intently the day Jesse was buried.

"And she patted his cheek?" Jane said.

"Yeah," I said. "It looked like they knew each other pretty well."

"I guess that makes sense. Jesse would've introduced his girlfriend to his best friends, right?"

"Sure."

Something in the tone of my voice must've alerted Jane. "Okay, Shannon, I know everyone is a suspect in your view, but I really like Althea. And Bob is a sweetheart."

"I totally agree. I'm just telling you what I saw."

"I appreciate that," Jane said. "But it sounds like they were having a completely innocent conversation. Probably just commiserating with each other. After all, both of them just lost a close friend."

"That's all it was, I'm sure."

"I can tell you're placating me, but I'm going to let it go. I like Althea a lot and I don't want to think that someone I care about might turn out to be the bad guy."

"I like her, too." That was the problem, I thought. I liked a lot of the people on my suspect list.

"Listen," she said. "Do you want to go out for an early dinner tonight?"

"Yes. I won't even talk if you don't want me to."

She chuckled weakly. "I won't hold you to that."

"Thanks."

I picked her up at five thirty, and we headed for our favorite spot, Bella Rossa on the square. Dinner was wonderful, as usual, and we chatted easily through the meal. Nothing heavy, no worries, just idle chitchat. I think we were both a little burned out by everything that had been happening lately.

But there was one thing I needed to talk about. "I know I promised to keep the conversation light, but I need to ask you something and I don't want you to get mad at me."

"Okay," she said warily.

"It's about Stephen. What's his deal? Is he going to live there indefinitely? I'm concerned that he's monopolizing your time."

She thought for a moment, choosing her words carefully. "It's odd having a man around who notices when I walk into the room. A man who watches my every move, who comes to my rescue when any little thing goes wrong. I spilled a drop of wine on the tablecloth at happy hour the other day and he instantly removed all the glasses and carried the cheese platter away. Then he whipped the tablecloth off and ran to the laundry room to clean it."

I frowned at her. "That's downright peculiar."

She shook her head. "It's sad. I always thought I would love to have a man pay attention and take care of me like that."

"Not like that."

"Now I wonder if I've been lying to myself all this time." With her elbow on the table, she rested her chin in her hand. "I thought I wanted that kind of deeply romantic care and concern from a man, but it turns out I don't. Stephen's behavior is a little disconcerting."

"No, Jane. It's downright creepy."

She grimaced. "Unfortunately I agree."

"Look, you can still have all that stuff you've always dreamed about. Just not with Stephen. He's nice-looking and probably a decent guy, but he's not the one for you, so it doesn't feel right when he behaves so obsequiously around you. Another man doing the same thing might make you feel differently."

"Obsequious," she said with a smile. "A ten-dollar word."

"Hey, I've got hidden smarts."

She laughed and sat back in her chair. "Enough about Stephen. Let's find something more interesting to talk about."

I took a sip of wine and swirled it for a moment. "Okay, let's talk about us. We're both healthy, our businesses are thriving, we have good friends, we live in a beautiful place, and of course, we're both totally hot."

She lifted her glass to mine. "Totally."

It was almost nine o'clock when I dropped Jane off at Hennessey House and drove home. I hoped she would be able to sleep tonight, but I was afraid she was too upset about Bob to be able to relax. It was too damn bad that all this horrible stuff with Jesse and the necklace had coincided with the opening of her B-and-B. There was no way for Jane to enjoy her moment in the sun when there was death and destruction happening all around her.

As I was locking up the house before heading to bed, the phone rang.

It was Jane. She was sobbing. "My things. My rooms. Everything's a mess! I—I've been robbed."

"Call the police," I shouted. "I'll be right there."

Mac caught me racing down the driveway and ran after me. When he heard what was going on, he jumped in the truck to go with me.

"This is about the necklace," he said.

"I can't argue with that."

We drove in silence until I pulled to the curb outside the B-and-B just as Eric screeched to a halt in his cop car. Tommy and two other officers drove up behind him and parked a few doors down.

Eric, Mac, and I ran inside and rushed upstairs. At the end of the long, wide hall, Jane's double doors were thrown open. I exchanged looks with Mac. This was just what I'd been afraid would happen if we revealed that the necklace had been found. But we'd been careful to specify that the necklace had been taken to a safe place. Okay, we didn't exactly identify the safe place as *my safe-deposit box*, but how smart did someone have to be to figure that out?

Did Jane's intruder not understand the part where we told everyone the necklace had been put somewhere for safekeeping? Did he actually think Jane would hide it in her bedroom?

So we weren't just dealing with your run-of-the-mill intruder. We were dealing with a stupid one.

I grabbed Jane and hugged her tightly. "We'll find whoever did this and they will pay."

"I hope so. I really do." She let go of me and leaned against the wall of her room, looking completely exhausted. This was one more horrific incident in her life, and I didn't know what to do to help her.

I stood inside the doorway and tried to contain my fury as I surveyed the mess. Jane's suite had been tossed quickly and without regard for any of her beautiful furnishings. Every last thing was on the floor, chairs were upturned, shelves and tables were flipped on their sides, and whatever had been on the surface of the tables and the bookshelves against the walls were now scattered across the carpeted floor.

"It can all be put back," Mac whispered in my ear. "If anything's broken, it can be replaced. Jane wasn't hurt. That's all that matters."

"That's right." I repeated his words over and over until they sank in. *Jane wasn't hurt. That's all that matters.*

Eric walked into the room and pulled Jane into his arms. "I'm sorry. Are you all right?"

She sniffed, but nodded. "I'm fine. Or I will be as soon as this nightmare is over."

"Were any of the other rooms touched?"

Jane's eyes widened. "I'm such an idiot. I didn't even check. When I got home I went to the kitchen and wound up talking to my chef for fifteen minutes or so. Then I came upstairs and saw this." She whirled around, gazing at the wall-to-wall chaos. "I have no idea if anyone else was robbed. I've got to check on my guests."

"You go ahead and do that," Eric said, "then come back here. I'll be looking around."

She rushed out of the room.

I didn't bother offering to go with her, because I knew she would want to visit each suite personally to assure herself that her guests were all safe and sound.

Instead I stayed in her suite, so livid on Jane's behalf I could barely take it all in. My gaze met Eric's and I could see that his anger matched my own.

"They were looking for the necklace," I said, saying what had to be obvious to both Eric and Mac.

Eric gazed at me. "We let everyone in town know it had been found and put in a safe place."

I shook my head in disgust. "I have a feeling someone didn't get the message, or if they heard it was found, they didn't hear that it was safely locked up. They must've thought Jane had it here. I can't think of any other explanation."

Mac looked around. "Who would be brazen enough to walk into a fully staffed and occupied establishment and try to rip off the owner's property?"

"Someone who's desperate to find a priceless piece of jewelry," I said, clenching my teeth to keep from screaming expletives up and down the hall. "The same person who would destroy Jesse's house looking for the same thing."

"Yeah," Eric said, his jaw tightening. "Okay, everybody out. I've got to get my team in here and dust for fingerprints."

"I wonder if they actually took anything," I said. "If they didn't find the necklace, maybe nothing's actually missing."

"We'll still need fingerprints."

"Okay." I frowned at him. "Just . . . don't leave, you know, that black powdery mess everywhere."

"Out," he said, pointing toward the hall.

Mac took my hand and pulled me away.

Mac and I stayed at Hennessey House until midnight, keeping Jane company while the police combed through her private suite and all her personal belongings. We started out in the communal living room downstairs, sharing a bottle of wine, and ended up in the kitchen eating ice cream. It was how all good parties progressed, except we weren't exactly in a partying mood.

I invited Jane to come home with me, but she chose to spend the night alone in one of the unoccupied suites down the hall. Eric allowed her to grab only her nightgown and toothbrush from her suite. That was it.

The following afternoon, Eric gave the okay for me to

return to Jane's rooms and help her begin putting her things back in order. When I walked into her suite, I was dismayed to see almost nothing had been put away yet. And even worse, every surface was covered in that nasty black powder residue.

Jane was in the sitting room, standing by the entry to her bedroom. She looked up when I walked in and I was shocked by how pale and vulnerable she appeared.

"Oh, honey," I murmured, and ran to give her a hug.

"Shannon." She was shaking and I wanted to kill whoever had done this to her.

Something had occurred to me when I couldn't fall asleep the night before. How had the intruder known that Jane wasn't home last evening? Had he been watching the place? Or staying there? Had he been following her?

It was too soon after the break-in to mention my thoughts to Jane, but I intended to talk to Eric and Mac about them.

Jane was able to steady her nerves enough to start putting her rooms back together. I was in charge of wiping away that damn sticky fingerprint residue off the tables and shelves. Jane was in charge of putting her books and knickknacks and clothes back in their proper places. We'd been working for almost an hour when Althea rushed in, out of breath. "I came as soon as I heard. I can't believe it. I want to help."

Jane gaped at her. "You heard about my break-in all the way down in Blue Point?"

"Yes." She tossed her bag and her sweater on the carpeted floor behind the door. "I have a number of customers from Lighthouse Cove. One of them was in this morning and told me about it." She surveyed the mess. "How awful. You poor baby. What can I do to help?"

"Nobody was hurt," Jane said, giving her a half smile. "I can't even tell if anything was taken, so I refuse to wail and gnash my teeth. We'll just clean up the mess and move forward."

Althea walked over and gave her a crushing hug. "You are impossibly brave and sweet. Not everyone would be able to go through something as awful as this and still be smiling."

"I'm faking the smile," Jane said with a shrug. "But I'm okay. I was pretty upset last night, but this morning I woke up determined to snap out of it and just do what needs to be done."

"Good," Althea said, saluting her. "Let's get to it."

It was fun having Althea around. She kept up a steady, light conversation and two hours slipped by before I noticed. The easy chatting helped Jane relax a little, too.

"Well, this doesn't look too bad."

I glanced up. Stephen Darby and his father stood in the doorway, wide-eyed, watching us work.

"Hello, Ned," Jane said, and walked across the room to give him a peck on his pale cheek. "It's so good to see you. How's Bob doing?"

"No change." He shook his head. "He's still in a coma, but they say his vital signs are good, so who knows? He could pull out of it."

"I'm going to hope and pray that he does," she said.

"I appreciate it. I already lost Jesse," he said wistfully. "If I lose Bob, I'll be one lonesome cowboy."

He really did look as though he'd lost his best friend. I said a silent prayer for Bob to wake up soon.

Eric walked into the room just then and looked around until he found Jane. "How're you doing?"

If I hadn't been looking toward the door, I would've missed Stephen's reaction when Eric strolled in obviously in charge. The man flinched visibly. Was he just caught off guard or did he have something to fear from the cops?

It seemed that Eric noticed as well. He expanded his chest and stared at Stephen for a good, long moment while Stephen pretended to be invisible.

"I'm going to be fine," Jane said, oblivious of the little drama. She stood up and gestured at me and Althea. "I have lots of great help, as you can see."

"Anything missing?" he asked, walking with Jane into the bedroom to speak privately.

I already knew the answer. Jane hadn't found anything missing. All of her important financial documents and legal papers had been placed inside her new safe-deposit box. Her jewelry had been tossed around, but nothing appeared to have been taken, thank goodness. I knew she owned some expensive pieces that her grandmother had given her.

Something occurred to me and I looked up at Ned. "Has Bob had diabetes for a long time?"

"Long as I've known him. He tests his blood and gives himself a shot every morning like clockwork." He sent Stephen a queasy look. "Not sure I could do that myself."

"You could do it if you knew it would save your life," Stephen said, rubbing his dad's arm affectionately.

Despite my wariness, Stephen was a decent son to Ned. The two got along well and Stephen appeared to be taking good care of his dad—even if he wasn't eager to live in the same house with him.

A while later, Eric walked out of the bedroom and approached Stephen. "Do you have a few minutes to talk?"

"Me?" Stephen blinked a few times, clearly agitated.

"Yeah." He pointed to the hall. "Let's go find a quiet place. I just have a few questions. We can do it here or down at headquarters."

"Uh, here is fine, but my father's waiting for me. I'm taking him to lunch."

Eric nodded at Ned. "Hello, Mr. Darby. We'll just be a couple minutes. Why don't we find you a comfortable chair until we're finished?"

"I can wait downstairs in that library room," Ned said.

"Okay. That's good, Dad," Stephen said. "I'll meet you there in a little while."

The three men left Jane's rooms, and Althea, Jane, and I gazed at each other.

"Stephen didn't look happy," Althea whispered.

I bit back a smile. "Neither did Ned. But I'm sure they have nothing to worry about. Eric is probably interviewing everyone who's staying here in case they saw or heard something last night."

She sighed. "That police chief is awfully handsome, isn't he?"

Now I did smile at her. "Oh yes."

We continued for another two hours putting Jane's rooms back in order. Tables were righted and beloved tchotchkes were placed where they'd been before. Althea eschewed the housekeeping staff and ran the vacuum cleaner herself over the area rugs and highly polished wooden floor. Pillows were fluffed and returned to the couches and chairs, books to their proper shelves, and eventually everything looked as pristine and perfect as it had before Jane's world was turned upside down.

She thanked us both and promised that lunch was going on her tab next week.

"Don't you worry about that," Althea said. "Just take care of yourself."

"I'm holding you to it," I said.

Jane laughed. "Good, because I mean it. I owe you both."

"When I get home, I'll call Palmer at the newspaper," I said. "I want to make sure everyone in town knows that the necklace is in the bank, okay? Like, put it in a headline so everybody gets it."

"Good idea," Jane said. "I don't know how anyone could've gotten the idea that it might be here."

"Whoever it is, they're not paying attention. They were still looking for it Saturday night at Jesse's house."

"Still?" Jane said. "But I had the locks changed and the police are still cruising the area, aren't they?"

"Yeah," I said. "We've got a determined intruder."

"Where is this?" Althea asked.

Uh-oh. I had forgotten she didn't know the whole story. I glanced at Jane. "Jesse's house. Somebody broke in."

"More than once," Jane added.

"We think they were looking for an expensive necklace he found a few years ago."

"Oh dear," Althea cried. "Did they break anything?"

I exchanged another look with Jane, then shrugged. Might as well share the rest of the bad news with her. "The first time they smashed a hole in the wall and generally made a horrible mess."

"That's disgusting." She pressed shaking fingers to her lips. "Oh my goodness. Poor Jesse."

"I'm sorry, Althea. I shouldn't have said anything."

"No. Don't worry about me. I'm not as fragile as all that. I'm just sorry to think of someone hounding Jesse even after his death."

"It's been pretty bad," I admitted. "And they keep getting away before we can catch them."

Jane punched her fist against her palm. "You'd think the word would've gotten out a long time ago, after we told our friends at our girls' night dinner."

"And you living right next door, Shannon." Althea gave me a worried look. "You must be scared to death."

"I have plenty of friends looking out for me."

Althea sighed. "You're very lucky to have so many friends."

"We both grew up here, so, you know, that's life in a small town."

"I grew up in a big city," Althea said. "Never thought I'd leave it. But now I love living in a small community."

"It grows on you," I said, and started itching, which made Althea giggle.

"I think our work here is done," Jane announced. "I'm so grateful to you both."

We had a sentimental group hug and then I took off to check out the Stansburys' home to see how the last segment of the roof was coming along.

That evening, Mac offered to grill steaks if I would make the salad. I hadn't had steak in a while, so of course I said yes, immediately.

We dined at my house because it was roomier and closer to the grill. Two baked potatoes were roasting in the toaster oven and the salad was made, so Robbie and

I joined him outside at the grill. While we chatted, Mac tossed a ball for Robbie, melting my heart. Of course, Robbie wasn't all that interested in the "bringing it back" part of the game, so it petered out rather quickly.

After Mac regaled me with the latest gossip in the fascinating world of New York publishing, the conversation naturally drifted back around to Jesse's murder and the subsequent break-ins and oddities that some of us had experienced.

"Whatever happened with that hotel suicide?" he wondered. "How does that fit in with Jesse's overdose?"

"You mean Jesse's murder?"

"The cops are still calling it an overdose."

"They're being ultracareful," I said, "but I know it was murder and Jane agrees. And even if he won't admit it, Eric agrees, too."

"Interesting," Mac said, sipping his wine. "And the hotel suicide?"

"Murder." I told him how all the fingerprints in the room were wiped clean. "How can that be suicide? Why would he wipe away his own fingerprints?"

"Good question."

"Because someone killed him," I said easily.

"Just like Jesse?" He flipped the two rib eyes over and I watched the meat sizzle and the fire spark. "Two homicides meant to look like suicides? That's quite a coincidence."

"I guess." I frowned. "I was suspicious of Andrew when he was hanging around Jane, but I can't really see a tie-in with the two deaths, can you?"

"If I were writing this as a book, there would absolutely be a tie-in. I try to avoid writing actual coincidences. Everything's got to count for something, and each action needs to be meaningful. So let's talk it out. You've got two people dead within a few weeks of each other. Both of them supposedly committed suicide. In one small town. What's the connection? Because there's got to be one."

"Okay. Jesse died of an apparent overdose, Andrew of

an apparent suicide by some kind of drug administered by syringe. Oh, and there's Bob. Not that it's connected, but he slipped into a diabetic coma yesterday."

"Bob? Jesse's friend? He's in a coma?"

"Yeah."

"Wow." Mac scratched his head. "Well, there's your third suspicious event. That can't be a coincidence. And look at the similarities. Nobody was killed in a truly brutal or 'in your face' manner," he said. "No gunshots, no strangulations. They're all nuanced attacks."

"Nuanced," I said, liking the word.

"Subtle," he added. "Their deaths could skim under the wire, be accepted as accidental. And the killer could get away with murder."

"Until you put them all together in one small town in the span of a few weeks," I said, getting angrier. "And then it's not nuanced at all."

"No. It's bold."

"It's 'in your face.'"

"Yeah." He sipped his wine. "I wouldn't actually write something like that, because it becomes obvious to the reader. The killer isn't necessarily obvious, of course, but the crimes are beginning to stack up. And still, it could just be a coincidence."

"But you don't honestly think so," I said.

"Nope, given the fact that there's somebody digging through Jesse's house and trashing Jane's hotel rooms, that pretty much adds up to *foul play* in my book."

"That's what I told Eric," I cried. "But he insists on following the rules, checking all the evidence, waiting for reports, blah, blah, blah. It's so annoying."

"I feel your pain. Why aren't you on his must-call list when he gets those reports in?"

"I don't know," I said, laughing. "Doesn't he know how important I am?"

Mac grinned. "You know, I've been given full access to those reports. I drive along with the cops to check out crime scenes and domestic disputes. I'm allowed to sit in on interrogations and interview the guys who're in jail.

But I still have a hard time getting any real information out of Eric."

"He's disgustingly circumspect." I stared up at the dusky sky with its ribbons of coral and pink streaming wildly across the dark blue, the last remnants of sunset fading slowly into nighttime. "I guess it didn't help that he and I started out on the wrong foot, so to speak."

"How so?"

"Remember when you first moved here and there was a rash of attacks? And I found the body of that guy I'd threatened to, well, kill?"

"Of course I remember."

"It didn't look good. And Eric was new in town and he didn't know me, so he automatically assumed . . ." I shrugged.

"That you were a cold-blooded killer." He laughed wryly. "Yeah, that's how I read you, Irish."

"I don't blame him, and we did become friends. But now there's another murder and I feel like I have to tip-toe around him to get any information."

"And that's where Tommy comes in."

"How'd you know . . . ?" Why did I bother to ask? Mac seemed to see all, know all. "Tommy's an old friend."

"That's what I hear."

"People in small towns have big mouths," I grumbled.

He laughed. "Bless their hearts."

Chapter Fourteen

Mac pulled the steaks off the grill and we went inside. He opened a bottle of wine while I took two steaming-hot baked potatoes out of the oven and gave the salad one more toss. We sat down at the dining table and he poured wine into our glasses. Robbie toed the line he wasn't allowed to cross, but let out a few soft whines in the back of his throat.

Mac lifted his glass. "Here's to small towns."

I smiled, tipped my glass against his, and drank. As I cut into my perfectly grilled steak, I said, "If you were writing a story based on everything that's happened since Jesse died, how would you approach it?"

His forehead furrowed as he thought about it. "Mainly, I would find a way to fit all these disparate elements together. They might not seem related, but they are. So what links these three people together?"

"You mean Andrew and Jesse and Bob, right? Are you sure Bob belongs?"

"Sure, he fell into a coma from some mistake with his insulin."

"True enough."

"Once in a while I might make a character like Bob a red herring. But for the purposes of my book, let's say they're all legitimately connected. Great salad, by the way."

"Thank you."

"So now we ask ourselves some questions."

"Okay."

He took a sip of wine as if priming his internal pump. "We've got our three victims. What do we know about them?"

We talked back and forth and laid out every detail that might be relevant, starting with Jesse, the most familiar victim to me, then Andrew, and finally Bob.

"So you found out about Andrew's death from one of the guys on your crew?"

"Right. My guy Douglas has a brother, Phil, who works at the Inn on Main Street and was in Andrew's room a few times."

"And he thinks the dead guy was having an affair? Why?"

I thought back to the conversation with Douglas. "Phil smelled a woman's perfume in the room a few times."

"Did he see the woman enter the hotel room?"

"I don't know. Douglas didn't say."

Considering, Mac asked, "Do you have Douglas's phone number?"

"Of course, but I shouldn't call now." I checked the clock on the kitchen wall. "It's almost seven thirty."

Mac gave me a cockeyed look.

"I mean, I'm his boss and it's nighttime. He won't love hearing from me."

"We need information. It's important."

"What if he doesn't answer?"

He raised one eyebrow. "He'll answer a call from his boss."

"True." I grabbed my phone and placed the call. When Douglas answered, I pressed the speaker button and set the phone on the table between me and Mac.

"Hey, boss. What's up?"

"Sorry to bother you, Douglas. This is unrelated to work, but I was thinking about how your brother found that dead guy."

"Right. Weird, huh?"

"Yeah. Phil said the guy was having an affair. Did he actually see a woman in his hotel room?"

Douglas chuckled. "Wow, boss. You sound like a cop."

"Yeah, sorry. I get a little carried away sometimes."

"That's cool. Phil's right here. Let me put him on the line."

"Great. Thanks."

"Hey, Shannon. How's it hanging?"

I gave Mac a blank look and he chuckled as he took a bite of potato.

"It's hanging like sunshine, Phil." Oh boy. I sounded like Mrs. Higgins. "Listen, I was wondering." I asked him about the possibility that Andrew Braxton had been having an affair.

"Oh yeah," he said. "There was definitely a woman in there."

"How do you know? Did you see her?"

"Didn't have to. I smelled her perfume."

Mac and I exchanged another look. "Perfume."

"Yeah. It was nice."

"But you never saw a woman go in the room."

"Nope, just smelled her," he said.

"Did you ask Mr. Braxton about her?"

"Nope. I just sort of gave him a wink, like, dude, you're an animal."

I rolled my eyes and Mac choked down a laugh.

It was probably stupid to ask Phil this question, but I forged ahead. "Did you recognize the scent?"

He chuckled. "Oh yeah. Sexy flowers. Nice."

Not helpful, I thought. "Okay, great. Thank you, Phil. I really appreciate your talking to me."

"No problemo," he said.

I ended the call and stared at Mac. "I worry about our youth."

"Don't. He was just being a guy."

"I worry about our guys, too."

He nodded philosophically. "You probably should."

After pouring us both more wine, Mac continued. "I'm sorry to dash cold water on Phil's story, but in my experience, the scent of perfume is best used as a red herring."

"Why is that?"

"Because while it's titillating to suggest that you could track down a killer by the scent he or she wears, it's problematic. First of all, a killer would have to be stupid to wear any sort of cologne while stalking his victim because scent is one of the strongest memory triggers. And we don't want our villain to be stupid. At least not in the books we read. In real life, definitely."

"I see what you mean," I said. "In real life, I would appreciate a dumber villain."

"Right. Another problem with scent is that you can't pinpoint it. One of the housekeepers might've been wearing perfume that day. Or she could've used an orange blossom dust spray on the tables. Or it could've been another woman walking down the hall and Phil thought he smelled it inside the room. It's all too inconclusive."

"Don't tell Douglas, but I'm hesitant to trust too much of Phil's story."

"Me, too." He grabbed a bite of salad before continuing. "Okay, we've got our victims lined up. So, who are our suspects? What are their motives? How does everything play out on our timeline?"

I shrugged shyly. "I made a list of suspects."

"You rock." He beamed at me like the proud father of a four-year-old. "Let's see it. We'll play the Scooby-Doo game."

"The what?"

"The Scooby-Doo game."

I found the list in the junk drawer—which was right where it belonged, given that two of the people on my list were now either dead or in a coma—and handed it to Mac.

"*Scooby-Doo,* the cartoon show?" I said. "I watched it a few times when I was a kid."

"I watched it constantly," Mac said with boyish excitement. "At some point in every show, Scooby and the gang gather around and analyze who might've done the crime and why, how they covered it up, and how the gang's going to get them to confess. Basically, they brainstorm."

"But . . . Scooby-Doo was a dog, right?"

"It's a cartoon, so anything can happen," he said.

"So the dog solves crimes."

"You need to let go of those prejudices."

I smiled. "Right. Sorry. So, where do we start?"

He waved the list. "See, you were already in Scooby mode a while ago."

"I just never knew what that was called."

He grinned. "Jargon matters."

"I see that now." I glanced at Robbie, who was inching forward on his belly. I made a tsk-tsk noise with my tongue, and without missing a beat, he backed up right to the dining room door.

"Okay, let's start at the top with Jane," Mac said.

"But Jane's not on my list."

"I know. But you need some practice until you get the hang of it. And besides, you need to establish a firm alibi for Jane." He swirled his wine and took a sip. "So, ask yourself, how did Jane kill Jesse? And why? What did she have to gain?"

"It's a little creepy to practice on Jane, but here goes." I took a moment. "Okay, because she wanted his money. His house. She was tired of his nagging."

"Did he nag her? Really?"

"No, but we're just practicing, right?"

"Yeah, but let's try to keep it realistic."

"Well, realistically, Jane wouldn't kill Jesse. But okay. Jesse got a little cranky sometimes."

"So she killed him?"

I thought about it for a minute, pictured poor Jesse sprawled on the couch in his boxers. And took a deep breath as another possibility occurred to me. "Jesse was dying of some horrible disease and didn't want to draw it out until he was too sick to get out of bed. But he didn't have the nerve to do it himself, so he asked Jane to put some sleeping pills in his beer or something. She did it to relieve him of the misery of a prolonged death."

"That's good," he said. "That's really good. A mercy killing. She'll still go to jail, but that was a real good motive." He patted his heart. "I'm so proud of you."

I laughed. "You're nuts. Besides, if that really happened, Jesse would've told her where to find the necklace before he died."

"True." Mac scowled. "Damn. That's where it's weak. But let's keep going because you're on a roll. What did she have to gain?"

"His house? His money?"

"Also kind of weak since Jane already has a huge house and it looks like she's got some money."

"Her grandmother left her some cash along with that gigantic house, which she turned into a beautiful bed-and-breakfast. And she's going to be very successful."

"Good. But she could still be after his money because some people just want more. But I'd say Jane is slipping down the suspect list."

"Good. I didn't put her on there in the first place."

He cut into his steak and took a bite. "Who's next?"

"Let's do Stephen now."

"You don't like him," he said, grinning.

"I guess it shows. I don't like how he moved in on Jane. He grabbed a room at the B-and-B and now it looks like he'll never leave. It's a little disturbing."

"Maybe he likes her."

"I wouldn't blame him. She's fabulous, but still, it's a little hinky. Jane's not too happy about it."

I related what Lizzie had heard from Ned. Namely, that Stephen had insisted on getting a tour of Jesse's house, until Jesse finally blew up over it.

"Ah, so Stephen was showing a little too much interest in the old man's property."

"Yeah. Don't you think that's weird? Or at least coincidental? Something doesn't feel right about him."

"Okay, yeah," Mac said, fiddling with his fork. "Let's go with that feeling. Why did he kill Jesse?"

"He heard about the necklace and thought he'd try to steal it. He needs money. His financial career failed miserably. When he tried to check into Hennessey House, his credit card was rejected."

Mac grimaced. "Can't hold that against anyone."

"Normally I wouldn't, but he was a financial adviser. You'd think he'd know which of his credit cards worked."

"Good point." He bit into a piece of steak. "How'd he kill him?"

"We already know how Jesse died, so we just have to figure out how Stephen got into the house and got him to swallow the sleeping pills."

"What's your best guess?"

I chewed on some lettuce while I thought about it. "I say he used his father to gain access. He came over to tell Jesse that Ned was sick and he was worried about him. Stephen tells him he just needs someone to talk to. Jesse invites him in for a beer and they get to talking. Stephen slips the drugs into Jesse's drink, and when he falls asleep, Stephen starts the search for the necklace."

"Sounds reasonable."

"And that same scenario can be played out with any other name on the list."

"Except Althea," Mac said.

I frowned. "Right. She had more access to Jesse than anyone else. So there's opportunity."

"Good one, grasshopper. Means, motive, opportunity. The holy trinity of homicide. So, tell me about her motive. Why'd she want him dead?"

"Because she wanted . . ." I was stumped. "What did she want? She wouldn't get his house or his money if he died. I guess if she somehow heard about the necklace, she might want it."

"Of course she would want it."

"But the letter we found with the necklace explained that if Jesse died, it would go to Jane. But maybe in a moment of weakness Jesse mentioned the necklace to Althea and she started lobbying to get it."

"Lobbying." Mac nodded approvingly.

"You know, dressing seductively and . . . oh, you know."

"Yeah, I know."

"And that's what Cuckoo was thinking, too. Now that Althea was in Jesse's life, the necklace would go to her—unless Cuckoo made his move."

"Okay, that's good for Cuckoo. But let's go back to Althea."

"Okay." I tried to think. "Why else would a woman kill a man?"

"Lousy in bed?"

I waved my hands in front of my face. "Noooo, Jesse was like my uncle. Don't paint that picture for me."

Mac's blue eyes twinkled with laughter as he took another sip of wine.

"It's really not funny."

"Of course not. Sorry." But he was still grinning.

I shook my head a few more times until the image of Jesse and Althea was tamped down, but I knew it would always be there, waiting for the right moment to appear again. "Here's the other issue about Althea. I never saw her before in my life until the funeral. Did you?"

"No. But I haven't been around that long."

"I lived next door to the man and I never saw her. She told us that Jesse preferred to travel to Blue Point to see her, rather than bring her to Lighthouse Cove. I wonder if she's even been inside Jesse's house."

"Good question."

"Don't you think someone would've seen her at some point?"

"Maybe somebody did."

"I know Bob and Ned met her a few times, but otherwise nobody in Lighthouse Cove ever saw her."

"How do you know?"

"Because if someone in this town ever got a good look at Jesse's girlfriend, it would've been front-page news within minutes."

"You're right about that," he said, smiling.

I thought about Althea for a minute. "And since the funeral, I see her all the time. So if she wanted Jesse dead and got her wish, why's she hanging around now?"

"Because of the necklace."

"Bingo."

He took another bite of steak before continuing. "Okay, let's move on. Bob is in a coma, so we'll give him a pass. But there's Ned, Stephen's father."

"Oh, but he's so nice."

"For a killer," Mac said, sticking to the program. "What's his motive?"

"The necklace. He was there when Jesse found it, right?" I gasped as something occurred to me. "What if Ned was the one who found it and Jesse stole it?"

"Scooby, that's brilliant."

"Ruh-roh."

He grinned. "You're getting the hang of this."

"I really am," I said, tickled that I'd remembered the big dog's signature phrase. "Okay, there's one problem. When I asked Ned about the necklace, he swore he'd never seen it before."

"He was lying," Mac said, adding, "For this scenario only."

"Okay. And Stephen plays a key role because he wants to help his dad recover what was rightfully his."

"Exactly."

"There are a few sticky wickets, though," I said, repeating an old expression my dad liked to use. "Jesse wouldn't have bragged about it to all those people if he'd stolen it, would he?"

"Probably not, so that might be an issue. On the other hand, you wondered why he was willing to sell it to one of those pawnshops for less than it was worth. There's your answer."

"Right. If he stole it, he would want to get rid of it quickly."

"Exactly. He couldn't afford to hold out for top dollar."

I grabbed my wineglass and took a quick sip. "Sadly,

this scenario is worthless because Jesse didn't sell the necklace. But wow, if he did, then good old Ned would've zipped to number one on my suspect list."

"See? Fun, right?"

"Very fun. Except for the grisly murder-suicide aspect of the thing."

"Yeah, but since we're on the side of truth and justice, it's okay to enjoy the process."

Staring at my suspect list later that night while waiting for Robbie to finish his business outside, I realized that Mac and I hadn't applied the Scooby process to Cuckoo Clemens or any of the other shop owners who'd admitted seeing Jesse's necklace. Of course, except for Cuckoo, I really didn't suspect anyone in that group.

It had been a long day and dinner was fun. Mac had stayed awhile longer because I offered him three different choices of dessert. I had all of them in my freezer because Jane had begged me to take home a bunch of the desserts left over from her open house party.

Once Mac left, I was so tired and full—thanks to the chocolate mousse cake I gobbled up for dessert—I barely made it up the stairs before falling facedown on my bed. Tiger gave my back a nice little massage before curling up on top of me and we both went right to sleep.

The next day I revisited my suspect list and wondered why I should've excluded those shopkeepers. They'd each seen the necklace and could be just as guilty as the next guy.

I also had come up with a great new way to gauge my suspects' guilt.

I found Mac in my garage, researching something for his next book that involved two of my torque wrenches. I just hoped it didn't have anything to do with torturing somebody.

I gave him an hour to work out his torquing issues and then tracked him down for some advice.

"I made this groovy chart," I said, showing him the

spreadsheet. "It lists all of the shop owners and their addresses and the distance each would have to travel to get to and from Jesse's place."

"Aren't you clever?" he said, straining to unscrew a bolt using the smaller torque wrench I'd given him.

"I have a socket wrench," I said, wondering if he'd appreciate me showing him how to do it.

"I know, but I'm trying to make this work with the torque wrench."

"You might want to use the bigger one, then."

"Nope," he said through clenched teeth. "Need to make this work."

"Okay, then. Anyway, I had this plan to sneak into the suspects' cars and check their mileage, but that wouldn't do any good because I don't have anything to compare it to."

He stared at me for a long moment, then set the wrench aside. "Unless the person who snuck into Jesse's house happened to take his car into the shop within the last two weeks or so. Then you might be able to get the earlier mileage from his mechanic and see if the mileage jumped more than usual."

"Right," I said, so loving how he got the way my mind worked. "Because of the extra miles he'd have to travel up here all those nights of the break-ins."

"It's worth a shot."

I thought of the logistics. Getting inside their cars. Checking out their mechanics. And even if I found someone with tons of extra mileage on their odometer, it would be inconclusive at best. "You're being kind. I'm grasping at straws."

"It gets complicated," he said sympathetically.

"I know. I should go pound nails."

"Don't take it so hard," he said.

"No, I really have to go pound nails. We're framing a house over on Chambord Street."

He grinned and grabbed me in a warm hug. "I love it when you talk construction."

*   *   *

Three hours later, Mac hunted me down at my construction site. He'd never done that before, so I figured it must be important.

"Guess what," he said, when I climbed down from the ladder.

"I have no idea."

"Then I'll tell you. Come over here." He walked me over to his big SUV and we climbed inside for privacy.

"Okay, what is it?"

"You know how I have access to police files and information."

"Yes, because the mayor loves you."

"Exactly." He grinned as he shifted in his seat to face me. "So listen. There are traffic cameras out on Highway 101."

"Oh yeah." I shook my head. "Everyone whines about those."

"They take pictures of cars and license plates."

"I know. Some people consider that an invasion of privacy."

"Listen to me," he said softly. "The state of California photographs every car and license plate that passes under those cameras along with the day of the week and the time of day. It's all recorded."

"I know," I said patiently, "and that's why—" I gasped. "Oh my God! They photograph the cars at the Lighthouse Cove turnoff."

"I know," he said, imitating me.

"We might be able to track down the shop owners and see if they came to town on the same days as the break-ins happened." I jumped across the console and kissed him soundly on the lips. "You're a genius! That's brilliant!"

I moved back to my seat, but he yanked me over to his side. "I'm a genius, remember?"

His kiss lasted longer and I had to admit it was much more satisfying than my first exuberant smack on the lips.

It was a few minutes later that he told me he'd requested and received a dozen grainy photos of cars belonging to Stephen and Ned Darby, Bob Madderly, and two of the shop owners I'd told him about. He'd put in a request for information on Althea, too, but her car didn't show up in any photographs.

That evening when I got home from work, Mac brought copies of the traffic photos over to my place. I ordered a pizza and we went through them together. We were able to see the comings and goings of those four people over the last month. Each photo was time-stamped. On the surface, there was nothing to get suspicious about.

But it was the *absence* of one person that raised my suspicions.

"Why doesn't Althea's car show up in any of the records? I know she must drive a car."

"Maybe it's registered under a different name," Mac said. "Was she married before?"

"I don't know, but I guess I could find out easily enough." I studied the other photos for another minute. "It might just be a case of her not liking to drive the freeways. Plenty of people don't."

Mac pulled out his phone, turned on the GPS navigation app, and followed it all the way to Blue Point. "Mileage-wise, Highway 1 is probably closer for her. But if she's driving at night, it's a lot more dangerous than the 101."

"True," I admitted. "But she might like the slower pace."

Highway 1 skirted the treacherous cliffs along the coast of much of Northern California. It was two narrow lanes often bordered on one side or the other by a sheer cliff that dropped hundreds of yards down to the ocean. There were hairpin turns that would cause even a professional driver some anxiety. On a clear day it could be terrifying, but it was even worse after a rainstorm when parts of the highway would tend to crumble and disappear down the cliff. One lane might be closed for miles and stay that way for months. The 101 was infinitely easier, wider, and safer, but it was a whole five miles inland. Many locals didn't bother to travel that "enormous" distance just for safety's sake.

"I'm going to go back over my calendar and double-check the dates of the break-ins. And I wonder if Jesse had a calendar that he wrote on."

"We can check."

"Should I still bother checking mileage? I was thinking if Jane could get into Stephen's car . . ."

"Good luck with that," he said.

"I'm really overcomplicating things, aren't I?" I realized that even though Jane thought Stephen was weird, she might not be willing to help me prove that her "guest" had been lying. "I'm going to let this theory go."

"Probably a good idea," he said reluctantly.

"I'm so tired," I said, realizing I'd been up since five that morning.

"Your eyes look a little red," Mac said, adding quickly, "But otherwise you're beautiful."

I laughed. "Thanks for qualifying that. No woman wants to hear how tired she looks, even if she's falling asleep at the table, which is what I'm about to do."

He, on the other hand, looked handsome and masculine and just a touch dangerous. He flashed me a wicked smile that made me want to melt, if only I weren't already dead on my feet.

"I'd better let you get some sleep," he said. "We've got that Planning Commission meeting tomorrow morning. Should be all kinds of fun."

"Oh, you don't know the half of it."

He chuckled and stood to leave, but paused to rub my shoulders.

"Please don't stop," I whispered, relaxing in my chair. He had strong arms, as I'd learned the first time we ever met, months ago when he picked me up and carried me to his car. My hero.

"You've got muscles, Irish."

"Some days they take a beating."

He leaned in and gave me a soft, sensual kiss on my

neck that sent a thousand tingles zipping through my system. Then he left. I had to admit I was getting tired of seeing him leave. I could acknowledge that much, even if I wasn't sure what my next move should be.

Robbie and Tiger circled my feet, reminding me that it was time for their evening treat. I spent a few minutes petting them. When Robbie rolled over for a belly rub, Tiger licked his face. Our happy little family.

As I washed my face and got ready for bed, I thought about what we'd discovered with the traffic photos. Not much, really. But I actually felt relieved that Althea's car hadn't been in any of them. I'd grown fond of the older woman and I knew Jane had, too. Althea seemed to genuinely care for Jane and I hoped her feelings extended to me, too—if only to get me a discount at her fabulous shop in Blue Point. But seriously, I was glad to know that Althea wasn't the one sneaking into town to kill Jesse and search his home. So who was?

Despite that question burning a hole in my brain, I climbed into bed and attempted to get some sleep.

Mac met me in the driveway the next morning and we walked to City Hall to attend the Planning Commission meeting.

What I'd hoped would take fifteen minutes to rubber-stamp took over two hours of wrangling and protesting before I was even allowed to speak on Mac's behalf. There was even one old guy carrying a sign protesting the destruction of the lighthouse.

I assured Teddy Peters, who was head of the Commission, and the other Commission members that we had no plans to change the facade of either the mansion or the lighthouse itself. "May I remind you all that the town allowed MacKintyre Sullivan to buy our lighthouse mansion because we knew he recognized it as a treasured landmark and would treat it with the proper respect? Let's not forget that Mr. Sullivan is a world-renowned author and a very important new member of our community. It would behoove us to do what we can to create a welcoming environment for him. It might attract more of his ilk to the area."

Mac reached out and pinched me at that point, probably for referring to his "ilk." I continued my impassioned speech and maybe I did gush a bit much.

When I finally sat down, Aldous Murch stood up and I had to suppress a groan.

"He might be famous," Aldous said, "but that don't give him the right to desecrate our sacred landmarks."

"I object," I said loudly.

"This isn't a court of law, Shannon," Teddy said mildly. "Let Aldous make his points and then we'll figure out where to go from there."

I let Aldous talk. In the end, he helped Mac's case by being so overly freaked out about any little improvement to the lighthouse mansion that the rest of the Commission members finally had to tell him to sit down.

My blueprints were approved and my applications were stamped and recorded.

Outside on the steps of City Hall, I gave a loud whoop of joy. "We did it!"

"You did it, Irish," he said, and grabbed me in a quick hug. "Thank you, from me and others of my ilk."

I laughed with him. "You're welcome. Thank goodness that's over."

On the walk home, we saw Eric heading toward us. All business, he held up his hand to stop us.

"Glad I ran into you two," he said. "Mind coming down to the station to talk?"

"I didn't do it," I said immediately.

Eric grinned. "Didn't do what, Shannon?"

"Anything. I swear."

Mac was chuckling and Eric's grin broadened. "I just want to show you both something."

I really liked Thor—aka Police Chief Eric Jensen—a lot. I mean, the guy was handsome and smart and had a great sense of humor—when he wasn't trying to arrest me. But anytime he flashed me that ultrafocused police chief look of his, I immediately wondered if I should call my lawyer.

"No problem," Mac said. "We'll walk with you." He obviously didn't suffer from the same guilty conscience I did.

"You go on ahead." Eric gestured toward the post office. "I've gotta buy some stamps. I'll only be a few minutes behind you."

"Okay, see you there."

As we headed toward the police station three blocks over, I fretted.

"What's wrong?" Mac said.

"Why does he want to talk to us?"

"I have no idea, but I wouldn't worry about it."

"He's the police chief and he didn't look happy. I worry."

"I'm right here. I won't let him arrest you." Mac wrapped his hand around mine and held it all the way to the station. It helped.

Five minutes later, Eric arrived and ushered us into his office. Once we were seated, he pulled a file off a small stack at the side of his desk, opened it, and turned it around so we could see what was inside. There were a number of dull color photographs that had been copied onto shiny paper.

"They're awfully grainy," I said. "Can you tell what they are?"

Mac grabbed one of the sheets to examine it more closely. "It's us."

"What?" I said, frowning as I tried to make out the two objects in the frame. The photograph had been taken inside at night with almost no lighting and no flash.

"It's you and me, inside Jesse's house." Mac looked at Eric. "Where'd you get these?"

He pressed his lips together, his tension palpable. "They were in Andrew Braxton's smart phone."

"What?" I was repeating myself, but I couldn't help it. "That's crazy." I grabbed the photo again and stared at it long and hard. Finally I looked up and saw Mac and Eric watching me closely. "I recognize the sweatshirt I'm wearing. This was taken a few weeks ago, the first time we went inside the house."

Mac's eyes narrowed. "That was the night I snuck up and scared you."

"Right," I said. "So Andrew Braxton was hiding inside Jesse's house almost two weeks before he ever showed up to check into Jane's hotel."

Chapter Fifteen

After leaving the police station, I decided to clear my head by taking an afternoon run along the beach. I got home and called both of my foremen to make sure the work on all our sites was going smoothly. It was, thank goodness, so I told them I'd see them tomorrow and changed into my sweatpants, long-sleeved T-shirt, and running shoes.

I locked up the house and jogged out to the sidewalk.

"Yoo-hoo! Shannon, dear," Mrs. Higgins cried from where she knelt next to a rosebush in her garden across the street.

I gave one brief thought to building myself an escape tunnel from my house so I could come and go without being hailed by neighbors. But that wasn't fair. Mrs. Higgins was a sweet lady. I was just feeling ragged and befuddled from seeing those creepy pictures of me and Mac inside Jesse's house. I still couldn't believe that Andrew Braxton had been hiding in the closet, snapping photographs. Why? We would probably never know. Had he killed Jesse? I doubted it, seeing as how he ended up dead himself.

Besides the shots of Mac and me inside Jesse's house, there were two photos of Jane taken at Jesse's memorial service a few days before that. I didn't remember seeing Andrew there. Had he been wearing a disguise? I had no idea what it all meant. Who was he? And why was he dead?

"Hi, Mrs. Higgins," I said, snapping out of my twisted reverie. "Your roses look beautiful."

"Don't they? They make me so happy." She pulled off her gardening gloves and stood. "I'm glad I caught you. I want to show you something. Come with me."

I followed her to the backyard, where her gargantuan fountain was madly humming and spewing water.

"See?" She pointed to the water at the base of the fountain where a small yellow plastic boat bobbed along the surface. "I decided the birds might enjoy a bath toy, so I bought this little boat for them."

"Isn't that fun?" I murmured.

"I think so. The birds love it."

I stared at the plastic boat being pelted with water spurting from the dolphin's mouth. If I were a bird and saw this colossal jumble of water-spitting statuary, I might fly in the opposite direction. But that was just me.

She tugged at my sleeve. "The little boat reminded me of something you asked me a while ago."

I smiled patiently. "And what was that?"

"About Jesse, remember? I told you he was in a good mood. And I just remembered why." She tugged a little harder. "He told me why he was so happy."

I gently peeled her hand away from my sleeve. "What did he say?"

"He said . . ." She moved closer and whispered, "He finally met a woman who loved the same thing he did."

I almost sighed out loud, it was such a bittersweet sentiment. Poor Jesse, I thought. And poor Althea, too.

"Boats!" she cried. Without warning, she yanked the yellow plastic boat out of the water and shook it in front of my face to make her point. "They like boats! I never knew Jesse liked boats. Did you?" She thought about that. "But wait. He was in the navy, so it makes sense."

"It sure does." I smiled as I wiped droplets of water off my face.

"Boats," she muttered, tossing the child's bath toy back into the water. "Did Jesse leave on a boat?"

She looked up at me then, and appeared a little lost. I wasn't sure if she'd forgotten her train of thought or if she was missing her old pal. Either way, it was a little heartbreaking.

"Thanks for that information. I really appreciate it." I patted her shoulder gently. "Let's go around and see your rose garden, Mrs. Higgins."

She grabbed hold of my arm for support and we walked slowly back to her front yard. We talked about the roses for another two or three minutes, and then I left her there and headed for the beach a block away down Main Street.

I crossed the wide expanse of sand and when I reached the water's edge, I turned south. The wet, hard-packed sand provided good support and I began to jog, dodging the puddles of water and remnants of waves that made it onto shore and into my path.

I breathed deeply as I increased my pace. I loved this place. The town, the beach, the water, the air. My friends. I couldn't imagine a better place to grow up than one block away from the beach at Lighthouse Cove. I'd spent my summers lying in the sun, dodging the waves, and swimming out to the old buoy that used to mark the boundary between safety and the murky depths of the outer bay.

Over the years, the pier and boardwalk had grown more upscale with chic restaurants and fashionable shops. But the old arcade continued to cater to kids and teens, and there was still a designated fishing rail at the end of the pier for a die-hard fisherman to catch a meal or two.

I slowed down when I reached the Lighthouse Cove Marina at the opposite end of the strand from the pier. Speedboats, sailboats, and power cruisers bobbed on the water, reminding me of the tiny yellow boat in Mrs. Higgins's fountain. And that reminded me of her words a few minutes ago. I thought of how happy Jesse must've been to finally find a woman who shared his enjoyment of boats—at least according to Mrs. Higgins. I assumed she knew what she was talking about in that moment, even though she occasionally dipped into sad little bouts of dementia.

Recently my father had told me that he'd talked to Mrs. Higgins's daughter, who was thinking of selling Mrs. Higgins's house and moving the older woman in with her and her husband. I wasn't sure what Mrs. Higgins would do without her rose garden and her behemoth bird fountain, but I supposed it would be good for my neighbor to live with someone who cared for her.

But it was still a little depressing. I picked up speed and concentrated on my breathing instead of on the sad fact that some of the people I'd known my whole life were growing old and would be moving away or dying— if they hadn't already. I was a pretty upbeat person most of the time, but once in a while, I could get bogged down by the unfairness of it all. Like now, when death was all around me. I hated that feeling. So I ran faster and focused instead on the sound of my feet hitting the damp sand, the feel of the briny breeze brushing across my face, the echoing of a halyard wire pinging against a sailboat mast in the marina nearby.

Boats.

And just like that, I was back where I'd started with Jesse and Althea and the thought of what might have been. If only.

I remembered that Jesse had owned a small powerboat ten or fifteen years ago and my dad and some of the other guys used to go fishing with him once in a while. But he sold it eventually and I wasn't sure why. With a sigh, I wondered if he might've considered buying a new boat after he met Althea. Or maybe she owned her own. I would have to remember to ask her.

Or did Jesse have a boat that I didn't know about? I made a mental note to ask Jane.

I slowed down and finally came to a stop. I rubbed my stomach and realized I was getting hungry. I had leftover pizza at home and couldn't wait to bite into it. That would teach me to go running on a completely empty stomach.

After a few minutes of stretching to cool down, I didn't have the energy to retrace my steps along the shore and all the way back to Main Street. Instead I took my old shortcut, going east two blocks to my street and then a quick three and a half blocks back to my house.

While I was showering, my thoughts were a jumbled mix, from Mrs. Higgins and fountains and boats, to Jesse and Althea and shortcuts and pizza. There was always pizza.

And traffic cameras, suspect lists, and stealthy photographs taken in the dark. Why couldn't the mystery of Jesse's death come together like a neatly arranged jigsaw puzzle? There weren't that many puzzle pieces: a priceless necklace, two suspicious drug overdoses, an enigmatic visitor who'd committed suicide—according to the police—and who actually might've been hiding here in Lighthouse Cove all along.

I poured myself a glass of wine and ate my leftover pizza dinner with only Robbie and Tiger for company. They took advantage of my melancholy by rubbing up against my calves, earning bits of cheese as a reward for their sympathy. I studied my suspect list spreadsheet and wondered again why Althea's comings and goings from Lighthouse Cove weren't recorded by any of the traffic cameras.

I'd forgotten to check whether she'd been married before or if her car was registered under a different name. I realized it was possible that she'd borrowed someone else's car. And if that was the case, then it was also possible that Stephen or Ned or any of the other suspects might've done the same thing. Anyone could've borrowed a car to get here.

I started a list of all the issues I needed to revisit. Borrowed cars. Different names. And where in the world had Andrew Braxton been hiding before he officially checked into the Inn on Main Street? Who was he?

I cleared my plate from the dining table and took it to the sink. Gazing out the kitchen window, I saw Mac's door open. My heart fluttered foolishly and I was about to run outside to say hello when a tall, stunning woman backed out of his doorway. Her arms were wrapped around Mac's neck and she was kissing the living daylights out of him. She was supermodel thin yet sexy, with long, wavy blond hair tumbling down her back.

I couldn't help it. I cracked the window open to hear their conversation.

Mac detached her arms from his neck. "Good night, Vivi."

"But—"

"Go now."

"I want to stay."

"I have to work."

She rubbed against him. "Sure I can't convince you?"

He chuckled. "Go."

She giggled and jogged away, clambering down the stairs and disappearing from sight.

It was stupid to feel this shattered. I'd known all along that Mac Sullivan had dated supermodels and sports figures and anchorwomen. His name had been linked to dozens of those ultrafabulous types.

I didn't know what to do with myself, so I took a few deep breaths, pointedly ignored the ache in my chest, and went back to work. In my office, I got my laptop and brought it out to the dining room table to give myself more space. I wanted to check the online version of our town newspaper to see if Palmer had obtained more information on Andrew Braxton. The fact that a stranger had been spying on Mac and me inside Jesse's house that night was deeply disturbing. The fact that he'd been murdered was even worse, but why? Had he been caught photographing someone who made him pay the ultimate price?

I scrolled down the search results for Andrew Braxton and decided to read his hometown obituary first. He was raised in Long Beach, California, outside Los Angeles. He attributed his success in life to his father, who was his hero growing up. They quoted a few lines from Andrew's touching eulogy at his father's funeral. I wanted to read more, so I clicked the link to Andrew's father, Harold Braxton, to see if I could learn more about him and his family.

An hour later, I rubbed my computer-weary eyes. I'd fallen down a Google-created rabbit hole, following one link after another, and another, but eventually I unearthed some chilling results.

It turned out that Harold Braxton had been a respected physician who patented a lifesaving product and made a ton of money. His wife, Joan, died when his boys were young and he remained a widower for almost twenty years until he met and married "the woman of my dreams," as one source quoted him saying.

That woman's name was Althea Mulligan.

"Wait. No." I shoved my chair back from the table to catch my breath. "Hold on a minute." I began to pace back and forth across the dining room. I needed to figure this out.

Andrew Braxton's father, Harold, had married a woman named Althea. Did that mean that our Althea was Andrew Braxton's stepmother?

I knew there were other women named Althea out there in the world, but this had to be the same Althea who'd been dating Jesse. I'd stopped believing in coincidences halfway through playing the Scooby-Doo game with Mac.

"Wow." I shook my head and sat down again. And wondered. Had Andrew Braxton killed Jesse because the old guy had been dating his stepmother? He'd somehow gained access to Jesse's house and had been spying on me and Mac and Jane and God only knew who else all this time. Why? Had Althea told him about the necklace? Or was he jealous of any other man making a life with Althea other than his own father?

Despite my burning eyeballs, I spent another hour searching more names and checking more backgrounds.

When I was finally ready to shut down my laptop, I had to ask myself whether the police knew any of this. Because if they did, there might have been an arrest made days ago and maybe a life could've been saved.

It was almost midnight. All the lights were off in Mac's upstairs apartment—not that I would disturb him. Not after seeing him with Vivi. He'd told her he had to work, but maybe he'd been too tired. Maybe she'd worn him out.

"Shut up," I muttered, pulling my hair back from my face. I shoved the image of Mac and Vivi away and tried to figure out what to do with the information I'd found. It was too late to call Eric. Instead I wrote all the information out in a document and sent it to his police e-mail address. I would contact him tomorrow morning, right after I checked on one more detail.

The next morning, I drove down the coast and discovered exactly what I was hoping to find. On my trip back to town, I called Eric to tell him what I'd just learned, but he wasn't answering his cell, so I left him a hurried message. I'd been afraid to mention anything earlier for fear that he would think I was so off base it was laughable. But now I was bubbling with excitement.

I called Jane and asked her to meet me at Jesse's house.

"You sound happy."

"I will be when this is over," I said. "Can you meet me at Jesse's house for a few minutes?"

"Why?" she asked. "I'd really rather not go back to Jesse's house. It's just too sad."

With infinite patience, I said, "I need to tell you something."

"I'm listening."

"I'd rather tell you in person." I tried not to grit my teeth. I wasn't about to announce who had killed her uncle on the phone. "Please, Jane. It's important. I just need a few minutes."

"All right," she said. "I'll be there in ten minutes."

*   *   *

I hadn't wanted to tell Jane who the killer was over the phone, but when she walked into Jesse's house, I realized that I didn't have to tell her a thing.

The killer was following right behind her.

My internal panic meter shot off the charts.

Maybe the killer was unaware that I knew. But then I shot Jane a wary glance and she returned it in triplicate. That was not a good thing. Now I understood why she hadn't wanted to meet me here.

Never let them see your fear, my dad always said, so I straightened my shoulders and slapped a smile on my face.

"Hello, Althea."

She nodded. "Shannon. Why don't you two ladies have a seat?"

"I'd just as soon stand," I said. "I've got to get back home to—"

"It wasn't a suggestion," she said, cutting me off. Pulling a small but deadly gun out of her jacket pocket, she waved it toward the two spindly wooden chairs facing the sofa. "Sit down."

I didn't budge, so Jane grabbed my hand and pulled me over to the chairs.

"Althea, you don't have to do this," Jane said. Her voice was shaking and I knew she was scared to death. I was, too, but I'd learned a few months ago that it was a good idea to try to keep someone talking if she was aiming a gun at you. Whatever it took to prolong the moment. I took a deep breath and plunged in.

"I've already connected some of the dots," I said conversationally, "but maybe you can fill in a few blanks for me."

"By all means," she said acerbically.

"Did you kill Andrew Braxton?"

"Ah, my devoted stepson. He lost track of me when I changed my last name and moved up north. I should've changed my first name, too, because that's how he finally found me. Through the shop."

"Why didn't you change your first name?"

"Because I love my name. It's pretty." Her bottom lip stuck out in a pout. "It was the perfect name for my shop."

I'd never seen her narcissistic side until now. It was illuminating.

"Why was he trying to find you?" Jane asked.

Althea sneered. "He had this romantic notion that I had somehow coerced his father into changing his will and leaving me all his money. And then I killed him, according to Andrew."

"Did you?"

"Harold was crazy about me," she said, her tone blasé. "And his greatest wish was for me to be happy."

"And once he was dead and you had his money," I said, "his wish came true."

"You've got a smart mouth," she said.

"Are you going to tell me you didn't have anything to do with Harold's death?"

"He had a heart attack and died, boo-hoo," she said flippantly. "I got the money and the boat and moved away. Andrew should've been happy to see the last of me, but no. He couldn't deal with not getting any of Daddy's money. He refused to let it go."

As long as she was willing to talk, I had a few more questions that had come up when I was doing my online research last night. "According to some accounts, you slowly poisoned your first husband years before you met Harold. Was that true?"

"*Moi?* Poison?" She splayed her hands and shrugged to indicate she was clueless about any such thing. "Nobody could ever prove that."

According to the old newspaper I found online, she was right. They never proved that she'd poisoned her first husband. But seeing her with a gun in her hand, I knew she'd done it. This would teach me to trust my first impressions. I'd been suspicious of her from the beginning and I should've gone with those feelings. Althea Tannis was a predatory psychopath, and now she didn't care if we knew it or not.

"Harold died five long years ago," she said easily as she walked over to the fireplace mantel and grabbed the roll of duct tape there. "I thought I was home free all this time, but eventually Andrew found me. I had no choice but to take care of him. He would've hounded me forever."

She had just confessed to killing Andrew Braxton, but frankly I was more concerned that she'd known she would find a roll of duct tape on the mantel. I exchanged a furtive glance with Jane. Had Althea placed the tape there ahead of time? Was luring us here her plan all along? I suddenly felt as though I'd played right into her hands, but that was impossible.

"So you killed him," I said, trying to keep the conversation going.

Her smile was crafty. "He had those drugs already in his briefcase. Who would've thought he was suicidal? But I guess he missed his daddy too much to go on living."

"The police already suspect it was murder," I said.

"Maybe so, but they don't suspect it was me."

"One of the hotel staff knew there was a woman in his room. It won't take the cops long to narrow down the possibilities."

She glared up at me. "That's bull."

"They smelled your perfume."

"Oh." She sniffed at her wrist. "I suppose it's a flaw of mine, but I can't help it. I do love my Valentino. Damn it, now I suppose I'll have to stop wearing it."

Althea handed the roll of duct tape to Jane. "Tear off four long pieces for me."

"No." Jane tossed the roll of duct tape across the room.

Without warning, Althea smacked her across the face. I screamed. The woman was horrible!

She retrieved the tape and handed it back to Jane. "You'd be smart to remember who's got a gun pointed at you."

Jane's jaw was tighter than I'd ever seen it. I was feeling pretty tense, too, as Jane began ripping off lengths of duct tape and handing them to Althea.

"That's better," the woman said. Slipping the gun into her jacket pocket, she circled around Jane, grabbed hold of both her arms, and yanked them backward.

Jane let out a shriek, pulled her arms away, and jumped up from the chair. "What're you doing?"

"Making sure you don't go anywhere." She yanked the gun from her pocket and shoved it in Jane's stomach. "Now sit down."

"You're sick!" Jane shouted.

"Quiet, or I'll shut you up permanently."

"You're going to anyway, so why should I care?" And Jane suddenly screamed louder than I'd ever heard her scream.

Althea smacked her face again. "I said be quiet!"

"Screw you!" Jane shouted.

Althea turned and pointed the gun right in my face. "Sit down, Jane, or I'll kill your friend right now."

I couldn't breathe. I was frozen in fear, but I'd never been more proud of Jane. I prayed that we'd both live through this and make Althea pay for every hideous thing she'd done to us. I cringed as I recalled thinking that my dad might actually like to meet Althea Tannis. I really needed to work on my taste in people.

Grudgingly Jane sat and Althea wrapped Jane's wrists together behind her chair. Then she knelt down and taped Jane's ankles to the wooden chair legs. This time, she kept the gun on the floor right beside her knee. I knew that if I tried to make a move for the gun, she would be able to grab it faster. God only knew what she would do then.

"That's a good girl," Althea crooned.

"Oh, shut up," Jane muttered.

Althea chuckled.

I wasn't sure I could speak, but I had to try to distract her from hurting Jane further.

"I figured out last night that you were coming here by boat," I said. "I went through the traffic camera reports and they'd never recorded your car coming or going from Lighthouse Cove. That's when I realized I had never seen you drive up in a car."

"Aren't you clever?" She pointed the gun at my head and handed me the duct tape. "I'm going to need more tape strips."

I had no choice but to start tearing off pieces and handing them to her.

"Now, hold still," she warned, and knelt behind me. I couldn't see her, couldn't see where the gun was, but I felt her taping my right ankle to the chair. I thought she planned to ignore my comment about driving, but then she began to talk. "When I first heard that they were installing cameras on the 101, I stopped driving that route. Besides, it's faster by boat. I pull in to the marina and—"

"It's only a short walk to Jesse's house," I finished for her. Earlier I had driven to Blue Point to speak with the harbormaster, who had verified that Althea traveled by boat almost every day. And for the past three weeks, she had taken the boat out almost every night around sunset and returned sometime before dawn.

"Right again," she muttered, clearly unhappy with me. She proved it by wrenching my left ankle painfully.

Instinctively I kicked back, hitting her hand.

"Watch it," she snarled, standing up and slapping my ear hard enough to cause my eyes to cross.

"You watch it," I snapped. It was a juvenile response, but I couldn't help it. She was a nasty bully.

Pointing the gun at me, she snarled, "Put your hands behind the chair." To help me along, she grabbed one of my arms and twisted it back.

I couldn't help but jerk my arm away from her.

"I'm going to give you one last chance to avoid having me put a bullet in your head."

I froze at her words, and she quickly wrapped the tape around my wrists. But she was agitated and in more of a hurry now, and I felt the tape give a little. If I could just squeeze one of my hands out, I could grab her gun . . .

Althea began to pace in front of us, waving the gun back and forth between me and Jane. "Andrew followed me to Jesse's house one night and confronted me. I have to hand it to the little putz. He had some nerve. He told me he couldn't prove it yet, but he knew I killed his father and he was never going to stop searching for evidence."

"So you killed him," I said.

"It would've been so perfect to kill him in Jesse's house," she said, "but in the middle of our argument, we heard someone scream outside and I ran out the back door. Andrew must've stayed inside, because I didn't see him again until he checked into the hotel."

I was the person who'd screamed, I thought in disgust. That was the night Andrew managed to snap a few pictures of Mac and me. So we had just missed Althea by seconds and it was indeed my scream that had alerted her, damn it.

"Why was he taking pictures?"

"He's always got that stupid phone. He posts photos of every little detail of his life on social media. He followed me to Jesse's house, but I got out of there before he could snap my picture. He was trying to build a case against me. And when he found out about Jesse, he figured I'd had something to do with his death. He followed me everywhere. He snuck into the memorial service and saw me talking to Jane. He checked her out and that's when he made that reservation at the B-and-B. All in hopes of gathering evidence to prove I killed Jesse. If he could prove that, then he could try to connect it to Harold's death. But he was too stupid to make it work."

"Wait a minute," Jane said. "Were you the one who canceled Andrew's reservation at Hennessey House?"

"Why, yes, that was me," she said smugly. "I was giving myself a little tour of your cozy little establishment and happened to take a peek at your guest list for the week. When I saw Andrew's name, I had to do something, so I walked outside and down the street to make the call. I told your little helper that I was a doctor in the emergency room."

"What good did it do to cancel his reservation?" Jane asked.

"It made me laugh," she said. "It felt good to screw with his plans."

She told us that she had showed up at Andrew's hotel room the first night he was there and threatened to destroy him if he harassed her anymore. He threatened to call the police and unmask her, so she left. But she came back a few days later and cajoled him into letting her come inside so they could have a heart-to-heart talk.

"He believed me. What a sap. First thing I saw was his open briefcase. When he looked away for a moment to check a text message he'd received on that damn phone of his, I grabbed a syringe and shoved it into his neck."

She didn't even know what was in it, she said, but she knew Andrew specialized in the latest opiates and psychotropic drugs. It did the trick. He passed out.

She checked some of the other drugs in his bag and found some strong barbiturates. She injected those as well, and within minutes, he was dead from some horrible multidrug cocktail. She left the syringe in his arm, carefully wiping it clean, then typed out the suicide note. After that, she cleaned up any surfaces she might have touched, including the keyboard, and then snuck down the back stairway and exited through the alley.

Jane and I sat in stunned silence for a moment while she strutted in front of us like some kind of conceited rooster. I wondered why she didn't simply use her gun to shoot us. Why bother with the duct tape? But in that moment I remembered what Mac had said about the deaths of Jesse and Andrew and the suspicious coma that Bob had slipped into. They were nuanced attacks, he'd said. She didn't like guns, but apparently she would use them to get what she wanted out of her victims. So how did she plan to kill Jane and me? The question disturbed me a lot.

"Why did you kill Jesse?" I asked finally.

She stopped and considered me for a moment. "I honestly didn't mean to. He was a sweet guy. And quite accomplished in bed."

I glanced at Jane, who stared at Althea with absolute hatred. I'd never seen that look on Jane's face before, but I didn't blame her one bit. The woman belonged in hell.

But I was determined to keep her talking. "Did you really meet him in an exercise class?"

"Are you kidding?" she said, and laughed. "No, that was a good little lie. We met two years ago when he was trying to sell the necklace. He came into my shop."

"But you sell clothing."

"And vintage jewelry."

Damn it! I'd seen the jewelry in her store and hadn't even thought about connecting it to Jesse. Stupid, stupid, stupid. I'd been so suspicious of Althea from the beginning, but when I walked into her shop, I noticed the clothing. The antique jewelry was a mere sideline.

I was the worst amateur investigator on the planet.

"The minute I saw that necklace," Althea said, practically crooning now, "I knew I had to have it. But I wasn't about to give him money for it. No, in that very moment, I knew what I would have to do to get it. I used a little reverse psychology, told him not to sell it, but to give it to his wife. He told me he'd never been married and had no children, but he had a beautiful niece he could bequeath it to."

"Oh," Jane sighed, and I knew another little piece of her heart had just broken.

"What would you have done if he were married?" I wondered.

She shrugged. "I'd have had to get rid of his wife."

Of course she would. I didn't know what to say to that matter-of-fact response.

"Anyway, Jesse told me how pleased he was to receive such unselfish advice." She snickered. "He also told me how attractive he thought I was. He gave me his phone number. Shortly after that, I called him and our romance began."

"That was two years ago?" I asked.

"I had a long-range plan," she said. "We used to stay at my house, but then I started telling him I wanted to come see him in Lighthouse Cove. He was reluctant because he knew people would talk, but I told him I'd come by boat and no one would ever see me."

"That must've appealed to him."

"You know it," she said in her self-congratulatory tone. "The man loved boats. And secrets. And me." She flashed us a coy smile. "He wanted to buy a half interest in my boat, so I let him."

Jane and I exchanged a quick glance. That was why Jesse had sold off three of the jewels in the necklace. He wanted to pay Althea for his half of the boat.

She told us she began staying at his house and drugging him to sleep every night so she could search for the necklace. She laughed. "Every morning he would tell me how well he slept. But then one night, he woke up too soon. He saw me going through his drawers, so I told him a little white lie, gave him a hug and a triple dose of sleeping pills." She shrugged. "It killed him. Too bad, too. I liked him. He was a pretty simple guy with his little white boxer shorts and that salty navy language he used sometimes. He treated me right, though."

I could feel Jane seething. "You will pay for that," she said.

I didn't blame Jane for going off, but I needed Althea to stay cool and keep talking. I prayed that Eric would get my e-mail message soon and track me down here. Maybe the police were waiting outside Jesse's house right now. If only.

I needed more from her. "Once Jesse was dead, you started searching for real, right? You punched a hole in the wall and pulled up the floorboard."

"I couldn't very well do that while he was alive," she said. "And once he was gone, I knew I had a limited window of opportunity. I started with his office because he spent a lot of time in there. And the kitchen was as likely a hiding place as any. I started getting anxious because he'd been dead for hours now. I checked all the bookshelves and the medicine cabinet and I even searched the basement, but I didn't like going down there."

Good thing, I thought, but didn't mention that the basement was where I'd found the necklace.

"How did you get inside after Jane had the locks changed?"

She snorted a laugh. "It was pitifully easy to lift her keys from her purse."

Jane gasped. "You stole my keys?"

"Don't worry, princess," she crooned sarcastically. "I brought them back after I made copies."

"Why did you hurt Bob?" I asked. I was desperate to keep her talking.

"Who says I did?"

"Oh, please. His falling into a diabetic coma has *you* written all over it." Especially after playing the Scooby-Doo game with Mac, I thought.

She patted her hair, apparently taking my accusation as a compliment.

"I was charmed by Bob, despite myself," she said. "Jesse apparently boasted of our affair to Ned and Bob, and Bob began living vicariously through his stories. At Jesse's funeral, Bob introduced himself and told me that he'd already fallen in love with me."

Ugh. Poor Bob. But then, we had all been fooled by Althea's personable outer shell.

"I had hoped for a little break after Jesse died, and then Andrew suddenly showed up. I just didn't have time for Bob." She chuckled again. "I told him I was grieving, and he understood. He said that whenever I was ready, he wanted to court me. Such a sweet, old-fashioned concept."

She said it derisively and again, I felt pity for Bob.

"Unfortunately Bob became obsessed and started following me. He saw me go into Andrew's hotel room but never saw me leave." She scowled. "When he heard that someone had died in that room, he put two and two together and approached me. I seriously didn't think he had that much on the ball, but there you go."

"Did he accuse you of killing Andrew?"

She chuckled. "Yes, but he wanted to protect me. He drove all the way to Blue Point to propose marriage. I realized he'd seen too much and I had to get rid of him. I accepted his proposal and then seduced him into his bed. Then I dosed him with a few extra shots of insulin."

Her words turned my stomach, but I had to ask, "Did you buy him the silk boxers?"

She laughed gaily. "Yes. I just love the feel of natural fibers against my skin. And as long as he was going to be rubbing himself against me, I figured I might as well enjoy at least one aspect of it."

I had to look away so she wouldn't see me cringe. Once, I'd thought she was so genteel, but now she sounded like some tacky broad. I suddenly remembered that I'd bought a jacket in her store! Ugh. If we got out of here alive, I would never wear it again.

"I'll miss the old guy," she said sentimentally.

I frowned at her. "He's not dead yet."

"Not yet," she quipped. "It's too bad he doesn't have money. I'm pretty sure I could convince him to leave it all to me."

Abruptly she stopped pacing and stared hard at me. "I'm going to need your key."

I looked up at her. "I don't have a key."

"Oh, really? You don't have your house key with you? You leave the doors unlocked? Good to know."

I had my kitchen door key in my jeans pocket, but I wasn't about to tell her that. "What do you want with my house?"

"Little Miss Jane tells me the necklace is at your bank, so I want your safe-deposit key."

I snorted a laugh. "You can take the key, but the bank won't give you access to my safe-deposit box."

She didn't like being laughed at and slapped me again.

I hated her for that. If I got out of this, I was going to give her one sharp smack across her arrogant little face.

Maybe two.

"Then you'll just have to come with me to the bank," she said, waving the gun to get my attention.

But now she needed me. Maybe I had some leverage. "What're you going to do if I don't go with you? Kill me?"

"No, I'll kill her." She turned and trained the gun on Jane.

"Stop!" Crap! I hated that she was one step ahead of us. I had to fight back. "If you kill Jane, you're not getting anything from me."

"We'll see about that."

Without warning, she slapped Jane's face so hard her chair fell backward. I screamed and so did Jane, who was unable to stop the momentum as she tumbled to the floor.

"You make me sick," I shouted over the hubbub.

"Oh, cram it." She moved behind me and ripped the tape off my hands. "We're going to the bank. If you try anything, I'll make sure Jane dies."

Suddenly there was a loud pounding on the front door.

"Who the hell is that?" Althea said.

"The police?" I suggested.

"I know you're in there, Shannon Hammer!" somebody shouted from outside. "Open this door right now!"

Holy crap. I recognized that voice.

"Whitney?"

Chapter Sixteen

Jane groaned at the sound of Whitney's shrill yelling.

"Who is that?" Althea asked sharply.

"She's a . . . a woman I know."

"Get rid of her."

"Easier said than done," I muttered.

"Make it happen," Althea snapped, and slipped behind the front door, still aiming her gun right at me.

"Go away, Whitney," I yelled, hoping that for once she'd take a hint.

Much to my shock, the door burst open instead and Whitney stormed in. Interesting to know it hadn't been locked all this time.

"There you are!"

"Whitney, what are you doing?" I shouted in her face. "Get out of here!"

"Stop yelling!" She shook her finger at me. "You have pissed me off for the last time."

Did she have a death wish? Sometimes I wondered. I tried to stay calm. "I said get out—now."

"I'm not leaving until I tell you exactly what I think of you."

"How did you know I was here?"

"I drove up just as you walked into this house, so I've been parked outside waiting for you to come out. And then Jane shows up with that old lady. And you still didn't come out. What're you all doing in here?"

I almost laughed at her term for Althea, but this wasn't going to end well. I could imagine Althea growing more enraged as she waited behind the door for Whitney to leave.

"We're playing a game," I explained. It was lame, but maybe she'd buy it.

"I don't have time for games."

"Then go home," I said evenly. "I can't talk to you just now." *Please get out of here and call the police,* I thought, trying to send her a mental message. But her head was too thick.

"How dare you?" she said, fisting her hands on her hips in irritation. "You'll listen to me and like it."

Could she not see the duct tape around my ankles? Or Jane strapped to a chair and lying on the floor? The woman was so self-centered, nothing else existed but her world and her problems. But since Althea had gone ahead and unwrapped my hands a minute ago, and since Whitney was blocking Althea's view of me, I took the opportunity to cautiously reach down and remove the tape around my ankles.

"Fine," I said, as I tried to rip off the duct tape without making noise. "Say what you want, and then you can leave."

Her eyes narrowed in fury. "How dare you tell Mrs. Perry about that cheap, ugly version of her sculptural masterpiece? She's heartbroken. Why do you have to be so mean?"

"Me?" Was she for real? This was the reason she was here? "I didn't tell Mrs. Perry anything. I haven't seen her since the party."

"Who else but *you* would hurt her like that? It's what you do. It's so typical of you, to not be able to tell the difference between trash and art."

"Oh, please. You thought it was trash, too. We both lied to make her think her ugly fountain was beautiful." I sat up straight, having managed to pull off the tape while Whitney blocked my view. "Never mind. I didn't do what you think I did, so you can go ahead and leave now."

Unfortunately she was on a tear, flouncing around and blathering about my thoughtless behavior. And now Althea could see me again. I sat rigidly in the chair so the woman wouldn't realize I was free to move. She still had a gun pointed in my direction, after all.

"You ruin people's dreams," Whitney cried. "Isn't it bad enough that you've been trying to steal my husband for years?"

"Oh no." I started laughing. "You're crazy—you know that? I don't want Tommy. I couldn't steal him away from you if I tried. He's madly in love with you, heaven only knows why."

But she wasn't listening. She was leaning around to see what was on the floor. "Jane? Is that you? What're you doing down there?"

"Whitney," I whispered. "Go now."

She frowned at me. "What?"

"You're in danger."

"Will you speak up? I can't hear you."

She'd never been the sharpest arrow in the quiver, but her inability to comprehend a threat was mind-blowing.

"Get out of here!" I whispered as loudly as I could without alerting Althea.

But instead of running, Whitney stopped and sniffed the air. "Is that Valentino? I love Valentino." She lifted her snooty nose higher to breathe in Althea's flowery fragrance.

"You are ridiculous," I muttered.

"Who's wearing Valentino?" She glanced around. "Don't tell me it's you."

"Just kill her," Jane muttered, and I was ridiculously happy to know she still had her sense of humor.

Whitney heard her and gave her a puzzled look. "Jane, what's going on? Is this part of the game?"

"Shannon, get her out of here," Jane whispered.

Jane was right. I had to make a move. Without warning, I jumped up from my chair and grabbed Whitney, pulling her into the kitchen. She screamed and tried to slap my hands off her.

"No, you don't!" Althea shouted, and darted out from behind the door. She caught up with us in the kitchen and yanked a syringe from her pocket. Good grief, what else did she have in her pockets?

"Whitney, run!" I grappled with Althea, trying to avoid that needle. But now Althea had a firm hold on Whitney's arm.

"Get your hands off me!" Whitney shrieked. "Who are you?"

In one swift move, Althea managed to stab Whitney's arm.

"Ow! What're you ... uuuh ..." Whitney's eyelids fluttered closed and she crumpled to the floor.

"What was in that?" I cried, horrified to see Whitney inert. My mind flashed on Andrew Braxton, murdered by deadly injection. Had she killed Whitney?

"Relax. It's just a tranquilizer," she said, waving away my concern. "At least it shut her up. You and Jane are annoying, but that woman just about pushed me over the edge."

"What is wrong with you?" I shouted. "You're like the doctor of death with your gun and your drugs and your lies."

"I'm forced to carry a gun, but I rarely use it. I prefer a nice clean syringe." She patted her hair back into place. "I think they're more ladylike."

"You are not a lady," I said, then cringed inwardly. As if insulting her would work in my favor.

"And you're starting to get on my last nerve. As I said, I prefer needles, but I'll use a gun if I have to." She pulled her gun out again, but before she could train it on me, I grabbed the first thing from the kitchen counter I could get my hands on and swung it at her. The toaster knocked the gun out of her hand and she went scrambling for it. I leaped after her and we both fell to the floor. Luckily I landed on top of her. She struggled beneath me, stretching her arm out to reach the gun. I was at least six inches taller, so I was able to get my hand on it enough to sweep it farther away.

I might've been taller, but Althea was more ornery

and she easily bucked me off her back. As she clambered to get her footing, she smacked the side of my head so hard I felt my ears ring. I reached out and grabbed her ankle and tugged, causing her to fall to her knees. She screamed in pain.

"I hope that hurt," I said, then winced. Damn, it hurt to talk. My head ached from that blow to my temple. I couldn't wait to return the favor.

She was still on her knees as she turned and glared at me. "I'll show you a world of hurt."

I believed her. She was a mean, scary bitch, and who knew what else she had in her pockets? Another syringe? A knife? But I could see the strain in her eyes and realized that Whitney was right—she was an old lady. I almost laughed, but it would've been too painful.

"You won't hurt anyone again," I said, and shoved her in the chest as hard as I could. Her arms flailed out, but she couldn't get her balance and fell backward. She let out a guttural scream as she lay helplessly on her back with her legs bent at the knee and splayed.

I jumped up and grabbed the gun, pointing it at her. "Don't move."

At that moment, I heard shouts from the front porch as a small army of cops stormed into the house. Heavy footsteps stomped through the foyer and dispersed into the living room and down the hall.

"In here!" I shouted. "Help!"

Despite having a gun pointed at her, Althea stretched out her leg and slammed her foot against my shin, causing my knee to buckle. I slid down and leaned against the kitchen cabinet, my leg throbbing.

"What is wrong with you? I've got a gun!" I didn't know if she was brave or just stupid, but she was definitely lucky I didn't shoot her.

"I need help in here!" I yelled again.

Tommy dashed into the kitchen and his alert gaze went straight to Whitney lying motionless on the floor.

"What's happened to her?" he demanded, his face pale with fear.

"Althea injected her with a strong tranquilizer," I said. "She passed out. You'd better get an ambulance."

He swore loudly, shouted to the others to get in here. Then he knelt and picked up his wife as gently as he could and whisked her out of the house.

Eric raced into the room. "I'll take the gun," he said, easing it out of my hand. That was when I realized my hand was shaking.

Eric turned to the cop right behind him. "Cuff her, read her rights, and get her out of here."

The cop yanked Althea up off the floor and hand-cuffed her wrists in one smooth action. Another officer joined him and the two of them led her out. She couldn't go without a fight and wriggled to get free while squealing that she didn't do anything, all the way out of the house.

I looked up at Eric. "Jane."

"She's okay. We've got her."

My knees wobbled with relief. Eric lifted me up from the floor and into his arms. It was the second time in a few months that a handsome man had swept me off my feet. Sadly, I was too shaken to enjoy it.

"Are you going to be all right?" he asked.

I tried for humor, but it was lame. "You mean, besides the post-traumatic stress of being tormented by a psycho killer?"

"Yeah, besides that."

I nodded. "My leg is throbbing a little and my head hurts, but I'm fine otherwise. You can put me down."

"I'm not sure you're ready."

"I am, really."

He set me down on the floor reluctantly.

"Are you sure Jane's okay?" I asked. "When Althea pushed her chair over, I think she hit her head."

"We'll have her checked out at the hospital, but she's feisty. She's going to be fine."

"Okay, good." I was so relieved to know that Jane would be all right I gave in to the dizziness and the throbbing leg and slumped over. In one smooth move,

Eric lifted me into his arms again and carried me out to the living room.

"I'm fine," I murmured, but my words sounded slurred. I was sure it was just a delayed reaction to the horror show we'd just experienced a few moments ago.

"Of course you are," he said quietly. "But I'd appreciate it if you'd humor me."

"Okay."

He set me down on the big chair next to the couch. Even though I was perfectly fine, really, I decided to stay put until I got my bearings back. Eric stood close by and we watched as two of the cops finished removing the duct tape from Jane's ankles and wrists and helped her up.

Mac rushed into the house, glanced around, and found me. I smiled, grateful to see him. But then I remembered seeing him with the supermodel and my smile faded. I wanted to cry, but that was probably just a delayed reaction to Althea's attack.

Mac's eyes narrowed in speculation, but he said nothing as he turned to Eric. "Is she all right?"

"She fainted," he said gruffly.

"No, I didn't."

Eric and Mac exchanged a dubious look.

"Really, I'm fine." I gazed at Eric. "You got my e-mail."

"Yeah," he said. "And if you ever leave me a message like that again without contacting me personally, I'll kill you."

Jane stood and Eric reached for her when she swayed.

"I'm fine," Jane said.

"I'm hearing that a lot," he said, glancing back at me. "But do me a favor." He led Jane over to the couch. "Sit here for a minute until you're better than fine."

Mac was still staring at me, his forehead furrowed with concern. Was he worried? Angry? Confused? I couldn't tell. Did it matter?

It *did* matter, I decided. Even if he was involved with someone else, I still wanted to be his friend. And although that thought was incredibly depressing, I would simply have to muddle through and live with it. I gave him a weak smile that he returned with a broad grin.

The pain was subsiding in my leg and I felt less dizzy, too. So after a few deep breaths, I pushed myself out of the chair, crossed to the couch, and gave Jane a hug. "I'm so proud of you, but you scared the hell out of me."

"Likewise," she muttered.

As police officers worked in the background, Eric explained that even before he read my e-mail, he'd heard back from the police chief in Long Beach, who answered his question about Andrew Braxton's next of kin. "He told me that besides his wife and kids, Andrew had a stepmother. Her name was Althea Braxton. It couldn't be a coincidence."

Eric had been about to go and arrest Althea when Mac called to tell him that he'd seen me walk next door to Jesse's house.

I looked at Mac. "Thank you."

He flashed me another grin but said nothing.

"By then," Eric continued, "I had uncovered most of Althea's murky background. Your e-mail filled in the blanks. My men and I raced over here to save the day, but it seems that you two were able to save yourselves."

"I guess we did," I said.

Jane smiled wearily. "Sort of."

Eric frowned. "I've just got one question. What was Whitney Gallagher doing here?"

"You really don't want to know," I muttered.

I figured I owed Whitney my gratitude for barging in the way she did, but I was pretty certain she wouldn't return my thanks.

A few hours later, after Althea was processed and thrown in jail, Eric caught up with me, Mac and Jane to commiserate over pizza and wine at my house. We were joined by Emily, Lizzie and Hal, and Marigold, who had all been worried sick about us after hearing through the grapevine that something awful had happened at Jesse's place.

Knowing the grapevine would travel with the speed of sound, I gave my father a quick call out at Uncle Pete's winery to let him know I was safe and sound.

"Damn good thing you called," he said. "Natty Terrell just showed up to taste Pete's new batch of Rusty Ridge Pinot Noir. She couldn't wait to share the story with us."

I sighed. Natty owned the flower shop on the square and had one of the biggest mouths in town. I gave Dad the quickie version of what had happened. It was all pretty bad, but the good news was that Jane and I were fine and Jesse's killer was in jail.

"Sorry if it disappoints Natty," I said, "but please tell her I survived."

"It won't disappoint her because she'll be able to say she got the scoop directly from the horse's mouth. With her spreading the news, I figure the whole town should know the story by midnight."

"Good." I smiled. "How's the Pinot, by the way?"

"You're going to love it, honey," he said. "I'll bring you a bottle if you'll do me a favor and stay out of trouble."

"It's a deal."

I hung up the phone and gazed at my friends. It was lovely to be with people who were celebrating the fact that Jane and I were alive and well.

I caught Emily's gaze and realized that I'd been so wrapped up in solving Jesse's murder that I'd neglected to talk to her about what had happened the other day at her house when Gus met the ghost of Mrs. Rawley. I figured she'd already heard it all by now, but I was wrong.

"Gus Peratti was at my house?"

"Yes, a few days ago," I said. "He said he was supposed to meet you there, but then he realized he'd made a mistake. He ended up going over to the tea shop instead."

"That's right. He came by the tea shop but didn't mention that he'd been at my house." She looked puzzled.

"You didn't arrange to meet him at your house?"

"Of course not." She stared at me intently. "What aren't you telling me, Shannon?"

Was it possible that Gus had been lured to the house by something other than Emily's request? By a lovesick ghost, maybe? Was there more going on here? Did Mrs. Rawley have powers we didn't know about?

I told Emily what had happened to Gus while he was at her house. I tried to, anyway, but how was I supposed to explain that the ghost of Winifred Rawley had somehow entered and *mingled* with Gus's physical body . . . or something like that? I still couldn't explain it.

"Good heavens," Emily whispered. "That sounds dangerous."

"To tell you the truth, Gus claims he felt pretty good after it happened. But he did rush off quickly and I haven't seen him since."

"How . . . fascinating. And you witnessed the whole thing?"

"Yes. And there's more." I told Emily about Winifred's diary and her secret shame, namely, the baby that resembled Giuseppe Peratti and *not* her husband.

By now, everyone in the room was engrossed in the story.

"Do you think that's why she remains in the house?" Emily wondered.

"I do," I said. "I think she's been waiting for someone to discover the diary, and now that she's got people working in the house, she's not wasting any time. I think she pushed us to find the diary."

"Spattering a can of paint onto the wall was probably a sign," Mac said as he sprinkled red pepper flakes on his second piece of pizza.

"But why did Gus show up out of the blue?" Lizzie asked.

"We did have an appointment," Emily said, as if that explained it.

"You were supposed to meet at the tea shop, not at your house." Marigold met our gazes, her expression solemn. "I truly believe he was meant to come by the house."

I shook my head, unsure how to respond to that. "Whether it's true or not is a question for someone with much more knowledge of the spirit world than I have."

"And who in the world would that be?" Jane asked dryly.

"Whoever it is that claims to be an expert," Eric said, "you can bet they're lying."

Lizzie ignored Eric's cynical stand in favor of Marigold's statement. "Do you really think Gus was enticed there by the ghost?"

Marigold looked at me. "Don't you, Shannon?"

I glanced around. "If I say yes, will you all think I'm crazy?"

"We already know you're crazy," Jane said, laughing.

I chuckled. "Maybe so. But I really do think our ghost is happier now that she's seen Gus and knows that we found her diary."

"Don't get me wrong, I'm all for having happy ghosts," Eric said, his voice only slightly mocking. "But I'm more concerned that the strange occurrences happening in the house might be the work of a human creature, not a spirit."

Emily blinked. "You mean, somebody's actually trying to scare me away?"

"I'm just offering an alternative theory." He gave her a thoughtful look. "If you'd like, I'll take a team and comb through the house to make sure there's nothing illicit going on."

"I would really appreciate that," Emily said.

I applauded Eric's offer, but I knew in my gut that he wouldn't find anything suspicious—of the human variety. I'd seen our ghost in action and I'd read her journal. I turned to Emily. "I still believe the ghost of Mrs. Rawley is residing in your house. Maybe she would stop carrying on if you were to ask Gus to come by every so often, just to calm her down."

"Would seeing Gus calm her down or rile her up?" Lizzie wondered.

Emily and I exchanged glances and she bit her lip. "It's my opinion that Gus would rile any woman."

My other friends giggled like little girls.

"I know the problem," Hal confessed in a world-weary tone. "I have that same effect on women."

Lizzie snorted and we all burst out laughing. I went to the kitchen to bring out another bottle of wine, and the men helped themselves to a third piece of pizza.

I was glad that Eric planned to search the house, just to give Emily some peace of mind on that front. As far as the ghost was concerned, though, I knew the issue of Winifred Rawley's spectral presence wasn't completely resolved. But after seeing her reaction to Gus and the discovery of the diary, I was almost certain Emily and my guys would be safe inside the house. Of course, that didn't mean I wouldn't continue to be vigilant for as long as we worked there.

A cell phone rang and Jane dashed to answer it. She spoke for only a minute and when she hung up, she looked around the table. "That was Stephen Darby. His dad called to say that Bob woke up out of his coma. The doctor thinks he's on the road to recovery."

I wanted to cry, I was so glad. "It's the best news we've had out of this whole ugly experience."

"I'm so relieved," Jane said.

"Me, too," Eric said with a firm nod. "Now he'll be able to testify against Althea."

Two days later, Jane called. "I tracked down Demetrius."

I'd forgotten all about him. Jesse had mentioned a lawyer named Demetrius in his letter to Jane. "Where was he? And what did he tell you? Is the necklace yours?"

"He's in Palo Alto," she said. "And why Jesse drove all the way down there, I have no idea—except that the guy is the son of another old navy friend."

"Ah, that explains it."

"He's also an expert in maritime law, another reason Jesse sought him out. Anyway, Demetrius told me there's a case pending in some district court somewhere that could change the law enough that the necklace would no longer be my property."

"Oh no. I'm sorry."

"No, it's really okay," Jane said. "I told him I wanted to have it returned to the Spanish royal family."

I sat back in my chair, surprised by her decision. "Are you sure?"

"Yes. If it belongs to anyone, it belongs to them. Lizzie's research concluded that it had to have been the property of the Spanish princess on board the *Glorious Maiden*."

Lizzie had once studied to be a librarian and was still a research geek. Jane had begged her to look into the history of the necklace, just in case it still belonged to the royal family or if it should go to the government.

"It even has a name," Jane added.

"The necklace has a name?"

"And the diamond, too."

"Wow. What are their names?"

"The necklace is known as *Martillo de Oro*."

"Do we know what that means?"

"It means Golden Hammer."

"Hammer?" I smiled. "I like it."

"I thought you would. Lizzie says the name was meant to imply that whoever wore the necklace held great power. The hammer is a symbol of power."

Of course the princess would have power, but I also wondered if that great power had anything to do with the fact that a necklace that beautiful would draw men's eyes to the woman wearing it.

"That's so cool," I said. "What about the diamond?"

"It was called the *Princesa Diamante*. The Princess Diamond."

"That's simple, but elegant."

"Isn't it? She was especially beloved by her people,

and the diamond was created just for her, apparently, according to Lizzie. So I guess the name fits."

"It does," I said. "And it makes your decision to return it to the Spanish royal family even better."

"I think so."

"And good for Lizzie for finding out all that great information."

"Better her than me, right?"

"Or me." The puny bit of research I'd done on Mrs. Rawley and the Rawley Mansion had been enough to last me for a while. Lizzie, on the other hand, might still be searching out new information on every passenger on the *Glorious Maiden*'s fateful voyage. She probably had a list of every stick of jewelry and clothing they'd brought with them, maybe even traced the family names all the way to the present day. Lizzie could be a little obsessive sometimes. In this case, that wasn't a bad thing.

I thought of something else. "Before you get rid of the necklace, we should take lots of pictures of it for the Lighthouse Museum."

"Great idea. I'll call the curators this afternoon."

"I'll miss having the necklace around," I admitted. "It's so gorgeous."

"I won't miss it at all," Jane said. "It's the reason Uncle Jesse was killed, so I'm perfectly happy to see it go away."

She had a point.

Four days later, we celebrated Valentine's Day in Lighthouse Cove. After all the weeks of contentious infighting between Whitney and Jennifer versus the rest of the committee members, the festivities went off without a hitch. I couldn't have been more proud or happy.

The colorful parade down Main Street drew our biggest crowd yet. The town square was festooned with beautiful red-and-white hearts and lots of red-and-white banners that decorated the dozens of booths that were lined up around the perimeter. The vendors had gotten into the spirit of the parade theme and were serving everything from Love Dogs to Sweetheart Sundaes. There were heart-shaped hamburger buns and cookies and pies and anything else they could conjure up and serve in the shape of a heart.

The biggest foodie hit of all was something the vendor dubbed Love Bites. These were tiny slices of rare Kobe beef served between two miniature glazed donuts with a dollop of creamy horseradish sauce. It sounded horrific, but it was melt-in-your-mouth wonderful.

I knew this because I had consumed three of them so far.

All of my friends who owned shops in town had their own parade floats advertising their various businesses. Emily's featured four little girls having a tea party in the back of the flatbed truck she'd rented for the occasion. The crowd was on their feet as our local fire engines rumbled slowly down the parade route. And the elementary school band thrilled everyone with their slightly off-key rendition of "Call Me Maybe."

The baton twirlers were my favorites, especially the youngest ones, the Baby Batoneers. Twenty little girls between the ages of four and six wore adorable sparkly pink costumes and could barely twirl those batons between their tiny fingers. But their enthusiasm was compelling and they gave it their all, even when a few of them slipped and fell while trying to chase down the occasional errant baton.

Whitney, still fragile from Althea's attack—and milking it for all it was worth—sat in the back of Tommy's official police department float. She was wrapped in a cashmere blanket and waved regally as though she were Queen of the Rose Parade. The fact that she was sitting on a bale of hay and surrounded by the twelve dogs owned by the police officers on the force took nothing away from her imperious debutante demeanor.

I was very proud of the homemade float I had created. Basically it was my truck, covered in crepe paper and gauzy red-and-white hearts and flowers, and an oversized banner that read HAMMER CONSTRUCTION COMPANY,

FOR ALL YOUR BUILDING NEEDS. Dad drove the truck and I sat in the back with a bunch of kids from the neighborhood. They all wore hard hats and tool belts and carried colorful plastic hammers, which they banged on every conceivable surface they could find. We waved and cheered and threw chocolate kisses to the crowd and we were accompanied by our pets, of course. Pets were a major theme this year, so I had Robbie and Tiger with me. Tiger didn't appreciate having to wear a leash, but she definitely enjoyed the adulation of the crowd.

The parade announcer highlighted our choice of Eric Jensen as grand marshal of the Valentine's Festival this year. He had been given the honor because he was our brand-new chief of police after forty years with old Chief Ray at the helm. Eric was an excellent choice because not only had he raised the morale of our police department, but he'd also solved several awful murders in the short time he'd been in the job.

And besides, who better to lead the Valentine's Parade than someone as handsome as Eric, who set hearts fluttering all along the route?

Every woman I'd seen so far today had thanked me for choosing Eric.

It was a relief to have everything settled and back to normal, I thought as I waved to the cheering crowd. I'd experienced more than my share of drama lately and I was so looking forward to taking a nice break from all that. Then I spotted Mac in the crowd. When he grinned at me, I tossed him a chocolate kiss, which he snatched out of the air. He followed that with a wink and my insides did a happy little flip—until I found myself glancing around, checking to see if a statuesque blonde might be hovering nearby.

And didn't that put a damper on the moment? I really had to get over it. I liked Mac a lot. I liked Eric, too, and sometimes I thought that with a little encouragement on my part, the police chief and I could have a nice relationship. When he wasn't suspecting me of high crimes, that is.

I glanced back at Mac and sighed. I guess I had a few

decisions to make. But not today. Today I would relax and take that break I'd been looking forward to. In the meantime, nobody said I couldn't be equally friendly with both men. So maybe I would. But oh, these matters could get complicated, couldn't they?

After the parade was over, the floats were parked along one end of the town square where they would be on display for the rest of the afternoon. Everyone in town with a pet took their dogs and cats and hamsters and bunnies—and one potbellied pig—over to the stage where the pet fashion show was about to begin. The audience was filling up and a lot of kids were already sitting on the grass by the stage, waiting for the show to begin.

I had Robbie on a leash, but I carried Tiger in my arms to keep her calm. Robbie looked dashing in his plaid outfit and I'd entered Tiger in the pet-owner look-alike contest. I didn't expect to win since our only similarity was the reddish color of her fur and my hair. But I knew it would be fun and that was what mattered today.

"So you dare to show your face here after what you did to me?"

I turned and almost groaned. Always the drama queen. "Hello, Whitney."

"I could've died and it would be your fault."

"No, it would be *your* fault. I told you to leave. I told you there was danger. Didn't you even notice that we were duct-taped to our chairs? What's wrong with you?"

"Don't talk to me like that. I was traumatized."

I took a deep breath. "I know, and I'm sorry. But that's Althea Tannis's fault, not mine. She's a cold-blooded killer and I hope you'll testify at her trial."

"I most certainly will."

"Good." I gave her a curt wave. "Okay, bye-bye."

"Not so fast. You—"

She was interrupted when Ralphie Smith, our town's perennial theatrical director, shouted from the stage, "Hey, Shannon, the fashion show's about to begin. We need you up here."

I had volunteered to announce the first part of the Pet

Parade Fashion Show. I waved to him. "Be right there, Ralphie."

"Oh my God," Whitney said, "I can't believe you're going through with that stupid pet fashion show. You have no class and I'm sick of you and Jane and those other women acting like you run this town."

"We don't run this town. We just organize the festivals. We enjoy doing it. And look around. Everyone's having a good time. Do you really have a problem with that?"

"I have a problem with your existence."

I shrugged. What could I say? That was pretty much the story of my life since high school when it came to dealing with Whitney. "Gotta go. See you around."

"No!" She grabbed my arm.

Tiger hissed and I held the cat tighter.

"I—I know the mayor," Whitney said, eyeing Tiger cautiously. "He'll let me take over the Festival Committee and I'll kick you out."

"But why?"

"Because y-you suck!"

"That's mature," I drawled. "Look, I know you've had a hard time lately, so I'll let that one slide." I moved closer and got right in her face. "But I know the mayor, too, and he's been pretty happy with the festivals lately. And let's face it. You wouldn't know the first thing about organizing a festival. And you'd hate it. But hey, you take your best shot."

"Best shot at what?" Tommy said jovially as he walked up sipping a beer. He wrapped his arm around Whitney's shoulders and nuzzled her neck. "Hey, gorgeous, what were you two ladies talking about?"

I gave him a bright smile. "Whitney was just telling me she wants to run the Festival Committee from now on."

"Aw, baby," he crooned, chucking her chin. "Are you still going on about that?"

My ears perked up. So Tommy had heard her grousing about the committee, too? I thought she was usually more discreet about her hatred of me when Tommy was around.

"She thinks she can do a better job than me and Jane," I added helpfully.

"Aw, honey, let it go," he murmured, and kissed her cheek. "You know Shannon and Jane are just better at things like this than you are."

Her eyes darkened and a small line of tension popped up between her perfectly plucked eyebrows. Suddenly I was worried for Tommy's safety.

"And just what do you think *I'm* good at?" she demanded.

He smiled that adorable smile of his and said, "You're good at being beautiful and sexy and you're a wonderful mother and wife and I couldn't be more proud of you."

Whitney stared at him for a long moment and then slowly flashed me the most superior look of cold satisfaction I'd ever seen in my life. "He's mine."

I wanted to laugh, but I didn't dare. Tommy had managed to shut her up in his own inimitable, sweet way and I couldn't have been happier to witness it. Except the part where Whitney still made me sick.

"Enjoy your little committee," she said in her most condescending tone, then flipped her hair and flounced off, clutching Tommy's arm possessively.

"Good girl," I murmured to Tiger as I stroked her soft fur. "We don't like her, do we?"

Tiger purred louder and I knew she agreed.

Jane joined me. She stooped to pet Robbie and we both watched Whitney and Tommy cross the park toward the food court.

"Trouble?" she asked.

"Not anymore," I said. "I don't think she'll be coming to any more committee meetings from now on."

"Don't toy with me," she warned as she stood up. "Are you serious?"

"Yes."

"Oh my God, that's great!" She clapped her hands and then grabbed me and Tiger in a hug. "Whatever you had to do to accomplish that, it was worth it."

"I agree." Even if I included the countless times I'd

been tormented and dissed by Whitney over the past fifteen years, it was worth it to have her off the committee and out of our hair.

I smiled as I straightened Tiger's collar and clutched Robbie's leash. "And now we've got a fashion show to win."

Jane and I were sharing announcing duties at the fashion show, so we walked together to the stage.

"Oh, look who's in the audience," I murmured from the stage stairway.

Jane glanced around until she saw the person I was talking about. "Oh yeah. Stephen's a Lighthouse Cove regular these days."

"He moved out of your place, right?"

"Yes, finally. He found a cute duplex on the other side of the square."

"That's not the only cute thing he found," I said, watching in shock as he kissed the woman standing next to him. "Is that Luisa Capello?"

"Yes," Jane said, smiling.

I frowned. "He's awfully fickle, isn't he? The last I saw, he was madly in love with you. He was like a little puppy following you around."

"I know. Lucky for me, he walked into Capello's Pizza last week and fell in love with their food and their daughter."

"Well, they do make a great pizza, and Luisa is darling." I cast another dark glance toward Stephen. "But he's still on my list."

Jane laughed and dragged me the rest of the way up the stairs.

The Pet Fashion Show was the biggest hit of the day. My Tiger and I won Honorable Mention in the Look-Alike category. Robbie scored the Second Place ribbon for the Most Dignified costume in his Royal Stewart tartan kilt and jaunty tartan cap.

I strolled to the center of the stage with Tiger and Robbie to proudly claim our ribbons with the other winners. The stage was packed with happy people and pets of every shape and size, mainly because we'd decided that every single entrant should at least win an Honorable Mention. Didn't want to hurt anyone's feelings, after all.

Without warning, an earsplitting scream arose from the other side of the park. I saw Eric and Tommy running toward the sound, just as one of the vendor booths erupted into chaos.

"Oh no." I clutched Tiger closer and tightened my grip on Robbie's leash. Glancing around at the other prizewinners, I shouted, "Hold on to your animals."

It was the no-kill animal shelter's adoption booth. The young assistant had lost control of her dogs and they were dashing across the park in every direction, many of them making a beeline for the Fashion Show stage.

"Maybe we should've let them participate in the show," Ellie, one of our fellow Festival Committee members, mumbled as she ducked behind me. "It looks like they're about to attack."

I laughed as a miniature schnauzer wiggled its way up the steps and onto the stage and started sniffing at Robbie. He sniffed back, clearly not minding at all.

"They just want to play."

Within a few minutes, most of the escapees had been rounded up, thanks to the kids who'd gone chasing after them. The way some of those children were clutching the animals, I had a feeling they wouldn't let them go without a fight.

Jane smiled. "There's going to be a lot more pet adoptions this afternoon than the shelter counted on."

"Isn't that lovely?" Ellie sighed.

"Hey, Irish."

I glanced down and saw Mac standing on the grass, holding a pretty black cat in his arms.

"Hey, yourself." I handed Tiger off to Jane and wound my way through the crowd to the stairs with Robbie tagging happily behind me. I hadn't spoken to Mac in almost a week, since he'd gone to New York for more meetings. I had tried not to miss him too much, and luckily I'd had the Valentine's Festival to keep me busy.

"Are you having fun?" I asked.

"This is the best," he said, gazing around. "Damn, I love this town. I missed it while I was away." He looked back at me. "I missed you."

"We all missed you, too," I said, smiling. I reached out and petted the black cat. "Who's your friend?"

"I named him Luke, short for Lucifer, because he's a devil of a cat."

"He's a beauty." But then I caught his words. "You named him? Is he yours?"

"Yeah, I just adopted him." He nuzzled the cat's soft neck. "I think we'll be good together."

I could hear Luke purring from where I stood. "Oh, that's wonderful, Mac. Welcome, Luke."

"Shannon," Mac said somberly. "I haven't had a chance to talk to you since I left for New York."

"Did you have a good time?"

"Yeah, yeah," he said, waving off the question. "But I wanted to tell you that the woman you saw in my apartment—and I know you saw her—she's . . . nobody. She's not important to me. She showed up here without warning and I tried to be nice, but I wanted her out of there. She's a little pushy."

"You don't owe me any explanations."

His gaze was focused like a laser on me. "I think I do."

"I'm . . . fine."

"Yeah, I know you are." Smiling, he brushed a strand of hair away from my cheek. "But I still want to apologize. I know you saw us that night and I think I hurt you, and . . . hell, I never want to hurt you, Irish. I—"

"There you are."

We both turned to see Eric walking toward us with a big, beautiful German shepherd on a leash. Instinctively I stooped down and picked up Robbie. At the same time, Mac grasped the short leash that was clipped to Luke's collar.

"This is Rudy," Eric said, grinning at the big dog who gazed with adoration at his human companion. "He's very well behaved."

"He's a beauty," I said, grateful for the interruption. "Where'd he come from?"

"I just adopted him from the shelter."

I laughed. "That's fantastic, Eric. He suits you."

"He looks formidable." Mac held on to Luke as he leaned over to pet the dog.

"He is." Eric frowned. "He belonged to a soldier who died in Afghanistan."

"Oh, poor Rudy," I said, and set Robbie cautiously on the ground. The two dogs began to sniff each other in greeting.

"He's trained for combat," Eric said. "I'm thinking he'd be a great addition to our K-9 unit."

I listened as the two men talked companionably about the virtues of cats versus dogs. Having one of each, I wasn't about to side with either one of them, but I laughed at their comments and barbs and my heart felt lighter than it had in weeks. I didn't have any decisions to make today, about men, about life, about anything more important than what to have for dinner. No, for now, I was content to simply enjoy the moment and the fact that I was in the company of two impossibly handsome, generous men, each of whom had just shown his true strength by adopting a sweet, helpless animal to love and care for.

Could this day get any better? I didn't think so.

The Bibliophile Mysteries return!
Don't miss the latest, *Ripped from the Pages*,
available in June 2015 from Obsidian,
in hardcover and as an e-book.
Turn the page for a peek at the opening pages,
when Brooklyn Wainwright returns to Sonoma's
wine country....
And *The Book Stops Here*, available now
in hardcover and e-book,
becomes available in paperback in May 2015.

Chapter One

"Won't this be fun?" My mother squeezed me with painful enthusiasm. "Two whole months living right next door to each other. You and me. We'll be like best girlfriends."

"Or double-homicide victims," my friend Robin muttered in my ear.

Naturally, my mother, who had the ultrasonic-hearing ability of a fruit bat, overheard her. "Homicide? No, no. None of that talk." Leaning away from me, she whispered, "Robin sweetie, we mustn't mock Brooklyn. She can't help finding, you know, dead people."

"Mom, I don't think Robin meant it that way."

"Of course she didn't," Mom said, and winked at Robin. Robin grinned at me. "I love your mom."

"I do, too," I said, holding back a sigh. Mom had a point, since I did have a disturbing tendency to stumble over dead bodies. She was also right to say that I couldn't help it. It wasn't like I went out in search of them, for Pete's sake. That would be a sickness requiring immediate intervention and possibly a twelve-step program.

Hello, my name is Brooklyn, and I'm a dead-body magnet.

Robin's point was equally valid, too, though. My mother and I could come very close to destroying each other if Mom insisted on being my BFF for the next two months.

Even though she'd raised her children in an atmosphere of peace and love and kindness, there was a limit to how much of her craziness I could take. On the other hand, Mom was an excellent cook, and I could barely boil water, so I could definitely see some benefit to hanging around her house. Still, good food couldn't make up for the horror of living in close proximity to a woman whose latest idea of a good time was a therapeutic purging and bloodletting at the new panchakarma clinic over in Glen Ellen.

I focused on that as I poured myself another cup of coffee and added a generous dollop of half and half.

A few months ago my hunky British ex–MI6 security agent boyfriend, Derek Stone, had purchased the loft apartment next door to mine in San Francisco. We decided to blow out the walls and turn the two lofts into one big home with a spacious office for Derek and a separate living area for visiting relatives and friends. Our reliable builder had promised it would take only two months to get through the worst of the noise and mess, so Derek and I began to plan where we would stay during the renovation. I liked the idea of spending time in Dharma, where I'd grown up, but live in my parents' house? For two months? Even though there was plenty of room for us? Never!

"It would be disastrous," I'd concluded.

Derek's look of relief had been profound. "We're in complete agreement as usual, darling."

"Am I being awful? My parents are wonderful people."

"Your parents are delightful," he assured me. "But we need our own space."

"Right. Space." I knew Derek was mainly concerned about me. He would spend most weeks in the city and commute to Sonoma on the weekends. His Pacific Heights office building had two luxury guest apartments on the top floor, one of which would suit him just fine.

Another idea had been for me to stay there with him, but that would've meant renting studio space at the Covington Library up the hill for my work. This would entail packing up all my bookbinding equipment and supplies, including my various book presses and a few hundred other items of importance to my job. Those small studio spaces in the Covington basement, while cheap, were equipped with nothing but a drafting table and two chairs, plus some empty cupboards and counters.

I'm a bookbinder specializing in rare-book restoration, and I was currently working on several important projects that had to be turned in during the time we would be away from home. The original plan of staying with my parents, while less than ideal, would've allowed me access to my former mentor's fully stocked bookbinding studio just down the hill from my parents. Abraham Karastovsky had died more than a year ago, but his daughter, Annie, had kept his workshop intact. She lived in the main house but had given me carte blanche to use the studio whenever I wanted to.

For weeks, Derek and I had tossed around various possibilities, including renting a place somewhere. That seemed to be the best alternative, and at the last minute, we were given a reprieve that made everyone happy. My parents' next-door neighbors, the Quinlans, generously offered up their house for our use. They were off to Europe for three months, and we were welcome to live in their home while they were gone.

We were willing to pay them rent, but all they required from us was that we take good care of their golden retriever, Maggie, and water their plants. It seemed like a darn good deal to Derek and me, and I was hopeful that sweet old Maggie and my adorable kitten, Charlie (aka Charlemagne Cupcake Wainwright Stone, a weighty name for something so tiny and cute), would become new best friends.

So last weekend, Derek and little Charlie and I had moved out of our South of Market Street loft and turned it over to our builder, who promised to work his magic for us.

And suddenly we were living in Dharma. Suddenly I was sitting in my mother's kitchen, having breakfast and wondering why I'd ever thought I could avoid seeing her every day simply because we weren't together in the same house. Not that I minded her visits on a regular basis. I joked about it, of course, but in truth, my mother was great, a true original and a sweet, funny woman with a good heart. All my friends loved her. She was smart and generous. But sometimes ... well, I worried about her hobbies. She'd been heavily involved in Wicca for a while and recently had been anointed the Grand Raven Mistress of her local druidic coven. Some of the spells she had cast had been alarmingly effective. She would try anything once. Lately she'd shown some interest in exorcisms. I didn't know what to expect.

"Do you want some breakfast before we leave?" I asked Robin. We'd made plans to drive over to the Dharma winery this morning to watch them excavate the existing storage cave over by the cabernet vineyards. It would eventually become a large underground tasting room. Cave tastings were the hottest trend in Napa and Sonoma, and our popular Dharma winery was finally jumping on the bandwagon.

Robin pulled out a kitchen chair and sat. "I already had breakfast with Austin. He had to be on site at seven."

Robin lived with my brother Austin with whom she had been in love since third grade. She and I had been best friends since then, too, and I loved her as much as any of my three sisters. I didn't get to see her as often as I used to when she was living in San Francisco, but I knew she was blissfully happy with Austin, who supported her sculpting work and was clearly as much in love with her as she was with him.

Austin ran the Dharma winery and my brother Jackson managed the vineyards. My father did a great job overseeing the entire operation, thanks to his early experience in the business world. Decades ago he'd turned his back on corporate hell and gone off to follow the Grateful Dead. Ironically, these days, Dad and four other commune members made up the winery's board of directors. He was also part of the group who oversaw the town's business. And he loved it. It probably helped that Dad was still remarkably laid-back. I sometimes wondered if Mom had cast a mellow spell on him.

I checked the kitchen clock. It was already seven thirty. The cave excavation was scheduled to begin at eight. "I'll just fix myself a quick bowl of cereal, and then we'll go."

Robin glanced at Mom. "Becky, are you coming with us?"

"You girls go on ahead," she said, pulling a large plastic bin of homemade granola down from the cupboard. "I want to put together a basket of herbs and goodies for the cave ceremony. I'll catch up with you later."

"What cave ceremony?" I asked as I poured granola into a bowl and returned the bin to the cupboard.

She looked at me as though I'd failed my third grade spelling test. "Sweetie, we have to bless the new space."

"Oh." I shot Robin a wary glance. "Of course we do."

Robin bumped my shoulder. "You haven't been away so long that you'd forget about the sacred cave ceremony."

"I've been busy," I mumbled. She was teasing me, but still, I should've known that my mother would want to cast a protection spell or do something to celebrate the groundbreaking of our winery's newest venture.

I could picture Mom doing a spritely interpretive dance to the wine goddess. She would chant bad haiku and sprinkle magic sparkles on the heavy tunneling machines and equipment. It would be amazing and the heavy equipment would turn our tasting cave into a magical space where all would be welcome. Or something like that.

"Oh, sweetie," Mom said, hanging a dish towel on the small rack by the sink. "While you're here, you should go to lunch at the new vegan restaurant on the Lane. They serve a turnip burger that is to die for."

I swallowed cautiously, hoping I didn't lose my breakfast. "I'll be sure to check that out, Mom."

She laughed, and her blond ponytail bobbed gleefully. "Oh, you should see your face. Do you really think I'd be caught dead eating anything so vile?"

"I . . . Okay, you got me." I shook my head and chuckled as I carried my bowl to the sink. "I was trying to remember when you'd turned vegan."

"I didn't, and I never will. And when did I ever serve my children turnips? Like, never."

"You're right, and I appreciate that. But I haven't seen you in a while. I was a little afraid you'd suddenly turned into Savannah." My sister Savannah was a vegetarian now, but she'd gone through several austere phases to get there, including a few months when she would eat only fruit that had already fallen from the tree.

"No, sweetie, I was just pulling your leg."

I smiled at her. "You still got it, Mom."

"I sure do." She grabbed me in a hug and it felt good to hold on to her. "Oh, Brooklyn, I'm so happy you're here."

"So am I."

As I washed out my cereal bowl, Mom left the kitchen.

"Let's get going," Robin said after I put my bowl away in the cupboard. "I don't want to miss anything."

"Wait a second, girls," my mother called from her office alcove off the kitchen. She walked out, holding two tiny muslin bags tied with drawstrings, and handed one to each of us. "I want you both to carry one of these in your pocket." Her expression had turned deadly serious. "It'll keep you safe."